COLUMBUS: FLIGHT
Project Columbus, Book 1

By J.C. Rainier

Columbus: Flight
Project Columbus, Book 1
Copyright © 2012 by J.C. Rainier
Original Publication: 12 September 2012
Second Edition
Published: 6 August 2013
ISBN: 978-0-9882482-6-7
Publisher: J.C. Rainier

In conjuction with Oakenbrand Press.

Currently Available by J.C. Rainier:

Columbus: Flight

Columbus: Ashes

Coming September 2013:

Columbus: Demeter

Please follow J. C. on Facebook or Twitter (@JCRainier), or check
http://jcrainier.com periodically for blog updates and sneak previews
of the Project Columbus series.

```
>BEGIN PLAYBACK|
```

Dr. Benedict looked out of the control tower windows, high above the grounds of the complex. Smoke hung thick in the air to the west, pocked with gouts of flame from the burning wreckage of trucks and buildings.

Blood and fire, thought Dr. Benedict, *Only appropriate for what I am doing.*

As the fires continued to burn, bleeding into the dying crimson sunset as night began to fall over the dark mountains, he turned back to the launch control stations in the tower. He knelt down over the lifeless body of Sergeant Henderson. There was no doubt to the doctor that the Marine never saw his end coming. A brave and strong man he was, dutiful and honorable. Benedict momentarily reflected on what a loss it was, being unable to include Henderson in his plans.

But your duty and honor were too strong. You would never have let me do this, and in doing so, your peoples' future would have been destroyed. Benedict spoke in a muttered prayer, "Lord, take this child unto Heaven. Bless him and his family, for they have done no wrong."

Benedict then rose and moved swiftly to the control stations. The massive rocket-powered transports loomed beyond like a giant steel grove. Staccato gunfire once again rattled from outside the compound, adding to his urgency. The scientist scanned the screens of each of the four computers quickly as he checked the guidance systems one more time. He paused, as the corner of his eye caught a glimpse of the Colt he had used to murder Henderson.

Did I have to become a murderer? Benedict began to think deeply. *I know it's fitting that I am a traitor. Are traitors and patriots the same thing? Are they mutually exclusive? Or is it all a matter of history's perspective?*

He reached for the Colt and traced his fingers along the barrel. *Benedict Arnold,* he mused. *The destiny of my name. And I never would have dreamed it, not in a million years.*

Truly, he had never meant for this to happen. He reflected on the events that lead up to his act of treason.

Dr. David Benedict was actually a humble man. His fifty eight years on Earth had seen many major political and world events happen. But early in life, the Apollo program had made a big impact on him, and he knew that his future was going to be that of discovery and exploration. He closed his eyes. Memories came rushing back, causing a moment of serenity.

His mind called up images of his mother who tried her best to provide for him, of serving in the Army to pay for college, and of his graduation from the University of Minnesota.

I had ideals back then, far beyond JFK, Apollo, and the Space Shuttles.

A loud blast from an RPG exploding inside the compound brought him back to his senses, and his hands went back to their work over the keyboards laid out in a compulsively neat line in front of him.

"C'mon, David. If the guidance calculations are wrong, even just a little bit…" he trailed off. *I wonder who is at our doorstep?*

Outside, on the tarmac just to the east, he saw hundreds of terrified civilians streaming from the compound, like birds scattered by a fox. Clustered near the rag-tag transports and the compound were solders in blue flight suits and green fatigues. Their mouths yelled orders that Dr. Benedict could not possibly hear. *A silent symphony of chaos. And about to understand what cattle feel like.*

His stare snapped back to the dizzying star field presented on the third screen. Earth was highlighted by a tiny blue dot, and overlapping colored parabolas emanated forth. His fingers repeatedly clicked keys as he entered calculations and alternated between the lines that represented each sleeper ship. As the gunfire and explosions became more intense, he wove the projections into one solid white line. Dr. Benedict sighed, and hit the "enter" key with great deliberation. Once again he closed his eyes.

We could have seen it coming. We should have seen it coming. We weren't invincible. But I was just a scientist, and the enemy was the political machine. Did they know they were the enemy?

If only they had more time to work. If only they could have made Faster than Light travel possible. As it was, the margin for error was far too slim, and he had to thank the government for that.

An explosion rocked the control tower, and David's feet came out from under him. His world went dark, and his ears rang.

Has the government figured out what I am doing? Have the Chinese made it this far east? Or do we have other guests?

America had been fighting wars for too long. Her economy was on its last legs. If ever there was a time to seize opportunity, it was two years ago. America's soldiers were just returning from the Middle East, and a drawn out war would have been disastrous. Yet that is exactly what she got. Even the use of nuclear weapons by both sides did not end the war.

David realized his eyes were open, looking up at the ceiling of the darkened control tower. He could hear a low rumble that started to crescendo in volume.

The boosters. Maybe there's hope for America yet.

He could see the inside of the tower again as an orange glow from outside the window clearly lit his surroundings. He picked himself off the floor, shook the shattered bits of glass from his sweater, and moved to the eastern window. He watched the rockets of his transport fleet burn trails into the sky. Three were already airborne, another had just lifted off, and the remaining six lit up with great flares of fire beneath their Atlas rocket boosters, scorching the nearly empty tarmac; a few scattered corpses smoldered where they lay on the ground.

Dr. Benedict stepped one more time to his consoles, only one of which remained powered on. The battery back up unit did not have much time left, he knew. *I hope they can get clear.* He punched up a command on the terminal, and a stopped timer appeared on the screen. *5 minutes. That's all I can give them.* One last time, he pressed "enter", and the timer started counting down. He nervously paced back to the window.

Another massive explosion rocked the control tower, and a burst of flame illuminated the compound. More gunfire followed, and a propane tank on the side of the compound building burst open aflame, hurtling debris across the grounds.

Now he could see seven trails of fire and smoke extending into the sky. The remaining three transports lifted their massive bodies off of the ground in a final, almost choreographed push. David watched as tracer fire ripped into the compound, missing the rockets beyond.

"Come on, fly! Fly and leave this world of deceit and death behind!" David yelled.

He could see the tracers inching nearer and nearer to the rockets as they screamed into the sky. David gasped in horror as he saw one of his transports raked along the side by a burst of machine gun fire. He held his breath.

No fire. No fire, they missed the Atlas booster. They hit the hull. Dear Lord, I pray that the hull is not breached. I pray for the men and women to remain safe on their long journey.

David glanced back at the timer. 3 minutes remaining. He reached into his pocket for his lighter and a cigarette. His hands trembled as he lit his last smoke. He drew a deep puff and walked over to the console and picked up his Colt. From downstairs, he could hear the voices of the invaders. Listening closely, he tried to pick out the intonation of their voices, trying to discern their identity.

Chinese, he thought. David looked one last time to the window at the dying light from the rocket boosters. *Godspeed, my children. And watch over them, Tadashi, my old friend.*

Dr. Benedict knelt behind the console and aimed his pistol at the doorway. He could hear the invaders' footsteps getting closer.

You're not the only ones who use nukes. And I'll be damned if my life's work ends in your hands. I am a patriot, not a traitor!

Dr. Benedict saw a shadow move in the doorway. He squeezed the trigger over and over, and his gun sent round after round into the doorway. The shadow dropped, and then he saw a muzzle flash in front of him. The doctor felt the slug rip into his chest. The cigarette fell from his mouth, and he fell backwards. He gasped for air, but couldn't seem to come up with any. He could barely see the screen of his console, yet he twisted his mouth into a smile as he watched the clock count down from 3. 2. 1…

. . .

```
1st Lt Haruka Kimura
USAF
16 August 2014, 20:10
Transport W04
>|
```

BRRZT. BRRZT. BRRZT. BRRZT.

Warning lights flashed in tempo with the alarm buzzer. The walls of the dim cockpit took on a faint red pulsing glow, throbbing with each pulse and squawk. Lieutenant Haruka Kimura looked at the console on her right and scanned each warning light and gauge quickly. "Captain, we've lost lateral thrusters five, six, and seven. Generator two has no reading, general system failure warnings in sections four, eight through eleven, and thirteen."

The transport groaned and rolled hard to the right. The three crew members pitched with the stricken craft, their harnesses biting their chests but keeping them seated at the controls. Haruka grunted, and looked to her left at Captain Bartrand. She watched as the captain gritted his teeth, and delicately manipulated his pitch thruster controls, keeping the nose stabilized.

"She's sluggish!" He shouted. "We must have caught some fire on the way up. Kimura, keep off of lateral one through four. Full burn on eight. We need 90 more seconds before we can dump the dead weight. Mancini, check with the sleepers, emergency alert request."

Haruka centered and locked her left control pair. She could feel her hands start to get clammy, but she gripped her rightmost control and deftly opened up throttle to the thruster. Nothing happened.

"M-M-MAYDAY, MAYDAY." Lieutenant Mancini stuttered nervously into his headset's boom. "Whiskey Zero Four, MAYDAY. We're hit, I repeat, we're hit. Requesting emergency status check from all sleeper ships." Haruka could clearly hear every word in a split-second echo from her headset's speaker.

Silence met them. The weight of gravity against the rockets' thrust, and the roll of the transport were starting to take their toll on Kimura. Her vision started to narrow. *No. You can't black out. Not now.* She reached to her console and switched off the blaring alarm.

"Sixty seconds. Kimura, ready on booster separation," barked Bartrand.

Slowly, transport Whiskey Zero Four started to ease off of its roll. The forces on the occupants lessened, but Haruka kept firm pressure on her thruster control. She watched as Bartrand eased off of the pitch control. Another massive vibration rocked the transport, and the nose started to dip. The captain once again eased onto his control, and carefully see-sawed the transport back to its original path.

Suddenly, the radio crackled to life. "Whiskey Zero Four, this is *Raphael* Control. We are ready for you. Any dock, proceed when ready." The male controller's voice was precise and calm, but Haruka knew they were not clear yet.

"F-fifteen seconds to booster separation," yelled Bartrand, his voice starting to crack. Gravity started to slack, and Haruka could see clearly once more. The clock display on the lieutenant's console ticked off the seconds. She turned a key on her console, and four missile switches illuminated red. "Separation in 5. 4. 3. 2. 1. Mark."

On cue, Kimura flipped all four switches. Once again the transport groaned, then heaved suddenly.

BRRZT. BRRZT. BRRZT. BRRZT.

Again the alarm rang in the cockpit. Kimura looked at the indicators, as the right roll they had been in stopped and the star field before them started to slowly pitch upward. Then the heavy ship began rolling hard to the left. Feverishly punching a sequence of buttons on her console, she backed off of her right thrusters, and quickly unlocked and fired her left thrusters. Moments later, the roll stopped. Captain Bartrand squeezed the pitch thrusters. His knuckles were as white as snow, and sweat began to stain his flight suit. He corrected the movement of the transport's nose, and once more the star field leveled out.

He stared at her, panic evident in his blue eyes. "What the hell was that?"

"Number four booster failed to separate. I forced the fuel shutoff switch as fast as I could, Captain. We still have general system failures in sections four and eight, and no reading on generator two. There's still nothing from thrusters five, six, and seven." Her gut felt like it was rising within her. *How much longer can we hold her together?* She backed off of the thruster control, and alternated sides, short bursts back and forth bringing the roll to neutral. Once more, she switched off the alarm.

"Mancini," barked Bartrand, "Reboot the secondary control system. I'll take the radio."

"Yes sir." Lieutenant Mancini unbuckled his harness and pushed, nearly weightless, to a console at the back of the cockpit. Haruka watched as Marco Mancini buckled his squat frame into the empty rear console station. *Hall should be there right now. But the damned fool wanted to play hero when the transports came under attack on the ground.* She could see in her mind the features of the young engineer's smiling face, the way he looked out of place with his short crew cut. He had been a pretty boy; but a boy, not a man. *Heroes get themselves killed; didn't anyone ever tell you that, Hall?*

"There's our ride." Bartrand pointed out of the front of the cockpit, to a great mass of gray metal in front of them, dull and barely lit by the light reflected from the moon. "Damn it, we need those thrusters back to make it." The captain nervously shot a glance over his shoulder. "Hurry, Mancini!"

They both watched as the giant sleeper ship *Raphael* became more prominent in their view. *She's huge. Reading the specifications are one thing, but being so close is just... humbling.* Then she saw the shining white silhouette of a transport, slowly spinning lifeless off the ventral starboard side of *Raphael*. *One of yesterday's transports, no doubt.*

"Reboot complete, Captain." Mancini said.

"Locking thruster control and switching to secondary feed, Captain." Haruka centered and locked her controls, then quickly keyed a new set of commands into her console. The machine processed for a moment. "Secondary thruster control enabled, running system check."

BRRZT. BRRZT. BRRZT. BRRZT.

Bertrand closed his eyes and grimaced. "What now, Kimura?"

"General system failure sections four and eight. Thruster seven failure. I have a reading from generator two, but it's fluctuating badly." She looked up, and grinned. "But hey, we've got two thrusters back."

The captain opened his eyes and ignored her attempted humor. "Can we eject that damned booster already?"

She looked at the radar screen between and did some quick mental math. She shook her head. "Negative, Captain. We might throw the booster into the stern of *Raphael.*"

"Damn it. Crippled, and dragging a bomb at our side," Bartrand said. He grabbed his controller. Haruka could see the color start to drain from his face. "This is going to be fun."

If your idea of fun includes exploding and killing hundreds of people, you're right, Captain. The Lieutenant could feel the sweat rolling down her brow and back. Her hands were already slick with sweat themselves, but she unlocked her thruster controls, took a deep breath, and prepared herself.

"*Raphael* Control, this is Whiskey Zero Four, emergency approach.

Heading for dock one." Bertrand spoke into his headset. "Firing retro rockets to slow approach."

"Acknowledged, Whiskey Zero Four. Assistance teams will be waiting, dock one."

As Captain Bertrand throttled up the retro rockets, the damaged transport once again groaned, and Haruka could see their view drift left as they began to fishtail. Deftly, she fired several bursts from her newly functional thrusters, and brought their momentum back to center. She pushed further, and then reversed thrust to the left to bring them once more to the centerline of *Raphael's* belly.

No room for error. She knew that with the added width of the stuck booster, there was precious little space to maneuver without hitting one of the sleeper's supply pods. And *Raphael's* docks only had a limited reach and flexibility, so she couldn't deviate more than a couple feet from the centerline or they would be unable to seal the airlock. Once again her vision started to narrow. She was suddenly aware of the adrenaline taking over her body, and she pulled her hands back from the thrusters to keep from inadvertently sending the ship careening to destruction.

She could barely hear the rockets burning to slow their forward movement. She could, in fact, no longer hear Bartrand. She could only stay focused on the beacon lights ahead, guiding her to their destination. They continued to creep closer, but at a slower pace. Haruka could tell by the clustering that the transport was listing slightly to the right, so she placed her hands back on the controls and gingerly gave two bursts in an alternating pattern from each side, and Whiskey Zero Four was righted again. The last beacon light passed over the canopy and out of sight.

She glanced at Bartrand and saw him completely frozen, fixated out into space, staring at another abandoned transport. She gasped. *He has pitch control, he has to land us.*

Haruka jammed her body forward against her harness, reaching across to the pitch control in front of Bartrand. With her arm extended as far as she could, she tapped the pitch stick as hard as she could, before her hand fell off of the control. The transport lurched slightly towards the sleeper ship, and with a groan and a shudder, came to a sudden stop.

She slouched back in her seat and stared at an abandoned transport spinning off in the distance. It was, in essence, a giant, glorified shipping container. *And I just flew one full of bullets into space.* Haruka shook her head to break her gaze, and surveyed the cockpit.

Marco Mancini, ghost white and closed eyes, was praying over and over. Bartrand was still frozen, staring into the great nothingness in front of him. "Captain?" she said softly. He didn't move. She looked backward again, "Marco?" Mancini opened his eyes.

"Kimura?" he said, nearly sobbing.

"Engage docking clamps and prepare the airlock."

"Y-Y-Yes ma'am," and he began to punch away at his station.

"Am I dead?" Captain Bartrand was now staring at Haruka. "Are we…?"

"Dead? No. Docked? Yes."

What the hell WAS that, Captain?

. . .

What the hell did Dad drag me into?

Countless voices echoed through the hold around Calvin. The worst were the children. Their cries rang harsh against his ears.

"Leave your belongings here. They will be collected and brought on board for you." Cal watched one of his dad's pawns hanging on a railing near the tunnel, struggling against the weightlessness. The man's flight suit was stained with vomit, but Cal didn't want to know whether it was his own or that of another so-called "passenger".

The airman continued directing traffic into the exit corridor. "Please exit the craft in a slow and orderly manner. If you need assistance with your children, please wait and you will be helped."

Cal rolled his eyes. *God, I don't want to be stuck here waiting for them to clear these kids out.* He unbuckled his restraints and pushed awkwardly off the wall, floating towards the throng of people exiting the hold. The lanky teenager ended up with a slight forward rotation and bumped his back against a broad-shouldered man with a rough, pocked face.

"Wait your turn, kid," the man snapped.

Cal scoffed, and grabbed the railing opposite the airman. He flattened himself against the wall as best as he could and glared into the crowd, eyeing each person as they passed. The only thing he could say for sure about them was that they had little in common with each other. *And nothing with me.*

He watched as a skinny guy, no older than 25 by Cal's estimates, tried to walk his way into the tunnel one-handed, while carrying a screaming toddler in his other arm. The glacial pace at which he moved was pure torture.

C'mon, Dad, where are you? I need you to explain why you dragged me away from my friends. With his free hand he lightly pounded the wall and reflected on how he got into this situation. *Kidnapped. I guess he knew I wouldn't come otherwise.*

Cal was supposed to go downtown that night, a week ago, with his friends. His friend Mike had fake IDs for all of them and they were going to tear up some bars, smoke some weed, and live it up a little. School was out, Cal had graduated, and it was time to live life. Then his father had sent some Air Force goons to get him and bring him to Wyoming. *Wyoming, for Christ's sake! What could he possibly want me in Wyoming for? And why was it so important that he had to abduct me?*

At first Cal thought that he was being sent to a ranch for some character building or some other nonsense. But he was placed on a bus with a bunch of nobodies, and sent to an isolated compound outside of Laramie that was full of massive rockets. It was at that point that Cal began to worry. He hadn't heard from his father, and from what he heard at the compound from the others that were there, they were all about to get shot into space.

Most of the officers there had no idea why Cal was there. One told him that his dad had placed him there "for his own safety".

As it turns out, his father's idea of sending him to Wyoming "for his own safety" made him laugh. Earlier in the day, he and the other passengers were herded into this rocket while someone was ripping machine gun fire at them.

My safety. If you had known this would happen, would you still have sent me?

Cal's father was a Brigadier General with the Air Force. The necessity of war had taken him away from his duties at home.

The War... Cal reflected on another aspect of his so-called protection. *Why would he have moved me closer to the front lines if he wanted me safe?* The thought was unsettling.

Calvin watched the last of the passengers scramble into the exit tunnel. He followed, his arms scrambling for traction as he pulled himself along. Peering down the tunnel he could see the cockpit door closed ahead and a bend just before where his band of shipmates slowly snaked and floated through.

In his mindlessness, Cal had come too close to the passenger in front of him. Her thick-heeled boot gave a glancing blow that hit his temple. He yelped and grabbed it in a vain attempt at soothing the pain.

The woman looked back, her ponytailed chestnut hair waving uncontrolled in the zero-G environment. "I'm so sorry, I didn't mean to..." she cut off when she saw Cal's grimace.

He growled for a moment, but bit off a caustic response when he saw her bright green eyes and the apologetic frown on her face. He recognized her milky white skin from the compound. The two had shared meals together, and even worked out at the gym several times.

Alexis, he recalled her name, and drew in a breath. "My fault; got too close."

"Did I hurt you?"

Cal withdrew the hand from his temple and said, "You'll have to try harder." His head throbbed, and he noticed blood stuck to the forefingers on his right hand.

"Move along." The voice was that of the airman behind him. He glanced back and sneered, then pulled himself along, using his palm where his right hand touched so as not to transfer blood to the walls.

He watched the green-eyed woman pull her way around the wall, admiring the tightness of her jeans and the gentle curves of her body. He also noticed that she seemed to move with unusual ease, despite not being bound to the floor.

Rounding the bend, he pulled himself into the airlock beyond, and then through the gaping airlock door. The air beyond smelled different. It was not the cramped, body-odor filled air of the transport, but rather a neutral, sterile air. He noticed the name "MICHAEL" printed in neat block lettering on the walls just inside. They quickly came to a T-junction, guarded by another floating uniform, this time with a clipboard.

"Names," she barked, her blonde bobbed hair unable to conceal her lieutenant's rank insignia.

"Alexis Decker," she spoke before Cal could open his mouth. Calvin measured her up and down. His eyes were entranced by her curves. She was neither slender nor overweight, but even weightless, her hips danced in a manner that hypnotized him.

The lieutenant tapped her clipboard with her pen. "Name, lover boy?"

Cal snapped his attention back to the lieutenant. He could feel himself blush. "McLaughlin. Calvin McLaughlin." He noticed her eyes get wide for a moment, and she cleared her throat.

"Very well." She scribbled something on the schematic on her clipboard. "Proceed to the gallery level." She pointed upwards. "Go right when you reach the gallery, you are both in sleeper pod twelve, section delta. Alexis Decker, you are in berth delta one four.

"Mr. McLaughlin, you are in berth delta zero eight." She looked at Cal as a nurse might look at a sick patient. "My condolences on your loss, sir."

Calvin paused and thought hard. "My what?"

"Your father, sir." She stopped, her jaw went slack, and she stammered, "Oh, m-m-my. No… no one… you didn't know? Oh my God."

"Know what?" Calvin started to feel sick to his stomach. The lieutenant shook her head. "Know what, Lieutenant?"

"Please... I..."

"TELL ME, LIEUTENANT!" he snapped.

"Your... your father..." she gulped. "Your father was killed in action, three days ago. I am so sorry."

Calvin floated in the hallway, unable to speak. His mouth dropped open. Alexis looked at him, her hands covering her mouth, her eyes starting to water. Bile started to rise in his throat, as did a great anger. His face turned red, and fists clenched tight. Pain began to throb in his palms where his fingers dug in, but it did little to dull the rage he felt.

"Calvin..." Alexis said in a soft tone.

"NO!" screamed Cal at the top of his lungs. He spun around violently to bang his hands on the bulkhead, but couldn't control the spin. He put his feet to the wall, lunged at the blonde lieutenant, tore the clipboard from her hands, and sent it hurtling end over end back into the transport. He pushed the shocked officer into the wall, in turn sending himself into the opposite wall. "DAMN YOU!"

As he looked out from the wall at the two women, he saw his own tears floating away from his face, unbound by gravity. With a hard push, he navigated deeper into the ship and found the ladder up into the gallery.

"Calvin!" He heard Alexis call from behind him, but he pulled himself up the ladder and into the gallery with two quick hand strokes, and pushed himself hard headlong down towards the stern of the ship, and sleeper pod twelve. He sailed over the backs of the other passengers, who were using hand rails built into the flooring to guide them along.

What the hell is this, Dad? Did you know what was going on? Why didn't you tell me? His thoughts raced, as he tried desperately to stifle the cries that were trying to burst forth from him. Some of his thoughts were terrible. *What about Mike? Rob? Brittany? Did you think about their "safety" too, Dad? Where are THEY?*

He saw the corridor ahead and to his left marked "12". Cal tried to alter his path, but with nothing to push off of, he simply flailed wildly. His awkward movement sent him into a slight spin, and he slammed sideways into a structural support, yelping in pain. He recovered, shot off of the support, and into the corridor to the sleeper pod. He pushed past another uniform, and quickly found his way to the delta section.

The immaculate sleeper section was full of men and women struggling to get into small berths, or trying to strap small children into their own berths. He looked for markings on the berths to try to find number eight. Upon doing so, he swiftly moved to pull himself in, with far more grace that his seventeen-year-old body had ever done anything before.

"Calvin!" Again he heard the voice of Alexis as she tried to catch up. He flipped onto his back and fumbled about for the harness restraint. "Calvin, wait."

"Leave me alone," he said, choking back more tears. Alexis peered into his berth from just outside. *LEAVE ME ALONE!* He screamed inside.

"No."

"What, is it time for a pep talk now?" He pulled himself back out of the berth and righted himself, looking her square in the eye. He could see his own blue eyes reflecting in her tears. *LEAVE ME ALONE! I don't want to listen!*

"I'm sorry. I.. I don't know you, or your dad. But I know you're hurting."

He smirked and rolled his eyes. *You don't know. LEAVE ME ALONE.*

Alexis continued. "Listen, I know you're going to go all macho tough guy now, and say you're fine…"

"I AM fine," he interrupted.

"No you're not. You're a mess, and that's ok. But don't bottle it up."

"Screw you, I've got it handled."

Cal flinched back as her hand came up. She gently brushed his temple, where her heel had caught him in the transport. Her touch was warm and soothing, but he brushed her hand away with a gentle swipe.

"I'm scared, Calvin McLaughlin." She said, point-blank. "I'm sitting in space, surrounded by strangers, thousands of miles from what should be my home." She looked down, then up again, and gave a nervous laugh. "I'm talking to a guy I accidentally kicked in the head, that I've known just a few days, who just found out his dad is dead, and trying to tell him something that he doesn't want to listen to."

He felt his anger flash again. "And what is it that I don't want to listen to?"

"That I appreciate your father's sacrifice." She was starting to raise her voice. "And that I think his son, who was sitting like a brooding emo kid in the cargo hold, might just be the person I need to keep sane around here." She gestured with her hands to emphasize the insanity of the situation.

"Brooding emo kid? Hey, what the…"

"Look around you, Calvin."

He stopped looking at her, and took in his surroundings once more. All of the people had entered their berths and were laying on their backs, a sea of anonymous silhouettes of silent flesh. The berths were being closed one at a time by the last airman he had knocked over.

"Do you know anyone here?" Alexis asked. Cal shook his head. "Yes you do. My name is Alexis Decker."

Alexis gently extended her hand. Cal looked at it and slowly, numbly, shook it. As he shook it, Alexis hugged him with her free hand, and gently kissed his forehead.

"I'm sorry for kicking you. And I'm sorry about your dad." She placed her hands behind him and gently pushed off, then twisted around and looked for her berth. As she pulled herself inside, she looked back at Cal. The glance of her green eyes felt as if they numbed the raging pain within him. He pulled himself back up, and with some effort strapped himself into his harness.

You win, Alexis. The berth door shut, and he surrendered himself to grief.

• • •

"Doctor Kimura, just letting you know that your initial passenger checks will start in fifteen minutes," Lieutenant Darius Owens said; his deep southern accent gave a slight lilt to his words. The glowing red orb on his computer terminal indicated that the com system was linked and active.

"Thank you, Darius. I am preparing for them now."

Dr. Tadashi Kimura's accent, on the other hand, was always a curious one for Darius. He knew the now eldest scientist from Project Columbus was Japanese, but the man had spent so long in the States that it had become muddled.

Darius tapped the orb on his screen, which dropped to a dark hue that indicated the system had closed the link. Next he keyed a few commands and locked his terminal, one of three ops stations on the bridge of *Gabriel*. Roger Miller, another lieutenant at ops, gave Darius a quick glance before he started a system check on the environmental controls.

Gabriel was a massive ship. Darius knew it would take him some time to reach the doctor's terminal within sleeper pod four. *Gabriel* had twelve pods, arranged in matched pairs on opposite sides of the gallery backbone. Darius was on the bridge which was joined to the front of the gallery by an airlock, and situated above the thirteenth sleeper pod. All areas forward of that airlock were designated for crew use only.

He unbuckled his restraint harness and gently kicked off of the console's casing. He did a graceful half roll to face the three stairs up to the command chair, grabbed the railing, and then pulled himself past the empty command chair to the end of the bridge. From there he made his way down the stairs and through the gaping airlock.

His eyes were met with only periodic dim strips of light from fixtures integrated to the ceiling. Darius clung to the edge of the airlock and waited for his eyes to adjust to the darkness. Once he was comfortable that no structural supports would ambush him from the black, he pushed hard off of the wall and aimed down the hallway as he tucked himself as straight as an arrow. Darius knew that he would probably need to find a hand or foot hold to regain momentum once the air slowed him down. Including the reactor, bridge, primary support, and propulsion systems, *Gabriel* was over half a kilometer long. His journey would be just shy of two hundred meters, a mere speck of the journey that he and the passengers had already taken. Yet the longest portion of their voyage had not begun.

And the price in blood has been high so far, he thought.

As Darius continued his aft ward flight, his mind drifted to the most prominent casualty of the day.

Dr. David Benedict was the head of Project Columbus and the lead astrophysicist on the research team. His vision guided the project to launch readiness and his brilliance helped achieve breakthroughs in many systems on the sleeper ships from navigation to propulsion. It confused Darius why such an active and resourceful man would stay behind to face certain torture and slaughter at the hands of the Chinese. Far more puzzling was why the fifty-eight year old scientist would do so when the Marines were there with a specific assignment to cover the escape of the transports.

Either he was suicidal, or knew something that I don't.

Darius reached the airlock separating pod four from the starboard side of the gallery. He maneuvered through the airlock and took a left at the T intersection and around another bend, past the door to the ES-AARC cockpit at the front of the sleeper pod. One more turn brought him to the hatch that led to berth section bravo, one of four in the pod. He used the hand ladder built into the ceiling to pull his weight one more time and he emerged into a brightly lit hallway.

Immaculate white sleeper berths stacked two high from floor to ceiling, and ten from wall to wall, on both sides of the hall.

Or is it two from wall to wall, and ten from floor to ceiling? Having no gravity certainly makes absolute directions more difficult, he thought.

Darius spotted Dr. Kimura, weightless and tending to a computer terminal built at the foot of the sleepers near the far end of the hall. His jet black hair was marred with streaks of silver. The years showed their toll in the lines on his face, but kindness showed in his smile.

He always seems to smile no matter what.

"Dr. Kimura, bridge reports all operational and navigational functions are in the green. Reactor temperature normal, cooling systems functional, no radiation leaks detected. Positive radio contact confirmed with *Michael* and *Raphael*." Darius paused for a moment. "Sir, Dr. Benedict…"

Dr. Kimura's gaze met his own, bloodshot, watery, and weary.

"I know, Darius."

Darius sighed, "I owe him my life, Doctor K. I think near everybody on this ship does. But why do we have to lose a smart man like that, when we could use him the most?"

"Dr. Benedict knew better than anyone that if you want to win, sometimes you have to stack the deck. Sometimes that means playing your opponents along, sometimes it means stacking aces and hoping you don't get caught cheating. You, your company, and every person on these ships are here for a reason, but it was his decision to stay behind." The scientist's soft voice still seemed loud in such a confined space.

Kimura went back to his work on the computer; an occasional chirp gave confirmation of his commands. Darius studied him for a minute or so as he thought.

He's not normally this evasive.

"So what ace did Dr. Benedict stack back in Laramie that made him stay?" Darius asked.

Dr. Kimura froze momentarily and blinked, as one would expect from a deer caught in the headlights.

"A dirty bomb."

"Excuse me?"

"Dr. Benedict wanted to assure that we had no pursuers. His intent was to detonate a nuclear device as soon as the transports were clear. Of course, the government was not going to give up any of the warheads they hadn't yet used in the war, nor were they keen on the idea of intentionally detonating such a weapon on American soil. Dr. Benedict had to make his own."

Chills ran down Darius's spine, and goose bumps dotted his ebony skin.

"Do I want to know how?"

Dr. Kimura turned his attention back to his work.

"The answer is moot, Darius. I don't think now is the time to discuss that. I need to make sure our passengers are in hibernation and do a full count."

Later then, Doctor. I suppose I have my own work to do.

"Darius, are you sure the programming for the crew units is set to correctly cycle out of stasis every five years?"

"Yes I am, sir."

"And the proximity program for final crew revival?"

Darius forced an uneasy smile. He wanted to be proud of his work, but hearing the details of Dr. Benedict's sacrifice kept his mind racing.

"The basic program is ready. I just need for you to define what proximity you want me to set it to."

"Point zero zero five light years, if you please, Mr. Owens." Dr. Kimura seemed to lose himself in thought. "Darius, so much of our mission depends on a number of variables being exactly correct. Anything we can do to improve our margin of error gives us an infinitesimal greater chance of survival. I want you to promise me something."

"Anything, Doctor."

"Should my berth malfunction and you find I am deceased, please make sure to reprogram Kayla Reid's berth to take my place. You will need her to check passenger status should I pass."

Darius stared in confusion. His voice cracked ever so slightly and he concentrated on not stuttering. "Oh… okay, Doctor. Yes sir. I need to get back to programming the proximity routine. See you later, Doctor K?"

Dr. Kimura nodded, half bowing at the same time. Darius pushed off from one of the sleeper berths and made his way to the hatch. From there he snaked his way out of the sleeper pod and back into the lonely gallery.

That was an odd request. Does he expect his sleeper to malfunction?

He slowly pulled himself along the handrails built into the floor until he could find a structural brace to push off of. He found a suitable platform and used his mighty legs to propel himself once again aft. He repeated this action several times until he reached the airlock that separated the gallery from the support section.

The hallway inside was nearly black, with only the light filtering in from behind him, and a single strip of LEDs many feet in front of him. Darius navigated by memory to a small terminal in the wall and swiped quickly over the display. A strip of LEDs illuminated softly, like a row of highway lane reflectors at night.

He moved cautiously along the hallway until he reached the door that provided access to the main computer core halfway down the hall. He keyed a code into the pad next to the access hatch, eliciting a reaffirming chirp. The hatch slid open and Darius pulled himself inside.

Racks of computers ran down the room in three parallel lines. Cables were neatly bundled and run into conduits at regular intervals, which lead to a concentration of networking equipment at the far end of the bay. A single workstation sat in solitary watch next to the net switches.

Darius made his way to the station and strapped in. He stared blankly for a moment at the prompts on screen in front of him.

XCS-02 MAINFRAME LOGIN:

He typed his account login into the computer, and his password when prompted.

XCS-02 LOGIN ACCEPTED. OWENS, LT. DARIUS. MAINFRAME ACCESS ENABLED. ENABLE VOICE INTERFACE?

Darius keyed an affirmative response.

The computer's voice was feminine, but undeniably artificial.

"VOICE INTERFACE ENABLED. COMMAND?"

"Access passenger matrix."

"ACCESSING. SEARCH PARAMETERS?"

"Reid, Kayla."

Darius could hear drives accessing behind him for a moment before the computer came back with a response. "SEARCH COMPLETE. REID, KAYLA. CIVILIAN. SLEEPER ASSIGNMENT ONE ALPHA SIX. COMMAND?"

"Modify revival parameters."

The computer spat back a disapproving bleat.

"AUTHORIZATION OF CIVILIAN REVIVAL REQUIRES OVERRIDE COMMAND. REQUEST COMMAND AUTHORITY FROM APPROPRIATE SOURCE."

Stupid computer.

"Override requested by Doctor Tadashi Kimura. Send confirmation request to his current terminal."

"STANDBY."

Darius scratched at his shaved scalp while the computer processed the request. It did not come back with an immediate response.

Doctor must be busy. Or this beast forgot which router to send the request through.

"Secondary process request."

"COMMAND?"

"Begin audio playback. Genre classical. Terminate process upon response from Dr. Kimura."

Gabriel's mainframe chirped once. A moment later, Darius heard the powerful, precise sounds of Beethoven's 9th Symphony flow through the speakers. He stretched out and looked at the ceiling as he listened.

He took deep breaths of the crisp, filtered air. His mind wandered as time slowly passed by.

Darius could not shake the thought that there was something more to Dr. Benedict detonating a nuclear device at the Laramie compound. The Chinese didn't have any air support. If they did, the large, slow rockets would have been easy prey.

Why was it so important to use that much power against ground troops? And riflemen at that. From the reports I heard, they didn't have any armored units. What did Dr. Benedict need to stay behind and protect that the Marines could not have bought time for?

The music stopped. For a moment, only the white noise of cooling fans echoed through the room.

"REQUEST ACKNOWLEDGED. PLEASE STATE REQUIRED MODIFICATIONS."

"Add conditional revival code. Primary condition, incapacitation of Doctor Tadashi Kimura. Corollary condition, synchronize with maintenance revival schedule."

The mainframe clicked and processed for a few seconds.

"MODIFICATION COMPLETE. COMMAND?"

"Access proximity revival routine. Set proximity value to point zero zero five light years."

Again the computer calculated.

"MODIFICATION COMPLETE. COMMAND?"

Darius considered his next task carefully.

Sometimes you have to stack the deck, Dr. Kimura's voice echoed within his mind. *So much of our mission depends on a number of variables being exactly correct.*

Darius drew a deep breath, held it, and then released it. *The computer is my variable, let's see if I can stack the deck.*

"Begin system audit. System status check, computers and network system. Graphical representation."

A picture of *Gabriel's* basic network structure appeared on the workstation screen. Darius zoomed in and viewed each link in the system meticulously, section by section. He had barely finished his audit of the crew pod and started on the bridge when he gasped and froze.

"Computer, identify this link," he said as he tapped a gray strand that radiated from the communications array back into the body of the ship.

"ANALYZING. SOFTWARE BRIDGE IN COMMUNICATIONS

SYSTEM."

"I can see that, but that link was removed in version 4.22 of the com software, not to mention the 1.61.C firmware update. Why is it there?"

With a sharp beep, the computer registered its disapproval in an almost disdainful way.

"COM SOFTWARE VERSION 4.22 CHECKSUM ERROR. FILE CORRUPT. CURRENT COM SOFTWARE VERSION IS 4.15."

Darius gasped. "What? Define current firmware version."

"CURRENT FIRMWARE VERSION 1.61.A. ERROR. REDUNDANT FIRMWARE FAILURE. AUTOMATIC FAILSAFE PROCEDURE ENGAGED. TERMINAL ACCESS RESTRICTED UNTIL REDUNDANT FIRMWARE CAN BE RELOADED."

With a negative chirp, the mainframe ceased talking to Darius and switched to a standby screen.

Well, better to find this out now so I can fix it.

• • •

Lieutenant Kimura placed another anonymous bag in the storage locker. This one was a green plaid soft sided carry-on style bag, the last one before it was a gray duffel bag, and the one before that was a small pink backpack. She closed the locker, pulled herself to the next one on her right, and opened the door to reveal the nothingness inside.

This is what is left of their lives, she thought. Mancini handed her another bag, this one an old surplus army duffel. She slid it in place at the bottom of the locker. *Another story to tell. Maybe I will see its owner, hear their story. After all, we don't have much left otherwise.*

She had been pressed into service moving the belongings and luggage of passengers from the last two transports to dock with *Raphael*. They were Whiskey Zero Nine and Whiskey Zero Six. *And they would recognize me as much as I them.*

Haruka received baggage from Mancini, who in turn retrieved them from a cart that floated nearby. This was the last of the baggage from transport Whiskey Zero Six, the last to dock. Elsewhere, she knew, the passengers were being settled and closed into their sleeper berths. The ship was nearly silent; only the whisper of air circulation and a low hum made by the support mechanisms were audible.

They finished their work, and Haruka closed the final locker, barely half full. With great care, she and Lieutenant Marco Mancini moved the cart out of sleeper pod fourteen, and secured it to the hand railings in the gallery. They were no longer being used by the passengers, as all had reported to their sleeper pods. She looked down the massive expanse towards the bridge, eventually fading into darkness.

Humbling from the inside as well as the outside. She's huge. Haruka knew the specifications well. Eight hundred meters long, two hundred meters wide, supply pods lining her belly stem to stern. Including the pod under the bridge, she had fifteen sleeper pods, two medical pods, a workshop pod, and a galley pod. Though her capacity was not much more than the other sleeper ships at 2400 people, *Raphael* was designed to be the first to land, to provide services to the entire colony. Like the other ships, she was supplied with everything a new colony might need: heavy machinery, power tools, fuel, medical and food supplies. There were even two special supply pods fitted with biostasis berths for domesticated animals ranging from horses to sheep to dogs.

Out of the darkness, a young man in a flight suit floated swiftly towards Haruka and Mancini. He was many pods away, but moved with a purpose. Haruka righted herself on the cart and awaiting the herald from the forward section of *Raphael*. It took a minute, but he arrived.

"The colonel wishes to see you, Lieutenant Kimura. You too, Lieutenant Mancini," the herald said.

"Thank you, Airman." The brown-haired youth pushed off and left the two behind, carrying on his duties. *Debriefing time. Hopefully she will let me sleep before giving me a new assignment.* Haruka was tired. She had not been given any time to rest after their near disastrous launch and docking, instead put to work directing and securing passengers and their baggage.

Haruka grabbed the cart and heaved off down the long gallery, with Mancini at her heels. She snapped her arms to keep air resistance down and keep her speed up. She knew that she would still have to give herself a few more speed boosts to get to the bridge. Tunnels to the sleeper pods passed right and left, and a ladder way down to the lower backbone and docking ports gaped darkly below her as she floated past. Minimal lighting was present in the gallery so the crew could move around, but the lighting in the lower levels was already turned off to conserve power.

As she approached the medical pods, Haruka knew she was barely halfway to the bridge. She grabbed a structural support as she passed and, pushing off with her legs, gave herself a great boost in speed. *We will be maintaining this whole ship with a skeleton crew,* she thought to herself. *That is a tall order. I wonder how long it will take us each cycle.*

The next set of pods contained the galley and workshop, and a crewman was securing a cart outside the galley. He briefly glanced as Haruka and Mancini floated by. She could make out the split staircase leading to the bridge and the crew's sleeper pod, just emerging from the darkness ahead.

They floated to another structural support and pushed onward. Another dark hole in the flooring signaled a ladder way to the lower levels. Two more sleeper pods drifted by, reminding Haruka of the task that would need to be done to maintain the ship. *Maybe the Colonel will let more of the crew come out of sleep to handle the work load.*

Minutes passed and little changed in the scenery. At last the duo reached the staircase. The right half led down into the crew's sleeper pod, the left side up to the bridge. Haruka straightened her uniform and pulled herself up onto the bridge, Mancini in tow like a puppy.

The bridge of *Raphael* was much larger than the cockpit of the transport she flew into space. There was ample room to move about, and stations for 10 crew, including the commanding officer. While navigation, engineering, and operations stations were grouped in clusters of three, the workstations themselves were not crowded. Overhead, a canopy of dozens of sections of glass extended all the way back to the top of the stairs and forward until it disappeared under the deck plating in front of her. The command chair sat on a platform that was elevated three feet above the crew stations, and surrounded by a railing. Three breaks were present in the railing and led to the clusters of work stations. Engineering was to the left of the command chair, operations to the right, and navigation was in front. In this arrangement, the commanding officer and the navigators had a full view of what was beyond the canopy. Though the steel hull created blind spots along the flank, exterior cameras could be called up on the nav stations to circumvent the issue.

As Haruka floated over the deck plating and forward, she could see Captain Bartrand seated at one of the navigation stations. He hunched over the station, reviewing screens of data, and observing the status of the navigation and propulsion systems. Over one of the engineering stations loomed the Chief Engineer, Captain Maynard. An eager young Lieutenant Shipp sat at an operations station.

"Elevation thrust please, Mr. Bartrand. Nice and easy, let's clear these transports," came a stern female voice from the command chair. "Lieutenant Shipp, let's get everyone up here, including the doctor."

"All crew to the bridge, all crew to the bridge. Doctor Nelson, please report to the bridge," Shipp's voice echoed over the general com system.

A hand came down to the side of the command chair, released a lock, and the chair swiveled to the side. With another motion, its occupant locked the chair's position one more time. Haruka could see that she was tall, but also very fit. She had hard lines, and her crow's feet and graying brown hair gave her a further air of distinction. Colonel Marissa Fox was all business, and it showed in every move she made.

Haruka and Mancini saluted. "Lieutenant Marco Mancini and Lieutenant Haruka Kimura, reporting as requested, ma'am," chimed Mancini.

They received a return salute. "Very well. It's time to get underway. After having to deal with the emergency docking of Whiskey Zero Four and the fact that we had one more transport to unload than the other ships, we're running late. Mancini, take an ops station please. Kimura, you're on nav."

"Yes ma'am" they replied in unison.

No debriefing. No sleep for the weary, either. Let's get this over with.

Harukaa grabbed the railing and pulled herself to a station at the nose of the bridge, just below the level of the command chair. She slipped into her familiar position to the right of Bartrand, and secured her harness. She glanced back over her shoulder to the right at Mancini belting himself in to an ops station. She then focused her attention on the controls fed to her station by Bartrand's terminal. *Main drive control, Captain?* She thought. Fixing her gaze out of the windows directly in front of her, she sighed quietly. *Let's hope Dr. Benedict's course calculations loaded correctly.*

Haruka heard Colonel Fox giving orders behind her. "Lander, Perez, engineering stations please. Overton, ops. Ellsworth, go to nav." Then she momentarily lost the harshness in her voice. "Doctor Nelson, please. Take my seat. This ride might be a bit bumpy."

"Thank you, Colonel." The doctor's voice was soothing, almost like a song. Haruka looked over her shoulder and watched the aging doctor take the command chair and strap in. Colonel Fox braced herself against the railing behind the nav stations. Airman Ellsworth took the final navigation console seat on the far side of Captain Bartrand.

"Are we clear of the transports, Captain?" asked Fox.

"Yes, ma'am. Clear of transports, elevation thrusters at station keeping."

Haruka looked down to the side of her station, where a large screen displayed the view beneath the ventral side of the crew pod. She could see one of the transports spinning slowly, far below *Raphael. A waste of material.*

The original operational plan of Project Columbus called for the transports to be brought up only two at a time. After docking and moving out the passengers, the crews of the sleeper ships were to strip all modular materials and certain sections of ship systems that were easy to remove, valuable, or could be used on the sleeper, before discharging the transport into space. However, time was of the essence. America was at war, and there was no telling if her enemies could destroy the sleepers if they tried to escape. Nobody within the project wanted to take the risk. *So we loaded the refugees on and shoved the transports off as quickly as possible.*

"Maynard, reactor status please." Fox was still a commanding presence, even while being cordial.

"Reactor online, Colonel. Cooling systems report normal. Reactor output restrict at 80%, ma'am. Generators online, all power systems registering normal."

"Increase reactor to 100%, Captain," she barked.

"Yes ma'am, bringing reactor to full." Maynard said quickly.

"Mancini, support systems check," continued Fox.

"Life support systems operational, system check acknowledges that Doctor Nelson's passenger checks are complete. Biostasis systems online, no errors."

"Shipp, com check. Do we have fleet contact?"

"Last report was three hours ago, ma'am. Receiving beacon signals from *Michael* and *Gabriel*. Negative on live contact, we may be too far behind them right now."

"Keep trying at regular intervals, Shipp. Ellsworth, radar check."

Airman Ellsworth peered at the screen in front of him. "Negative contact on forward radar. Ventral radar confirms *Raphael* is clear of all transports."

"Captain Bartrand, have you made the corrections to the navigational calculations?" asked Colonel Fox.

Corrections?

"Yes ma'am, nav calculations projected based on new speed," the captain stated. His eyes narrowed as he looked over the data one more time.

"Kimura, bring the plasma drive online. Begin full thrust on Bartrand's command."

Haruka responded, "Yes ma'am." She punched commands into her terminal. *What corrections? New speed? What did the Colonel have planned?* Her indicators changed, and the computer chirped a confirmation. "Plasma drive online, Captain Bartrand. Ready on your command."

She looked to her left at the captain, who once again input information into his control system. "Burn calculations complete. Transferring to your terminal, begin burn in 5. 4. 3. 2. 1, full thrust!" He punched one last button on his terminal. In unison, Haruka triggered the plasma drive. Slowly, the transport below started to move towards the rear of the under canopy, then finally disappeared out of sight.

Ellsworth spoke, "Radar confirming forward movement. Fifteen meters per second, and climbing."

Raphael continued to move forward, nearly silent but for the sounds of the computer terminals and their operators' breathing. Kimura watched her console as the main drive system quickly reached its full impulse. A minute ticked by quietly.

"Forward momentum three five zero meters per second and accelerating, Colonel," Ellsworth broke the silence.

"Easy, Ellsworth. We're not going to try to break escape velocity without a little help," snapped Colonel Fox.

Raphael continued to plod along, her acceleration very gradual. The transport dock site was now far behind, and ahead the sun burned brightly. To the port, the stark contrast of the Earth's terminator was breathtaking.

"Captain Bartrand, you may begin your thrust procedure for low orbit slingshot maneuver. Lieutenant Kimura, maintain thrust impulse."

"Yes ma'am," acknowledged Bartrand and Haruka simultaneously. She flashed back briefly to the docking of Whiskey Zero Four. Bartrand had frozen up, and she had to reach his controls to save the transport. Glancing over at the nav console in front of him, she realized that she could not even read his screen from her angle. She dreaded another lock up of the captain. She knew there were risks even in the original high orbit slingshot. Haruka tried hard not to consider the consequences of *Raphael* crossing deeper into the Earth's gravity well.

Raphael is massive. She's also got a nuclear reactor and over two thousand souls on board now. What is Colonel Fox planning?

Bartrand clenched his jaw and deftly manipulated his controls. His knuckles tensed, and Haruka could see them pale. *Raphael's* nose glided smoothly onto a steady course, and the gravity of Earth started to accelerate her even faster.

Raphael began to shudder. The dark side of the Earth could no longer be seen, as the terminator dropped from view. Earth loomed out the port side of the canopy like a giant blue and green mural, growing so large that Haruka had to crane her neck upward to see Siberia.

The giant sleeper ship groaned and bumped, and Bartrand rotated his thruster control several times to hold the course of *Raphael* steady. The sun roared across the side of the bridge, and disappeared out the view of the side of the canopy with little fanfare. The Earth continued to dominate the canopy view on the port side.

The shuddering and vibration continued, and Haruka could see the bow of the ship bathed in a blue, whisp-like light. *Plasma charge. We're too close to the Earth!*

Captain Bartrand countered the thrust hard. The ship groaned once more but her nose turned away from the looming planet, and the Earth began to drop away out of view. Finally, the light abated along with the vibrations.

"Slingshot complete, Colonel," he said, his hands relaxing from the controls.

Fox grinned, "Ellsworth, confirm forward momentum on radar."

Ellsworth looked at his console and blinked. His eyes opened wide in shock, "Colonel, forward momentum one nine kilometers per second and still increasing."

"Escape velocity for Earth's gravity has been exceeded, Colonel," grinned Bartrand. "On full thrust, we will easily gain escape velocity from the Sun as well."

The colonel pulled herself up straight by the railing. With an air of pride, she spoke. "We'll catch the rest of the fleet soon enough. Bartrand, begin thrust corrections. Exit course to Alpha Centauri B, if you please."

. . .

"Kimura to bridge." The doctor's voice had an extra nasal quality when it came through the headset.

"Bridge, Lieutenant Owens speaking. Go ahead, Doctor," he replied as he adjusted the slender boom.

"Passenger checks complete. Excluding myself and the crew we have one thousand nine hundred and nine passengers, all confirmed in bio-stasis."

Almost a full load, Darius thought. *That's good news.*

"I will inform the Colonel, Doctor." Darius lowered his voice a bit. "Doc, have you eaten yet?"

Doctor Kimura laughed tiredly. "That is one thing that is not on my checklist."

"Where are you?"

"ESAARC cockpit in pod four."

Darius knew the place. "Stay where you are, I'll join you soon."

Darius finished logging the info the doctor had given him, and then took off his headset. His stomach suddenly roared with hunger, reminding him that he hadn't eaten recently either. He unbuckled his restraints and pulled himself to the command chair.

"Sir, Doctor Kimura reports all passengers are in stasis and stowed successfully. I've logged the final counts, and sent them to your terminal. Permission to grab some chow?"

The chair swiveled. Colonel Eriksen's square frame dominated it; his receding red hair and thick beard were marred by streaks of white. Eriksen nodded cordially. "Permission granted. You're relieved for a 10 hour shift, Mr. Owens. Get some rest."

"Yes sir." Darius saluted, and then started for the airlock when Colonel Eriksen's voice stopped him.

"Doctor Kimura can have a packet of my tea, if you can't find a substitute."

Darius looked back at the Command chair, but Eriksen had already turned back to his duties. Darius smiled.

Either Dr. Kimura has become too predictable, or I have.

"Thank you sir," Darius responded.

Darius turned away from the airlock before him, instead choosing the staircase behind him leading to the crew pod. After a few turns he found a bank of lockers and opened one. Neatly banded bundles of meals lay within, jostled and canted at various angles from the motion of the ship.

Darius paged through the meal packages for a combination that he believed Dr. Kimura might enjoy. He muttered and grimaced at most of the selections and then came on a package that he quickly plucked out. He grabbed the adjacent pouch for himself and bundled the remaining meals together. He secured the locker and then rummaged within another one.

C'mon, Colonel, where did you hide it?

Darius reached almost to the back wall of the locker just below the second shelf and brushed up against something soft and plastic. He grinned and grabbed the soft pouch, pulling it out for examination. The markings on the pouch confirmed its contents and Darius quickly ripped open one of the meal bags and exchanged the tea for the reconstituted sports drink within, and then secured the second locker.

After his success, Darius departed from the crew pod and made his way down the spine of the ship to pod four.

The ESAARC cockpit door opened swiftly once Darius keyed his code into the pad next to it. Dr. Kimura was looking over his shoulder when Darius entered. Darius floated up to the empty seat next to Kimura, carefully carrying the two meal packs. He handed the open pack to the doctor and then navigated himself into the other seat. He juggled the remaining pack between his arms as he loosely slipped into the restraints.

"Thank you, Darius. I'm starved. What's on the menu today?"

Dr. Kimura peered inside the food pack and pulled out a neatly sealed ration bag.

"Beef sandwiches, potatoes, and orange drink." He saw Dr. Kimura wince at the last item. "I know you don't like that stuff so I traded the colonel for his tea, with his permission, of course."

"That's very kind of you." Dr. Kimura paused. "Will you be able to stay?"

I thought you might ask, he thought. Dr. Kimura had often taken meals with the military personnel back at the compound, especially with his daughter Haruka or with Darius. "Sure, Doc. I'm off duty for now." Darius sat down and opened his sandwich packet. "You know, some odd stuff has been happening up there."

Kimura paused in the middle of his bite.

"What do you mean?"

"Well, you know *Raphael* got delayed, right?" Darius bit a large chunk from his sandwich.

"I hadn't heard. What happened?"

"Well," he said through the food as he chewed, "some transport was damaged by enemy fire on the way up and they had to take it on and evacuate it; that took some time. Then they had four transports to take on total, not three like us or *Michael*. That made them even later."

"Wait, which transport?"

Darius concentrated for a moment as he recalled the information.

"Whiskey… Zero Four, I think. It was bound for *Michael* originally."

The color began to drain from Dr. Kimura's face.

"What happened, Darius? Did everyone survive?"

Darius looked over and stared into the doctor's wide eyes.

I've upset him.

"Doctor Kimura, are you ok?" They stared at each other. The silence was only a few seconds, yet the discomfort was palpable. "As far as I know they're alright."

Dr. Kimura sighed loudly and his eyes closed for a brief moment. "That is good to hear." His eyes opened again and his lips gave a tired smile. "I'm sorry, I didn't mean to interrupt. Please continue."

Darius put his lips to the valve on a small pouch and took a sip of his orange drink as he watched Dr. Kimura with measured concern. "Well, the strangest thing happened just a little bit ago. We got positive radio contact from *Raphael* again. And then they passed us."

"Passed us," Kimura repeated.

"That's right. And they didn't just creep up on us all slow like, either. They shot past us. The last we heard from her, their passenger count was complete, all verified asleep, and that Colonel Fox intended to have *Raphael* waiting for us at our destination, as she was designed. I wasn't too sure what to make of it. But Doctor," a big grin crept over his face, "you should have seen the look on Colonel Eriksen's face. Don't get me wrong. I think the colonel's a good man. It's just that I never thought I would see my CO lost for words, with his jaw on the floor."

Dr. Kimura gave out a good chuckle. *I don't know, maybe he's okay.* Darius considered the doctor's behavior. *I still get the feeling he's hiding something, that he's putting on a front.*

The two sat, staring at the stars as they ate lunch in silence. Once they completed their meal, Darius collected the packaging and stowed it all in a small locker under the console.

Darius broke the silence with a hushed tone, "Doctor Kimura, can we talk some more?"

"Of course, Darius. What's on your mind?"

"You said that everyone here was chosen for a reason, that you and Dr. Benedict had a plan for why we're here."

Kimura nodded and stared at him.

Let's see if he hides when I bring him into the open.

"How were we chosen? What were you looking for?"

Dr. Kimura avoided Darius's curious gaze and took a long look out of the windows.

"There is much to this subject, and some of it may disturb or upset you. Are you sure you want me to tell you?"

Darius considered this carefully. Something almost like fear tingled down his spine. Despite his better judgment, he motioned for the doctor to continue.

"Very well. Years ago the Project Columbus research team proposed and designed a computer algorithm to search out individuals that would be beneficial to establishing a colony. Because we were faced with low initial population numbers we had to create parameters capping certain characteristics of potential inhabitants, most notably profession."

"Okay, that makes sense. So what's the catch?"

"Did you get a chance to take a good look at the passengers when they assembled at the Laramie complex?"

The question made Darius stop. His jaw slacked ever so slightly as he attempted to recall.

"Well, I was busy with my duties so I guess I didn't take a real good look."

Dr. Kimura rolled his head back to look out the two dorsal windows at the splattered, twinkling mass of stars beyond.

"You will come to notice that there are almost no people my age. In fact, the vast majority of the passengers are between eighteen and thirty five."

"Why's that, Doctor?"

"Ah, this is where the design starts to get distasteful. If you consider an older person as someone's mother or father, or possibly grandparent, they become an indispensably intertwined part of a life. If you consider that same person for their skills and ability to contribute genetically to a colony then their value, shall we say… diminishes."

Darius curled his lip slightly. Kimura glanced at him.

"An understandable reaction, Darius. However, we also intentionally sought families. In particular, we wanted ones with small children."

Finally, a silver lining. He continued to process what Dr. Kimura was telling him. Darius still could not shake a nagging feeling, however.

"The ships could not be operated by the scientists," the doctor continued. "Untrained civilians would fare no better at that task. Furthermore, the colony will need some order and protection. This adds the Air Force into the equation; you and your peers gained passage for this reason."

Kimura shifted in his seat, and looked at Darius. His eyes seemed to betray the faint smile.

He still hides something from me. Doctor, I'm your friend. What is it that is that you feel you must protect?

"There's more, isn't there, Doctor? Something you haven't told us. Why?"

Kimura sighed, his body rising and falling as if he stretched from within.

"Yes, Mr. Owens. And now that we are on our way to what will hopefully be our new home, there is no point in hiding it. If you take me into custody and present me to Colonel Eriksen, I understand completely."

Darius blinked, and stared at him, unsure of how to interpret what was just said.

Now I don't want to know. Damn it, why did I ask?

"In essence we stole these sleeper ships from the United States government. We hid our intentions as long as we could, and we reprogrammed the algorithm. We deleted every politician from the database. We drastically cut back certain other professions. We then reassigned a few the remaining open positions to our own families. There were a few trusted officers in the Air Force that helped us move the replacement passengers to Wyoming. Additionally, they covered our tracks as long as they could."

Both men sat silently in their seats, staring at each other.

Don't ask, Darius. For the love of God, don't ask. Keep your mouth shut.

"Why, Doctor?"

"Because I was afraid. Dr. Benedict and Dr. Fairweather were as well. We feared that the government would simply export its own failure and collapse onboard these ships. But more ashamedly, I had a selfish fear. I feared that my family would be left behind, and I would be sent to the stars to wonder about their fate in the darkness."

Dr. Kimura hung his head and his voice cracked. "Do as you must, Darius."

Darius placed his massive hand on the doctor's shoulder.

"No man is an angel, Doctor. Fear and grief are very powerful persuaders. You still saved many lives. Ones I know will be eternally grateful for what you and Dr. Benedict have done." Darius sighed heavily, "However, my duty is clear, Doctor. I will report this to Colonel Eriksen when I next report for duty. Please report with me. Resisting will only make it harder on you."

. . .

"Course corrections complete, Colonel. Exit course to Alpha Centauri B, gravity compensated. We should be on an intercept course for planet Demeter." Captain Bartrand's eyes were bloodshot, and his fatigue was evidenced in his voice.

"Very well, Captain," said Colonel Fox. "How long do we estimate we need to run the plasma drive to achieve escape velocity?"

Bartrand rubbed his eyes, looked at his screen and punched in another set of data to his calculations. He blinked mindlessly at the screen a couple more times, and then spoke, "Three more minutes, Colonel. But we're a long way off from our target speed."

"I understand that, Captain. I want to power down the plasma drive for a bit and back the reactor down on power to give them a break. We've passed the fleet, we can afford ourselves some time to make sure our equipment is working properly." The tone in her voice was harsh, and Haruka could only imagine how the colonel would react to the story of Bartrand's near fatal hesitation.

But she has to know, for the safety of the ship. I have to tell her what happened to Bartrand on the transport. Haruka pondered the wisdom of bringing up the point with Fox, especially in her sleep deprived state. *No. We need to sleep first.*

"Kimura," the colonel barked.

"Yes ma'am?" Her voice cracked as she responded.

"Shut down the main plasma drive. Make sure the second watch is awake, and feed them. Send them to the bridge, and then get some sleep."

"Yes, ma'am." She let out a quiet sigh, switched off the power to the main drive, and unbuckled from her workstation harness. *A long overdue rest.*

She fumbled her way to the bridge railing, and pulled herself up. She could see that the colonel was extremely tired as well, but staring intently ahead, as if to burn a hole in the ship's bow with her gaze. Colonel Fox continued to give orders to the bridge crew. Haruka pulled herself to the end of the bridge, and all the way down the stairwell into the crew sleeper pod.

The second watch was assigned to sleeper section bravo, and Haruka bumped and floated her way into that section. In the minimal lighting of the hall, she was able to make out several crew members, weightlessly moving about their routines. Some were eating out of meal pouches, others changing flight suits.

A spindly, gray-haired major drifted up to Haruka. "Do you have something to report, Lieutenant?"

She straightened and saluted, and received a salute in return. "Yes, sir. Colonel Fox requires second shift to report to the bridge immediately after meal, sir."

"Very well Lieutenant. As you were."

Haruka pulled herself through the hatch and maneuvered to a storage locker. She opened it, retrieved a meal pouch, and then proceeded to section alpha. *Home, sweet home.* Her fingers fumbled as she tore open the outer bag, and the individually sealed contents scattered about the compartment.

"Damn it," she cursed under her breath. Haruka reached her arm out and plucked a portion of food out of the air as it tried to escape her reach. She analyzed the package. *Applesauce.* She loosened the top open, and squirted a stream of the contents into her mouth. The food hit her tongue, and she began to slurp it down. The flavor was pleasant and sweet, and the kick of cinnamon was evident. *Far better than what they ever served us in boot camp, that's for sure.*

As weary as she was, even the small packet of applesauce gave her a boost in energy. She gave a gentle push to and collected the remaining food packets that had scattered. She spun again and came to a rest with her back against the opposing wall.

What else do we have? Burger. Mustard packet. Lemon lime drink. She opened the burger package, folded one edge of the bun up, and slathered it with mustard. She released the mustard packet, using every bit of coordination she had left to keep it floating next to her.

The burger was dry and mostly tasteless, and she had not expected anything else. Haruka was so hungry, it didn't matter in the least to her. Once she finished consuming the food, she moved on to the drink packet. In slow, measured bursts, she squirted the liquid into her mouth.

Dad never liked any of these flavored drinks. She laughed for a moment, imagining him having to choke down a sports drink pouch in zero-G.

Haruka finished her drink, then collected the wrappers and rolled them up inside the outer pouch, stowing it away in a trash locker. As she closed the locker, she saw Marco Mancini pull himself into the hallway, a meal pouch in hand.

"Hell of a day, huh Kimura?" he said as he wrestled with the pouch.

Haruka watched as the stocky, brown-haired lieutenant opened his meal. "I'm not going to have any trouble sleeping, that's for sure." The pouch split open and the food packs within shot out in every direction. Haruka caught a small package of food that floated towards her. She read the label on it, then tossed it gently back to Mancini. "Cheese paste. Let me guess, you've got flatbread and pasta?"

Marco caught the packet, and grabbed another one near by, looking at it. "Yup. Sometimes I wonder who puts these things together. Thanks, Lieutenant." He proceeded to open a small clear pouch, and produced a plastic fork.

She watched him eat for a moment as she replayed the events of the day in her head. "Marco," she said. "What do you remember of the last minute or so before we docked the transport?"

Mancini chewed his pasta slowly, a look of deep thought on his face. He took a gulp from his drink and cleared his throat. "Let's see, I rebooted the control system, you switched to secondary thruster control. The system alarm went off, we went sideways again. Uh, I think I closed my eyes and started praying to God at that point. Next thing I knew, we were stopped, you told me to secure the docking clamps, and the captain looked like he was going to throw up."

He didn't see it, did he? Haruka frowned. "Did you see what the captain was doing right before?"

"No, like I said I was praying my ass off. But I guess you and Captain Bartrand brought us home safe, right?"

Haruka looked off into space and said nothing.

"Haruka?" asked Mancini. "What's on your mind?"

She looked back at him. He was staring at her, and had forgotten all about his meal. His eyebrows were arched and his eyes were open wide.

"What if I told you that the captain froze up?"

He cocked his head, and his hands dropped to his side. "Bartrand?"

Haruka nodded. Mancini looked away for a moment, and then exhaled with a loud huff. Then his eyes narrowed, and his jaw slacked. "Wait a minute. He's been doing nav calculations all day." His eyes snapped up to meet Haruka's. "Dear God, if he's made any mistakes…"

"I know, Marco." *I know all too well. He could run us into an asteroid, or get us sucked into Jupiter's gravity well, or overshoot our target altogether.*

"You've gotta tell Colonel Fox. She needs to know this, if he…"

Haruka interrupted him. "I know. I'm going to bring it up with her, but we're all too tired right now. If I approach her like this, or when she's just as tired, she might just stuff me in an airlock."

"Yeah, you're right," said Mancini. "So what do we do?"

She smiled, and she could feel her eyes to start to droop shut from fatigue. "I'm glad you said *we*, Marco. I need you to back me up on this. But for now, finish your dinner and get some sleep."

"You got it. And don't forget to sleep yourself, Kimura." He knocked on the hatch of a sleeper berth. She opened the portal to her unit. As she prepared to pull herself inside, she saw Ellsworth, Bartrand, and Perez enter the sleeper section, heading towards their berths. She yanked her slight frame into the cubby and secured herself in her harness, then pulled the hatch shut.

Haruka closed her eyes and thought about how she would approach the colonel on the next watch. As much as she tried to formulate a plan, it was too difficult in her state. She relaxed, and her thoughts changed to memories of her family. She could see her sister Saika's toothy smile as Lieutenant Reid, Saika's husband, kissed her. She could see her mother's face scrutinizing the hem of a dress as she sewed. And yet, when her thoughts turned to her father, she always saw him as a slender black haired giant, as she did when she was a little girl.

I hope you're having an easier time than I am, Dad. I could really use another friendly face around here right now. The lieutenant fell fast asleep.

· · ·

"If what you're saying is right, that's treason."

Despite being whispered, Colonel Eriksen's words of condemnation were no less cutting.

I can't believe I am betraying my friend like this.

Darius continued in a hushed tone as he hovered next to the colonel's ear, "I've never known him to lie, sir. Whatever is going on is big. I'm sure there's an explanation."

Even if we don't want to hear it.

He glanced up. Dr. Kimura held on to the railing of the bridge as he drifted near the command chair. His head hung like a puppy that had just been scolded. Darius moved to the side of the chair as Eriksen unlocked it and swung quickly to face the doctor. Colonel Eriksen stared at Dr. Kimura with ice blue eyes; his square jaw and furrowed brow registered his disapproval.

"Lieutenant Miller, please begin a log and activate bridge microphones for recording."

"Yes sir," replied the lieutenant. He loaded a sequence of codes into his station. The computer responded with a chirp. "Log recording, Colonel."

Eriksen tugged at his flight suit once to straighten it.

"*Gabriel* bridge log, entry August 17th, 2014. Time 14:09. Bridge microphones are on for recording the following proceedings. Present at this time are Doctor Tadashi Kimura, Lieutenants Darius Owens, Roger Miller, and Brandon Reid. Also present are Captain Tyler Quinn, Airman Patrick Camp, and Colonel Charles Eriksen."

The commanding officer cleared his throat and continued, "Doctor Tadashi Kimura, you are being placed under arrest. The fact that you turned yourself in will be noted. You are suspected of treason, subversion, sabotage of government property, and theft of government property.

"As you are a civilian, I am obligated to give you your Miranda rights. You have the right to remain silent. Anything you say can be used against you in a court of law. You have the right to an attorney. Should you be unable to afford one, an attorney will be provided for your defense. Do you understand, Doctor?"

Dr. Kimura's voice was barely more than a whisper, "I do, Colonel."

Every man on the bridge had locked their eyes on the doctor, save for Darius. Nearly all of them had a look of disbelief on their face. The colonel scowled, and Lieutenant Reid's eyes looked as if they would burst from his head at any moment.

"Very well. Mr. Owens, can you please state for the record what Doctor Kimura told you about Project Columbus?"

He breathed in and nodded as he tried to force down the lump that had formed in his throat. *I'm sorry, Doctor. I know you said I should follow my duty, but this still feels wrong.*

"We were eating lunch, and I had asked Doctor Kimura about how people were chosen and placed on the ships. He described the basic computer algorithm, designed by the Project Columbus research staff. He proceeded to tell me about how they altered the program to remove certain professions from the database and altered the proportions of other professions within the algorithm. He also mentioned that he had sympathizers within the Air Force that assisted them with hiding evidence and transporting the replacement passengers to the Laramie complex."

Silence engulfed the bridge. A puzzled look crept over Eriksen's face, and he scratched at his receding red hair.

"Doctor Kimura, it would be considered further cooperation if you answered my next questions, and answered them truthfully. I remind you, however, that you have the right not to answer," said Eriksen in a tone of solemn warning.

"I understand," Kimura replied. His head raised and he looked the colonel square in the eye.

Don't hide anything, Doctor, thought Darius.

Eriksen's hand moved to his jaw and he scratched at a streak on his beard. "First, do you object to anything that Lieutenant Owens has said, or do you wish to give a corrected statement?"

"I have no objections, but I do have two clarifications to make. "

"Go on."

"The algorithm was suggested, but not designed, by Dr. Weiss. Also, Dr. Robert Fairweather was involved in the algorithm's design, but Dr. Jonathan Fairweather was party to the modification. These changes were made well after his father and Dr. Weiss passed away."

"So noted. Mr. Owens mentioned that you have sympathizers in the Air Force. Who are they?"

Dr. Kimura had drifted slightly, so he righted himself. "Our primary sympathizer is Brigadier General Andrew McLaughlin. Most of the remaining are officers under his direct command."

"Were," Colonel Erikson interrupted.

The doctor paused and tilted his head slightly. "Were, sir?"

"General McLaughlin was killed in action four days ago, Dr. Kimura. Much of his command was destroyed as well."

An expression of shock shot across Kimura's face. "I… I see."

"Are there any other sympathizers, Doctor?"

"Yes, Colonel. Major Dan Forrest, and Lieutenants William Shipp and Brandon Reid."

As if they were tied together, all eyes in the room shifted from Kimura to the young lieutenant, who sat dumbfounded at his nav station. Silence once again fell over the bridge. Reid opened his mouth as if to speak, but the doctor shook his head at him. Darius's heart dropped suddenly.

Dear God, no. There are conspirators on the sleepers?

Colonel Eriksen turned back to Dr. Kimura. "Why, Doctor, did you do this? What possible motivation would you have to condemn those you removed from the database?"

"I was afraid, both for humanity and my family. The latter was purely selfish of me, I realize. But there is information about the algorithm that must be made known." Dr. Kimura nervously tapped his foot on the railing and his eyes darted between Darius and Eriksen.

"Go ahead, Doctor."

"The original algorithm was stacked so that the majority of the selected people would be between eighteen and thirty five, and worked in a trade or basic services industry. Children were encouraged in this age group. We felt it would be necessary to have both an existing young generation as well as adults that could continue to have children. The mix of professions was created so as to maximize any colony's chance of survival by having people who could build, farm, and take care of the ill.

"We completed the algorithm in 2002. By the language of the contract we were working under, however, we were required to submit the details of the programming and operation of the algorithm to scrutiny by Congress. It went to committee, was debated, modified, sent back, debated some more, and so forth. By the time it was approved in 2007, some of the original parameters had changed.

"At first we didn't think anything of it," Kimura continued. "But we started simulation of the algorithm in 2010. What we found was unsettling." He paused long enough that a feeling of suspense became thick in the air.

"Well, what did you find?" Eriksen's voice betrayed a hint of impatience.

Dr. Kimura took on a sudden grave tone, and his speech slowed. "Time after time it resulted in an abnormally high number of politicians. Moreover, we found that the same four Congressmen and their families ended up on the passenger list every single time we ran the simulation. Thorough analysis of the numbers indicated that between 25 and 30 percent of the total passenger capacity would always be selected as politicians and their families."

Darius felt a shiver run down his spine and the hairs on his neck stand up. He realized what the doctor was really saying. *We were betrayed first, by our own government.* He scanned the faces of his colleagues and saw nothing but shock.

"Dr. Benedict suggested we alter the algorithm to be a slight variant of the original. We eliminated or drastically reduced certain specific professions, and manually entered individual persons to fill voids." Kimura's eyes locked on to Lieutenant Reid. "In most of these cases, the individuals were related to the research staff, or to our sympathizers. The total number of these positions was limited to one percent of the total passenger capacity, compared to the 25 percent that was given to us in the modified algorithm."

Again, a blanket of silence descended. Darius watched as the doctor again switched his gaze, this time moving between Reid and the Colonel.

"Do you have any further statements, Doctor Kimura," asked Eriksen as he once again scratched at his beard.

"No, Colonel."

Eriksen swiveled his chair to face Reid. "Lieutenant Brandon Reid, you are under arrest for conspiracy to commit treason and conspiracy to commit subversion. You will be held until a court martial proceeding can occur. You are relieved of duty and confined to your berth for the duration of *Gabriel's* travel." Reid blinked and his head bobbed. "Captain Quinn, escort the lieutenant to his berth, and activate his unit. Mr. Owens, remove him from the maintenance cycle revival list. Replace him with Lieutenant Schneider."

"Yes, sir," both men responded in unison. Darius couldn't help but wonder what Reid was feeling at this moment, having been turned out for discipline by his own father in law.

"Doctor Kimura, it would be considered a further mitigating factor if you continued to serve your original role in monitoring the passengers and biostasis systems during this mission, until such time as you are charged or tried with a crime. Can we count on you for this?"

Kimura's response was without hesitation. "Of course, Colonel."

He is not placing the doctor in stasis?

The colonel continued, "The record will show that Dr. Tadashi Kimura will not be removed from maintenance cycle revival. He has critical knowledge and experience that cannot be ignored. We are in an enclosed ship in the vacuum of space; he has no possibility of escape. Although he is suspected of a capital crime, he has not shown aggression or malice to any person on board this vessel. Lieutenant Miller, please end recording."

Miller punched a button, and the terminal chirped. "Recording off, sir."

Darius and the red headed Captain Quinn moved to the nav consoles. Darius reached for the accused man's arm, but he held up one hand as if to indicate compliance. Reid rose up with his head bowed and made his way toward the end of the bridge. Darius and Quinn followed. As he passed the command chair, he saw that the colonel had risen up and was whispering something to Dr. Kimura, through clenched teeth and a sneer. Kimura's eyes were closed and his head once again drooped as he nodded at the colonel.

As they departed the bridge, Darius could hear Colonel Eriksen giving orders to contact the rest of the fleet about the other conspirators. The trio silently made their way down the staircase and into the crew pod. They reached Reid's sleeper berth within hallway alpha. It was anonymous, no difference separating it from the others flanking it.

But it will be a prison, unlike the others. Is that really fair to him?

Reid broke the silence with an unsteady voice. Darius could tell he was fighting back his emotion. "Tyler. Tell Saika what happened. Tell her I did it for her, for us. Tell Kayla, too. She needs to know that I was trying to save her life."

Captain Quinn's face looked as if he had aged a decade in just a few seconds. "Brandon, don't..."

"Promise me, Tyler! No matter what happens, my wife and sister need to know what happened."

"I... I promise."

Darius felt a lump rise within his own throat.

How can they possibly understand? Reid, what were you thinking?

Darius and Quinn watched as Lieutenant Brandon Reid pulled himself into the darkness of the sleeper and fastened his restraints. With one last nod between Reid and Quinn, the captain closed the berth. Darius drifted to the console at the end of the row and activated the berth.

Darius and Quinn glanced once at each other. Without a word, the two went on their separate ways.

. . .

```
Calvin McLaughlin
Date and time unknown
Michael
>|
```

"C'mon, Cal! You can hit harder than that!" Mike's voice called to him from somewhere behind him. His voice was almost drowned out by a low rumbling that couldn't quite be made out.

Mike? Mike, where are you?

There was a baseball bat in Calvin's hands, its shape not wholly defined, but rather hazy instead. A warm breeze licked his cheeks and then was gone. Out in the darkness ahead, a faintly lit metal shape started to slowly float towards him.

"Hit this one out of the park, dude!" Rob was there too, somewhere. His voice was full of laughter.

Rob? Mike?

The metal object was closer now, and Cal thought he could make it out. *Is that a mailbox?* As it approached, Calvin did indeed decide it was a mailbox, although it was hazy as well. He felt his arms swing, and watched the bat smash into the mailbox. With a metallic crunch, the mailbox flew out into oblivion.

Laugher echoed through his ears, and then the rumbling rose quickly in volume and pitch, accompanied by a squealing noise. He felt himself pitch backwards slightly. *Rob's truck? Where are they?*

He felt someone lift the bat out of his hands. "He still hits like a girl. Hey Cal, watch this girl hit harder." *Brittany.*

He looked over his shoulder, and saw Brittany holding the bat, her long blonde hair obscuring her face. *That can't be, the wind would blow it out of her face, not into it.*

The bat swung again, and another mailbox hurtled at Cal, just over his field of vision. "Did you see that, guys?" She laughed, and the other boys joined in chorus.

Calvin turned around, and there was nothing anymore. The bat was gone, the noises of the truck's engine and the laughter were gone, and he floated in the dark silence.

It's a dream. I'm asleep, I must be dreaming. He thought to himself.

Turning once more, he found himself weightless in a vast, dark corridor. He moved aimlessly toward an end that he could not see. The floor beneath him had endless rungs built into it. The dark shapes of structural braces loomed in front of him, and tunnels to his left and right led into darkness. "Hello?" he called. He was greeted by his own hollow echo.

The ship. I was just in this hallway. But there were people.

"What is your problem, Cal?" barked a familiar voice from behind him. Cal spun around, and was face to face with his father. The general defied gravity, and stood firmly on the deck in his immaculate dress blues, hat tucked under his arm.

"Dad?"

"You screwed up again, son," scowled his father.

"What? What did I do, Dad?" Calvin was puzzled. *You're the one that sent me here, remember? I didn't do anything!* Cal thought he was speaking, but realized his words were only in his mind.

General McLaughlin's face furrowed even more. "Don't act innocent. And don't give me that crap about not smoking pot or drinking. You were in the truck with your so-called friends. The cops said you were drunk. Why the hell are you doing this to yourself?"

This isn't about being blasted into space, is it Dad?

"You'll never be a real man if you keep up this loser shit, Cal. You need to pull your ass together and do your school work so you have a chance at college. God knows even the Air Force wouldn't take you like this."

Anger began to well up inside of him. He tried to control it. He didn't want this anger, not now.

"Fuck you, Dad." As quickly as it came, his anger stopped and was replaced by numbness. *That's not what I wanted to say! Oh God, Dad...*

He felt himself turning around and moving away from his father. *No, wait! I can't leave it like this!* His body would not comply though, and he found himself drifting down the corridor. It was no longer lit as he approached the end, and Cal drifted into the blackness.

What did you know, Dad?

A soft orange glow appeared before him in the distance, as tiny as a penny. As he drifted forth, it grew in size and morphed into a fire. Cal could see three figures, barely illuminated by the flames. Once more, familiar laughter could be heard, dancing in his head.

"Did you bring the booze, Cal?" Mike's disembodied voice drifted forth.

He looked at his hands, now holding two surreal bottles of liquor. "Yeah, dude. He's got it." Now the voice was that of Rob. "Dude, get over here. It's time to get wasted."

He floated forward some more, and could see the faces of his friends, although they still looked distorted as if through frosted glass. Cal's hands stretched out, and Rob and Brittany grabbed the bottles from him. Calvin could see Mike lighting a cigarette.

No, that's not right. It was a joint.

Cal was standing next to the fire, but he felt no heat. He watched as his friends drank and smoked. They talked and laughed but their words had no meaning to Cal. All three turned their attention to him, and it seemed their laughter was directed at Cal. Mike's arm extended, and offered the joint to Cal. His attention focused on the burning roll in front of him. The situation became more familiar to him.

The first time.

"C'mon, dude. You've said no every time. I'm not taking no for an answer this time." Mike beckoned one more time. Cal's arm reached out, against his will. He picked up the joint, and scrutinized it. *No...*

Brittany's voice rang out. "He won't do it. He's too chicken." She giggled, then said, "not a man. Not like Robbie here." He watched Brittany lean over and give Rob a wet kiss. Once again, his anger flashed.

She was supposed to be mine, you ass. Without thought, his hand rose to his face, and Calvin took a drag, holding in the smoke for a moment before coughing it out. He felt nothing but the emptiness within himself.

Another round of cackling rose from his friends, and a bottle was shoved in his hand. His mind fought against his hand as it came up to his lips, but in vain; he took a deep swig of the liquor. A bitter taste filled his mouth. Cal turned to vomit, but he couldn't. The light grew dim again, and when he turned back, his friends were gone.

"Can you stop trying to sabotage yourself for just one week, Calvin?"

He spun around and again was face to face with his father.

"Dad..." was all he could manage.

"That's twice you've been arrested. Are you trying to ruin your future?" Cal could see the anger written all over General McLaughlin's face. "These friends of yours are no good punks, and they're dragging you with them."

Cal heard himself scoff. He dreaded what he knew he would say next.

"Yeah? Better to have shitty friends than no friends at all, Dad. How does it feel to come home to an empty house? To go to a bar and drink alone? Huh, Dad?"

No, Cal. Why did you say that to him? The gravity of his words now seemed even harsher in retrospect. They stood there, staring at each other. Cal saw the veins in his father's head bulge. Numbness gave way to feelings of guilt and exhaustion. *Even in my dreams I'm tired.*

Calvin turned away, unable to bear the look on his father's face anymore. He moved forward with his head drooped. He looked back talk to his father but found he was alone again, floating in the darkness. Slowly, Cal drifted towards a dim light in the distance. He found himself once more in the darkened gallery of the sleeper ship.

Ahead were three dark figures, their backs were turned to Calvin. His head began to throb as he approached, and he heard laughter. They saw him, and started to move off.

"Rob, Mike, Brittany. Wait!" he shouted.

Try as he might, he could not catch up to them as they moved off. Cal floated to a stop. A gentle light from the ceiling overhead bathed him in a soft glow. He sat, alone with his thoughts, wracked with guilt and loneliness.

Minutes seemed to pass into hours. Then he felt something brush against his throbbing temple. He turned around.

Alexis.

. . .

Haruka floated in the empty sleeper section, the cold air within causing goose bumps to rise on her bare skin. She cast off her dirty flight suit, and unfolded one that she had retrieved from a storage locker.

Colonel Fox needs to know about Bartrand's freeze up. She shuddered at the idea of the consequences. *Far too much at stake, we need to make sure someone is there to back him up at the controls.*

She slipped into the flight suit and covered her nearly naked body. Haruka zipped up the suit just as a sleeper berth opened. Mancini pulled himself from the opening, his eyes barely open.

"Good morning, Lieutenant," she said.

Mancini managed to grunt an acknowledgement, and then floated off in search of food. Haruka herself had already eaten a package that contained scrambled eggs, sausage, and a thick hot sauce paste for garnish. While the food was decent, the instant coffee drink left much to be desired.

Another sleeper opened, and this time Captain Bartrand emerged.

"Good morning, Captain," she chirped, trying to mask any concern in her voice.

He nodded. "Lieutenant, good to see you. Did you sleep well?"

"Yes, sir," she lied.

"Good. See you on the bridge, Lieutenant."

"Yes, sir."

Haruka pushed off of the sleeper berths and navigated out of the pod. She encountered Mancini in the stairway connecting the pod to the gallery and bridge. Great rings under his eyes showed his fatigue, and he was attacking a food ration like a starved dog. As she passed on her way up the stairs to the bridge, he nodded to her. When she reached the top, Haruka paused for a moment to take in the panoramic view afforded by the bridge's glass canopy. Thousands of stars stretched in every direction, impossible to count.

Colonel Fox floated her way up the staircase past Haruka. "Colonel, may I have a word, please?" Haruka asked. Fox grabbed the railing to stop herself.

The colonel acknowledged Haruka with fiery eyes. "Yes, Lieutenant?

What is it?"

Here goes nothing. Or everything. She straightened her flight suit and took a deep breath.

"Ma'am, I have a concern about Captain Bartrand."

She saw Fox's eyes widen, and then narrow slightly. "What kind of concern, Lieutenant?"

"On the flight up to the sleeper ships, when Whiskey Zero Four was damaged, Captain Bartrand froze up on final approach," she stated, trying to keep her voice down. She saw Bartrand, Perez, Shipp, and Maynard floating past, to their stations.

"What do you mean froze up?"

"The captain did everything correct through most of the flight, but after the retro rockets were fired and we approached the dock, I noticed the transport pitching down slightly. When I looked over, the captain was off his controls and staring straight off into space."

Fox's brow furrowed into a sinister looking V, and Haruka could see anger flash over her. "And I suppose you're going to tell me you landed the transport, then?"

Haruka sighed, "Yes ma'am. I'm not trying to…"

"Save it, Kimura. I won't have any glory hogging. This is not the time or place for such childish…"

She was interrupted by a lieutenant manning an ops station. "Colonel!" he yelled. "Receiving a transmission from *Gabriel*. Colonel Eriksen ordering the arrest of Lieutenant William Shipp, charges of conspiracy to commit treason and subversion."

A stunned silence descended upon the bridge as, for a second, all eyes focused on Lieutenant Shipp. Shipp then sprung from his ops console and made way for the exit.

"Seize him," ordered Bartrand.

As Shipp attempted to pass the Colonel, Fox reached out and grabbed him by the collar. She yanked at his suit, and sent him face first into the railing. Shipp yelped in pain, and then stammered, "O-o-okay! I give!"

Maynard and Bartrand moved up and grabbed the lieutenant roughly as the colonel let go.

"Lieutenant Singh, send a request to *Gabriel* for more details on the charges against Shipp," Fox snarled.

"Ma'am, there is no need for that," said Shipp, his voice eerily calm. "I'll answer any questions you have."

All eyes were once more on the young Lieutenant. Blood began to float away from a cut on his forehead. Colonel Fox gritted her teeth, and then began the interrogation.

"What were you doing, Lieutenant? What is the nature of this charge against you?"

"We were protecting the future colony. We were trying to restore the correct balance of skills within the passenger lists to maximize chances of survival," he said, wincing in pain.

Maximize chances of survival? But that's what the algorithm was supposed to do.

"Bullshit, Lieutenant. I was briefed by the research staff as to what the selection algorithm was supposed to do," snapped Fox. "They assured us that it would pick passengers based on their ability to contribute to the security and health of an isolated colony. Try again."

Shipp countered, "No, Colonel. The algorithm had been compromised. Someone had altered it. We were just changing it back the way it was."

She scoffed, "That sounds like a computer glitch, not treason."

The lieutenant shook his head. "No, ma'am. This was not a programming error or glitch. This was the final algorithm that Congress approved for use in the program. Dr. Kimura said that it changed how the computer selected people, and filled up the ships with a bunch of people who would be useless to the mission."

"That's a hell of an accusation, Lieutenant. So you and your conspirators go and change a computer algorithm that could potentially say who lives or dies based on what, a hypothesis by Dr. Kimura?"

Dad would never level such an accusation... Butterflies began to form in Haruka's stomach, and her hands became clammy.

Again, Shipp shook his head. "Doctors Kimura, Benedict, and Fairweather ran many simulations of the algorithm and found what they called serious flaws in it. They said that the original algorithm had been altered so much, they were unsure if a colony could survive anymore. That's why they asked for our help."

WHAT? Dad.. oh no!

Fox's jaw nearly dropped to the floor. "Lieutenant, did you just accuse the doctors of being a party to this?"

"Yes, ma'am. In fact, I received my instructions directly from Dr. Benedict."

The colonel spat back, "Convenient to blame a dead man, don't you think, Lieutenant?"

He shrugged. "Contact *Gabriel*. Have them verify with Dr. Kimura, or Lieutenant Reid. Heck, contact *Michael* and have them ask Major Forrest or Dr. Fairweather."

Haruka's stomach turned. She had to fight the sudden urge to throw up. *Dad? Brandon?*

"Colonel," a soft voice interrupted. Lieutenant Singh had his hand up to his headset, listening to an unheard conversation within. "Lieutenant Shipp speaks the truth. Dr. Kimura confessed yesterday afternoon."

Tears began to well up in Haruka's eyes, and she bit her lip. *NO! Dad, what have you done?* She grasped the railing tighter, her knuckles turning white as snow. Colonel Fox looked sternly at Shipp, then Haruka, and back again to Shipp. *No, Colonel. No, I didn't do anything!*

"Maynard, Bartrand. Get these two off my bridge. Put them in stasis until we can court martial them," she growled harshly.

Bartrand was at Haruka's side in an instant, and dug his fingers into her arm until she screamed out in pain.

"Let her go, Colonel! Lieutenant Kimura is innocent!" yelled Shipp, as Maynard started to push him towards the stairs.

"Innocent my ass. If Dr. Kimura was in on it, certainly his precious daughter, an Air Force officer, was his right hand," Fox sneered.

Haruka cried out, "Please, Colonel!" Bartrand gave her arm another yank, and it came free from the railing.

Shipp pleaded once more, "She's innocent. I swear to it. I've answered everything truthfully, you can believe me."

The plea fell on deaf ears. "If this little harpy was innocent, she wouldn't have tried to tell me that Captain Bartrand froze up while flying that death trap they came up in. She's just trying to play for power."

Bartrand's grasp loosened slightly, and Haruka could see a moment of fear in his eyes. *He knows that he froze up. Tell her, Captain!* But once more, Bartrand's fingers tightened as his lip curled.

"No, Colonel. Lieutenant Kimura is right about Captain Bartrand. I was there," Marco Mancini's voice floated up the stairway. *Marco, thank God. I needed backup.*

Everyone stopped for a moment. A puzzled look came across Colonel Fox's face for a second, but then melted away once more into anger.

"I suppose you're right, Shipp," she spoke with daggers in her voice. "I don't have enough evidence to arrest Kimura. But I'll be damned if she's on my bridge crew. Bartrand, release her."

J.C. Rainier

The captain stared at Haruka for a moment, and then released her arm with a slight shove.

Fox looked back at Shipp. "Get this piece of garbage off my bridge and put him in stasis. Remove him from the maintenance revival list."

"Yes, ma'am," responded Maynard and Bartrand in unison.

Now Haruka drew the stare from the colonel. "Lieutenant Kimura and Lieutenant Mancini, you are both relieved of your current duties." They both gasped loudly. "You will be reassigned to propulsion maintenance duties. As there is no work to be done until the next maintenance cycle, you are to report to your berths immediately to be placed into stasis until the next cycle."

How can she do this? She started to speak feebly, "Colonel…"

"Silence," screamed Colonel Fox. At once the bridge was silent again. "I will not tolerate insubordination from anyone on board this ship, do you understand?"

A resounding chorus of "Yes, ma'am!" came from all on the bridge.

Haruka floated still for a moment. "Now, Kimura!" Fox yelled, spit flying from her lips.

She pushed off and down the stairs. Mancini clung to the railing below, slack jawed and aghast. She stopped and they exchanged looks of despair with each other. Both proceeded in silence to the sleeper pod.

"Well, this is a fine pickle we're in, right Kimura?" Marco remarked.

She sniffed and wiped at her eyes, trying to hold back her tears. "I'm sorry, Marco. I didn't mean for that to happen."

Mancini rested his back against a berth. "I'm still trying to figure out what the hell just happened to begin with. I mean, can she even do what she did? And what's all this stuff about your father? I can't believe that he would involve himself in any treason."

"I don't know if she can, but she just did. I doubt anyone will oppose her, and now Bartrand is firmly with her." She gave a deep sigh. "Thank you for saying that about Dad. I don't believe a word of it either. Nor about Brandon."

Marco looked puzzled. "Brandon?"

"Lieutenant Reid. My sister's husband. Shipp said he was in on it too, if he can be believed." She paused to think. *Saika, do you have any idea what's going on?* Her attention went back to Mancini. "Hey, thanks for backing me up. I didn't realize we'd get in this much trouble."

Mancini laughed quickly and said, "Don't worry about it. Remember back when we did the flight sims for the transports? I told you I'd follow you to hell and back, right?"

She smiled at him. "Yeah, I remember."

Marco grinned devilishly. "Yeah, well if we don't get our butts into these berths and into stasis, I might have to do that for you. Colonel didn't sound like she had much fuse left."

Haruka laughed once more as she wiped away the last of her tears. "Yeah, we probably should. I'm probably going to need you to back me up when we get to this planet of Benedict's, can't have her chewing you up and spitting you out just yet."

With one last shared laugh, the two lieutenants pulled themselves into their respective berths and strapped their harnesses. Haruka closed her hatch with a resounding *click*.

As she lay in the darkness awaiting sleep, she thought of Shipp and her father. *Shipp's lying, right Dad?* Her thoughts raced about what might happen to her father and Brandon, then to her sister and mother. She was concerned about how the two might react if they were to wake up and find their respective husbands under arrest.

In her thoughts of her family, she forgot about Bartrand.

• • •

Darius reached for his drink pouch and took a deep swig. The sweet orange liquid soothed his dry throat as it went down. He batted away a few stray drops from the air next to his face.

The mainframe room was cold and the air filtered. This was done to extend the life of the equipment contained within. Each of the three banks of servers were also exact copies of each other; Darius knew this was to provide redundancy should a blade or even a rack fail.

He focused his attention back on the workstation screen before him. Programming code littered the panel in an almost chaotic jumble. Darius scrutinized each individual line on the page.

Lord, this is taking a long time. This file is more broken than I thought. It doesn't help that the original programmers didn't tag any code.

Darius had been working off and on for a month attempting to repair the corrupted file. He was making progress, but there was no way he could finish before he needed to go into hibernation.

A section of damaged code came up as he scrolled to the next screen; he quickly erased the errant symbols and then painstakingly recreated the original commands from memory. Once he had placed the new statements, he ran a debug program. He grunted when the program came back with errors, and he began the editing process over again.

Periodically he glanced over at a small insert of his screen that was flashing between sets of passenger data. Or, at least, it was supposed to be flashing between them.

Halfway through the hour it took to repair that single page of code, the smaller inset seemed to get stuck. Darius had ignored this to push through and complete his work. Finally, the debug routine came back with no errors. Darius saved his progress and rubbed his great, dark hands up and down his face.

Time to check on him and see what he's up to.

The click of the buckles echoed through the room as he released his harness. He stretched out and his joints creaked from all the time spent hunched over the screen. He neatly rolled up and stowed the remnants of the meal he had just consumed, and then exited into the dark hallway of the propulsion section.

Darius made his way forward, passing the looming sentinels of the internal braces as well as an ominous black hole in the floor leading to the cargo pods. He paused briefly outside of pod four before snaking his way to Dr. Kimura's berth. Kimura was drifting in front of the terminal at the far end of the hallway.

Darius watched Dr. Kimura for several minutes. The Japanese scientist no longer looked like the wise man that Darius had always seen. Instead he had closed eyes and a face devoid of any expression at all. That, and he hadn't moved in quite some time.

"Doctor, is everything alright?"

Dr. Kimura jerked alert like a startled rabbit. His eyes darted to Darius before resting back on the terminal screen in front of him.

"Pardon?"

"Those passengers, Doctor. You've been looking at their vitals for almost a half hour now."

The doctor took a deep breath and rubbed his eyes quickly. He pressed a button and the terminal cycled to another set of passenger vitals.

"Everything is fine, Darius. I must have nodded off." Kimura stopped for a moment and one of his eyebrows shot up. "Are you monitoring what I am doing on my screen, Darius?"

Darius nodded. "Colonel's orders."

Which is silly. I know you're not going to just give up on your work.

Dr. Kimura shrugged and resumed his task, "I can understand his apprehension. He's no fool. All things considered, I believe he is handling this situation well."

It had been a month since the doctor was arrested and Lieutenant Reid placed in stasis. He knew it would not be much longer before the rest of the crew would place themselves in stasis. *Gabriel* was already at cruising speed, and the Oort probe had been launched a week prior to verify that their trajectory out of the system would not be obstructed by any comets or asteroids. Data was already returning from the probe and the collision warning system had been synchronized with the probe's data stream.

Dr. Kimura had told Darius that he wanted to check the passengers' vitals one more time before the first hibernation cycle, and Darius had convinced Colonel Eriksen to allow it.

Besides, I might get a chance to put more time into fixing the corrupted com system software.

Darius became aware that he was staring at the doctor, as he had turned around to return what was almost a glare at Darius.

"Is there something I can do for you, Mr. Owens?"

"Doctor, there's something wrong. I can tell. Others might not be able to see it, but I can. Your behavior has been strange all month."

Kimura sighed as he wrung his hands. "I have only compounded my fears, Darius. I had feared leaving my family behind, but now I fear I have put my family in jeopardy by bringing them with me."

Now if that's not the oddest thing he's ever said to me, I don't know what is.

Kimura continued, "There were certain functions of the stasis system that we could not test or project. Our algorithm was programmed to eliminate these variables from the selection pool. Try not to be upset, Darius, but one specific variable was pregnancy."

Crap. Just when I thought this damned program couldn't get any worse.

Darius felt his fists clench slightly. For the first time ever, he actually felt like he could bear animosity towards this man. "That's pretty low, Doctor."

"I understand the reaction and, frankly, I agree with you. However, there was a great measure of uncertainty surrounding how pregnancy would affect a human in biostasis. Our tests in rats showed a marked increase in the mortality rate of both the mother and the offspring. Similar tests in other animals contradicted the original findings."

So the tests were inconclusive. That doesn't mean...

"We couldn't ethically test this on an actual woman, and one human pregnancy would have made for far too small of a sample size in any case. We believed that this wouldn't cause a problem for the colony since young women would be able to get pregnant and give birth after our arrival."

Darius considered this carefully. "So your conscience is catching up to you, and you're regretting this decision?"

Kimura shook his head with fervor. "No. I cannot have the luxury of analyzing individuals, either passengers or those excluded from the program. I cannot even have the luxury of getting to know any passengers until we arrive and a colony is established."

Darius grew impatient. "Then what is it?"

Dr. Kimura sighed and his eyes looked sad. "I have become aware of a pregnant passenger."

Darius shuffled his hands along the wall and sniffed. "So? You said you don't have the luxury of caring, right?"

"I wish that was the case, Darius. It's Saika Reid, my daughter."

Darius stopped and looked at Kimura. There was no way he could hide the shock evident on his face. The two men floated in the silent hall for a brief moment before the doctor abruptly turned off the computer console and opened his sleeper berth.

"Doctor, wait." Darius reached his hand for the old man's shoulder but stopped short. He was upset with the doctor, but at the same time knew of his need for comfort.

"Yes?" Kimura struggled to mask the emotion in his voice.

Darius tried to speak, but could not form any words. Dr. Kimura pulled himself into the sleeper berth and strapped in as Darius looked on. Darius struggled to find something to say, but it all eluded him.

"Good night Mr. Owens. I will see you in five years." Dr. Kimura closed the sleeper berth hatch and Darius heard the lock click.

Darius was left alone in the hallway, thoughts and emotions ripping through his mind like a great torrent. He grimaced and made his way to the terminal that Kimura had been using. He flipped the unit on and searched for a sleeper berth. A graph showing a strong heart beat and respiration functions cast a glow on his face. His finger hovered over a large button marked "Activate".

I'm sorry for your pain, Doctor. But I will see you in five years, just as you promised.

Darius pressed the button firmly. The computer flashed a confirmation on the screen and Dr. Tadashi Kimura's sleeper unit began its biostasis routine.

. . .

Calvin felt his eyes open slowly. He could not be sure if he was awake or dreaming, as he continued to float in near total darkness. His head felt as if it was spinning. A dim red light pulsed from somewhere nearby.

He turned his head to his right, and saw a button throb on the wall of his berth. He extended his finger and pressed it. A display came up, at first just appearing as a jumble of numbers in Cal's blurred vision. He blinked and rubbed his eyes. Cal realized how clammy his hands were.

9-22-2019 06:04.

Cal blinked and thought for a moment. *Another dream. Will these never end?*

The terminal display went dark, and Cal could faintly make out a soft, diffuse light from just beyond. He went to reach for it, but something kept him from moving. He lurched again, and again was stopped. Cal grabbed at his chest, and felt the straps and buckles of his harness. His stomach churned hard.

Scrambling with his fingers, he frantically tried to unlatch his harness. For a moment, his clumsy fingers worked against him. He felt panic rising within him, and he held his breath. With one more try, he was able to release the straps. Cal reached around in the dark, and found a latch next to the display. Jerking and twisting it, he managed to open it and the hatch of his sleeper berth opened. He blinked at the soft, pale light that filtered in.

"What the…" he began, but cut himself off. His mouth watered and his head spun like he was in a washing machine.

Calvin pulled his head out of the berth in the nick of time as his stomach revolted. Cal vomited; the giant glob floated lazily away from him. He breathed in and recovered for a moment, then sent forth another mass of vomit. He could feel his throat start to burn, and could taste the bitterness in his mouth.

Crap, this isn't a dream.

Cal continued to breathe in deeply. He felt his stomach churn again, but he managed to hold back from throwing up a third time. He pulled his head back into his berth, closed his eyes, and concentrated on breathing.

Time passed as Cal floated in his sleeper. The spinning in his head subsided and was replaced by a dull throb. Cal tried to process the situation. His mind went back to the display panel. Opening his eyes, he pressed the red button on the terminal once more.

9-22-2019 06:33.

2019? Five years? That can't be right.

He hoisted himself out of the sleeper. Sleeper units on both the far side of the hallway were splattered with his vomit, and yet more still floated in aimless morphing balls. Disgusted, Cal pushed off of the sleeper wall and into the adjoining hall beyond. He then proceeded through the connecting hall leading to the gallery level.

Cal looked both ways, and could only see emptiness and eventual darkness in the dimly lit gallery. Carts chained to the hand railings on the floor floated like silent metal guardians near the pod's entrance. Cal floated over to a cart and stabilized himself on it, listening for signs of activity. His efforts were in vain, as only a ventilation fan kicking on nearby greeted his ears.

The other passengers should be waking up any time now, he thought to himself. *Then I guess we find out where we are.* Cal floated alone in silence for several minutes. Except for the dim lighting of the gallery corridor illuminating the way along the backbone and the sound of the fan, there was nothing. He saw no one, he heard no one. His skin began to crawl.

Something is wrong.

He wiped his lips and looked at his hand. Cal saw the flaked off remnants of his earlier vomit session on his hand, and could still taste it in his mouth. He looked down and saw spatter all over his shirt as well. Grimacing, he turned back into the sleeper pod. He noticed storage lockers along many walls inside the pod as he navigated his way inward.

I guess I was too busy to notice those on the way in. I wonder what they contain?

Calvin opened a locker. Within he could dimly make out rows of small plastic pouches neatly bundled together, completely packed from floor to ceiling. He reached in and struggled with the bundle for a moment, finally slipping a package out from within. He read the label aloud, "Standard Space Ration, menu 8A. Contains penne with meat sauce, vegetable medley, lemon-lime drink." He flipped the package over once, then back again. With an "hmm", he tucked it under his arm and closed the locker.

Cal continued to open and look through lockers in a search for fresh clothing, though he found only lockers containing more food packages. Still others were locked. At the end of one hallway, he encountered a pair of skinny lockers flanking a door marked "AUTHORIZED PER-SONNEL ONLY".

He tried the right locker first, and loosely packed trash floated within. A wrapper from a food package tumbled in slow motion toward Cal's face. Cal pushed the garbage back inside and closed the locker, then proceeded to the other. Inside was a dark, rumpled bundle of clothing. He reached inside and pulled out the clothing, examining it. It was a flight suit, and did not appear to be soiled. Grinning, he gently maneuvered his food package and the suit into the locker, and awkwardly began undressing himself in the hallway.

Removing his shirt was difficult, and the effort sent him spinning. He flung his arms out, banging one on the locker. He winced in pain, but managed to steady himself once more. Cal unzipped his jeans, and tried to carefully peel them off. He got the cuff caught at his ankle, and ended up slowly flipping head over heels. Alarmed, he jerked his pants free, and his feet flung into the door. He flailed once more, like a cat falling from a tree. This time his right hand caught on the edge of the locker, and he screamed out as the back of his hand tore open.

He managed to stop his rotation once more, and looked at his hand. Blood was starting to well up from the shallow gash. He sucked on it, tasting the acrid iron of his blood. Cal withdrew and examined his hand. Blood once more filled in the wound, and a few drops managed to escape the pool and float away.

Damn, that hurts. He winced and sucked in a deep breath.

Cal looked at his scattered clothing floating in the hallway. He sighed, collected his stained t-shirt, and maneuvered to the door jamb. He braced himself between the lockers and tore a swath from the cleanest part of his shirt, then wrapped it around his hand three times and tightly tucked it in on itself.

With the cut bandaged, he grabbed the flight suit and carefully donned it, then zipped it up. Cal flexed his arms and legs a little bit to determine the suit's fit.

Good fit, this should do.

Cal pushed himself up and retrieved his food pouch from within the locker. He tore it open, scattering four individual pouches within into the hallway. He growled, and retrieved each package. The smallest was clear plastic, and contained a napkin, fork, spoon, and a single-serve package of breath mints. He opened this pouch with measured caution, and was relieved when none of the contents flew outward.

Good. I'd rather not die in space with a fork stuck in my eye.

He was starting to get better at opening the packages. When he opened the largest one, he saw a packed mess of pasta and meat within. Poking at it with the fork, he found it easy to break apart and control. He consumed the entrée slowly and then moved on to his vegetable package. He found these somewhat more difficult to control, and several kernels of corn eluded him and ended up in various parts of the hallway, or inside the locker.

Finally Cal turned his attention to the drink pouch. It stymied him for a minute as he tried to figure out how to drink without spraying the contents all over his face or suit. Content, Cal opened the mint package and popped them in his mouth. He collected the trash and his stained clothing, stowed them in the locker, and shut it.

Food wasn't too bad. And mint is definitely better tasting than barf. He rolled the mints within his mouth as he pondered some more. *But no one else is around. What the hell happened?*

Cal bit into the mints and finished them off, then maneuvered himself back into the dimly lit gallery. He looked around and could see no signs of life. He rubbed his hair with his good hand, and thought for a moment before pushing himself to the railings on the floor. Slowly, he pulled himself back towards the end of the ship that he recalled entering from. His legs rose up as he used his hands to walk along, and he had to stop and reposition himself.

Minutes passed as he continued along the seemingly endless corridor. He had passed a gaping black hole leading to the bowels of the ship and two more corridors leading to sleeper pods on his right. His arms ached from pulling him along, his right hand stung from the sweat, and the work was making him pant for air. Cal grabbed the handle of a nearby cart, steadied himself and rested.

As he sat, waiting for his arms to give him a reprieve from fatigue, he heard a faint, almost echoing chirp. Cal looked around, but there was no change to the scenery. Again he heard a chirp. He peered over the cart and strained to listen.

Once more, the chirp came to his ear. Calvin saw another pod entrance ahead of him, and the sound seemed to come from within. He worked his way around the cart, crouched, aimed his body carefully, and shot off toward the sleeper pod. He reached the connecting hall, slowed himself down, and slowly walked his way along the walls with his hands.

The chirping was much louder now, and Cal knew he was in the right place. He paused and listened again to find out the direction of the sound. The sound came once again, and he knew that it was coming from the sleeper hall directly ahead of him. He pushed off of the wall and around the corner.

Ahead of him, a woman was floating and punching commands into a terminal built into the wall next to a bank of sleepers. Her long, gray hair was banded into a pigtail that snaked like a flag in a lazy wind.

"Excuse me," Cal said softly.

She spun around and screamed in alarm, and Cal jerked backwards, his own shocked scream escaping his lips. Cal's back hit the wall with a *thud*, his head following immediately after. As she face him, Cal could see that the woman was old, her crow's feet clearly defined and her brow wrinkled. She placed her hand over her heart, and gasped.

"Damn it, Airman. Don't sneak up on me like that," she berated. "If you give me a heart attack, I'm sure the colonel might stuff you in a sleeper for the rest of the trip. Or maybe out the air lock, I don't know."

Cal stared back at her brown eyes in shock. She glared at him for a moment, then shook her head and turned back to her work.

"What do you want, Airman?" she asked.

"A-a-airman?" Cal stuttered.

"I'm sorry, did I get it wrong? Are you a lieutenant?" she questioned, continuing her work as if he wasn't there.

He looked down at himself and it dawned on Cal what he was wearing. He let out a soft chuckle and watched her quietly for a moment. She continued work, but paused and turned after a moment.

Cal asked, "What are you doing?"

"My job. Checking on the passengers. What did you think I was doing?" she asked with a hint of sarcasm. She turned her attention to him and it seemed as if her gaze was trying to pierce him. "You're not Air Force, are you?"

Cal shook his head.

She backed up slightly, reached towards the console, and then asked, "Who are you? What are you doing here?"

Cal was unsure of what she was going to do, but something inside him urged him to be forthright. "My name is Calvin. I guess I'm a passenger on this ship."

The woman's eyes widened and her hand dropped slightly away from the console. "A passenger? What is your berth number?"

"My berth?" he asked nervously.

"Do you know what pod you were assigned to? What section and berth?"

Cal strained to remember. "Pod twelve. Section delta. Berth..." he trailed off.

The woman looked over her shoulder and tapped several buttons on her console. "Berth number?"

He squinted as he tried to recall once more. "I'm sorry, I can't remember. My brain, it's just..."

She nodded at him. "You're probably a bit disoriented. To be honest, with how well you are moving and how much you do remember, I'd say you are doing quite well." Once more she turned to the screen and tapped buttons. "Number eight?"

"Yes," he replied quickly. "That's the one."

"Excuse me one moment, Calvin," she said. Her finger floated over a small red button on the console. She tapped it, then spoke one more. "Doctor Taylor to bridge."

A tinny male voice responded through the com system, "Bridge here, Lieutenant Ceretti speaking."

"Lieutenant, please notify Colonel Dayton that I need an engineering check on one of the sleeper units," she requested, a hint of Midwest audible in her voice.

"Yes, Doctor. Do you have more specific information to report?"

"There are no passengers in danger, if that's what you're asking. I think there might be a minor programming glitch on one individual berth. The engineer can meet me in pod six for more information."

"Very well, Doctor. Bridge out." The com system light dimmed once more.

The doctor turned to Cal and looked at him top to bottom. "You're a bit beat up, I might add. These wounds don't heal well during biostasis, I'm afraid. Come here and let me take a look at them."

Calvin looked down at the bandage on his hand, then back at the doctor. He pushed off of the wall gently, and then braced a foot out in front of him to stop gently along the wall next to her. He offered his right hand to her. She undid the makeshift bandage and pulled it off, causing a slight amount of pain when the bandage tore part of the fresh scab from the back of his hand.

"This one is fresh," she said, examining it closely. "Did you get this before or after your sleep?"

"After. Uh, about a half hour ago, I think," Cal said.

"This is more of a scrape than anything. A big scrape, but it won't need stitches. I just need to clean it and give you a better bandage. It's probably going to sting like the blazes until it heals, though. Not much I can do about that."

She reached for his head, and he flinched. "Hey, what are you…" he started.

She firmly grasped his skull in her hands. "Hold still, let me look at it. Was this one before or after your sleep?"

"Before. How can it still be there? It's been five years!" he exclaimed.

The doctor paused a moment, then let his head go. "How do you know how long it's been?"

"The clock in my berth. It's September 22nd, 2019, isn't it?" Cal retorted as he rubbed the scab on his head.

"I see." The doctor examined his head wound again. "Well, it's started healing. It probably should have had a few stitches, but nothing more I can do at this point except make sure it doesn't get infected. You're probably going to have a bit of a scar there once it heals. The reason it hasn't healed is because you've been in biostasis. All of your body's functions, including repair and metabolism, slow to a crawl. Five years in biostasis is equivalent to about four days outside, give or take."

Cal raised his eyebrows, then sighed and smiled. "Thanks, Doc. Uh, what's your name?"

"Taylor. Doctor Heidi Taylor." She extended her hand, and Cal timidly shook it. "I'm not sure if you were ever given a formal welcome, so I will just in case." Dr. Taylor straightened her clothes. "On behalf of the crew and Project Columbus, I bid you welcome to the sleeper ship *Michael*."

Cal chuckled, "Yeah, I know a little bit about this ship."

Dr. Taylor raised her eyebrows. "Oh, how so?"

"Family projects," he said emphatically. "My grandpa was part of this thing from day one, from what I understand. Dad used to say he trained astronauts or something for a big government project. Later on I found out it was called Columbus, and had something to do with colonizing outer space."

Dr. Taylor's mouth slacked, and she was at a loss for words. Yet, her eyes showed a spark of recognition.

"What?" asked Cal.

"You're Calvin McLaughlin, aren't you?"

Cal was stunned. He rubbed his hand through his hair again. "How do you know me?"

"I worked with your grandfather for years. He didn't just train astronauts; he also trained the medical staffs chosen for the space flights. Between systems training and zero-G training, it was very intense. He always demanded everything you could give, but would never over work you, and was never unfair to anyone."

Sounds like she knew him better than I did. I guess that's because he died when I was so young.

"Sounds like a great guy. I guess I wish I knew him better." Cal shuffled a foot nervously along the berth wall.

"That he was. I'm sorry he is no longer with us."

Cal shrugged. "I really don't remember much about him. I think I was five when he passed."

Silence crept into the room, and Calvin's thoughts raced. *Alone. All alone out here, Dad and my friends long gone.* A memory flashed across his mind.

"Doctor, would it be too much to ask a favor of you?" he asked.

Dr. Taylor smiled brightly. "I suppose I can manage a favor for a McLaughlin."

"Can you tell me the status of pod twelve, section delta, berth fourteen?"

A puzzled look crossed the aged Doctor's face. "I suppose. Someone you know, I gather?" She punched a command into the terminal, and a set of vital signs appeared on the monitor. "Perfectly normal."

Calvin smiled.

. . .

Haruka hunched over the screen of her workstation, rubbing her temples gingerly. Her stomach was still churning from the hibernation sickness. As much as the light of the screen gave her a dull, throbbing headache, and her guts were trying to betray her, she thanked her lucky stars that she had not actually thrown up.

Marco wasn't so lucky, she thought. Fifteen minutes ago, she had left the poor lieutenant in the crew pod as he was retching violently. She had wanted to stay and help him, but the lack of gravity assured that his vomit splattered the hallway liberally.

Although not completely silent, the propulsion control room was much more pleasant for the moment. She was alone, strapped into a seat in front of one of the three workstations in the room. The room was kept much colder than the rest of the ship, giving her goose bumps and causing her to shiver.

Propulsion maintenance was known to be scut work on the sleeper ships. The nuclear reactor was equipped with an automatic refuel system, but the generators needed to be taken offline one at a time, cleaned, and inspected. The worst part of the work, however, was inspecting the plasma drive and thrusters. Although kept offline for most of the journey, they needed to be inspected and test simulations run to assure their operation for arrival.

I'm not sure that I'd rather do this than be put into stasis for the rest of the journey.

Haruka stared at the terminal screen. Displays indicated the fuel status, reactor temperature, and output level. All parameters were normal. She keyed in a sequence of commands and brought up the automatic refuel system's log. Haruka checked for errors, but none were to be found.

"Good morning, ma'am," came a woman's voice from behind Haruka.

She looked over her shoulder, and watched Airman Nova Weyler make her way into the control room. The tall, blonde airman was a fit and solidly built girl. She was young, too, at nineteen. *From what I hear, she picked up her training extremely quickly. Remarkable.* Haruka noticed that Nova had not changed her flight suit, grease marks staining the chest and legs. *Smart. No need to soil another suit with what we're about to do.*

"Good morning, Weyler. Anything to report?" asked Haruka.

Nova sighed. "Well, it looks like we may be a bit short staffed for a while, ma'am. Lieutenant Mancini is real sick, he's trying to find Doctor Nelson right now."

Haruka nodded. "Anything from the bridge?"

"No, ma'am."

"Very well. I'm going to take generator one offline now, we'll start there."

Haruka turned back to the terminal in front of her and began the shutdown sequence for the first generator. The computer processed, and after a few moments acknowledged the shutdown request. The shutdown procedure would take time, as the gas feed from the reactor had to bypass the generator, which then had to cool and spin down. Haruka began to pick nervously at her finger nails as the process moved forward.

Nova Weyler moved to a storage locker and opened it. Haruka watched as she lifted a large tool box from within and effortlessly floated it to a chair. The young woman then opened the box and inventoried its contents, checking the ratcheting tools for proper operation.

Haruka rubbed her hands against her arms and shoulders to help warm up. "How are you feeling?"

Nova did not look up from her task, "Just fine. Frankly, glad to be away from Lieutenant Mancini for a while. Don't get me wrong, I've got nothing against him, but I'd rather not be wearing his stomach, if you know what I mean."

"Of course. I can't blame you there," Haruka replied with a soft smile. *I don't think Marco even wants to be around Marco right now.*

Nova pulled a small bundle of screwdrivers from the tool box and loosened the strap binding them. She separated them out, making sure that there was a proper mixture of Philips and flathead drivers, as well as a socket handle for interchangeable bits.

"Ever take one of these generators apart, Weyler?" asked Haruka.

The airman nodded, "They had one of these back at Sheppard, among lots of other things I learned to work on."

"Propulsion school?"

Nova nodded, then bundled the screwdrivers back together and gently placed them within the toolbox, using the Velcro lining within to secure them. She paused, then said, "It was odd, ma'am, now that I think back on it."

"What do you mean?"

"Well, I know I tested highly on the mechanics stuff. So here I am, having just finished my training at Sheppard, and I get orders to go, of all places, to Virginia. To the shipyards," Nova closed the tool box and latched it.

"Wait, the naval shipyard? Why would they do that?" Haruka looked confused.

"I had no idea at the time, ma'am. But they wanted me to learn how to maintain a nuclear reactor. The Lincoln was down there for refueling, so I got lots of hands on work there. Just when I was starting to get used to where I was, I get reassigned again."

Haruka nodded, "To Laramie, right?"

"I had never heard of an Air Force base out there, but I figured they had sent me to a Navy shipyard, so what the heck. So I fly out to Wyoming and get myself tossed into a crash course on sleeper ships," Nova shook her head and shrugged. "I wonder how long they had been planning to take me out there."

Haruka pondered for a moment, and then glanced back at the screen. The gas feed was bypassed, but the reactor was still spinning, and far too warm to work on. She continued, "I have no doubt that your talent caught the eye of those in charge of Project Columbus."

"Like your father, ma'am?"

Haruka stopped and looked Nova straight in her deep brown eyes. She could see Nova's right eye twitching slightly, along with the corner of her mouth. She began to get an eerie feeling in the back of her mind. She could not place it, but her skin began to crawl.

Is she Fox's pawn?

Nova continued counting tools, this time a strip of assorted sockets. Silence descended upon the control room for a moment. Nova stopped and looked up, "Did I say something wrong, ma'am?"

If she is, Haruka thought, *let's see if I can get some information out of her first.*

She turned back to the screen and pretended to work. "What have you heard about my father, Weyler?"

"Not much. I over heard Lieutenant Singh talking to a couple other bridge crew, and he said something about how he's under arrest." The blonde stopped counting tools and looked at the doorway. "Then I swear Singh said the oddest thing."

"Oh? What's that?"

"That the CO of *Gabriel* is still letting your father work until they reach the planet."

Haruka stopped her false typing, and began to process that. "Doesn't sound too odd to me. Dad helped design the sleeper units, there's nobody on these ships that knows what effect they have on the passengers better than he does."

"Well, all the same. Sounds like there's going to be a few trials when we get there. I just hope we chose the right judges," Nova said as she placed the last of the tools back within the box.

"Wait, what do you mean by that?"

Nova looked up, and Haruka could see her right eye and the corner of her mouth twitch for a moment as she replied, "By what, Lieutenant?"

She knows something.

"We chose the right judges, Airman. What do you mean by that?"

Nova once more looked at the doorway and her eyes widened, "I… I misspoke, Lieutenant."

"No you didn't, that was a deliberate choice of words. You say that like there was some sort of fix-up in the selection process of the passengers. Not only that, but you say it like you had direct involvement."

"Involvement in what?" asked a familiar voice. Haruka turned toward the doorway and saw a ghost pale Marco Mancini floating within, one arm holding his stomach.

Nova was now visibly upset. Haruka could see her eyes were watering, and her mouth was twisted in an attempt to hold back her emotions.

I've got her now. Fox never should have sent this girl to try to deal with me.

Choking up, Nova blurted, "Please, Lieutenant Kimura. I don't want to get in trouble. Colonel Fox won't care how well I…"

"I don't care what Fox sent you here to do," she interrupted. "Now tell me what you meant."

Mancini tried to step in. "Kimura, stop it. Leave her be and let's…"

"Stuff it, Marco," she snapped. "She knows something. It's written all over her face and in what she says. Fox sent her to spy on us, probably trying to find an excuse to stuff us in our sleepers for the whole trip and court martial us."

The two lieutenants stared at Airman Weyler, who was now sobbing. She looked pitifully back at Haruka as tears floated away from her cheeks.

"No. Please, Lieutenant…"

"ANSWER ME!"

Nova let out a frustrated scream and began to cry louder than before. Haruka crossed her arms victoriously and let out a slight grin. Marco entered the control room and closed the heavy metal hatch behind him.

"Jesus, Kimura. They can probably hear us all the way on the bridge," he said.

Haruka glanced at her terminal briefly, verifying that the com system was turned off.

"They're a kilometer away, Marco. She can cry and scream all she wants, Fox will never hear her." Haruka turned back to Nova and repeated, "Answer me."

Nova just continued to sob, stopping only to blow her nose on a cleaning rag she produced from her flight suit. Haruka tapped her foot impatiently on the deck plating as she waited for an answer.

"Haruka, what on Earth do you hope to get out of her?" Mancini pressed.

She ignored him, "C'mon, Weyler. What is Fox really going to do to you, huh? Now answer me."

Nova screamed once more, this time Haruka heard the anguish within it.

"She will have me court martialed, Lieutenant! Don't you get it? I don't work for Colonel Fox."

Haruka's heart sank. *Wait, if I'm wrong about Fox, then... Oh, shit!*

"You want your answer, Lieutenant Kimura?" she screamed. "You want to know how I know that the judges were selected?"

Now I'm not so sure that I want to know.

"Yes, Airman."

"Do you know who Major Dan Forrest is, ma'am?" she asked, her voice broken by her sobs.

She paused a moment to recall, "He's an engineer. He was assigned to *Michael*, correct?"

"He was SUPPOSED to be assigned to *Raphael*, but two days before we started the passenger launch, Colonel Fox pushed through a reassignment. She put him on *Michael*, and brought Captain Maynard over to *Raphael*." Nova took in a deep breath, calmed herself a bit, and stared back at Haruka.

"It was from him that I found out about the alterations that were made to the final approved passenger algorithm. It was from him that I found out that, specifically, judges were manually chosen. And it is because of that, and because of what has happened, that I hope that the selections were fair and just men. Not just for you and your father, Lieutenant, but for Dan as well."

Oh, you silly girl, what have you gotten yourself into?

"Wait, so that means that Fox screwed you, right?" asked Mancini bluntly.

"Marco!" Haruka said, horrified.

Nova sniffed and wiped her eyes. "No, he's right. She separated Dan and I. We were supposed to be together, that was the plan. Now I won't see him again until we reach the planet, and even then…"

She began to sob once more.

"Even then what?" prodded Marco.

"Marco, shut up," Haruka shot back.

"What? What did I say?"

Haruka gave an exasperated sigh, "Because when we get to the planet, she's got at least two problems. First, we're going to arrive before the other two ships, so she will have to wait around for the major to land."

"That's not so bad. What's the second problem?"

"They're going to court martial him as soon as they land."

Upon hearing those words, Nova Weyler once again broke out into a fit of crying. Haruka blinked long and frowned. *Damn it, she didn't need to hear that from me.*

Marco intruded once more, "Yeah, I know. They're going to court martial Shipp and Reid too. But why the water works?"

"Because I'm in love with him, you ass," wailed Nova.

Mancini's jaw dropped, and he began to stammer, "I-I, I'm sorry. I-I didn't mean any disrespect."

Haruka unbuckled from her seat, retrieved the tool box from Nova, and shoved it roughly into Mancini's arms.

"Go make yourself useful, Marco."

"But…"

"Go."

He sighed, and then made his way to the hatch leading down to the generators. He opened it, took one forlorn glance back, and made his way with the toolbox down into the black below.

There was silence for a minute after Marco's departure. Haruka watched Nova as she sobbed, wiped her eyes repeatedly, and finally calmed down. She could tell that Nova was still distraught, her eyes watery and bloodshot and her cheeks flushed.

"I'm sorry about Marco. He's a good guy, but sometimes he just doesn't get it."

Nova sniffled and managed a weak smile, "At least you know how to handle him, ma'am."

This poor girl. I've made a terrible mistake today. Haruka started to move her arm towards Nova, but hesitated, unsure of herself. She smiled, and then placed her hand on Nova's hand. The young blonde looked up at Haruka.

"I'm really sorry that I jumped on you like that. I thought that maybe Colonel Fox sent you to spy on Mancini and I. After all, she stripped us of our positions simply because she thought that I was involved in whatever my dad is accused of."

"I know she did. I thought of all people that you might understand me. I need a friend out here, someone to talk to, and I thought that maybe you'd be the one," Nova said, her voice still cracking. She pounded her free fist on her thigh, "I'm so stupid. I never..."

"Hey, hey, hey. Don't beat yourself up. We've both probably made mistakes today, but that's ok. How we handle them now is what's important."

Tears began to well up again, and Nova's voice squeaked, "But now you know about me and Dan, and that I know about the algorithm. Oh God, Lieutenant, don't tell her. I don't want to be court martialed!"

Haruka squeezed her hand harder. Her voice softened even more, "Hey, Nova. Your name is Nova, right?"

Nova bit her lip and nodded quickly.

"Hang in there, Nova. Wait until we get to the planet, then we can see about getting my dad and Dan cleared up of this mess, ok?"

And Brandon, too.

Nova smiled and wiped her eyes one more time. Drawing in a deep breath, she said, "Thank you, Lieutenant, you're right."

Haruka returned the smile, "Please, we both know Fox isn't going to come back here for any reason. No need to salute me, Nova. Call me Haruka."

"H-Haruka. Thanks. Does this mean..."

"You've got the friend you're looking for."

"Now isn't that just a touching moment," Marco Mancini's voice rang impishly in her ears. The two looked over and saw him, grinning wide, half of his body visible in the hatch to the generators.

"Marco, you dork, how long have you been there?" she grabbed Nova's cleaning rag and tossed it at him.

"Long enough to hear you two serenade each other," he laughed. "Now let's get to work, these generators aren't going to clean themselves. And I ain't gonna to do it all while you polish each others' nails, ladies."

The two women laughed, and followed Mancini down into the darkness.

. . .

A light flickered on the computer screen and the com system came to life.

"Quinn to Lieutenant Owens."

Darius tapped a button on his headset. "Owens here, go ahead Captain."

"Mr. Owens, I need to report to the propulsion section. Are you available to monitor Doctor Kimura?"

"Yes, sir. I'll switch my terminal to monitor him." He turned off the com system and then brought up a split screen view. In the smaller corner window he brought up the link to Dr. Kimura's work. After he watched several pages of data pass, he turned his attention back to the broken com software.

He skimmed two pages of good code before coming upon a third that had significant damage. Chunks of programming had been replaced in the system by various symbols and almost unrecognizable characters.

I don't think the com system runs well on emoticons and accented vowels, he mused.

Darius removed the entire middle third of the page and recreated what he believed went there. A pass through with the debugger told him he was wrong, and he edited his work one line at a time until he got a positive result. He glanced at the inset window and noticed that the doctor had not advanced his work in around fifteen minutes.

Again?

He sighed as he unbuckled from his bridge station. As he maneuvered towards the bridge exit, he felt the eyes of Colonel Eriksen lock on him.

"I'm going to see what the doctor needs, Colonel."

He received a curt nod from his commander before proceeding off the bridge and towards Dr. Kimura in pod four.

I understand he's got problems right now, but if he plans on working through the whole trip, he's got to stop doing this.

Darius reached the inner hallway where Kimura was set up to work. He spoke in a voice barely more than a whisper, "Doctor Kimura, you're daydreaming again."

Dr. Kimura shook his head and focused on the computer screen before him. He rubbed his hands over his face as he took a deep breath, "Sorry, Darius. I'll get back to work."

"What do you keep thinking about, anyway?"

"Sometimes about my family. I still worry about Saika, but there is nothing more I can do for her. I miss Haruka and Sarah, and again there is nothing I can do..." his voice trailed off.

Darius waited for the doctor to continue, but he didn't. "But?"

There was a great sigh. "But I keep thinking of Project Columbus, of Dr. Benedict. Every time I find one of the few empty sleeper berths, I think of his sacrifice. I think of everything that he has done for the passengers of these ships. Worse, the consequences if he failed."

A sudden chill ran down Darius's spine. *This sounds even worse than the dirty bomb.*

"What do you mean by that?"

Kimura stared blankly at Darius. "How many personnel from the military are on board these ships?"

"Forty each on *Gabriel* and *Michael*. *Raphael* has only thirty nine; they reported a casualty back on Earth."

"And do you have a count on the Marines that made it on board?"

There was an uneasy silence for a moment. Darius knew the answer was unpleasant, but he couldn't deny the doctor's request.

"Seven."

"Seven," echoed Kimura.

"Out of one hundred twenty four."

The rest were either killed by the Chinese or by the bomb, no doubt.

"You know this war will end civilization as we know it. In the time we were in biostasis, it probably already has," Kimura continued in a dead tone.

"I had a feeling after the first three cities were leveled by nuclear weapons."

The other fifteen were just humanity's painful reminder of that fact.

"Tokyo, Seoul, and Pyongyang weren't even the tipping factor for Dr. Benedict. Washington and Beijing were. There was no going back after that, there was no way we could let Project Columbus live after those cities were burned to ash."

Darius could feel his heart beat through his chest.

"What do you mean, couldn't let it live?"

A frown crept across the aging man's face.

"We could not allow for the possibility that another sleeper ship could be built, especially not by an enemy. If so much as one sleeper ship were to follow us, carrying soldiers..."

They would easily conquer the colony. The very thought made Darius cringe. Dr. Kimura nodded slowly.

"Now you understand why Dr. Benedict stayed behind; to destroy all plans and records for Project Columbus. David had always struggled with the thought of being labeled a traitor, but in the end he said this would be his ultimate act of patriotism."

"And you're not so sure?"

Kimura shrugged. "It was for him. Martyrdom will probably go far in redeeming his image when history writes this chapter. I gain some personal justification from the fact that the government betrayed us all first, but I do not deny that I will be labeled as a traitor."

Darius sized up the doctor. He seemed to have aged in those five years, even though they had all been in stasis and should have effectively aged only a few days or so.

"You are no doubt under a lot of stress, Doctor. Should I revive Miss Reid?"

"Heavens no, Darius. If you wake her up, she will find out about her brother's arrest. She had no knowledge of what was going on, and it would be an undue strain on her to revive her early, force her to work, and give her knowledge of the depth of trouble that Brandon is in."

Darius furrowed his brow slightly. "But you yourself are dealing with the same issue."

"I've been preparing for the possibility of my own arrest, or the arrest and punishment of those around me for years, Darius. Yes, I have some stress to deal with, but I knew it would be there."

Darius shifted his weight against a sleeper berth as Dr. Kimura continued to cycle his screen through sets of passengers. Darius could see the doctor's face bore a flat expression and his eyes seemed listless.

His heart isn't in it anymore. I don't know how much longer he thinks he can take this.

"Darius, do you have a copy of the passenger manifest matrix?"

"Of course, Doctor, why?"

"May I look at it? I need to find a passenger."

Darius shook his head solemnly, "Sorry, Doctor Kimura. Your access has been restricted to the passenger vitals routine and com system only. Colonel's orders."

"I understand. In that case, can you please ask Colonel Eriksen to come speak with me, as I am also restricted from the bridge?"

Darius raised his eyebrows, "You don't want me to ask him for access for you?"

Kimura turned and looked directly into his eyes. "This is not a slight against you. I have the utmost respect for you, my friend. However, I feel it is best if I speak my request directly to the colonel. He said that my cooperation will be a mitigating factor at my upcoming trial. In that spirit, it is best that I make any special requests directly to him."

Darius considered the point for a moment and then nodded.

I hope he listens to you, Doctor.

"My gratitude, Lieutenant."

Darius pushed himself off of the sleeper berth, and then pulled his great frame through the hatch and out of the sleeper pod. His mind raced with terrible scenarios of Dr. Benedict failing to destroy the design records.

Images of lush greenery and rolling hills flooded his senses, and he could almost taste crisp spring air. The taste soon became bitter as he saw plumes of dark smoke rising in the distance beyond, the telltale sign of destruction.

Focus, Darius. Do your work.

He moved in silence towards the bridge, trying to stay one step ahead of the nightmare image.

. . .

Calvin stared in wonder at the endless field of stars beyond the massive glass canopy. Thousands of tiny points of light twinkled and pulsed in a cosmic symphony. This was one performance that was beautiful despite lacking sound. The gravity of the sight was not lost on him, either.

I'm one of only a few dozen people who will ever see this in their lives.

He felt a hand touch his bandaged right hand as it grasped the railing of the bridge. He looked over and saw the gray-haired Dr. Taylor smiling at him. "Amazing, isn't it?"

Cal returned the smile and nodded. He still wore the flight suit he had scavenged earlier in the day. He was flanked on either side by Dr. Taylor and Lieutenant Hunter Ceretti, a young man with dirty blonde hair and a matching dirty flight suit. Cal glanced to either side of him, then down at his own clothing, and gave a soft chuckle.

One might think I belonged here.

Cal quickly scanned the bridge. There were three clusters of three terminals in a horseshoe shape around a raised section that contained a single chair. Each cluster of workstations only had one occupant at this time. The occupant of the raised chair was a slightly chubby brown haired fellow with tufts of gray around his temples and a short, neatly trimmed beard that likewise had a matching pair of gray streaks. His brown eyes scrutinized Calvin from head to toe.

"I understand your name is McLaughlin, is that correct?" asked the chubby commander, his voice dripping with a thick northeastern accent.

"Yes, sir," Cal replied politely.

"How old are you, son?"

"Eighteen, sir."

"Eighteen," the colonel repeated. "Are you in the armed forces, son?"

"No sir."

"I see. Then why do you call me 'sir'?"

"My father and grandfather, sir, were both in the military. They taught me respect for officers."

The ship's commander nodded slightly. He looked at the lieutenant next to Cal and asked, "Ceretti, can you explain why he's wearing Forrest's flight suit?"

"I believe so, Colonel. When you gave the order to arrest Major Forrest, he was in the propulsion section. Since the order was to place the major in immediate stasis, we took him to the nearest empty sleeper berth, which was in pod twelve. We allowed him to change suits before placing him in stasis. His dirty flight suit was stowed within the pod. I believe that Mr. McLaughlin here found the flight suit after he came out of hibernation,"

"Very well, Ceretti. Is Captain Hartley looking into why Mr. McLaughlin's berth revived him early?"

"Yes, sir. He said he's almost done."

The Colonel turned his attention back to Cal, "Why were you placed on this ship, Mr. McLaughlin?"

Cal grimaced, and memories of his ordeal started to come back. "Because I had no choice."

He received a puzzled look in return from the colonel. Questioning resumed. "Can you please tell me what you mean by that? Was there a different choice you would rather have made, given the options?"

"At the time, sir?" he retorted. "Yes. I wanted to go and party with my friends back in Dallas. We were going to celebrate getting out of high school, but a few minutes before my friend Rob was going to pick me up, two guys from the Air Force came into my house and dragged me to a waiting Humvee. They took me to the airport, where I was shoved on a plane with a bunch of other scared people, and flown to Laramie. We were all put on a bus and driven out to some complex with a bunch of barbed wire and guys with guns."

The chubby colonel scratched at his beard while he considered the information. "What did your father tell you about Project Columbus?"

Cal stopped, confused. "My father, sir? Don't you mean my grandfather?"

"No, I mean your father. General Andrew McLaughlin. What did he tell you about the project?"

"That my grandfather used to train astronauts for it," he replied sharply.

"That's it?"

"No disrespect, Colonel, but my dad didn't have anything to do with Project Columbus. I mean, he was a combat pilot before he was a General, right? Why would he know anything about something he wasn't assigned to?" Cal started to feel frustration rise.

Again the colonel considered the response for a moment. He pushed a button on the arm of his chair and spoke, "Dayton to Hartley."

"Hartley here. Yes, Colonel?" came a voice from the com system.

"Have you finished your analysis of the failed sleeper unit?"

"Yes, sir. I wouldn't exactly call it failed, however."

"Explain, please."

"All of the hardware is working properly. There appears to be a glitch somewhere in the system that activated the unit when we placed Major Forrest into biostasis. I'm not sure if it's software or firmware, but I wouldn't use this unit until we sort it out, sir."

"Could it be sabotage?" asked Colonel Dayton.

"Negative, sir. While the trigger is specific, so is the unit number that the system defaulted to. This isn't sabotage unless whoever created the glitch also specifically intended for Mr. McLaughlin to be revived. The only way that is even possible is if someone knew which unit he was assigned to, and had modified the program after we were under way, and I'm just not seeing any evidence of that."

"Thank you, Captain. Dayton out," and he clicked the com system off.

"Colonel," interjected Dr. Taylor.

"Yes, Doctor?"

"I would be remiss if I didn't bring up that Calvin asked the status of another passenger when he came out of biostasis."

Cal gave Dr. Taylor a shocked look. Colonel Dayton's eyebrow raised, "Which passenger?"

"I don't know who it is, but they are in pod twelve, section delta, berth fourteen. The passenger matrix should bring up data on them," replied Dr. Taylor.

Colonel Dayton unlocked his chair and swiveled to face a workstation to his left. He spoke to a young black haired fellow sitting at the console, "Mr. Drisko, call up the passenger matrix and give me all data on that passenger."

"Yes, sir." He typed a sequence of commands into his workstation.

Cal stuttered, "S-sir, she's j-just a girl I met at the compound."

Colonel Dayton turned his seat to face Cal once more and locked its position. "As far as I can tell, Mr. McLaughlin, you have been telling the truth. If you still speak the truth, you have nothing to worry about." The colonel's tone gave a hint of warmth that Cal had not heard before.

There was an audible chirp, and Drisko spoke, "Passenger data for twelve delta fourteen ready, sir."

"Go ahead, Sergeant."

"Alexis Decker, a line cook from Portland, Oregon. Age nineteen at time of launch. She was selected by the algorithm from a refugee camp in Denver, with priority markers based on age, occupational skills, and known hobbies. No known criminal history. The matrix indicates she has military background in her family, but she herself has never served," Drisko read from the terminal screen in front of him.

Alexis. Cal closed his eyes and conjured a memory of her surprising kiss in the sleeper pod. A genuine smile came across his face, and he opened his eyes to look at a pensive Colonel Dayton.

"Curious," responded Dayton. "She doesn't sound like the kind of person who would have the skills to reprogram the sleepers. I think we've just got a glitch and a wild goose chase here, gentlemen. He doesn't seem to have any more connection to this conspiracy other than a blood relationship. If what Doctor Kimura said is true, I think we will find that to be the case with other similar relatives of the conspirators."

"Conspiracy?" Cal blurted. "What conspiracy? What do you think my dad was involved in? Who is Doctor Kimura?"

"I'm sorry, Mr. McLaughlin, I can't discuss anything about the investigation with you," said Dayton sincerely. "All I can share with you is that one of my crew is under arrest and has been placed in biostasis until we reach our destination."

"And that's this Forrest guy you're talking about?"

"Correct."

"So who takes his place on the crew?"

"Captain Hartley has already taken over his responsibilities. Now if you will excuse me, I have duties to attend to. You may go."

Calvin nodded. He turned toward the railing, grasping it with both hands. He hung his head and closed his eyes.

Not a man, he heard Brittany's taunting voice echo from the past. He gripped the railing tighter, until his knuckles turned white and the bandage rubbed on the raw back of his hand. He could hear the bridge crew talking, receiving orders from Dayton and giving responses back, but Cal ignored all of it.

They're dragging you with them, his father's voice came to his mind. *You'll never be a real man if you keep up this loser shit.*

I wasn't the only one who was angry, was I, Dad? he asked himself.

Cal tried to bring an image of his father to his mind. He needed to see him once more. Perhaps he could reconcile at least his own guilt. Cal envisioned a tall man in dress blues with a short, blonde buzz cut. Something seemed out of place to Calvin. *Dad didn't have a crew cut. His hair was short, but never that short.*

The vision looked like his father, sure enough, but yet the hair cut was wrong. There was something else, too. It took Cal a while to put his finger on it, but the man in his mind was much older than his father. Cal soaked in every detail he could. He then realized that the uniform was the wrong cut for the 2000's, and it did not bear the rank insignia of Brigadier General. Instead, it was that of a colonel.

Grandpa?

The figure just stood in his mind like a photograph, unmoving, given life only by the image it was taken from. Calvin held the image in his mind, processing it over and over. His grandfather was a tall, proud, stoic man in this picture. It occurred to Cal that he had seen this photograph dozens of times as a child, mostly at his grandmother's house.

Cal nodded away the vision and opened his eyes. The bridge crew was still occasionally giving clips of data or responding to orders. Calvin straightened himself up, straightened his borrowed flight suit, and cleared his throat.

"Colonel Dayton, sir," he said confidently. The bridge fell suddenly silent. The command chair unlocked and Dayton turned to face Cal.

"I said you could go, Mr. McLaughlin. Is there something else you need?"

"Yes, sir. Do you have any jobs for me to do?"

Dayton looked at Cal, stumped at first. He paused for several seconds before responding. "Come again, Mr. McLaughlin?"

"I would like to lend a hand, Colonel. What can I do?"

"You should probably prepare yourself for hibernation again."

"I can't, sir. Didn't Hartley say my berth is unusable? What am I supposed to do? Where am I to go?"

Colonel Dayton tapped his fingers on his armrest for a moment. "I appreciate your offer, Mr. McLaughlin, but I don't believe you're trained on any of *Michael's* systems. We would have to train you from scratch. As it is, we have nearly thirty spare crew members in stasis. You may use the crew gym, and there is a cargo pod that contains a small library. It may be a little cold if you go down there to retrieve something, and I can't vouch for the excitement of the books, but it's better than nothing."

Cal frowned in disappointment, but nodded, "I understand, thank you."

"While we make arrangements for you, I want you to be our guest. Lieutenant Ceretti will create an access code in our system for you to use. You will be able to go anywhere on the ship you would like, except the propulsion section. This includes access to the bridge, but I would ask that you not disturb any of the crew while they are working," added Dayton.

Well, that's a start.

"I appreciate it, sir. Thank you." Cal floated his way off the bridge and into the gallery. He made his way past the lonely entrances of pods one and two. The air was very cool inside the massive hallway, and long strips of lighting cast a dim glow on the walls and floor. Where there was a break in the lighting, shadows crept in, giving parts of the gallery an eerie feel.

"Can I have a moment, Calvin?" Dr. Taylor's voice almost made him jump.

"Yeah, Doctor. What's up?" He turned to face her as she swiftly made her way down to him, her gray braid of hair straight as an arrow behind her.

"I just want to make sure you don't get bored while you're waiting around. Do you want to work, or do you want to find something else to occupy your time?"

"The colonel said he doesn't want to train me."

"Colonel Dayton is responsible for the operation of the ship, but the passengers are my responsibility."

Calvin tried to think of what she meant. "What are you saying?"

Dr. Taylor smiled wide, her teeth perfect and white. "Want a crash course in biostasis?"

. . .

1st Lt Haruka Kimura
22 September 2019, 16:11
Raphael
>|

The turbine of generator one began to spin faster. Its vibrations echoed in a great cacophony that eventually subsided to a harmonic hum as it matched speed with the second generator.

"One down, one to go," Nova remarked as she tapped on the long, domed steel casing with her ratchet. "Do you think you two can do the other one while I check the reactor?"

Mancini gave her a cheeky smile. "Bring it on. I'll show Lieutenant Kimura how it's done."

Nova gave a quick smile back as handed the wrench to Mancini. She swiftly turned and floated her way to the aft of the room.

Haruka gave a disapproving *tsk* at Mancini. "Don't even think about it."

"What? I didn't say anything."

"I know you, Marco. I know that look."

"I don't know what you mean." His voice was thick with sarcasm.

Haruka rolled her eyes. "Uh huh. Yeah, the look you give when you're looking for trouble. Usually with a woman."

"What? I can't help it, she's kind of cute."

"And heartbroken because of what happened to her boyfriend, I might add," she scolded. "Leave her alone, for the sake of both of you."

Assuming he's her boyfriend. What does it matter? Boyfriend or lover. I never asked specifically. I really don't want to know, their relationship is inappropriate to begin with.

"Ah, you never let me have any fun," he sighed.

Haruka let out a laugh that was almost a snort. "I let you do what you want. I just drag your ass out of the fire when your so-called fun is about to get you punched in the face."

A mocking scowl twisted Mancini's face. "That only happened once."

"Twice. And you can thank me for that small miracle. I swear, right after we passed the transport sims, you were trying to make it happen every single week." She counted off the last three words on her fingers to drive the point home.

He grinned, "See? We've got each other's backs, to the end." He collected the toolbox, pushed off of the casing and shot like an arrow towards the second generator.

Haruka scoffed as her counterpart moved off. *Incorrigible.* She turned her attention to the terminal in front of her and initiated the shutdown sequence for generator two before making her own way to the unit.

The deceleration of the turbine once more threw the mechanical symphony into discord. Haruka and Mancini both pressed their hands over their ears in a vain effort to drown out the nearly painful noise. Neither of them attempted to speak, as it would have been futile. Minutes passed as the generator slowly wound down and the noise abated.

Mancini loosened the bolts on the access cover one by one and softly floated them over to Haruka after each one was freed from the assembly. He then slid the access cover open and crawled inside.

Haruka stretched and looked around. She was alone outside the generator, but could hear Mancini working within the housing. Her mind wandered for a moment. The light in the control room above reminded her vaguely of the bridge, and of the duties that had been stripped from her.

"You okay in there for a bit by yourself, Marco?"

"Yeah," his voice echoed from the opening.

"I'll be back in a little bit, try not to hurt yourself too badly."

She heard a giggle from inside the generator. Haruka propelled herself to the ladder and made the climb to the control room. Once inside she strapped into the seat closest to the window and called up a security routine on the computer. A diagram of the ship came up with several small dots. She pushed one that was located near the rear of the bridge and was prompted for an access code. Haruka typed in her security code and a window popped up with a view looking forward on the bridge toward the nav consoles and space beyond.

Haruka looked for the star field off of the bow, but the resolution of the camera was too low to pick up the tiny dots over the bridge's lights. She let out a defeated sigh, leaned her head back, and closed her eyes.

I should be up there gazing at the stars, not down here cleaning gunk out of the engines. All of the words and accusations came back to her in a rush. She felt a lump rise in her throat and her eyes start to water. *Mom, Dad, Saika... I've never missed you this much in my life.* Her breath stuttered for a moment, but she bit her lip hard and the pain kept her tears at bay.

Another memory flashed through Haruka's mind. She couldn't tell what it was at first, but something about it felt comforting. She relaxed and tried to hold on to it. There was blue all over, she recalled.

The sky. Three small, fluffy clouds. Definitely the sky.

She took a deep breath and let the memory and feelings flow back to her. More blue, this time around her. She smelled a tang of salt and recalled a faint breeze.

The sea. This must have been one of our trips, but where? It feels beautiful...

The image in her mind sharpened, and she could see a massive white steel structure behind her, a short linked fence bordering a platform she was standing on, and a green mass of land on the horizon in front of her, one massive rolling chain of hills. She could see her mother and sister conversing next to the fence, occasionally glancing off at the land beyond. Haruka felt a hand on her shoulder.

"I'm glad you could make it. I was beginning to worry that your training would never end. This trip just wouldn't be the same without you. I am certain that your mother would have been in tears over it," her father said with a smile.

I remember now. Two years ago, our camping trip to Puget Sound. This was the ferry we took.

The memory brought her warmth that cut through the cold reality of *Raphael*. She held on to it and tried to draw it closer. As she did, the image changed. It was dark, but there was a camp fire in front of her with bright, glowing embers. She watched as her family roasted marshmallows and caught up on years of stories from Haruka and Saika.

Haruka embraced the memory as long as she could. It seemed as if it could go on for an eternity, and she did not mind in the least. She smiled for a long time as she reminisced, but the warmth eventually faded and her eyes opened once more to the cold steel roof of the control room. She looked down at the time on the console. Two hours had passed.

Damn. She sat bolt upright and unstrapped. Haruka opened the hatch and tore down into the propulsion room as quickly as she could, finding her way to the dimly lit gap in the casing of generator two.

"I'm back, how're we doing?"

Mancini's voice gave a ghostly query, "We?"

"Yeah," she tried to play it off.

"Where the hell were you?"

"I'm sorry, Marco. Time got away from me."

"Yeah, just enough to miss all of the damn carbon build up and other muck in here," he grumbled.

"Hey, you're still alive. And the generator didn't punch you in the face, did it?"

"Not today. But I wasn't hitting on its sister, if that's what you're getting at."

Haruka laughed. "Well, that's good news. But seriously, where are we at?"

"Final inspections. Five, maybe ten minutes."

Haruka looked around and saw the cleaning rags that Mancini had been using floating around the generator. She collected these and deposited them in a trash locker along the far wall and then returned to the steel dome.

"Bridge to Kimura," Colonel Fox's voice was barely audible over the whine of generator one, "Why isn't generator two back online yet?"

Haruka braced herself against the outer casing of the massive turbine with her left hand. Clutching a ratchet in her right, she reached for the control panel at her side. She tapped the ratchet on the com system button.

"We're just finishing final inspection of the power transfer grid, Colonel. We should have number two back up in about five minutes"

"I want a report the instant they're done, Lieutenant. Fox out."

As the com system light went out, Haruka pulled herself back over to the open access panel.

"I don't see why she's in such a big rush. It's not like we will get there any faster if we hurry maintenance."

"I'm telling you, Kimura, it's the Fox way or the highway. It doesn't matter if the problem is relevant or not," Mancini's voice echoed from within the dimly lit cavity. A greasy hand and matching sleeve outstretched from the opening, palm up and fingers splayed. Haruka placed the ratchet in his palm, and he promptly retracted his arm to within the confines of his workspace. The walls of the generator made the wrench sound like dozens of arguing crickets.

"I don't know, Marco. Maybe there is something to getting done with the generator and the inspections faster."

"Yeah? What's that?"

"Going back to sleep so I don't have to listen to her yapping anymore."

"C'mon, she's a Fox, not a dog."

"My bad, I won't have to listen to her howling any more. Is that better?"

A chuckle from within the casing affirmed her answer. Haruka gazed across the long room, past the reactor, at generator one in the distance. Nova shot like an arrow from between the two, and caught the ladder up to the propulsion control room.

Haruka raised her voice to overpower the whine, "Where are you going, Weyler?"

Nova stopped briefly, her eyes meeting Haruka's.

"I thought I'd get started on the thruster inspections, Lieutenant."

"Alright, that's fine."

Nova crawled hand over hand up the ladder and out of sight. Haruka resumed her gaze across the room. She became fixated on the bright purple glow emanated by the reactor. Shivers ran down her spine, and goose bumps rose on her skin. She turned back to the terminal and brought up a screen of readings from the reactor.

Correct temperature, no radiation leaks. Her eyes fell once more on *Gabriel's* power plant. *Still, the sooner we're done and away from this reactor, the better.*

"There we go. All buttoned up."

Haruka's attention snapped back to the generator, where Mancini was securing the thick, curved metal of the access port. She placed her finger on the com system button and gently tapped.

"Lieutenant Kimura to Colonel Fox."

"Fox here, are you done yet?"

"Yes, ma'am. Airman Weyler has already started thruster inspection; I will be joining her shortly while Mancini starts the inspection of the plasma drive."

"Very well, Lieutenant. I want another report in an hour when your shift ends. Fox out."

Haruka grinned at Marco. She raised her voice an octave and spoke through her nose, "Yes, ma'am. Right away, ma'am"

Marco's mouth widened into a broad smile and his brown eyes gleamed. He cupped his hands to his lips and gave a short howl.

. . .

"Colonel Eriksen will be here in just a minute," Darius announced. Dr. Kimura gave a gentle smile. "Are you sure you don't want me to talk to him, Doctor?"

"No, thank you. I feel as if I am imposing on you as it is."

Darius shrugged. "Well, you're not. Sorry it has taken this long; he didn't seem too keen on leaving the bridge while he was on shift."

Just then, Colonel Eriksen pulled his way into the sleeper hallway. His beard made his expression look grimmer. He pulled himself upright and tugged at his flight suit.

"You wanted to see me, Doctor?"

Dr. Kimura fidgeted slightly and looked at the floor. "Yes, Colonel. I need access to the passenger matrix."

Eriksen stared at Dr. Kimura and opened his mouth, but seemed to be unable to find words at first. His eyes narrowed and his crow's feet seemed to stretch almost to his ears.

"You want access to the matrix to do *what*, Doctor Kimura?"

The scowl on Colonel Eriksen's face was as hard as the day of the interrogation on the bridge. Darius wondered if that made this request any more uncomfortable for Dr. Kimura.

"To find a new secondary doctor," Kimura said, unflinching.

"So let me get this straight. You stand accused of treason, and you want me to let you pick a new backup for you?"

"Yes, Colonel."

"And why on God's green earth... or black space, or whatever the hell," Colonel Eriksen's face started to turn red and he seemed flustered. "Damn it, why should I let you do that?"

"Because of who the current backup is, sir."

Eriksen's face remained quite colorful, but his expression changed to that of utter confusion. "I have no time to speak in riddles, Doctor. Just tell give your reason so I can make my decision."

At least he's going to hear him out. Maybe Dr. Kimura will get what he needs after all.

There was a brief pause inside the sleeper hallway that the three men weightlessly floated in. Although there was plenty of space to move about, there was something about the colonel's voice that made Darius feel as if they were all stuffed in a can.

Dr. Kimura stared intently at Colonel Eriksen. "Very well. The secondary doctor is Kayla Reid, the sister of Lieutenant Brandon Reid, and my daughter in law. I will state, for the record if it pleases you, that she was given this position because of her relationship to me. She was given minimal systems training back at Laramie shortly before the launch of the transports."

"Wait," Eriksen cut in. "Why was she given last minute training? Wasn't there already another doctor in place?"

Dr. Kimura squirmed and his brows rose in a worrisome manner. "There was a time gap between the disappearance of Doctor Lang and the arrival of the passengers. She was given training so as not to... ah... disturb any of them when they arrived. We knew she could be trusted to handle the task."

Eriksen rubbed his hands through his hair. "Okay, fine, but why replace her?"

"Because she will be useless if she has to come out of stasis. At least unless you plan to hide the fact that her brother has been arrested and accused of a capital crime, and that he could be executed."

"He chose his path."

"But *she* didn't," Kimura retorted without skipping a beat. "Please remember that anyone who is not, as you say, a conspirator, has no knowledge of what is going on. This will all come as a shock to Miss Reid when we land. Do you really want to risk the passengers and crew on a secondary doctor who could potentially become panicked, should I become incapacitated?"

The two men locked each other in stares. Darius caught himself holding his breath, but he dared not exhale and draw attention to himself.

"No," Eriksen replied with a stern voice. "Miss Reid will not be replaced. You'd still have to pull a civilian doctor out of stasis to train them, and that alone could give them concerns as to why. The last thing I want is an antsy civilian doctor who can revive the passengers and doesn't know why he's awake."

The wrinkled scientist's mouth curled down. "If we are to train a civilian doctor from the passenger manifest, I can keep him quiet. There are factors to consider."

Eriksen's tone took on a sudden gruff quality, "You forget the situation that you're in, Doctor Kimura. You're only awake because of your skill with the sleeper berths. You don't get to tell me what to do on my ship. You don't get to make assumptions about what needs to happen next. Keep your eyes on the screen and do your job."

"But if I'm unable to continue for some reason, Miss Reid will be under too much stress."

"Then train Lieutenant Owens."

What? Me?

"What?" Kimura cried out.

"Lieutenant Owens will be keeping up the computer systems anyway," Eriksen grunted. "From what I've seen of your job so far, it doesn't look too hard. Teach him how to do your job. Miss Reid can help him if you can't work, but I am not bringing another civilian out of stasis before we arrive. End of discussion."

Dr. Kimura bowed his head to Eriksen before the commander departed the sleeper pod. Darius let out his breath in a loud rush. There was an awkward moment of silence before he moved to the computer terminal and brought up the passenger matrix.

"I am sorry to have burdened you with my request, Darius."

He shrugged. "It's no problem for me. It's not like the colonel is going to shoot the messenger."

"Nevertheless I appreciate your assistance."

"Again, no problem. I'm sorry that you didn't get what you needed from him." Darius turned to go.

"You're not going to stay?" Darius could hear the disappointment in Kimura's voice.

"I'm sorry, I've got a project that is eating up too much of my time. I've got to get back to the computer core."

"Nothing serious, I hope."

Darius grunted and turned back to face the doctor. "I don't know. I found that the com system software was corrupted and rolled back to another version. I've been trying to repair the software, but it's going slowly. To be honest, I'm not sure I can fix it all this cycle."

Kimura looked at Darius, raising a brow on his wizened face. "You're rebuilding the whole file?"

"Pretty much."

"And you know what problems the old version had?"

"Yeah." Darius brought his hand to his temple and rubbed slowly.

Crap, why didn't I think of that sooner? "And I'm pretty sure I know what you're going to say next."

Dr. Kimura smiled gently. "Then, if you please, we are even for your previous assistance. When you have time, return and I will teach you what Colonel Eriksen wants you to know."

Darius returned the grin, his white teeth contrasting starkly from his black skin. He turned once more and departed from pod four and into the desolate gallery. His mind began to form ideas on how to structure the task at hand. *I don't need to rewrite the whole file yet. All I need to do is patch the existing one to plug the hole for now.*

He made his way into the computer core and secured himself to the workstation chair. He called up the active com software this time, and with a renewed purpose he read the code and inserted new lines every few pages. *So just cap this off...*

His fingers became a blur to him as he stared intently at the screen. A grin crept across his face as the minutes passed and he neared the end of the file. At last he reached the final code insertion. He paused and considered. *What do I do with the incoming communications?* Darius drummed his thumbs at the edge of the screen.

A null mailbox. That should do the trick. He created a secured mail file that he could access and directed the com system to dump incoming transmissions from the main array into this new box. *That will allow me to review anything that comes in and make sure it doesn't accidentally shut off any systems.*

Darius stretched and rubbed his eyes.

But first, I need to sleep.

. . .

"What about these two?" Dr. Taylor asked, looking at Calvin instead of the vital signs on the terminal display.

He glanced quickly at the first set, but his eyes swept back and forth over the readings for the second passenger.

"The top one is dead, a complete flat line. But the second one..."

"Take your time"

"No, I got it. The temperature on the sleeper unit is too high. If it's not reduced, this passenger will be subject to sulfide poisoning and can die of respiratory failure or... or... cardiac arrest?"

"Very good. What do you do if the sleeper's thermal control has failed and you can't reduce the temperature?"

Cal's fingers hovered over the touch screen, and made their way to a red button with a large "X" imposed on top. He tapped the button, the terminal registered a loud buzz, and then the display changed the available commands to a set of four new buttons.

"First I turn off the hibernation routine with these two buttons, then I turn on the amyl nitrite injector here," he pointed to each command in sequence.

"Good. You're a quick learner, Calvin."

"But that will wake up the passenger, right?"

"Of course, but that's what you want if their unit is failing. Here, let's try another set." She keyed a set of instructions into the terminal, and two fresh vital signs appeared in front of Cal. He studied them for almost a minute each.

"The first one is normal hibernation, but the second has a fast heartbeat. The temperature of the unit is normal, so this is sulfide poisoning, right?"

Dr. Taylor pursed her lips, and then frowned slightly.

"See the regular respiration? Also all of your indicators show the unit is functioning properly. This is actually a child in hibernation. They can have higher heart rates than adults and not be in any danger."

"OK, I understand."

"So are you ready to try it with real passengers?"

Cal drew a great breath in and closed his eyes. He collected himself for a moment, exhaled, and nodded. Dr. Taylor exited the simulation program and called up the first pair of passengers with a short series of touches.

Cal opened his eyes. Though his gaze looked forward, he was keenly aware of Dr. Taylor watching him. Slow, regular signs of life showed on his screen.

"These two are normal," he said.

"Correct. Push that arrow to move to the next set," Dr. Taylor said as she pointed to a green triangle on the screen.

Cal moved to the next set of vitals and studied them for a minute.

"First one is normal, second one… a child?"

Dr. Taylor's eyes momentarily left Cal and went to the terminal screen.

"Correct."

Cal summoned another pair of vitals to the screen. "These two are also normal."

"Correct."

"So you really sit here all day and scroll through looking at nothing, Doctor?"

She turned away from Calvin and moved to another terminal at the far end of the sleeper unit's hallway. Dr. Taylor turned it on with a keystroke and called up the passenger monitoring program. "It may seem like tedious work, but it's extremely important. If something goes wrong with a passenger or a sleeper, we can catch it and possibly save their life."

"I understand."

Not exactly the kind of work that I was expecting, but maybe I can make myself useful.

The pair worked in near silence, only broken by the occasional chirp from their terminals as commands were processed. Cal worked significantly slower than the doctor, his inexperience preventing him from doing more than six passengers every minute. As the minutes ticked away, Cal found his mind wandering from the tedium. He thought of the passengers within the sleeper units and wondered if they were dreaming.

I had a dream when I was in hibernation, and it wasn't pleasant. Are they all terrified, or do they have pleasant dreams? Was I just torturing myself?

He realized that his thoughts had wandered, and brought his full attention back to his work. Cal glanced briefly over at the aging doctor, and noted to himself how quickly she could read the vitals. He turned back to the terminal and continued his analysis of the passengers.

The duo finished their work in forty minutes. Cal's neck had become somewhat strained as he was unaccustomed to working in zero-G. He rubbed his hand on his neck in a vain effort to relieve the tension.

"And thus concludes my work, for now," Dr. Taylor said.

"How often do you do this?"

"At least twice a day."

"Twice a day? Doesn't that leave you with a lot of down time?"

Dr. Taylor shut off her terminal, navigated over to Cal, and turned his terminal off as well. "You find things to keep yourself entertained. My next stop is the gym. It's extremely important for the crew to exercise while they are awake."

Cal stretched, causing himself to slowly pitch backwards. He steadied himself on a sleeper berth, and then rubbed his hair.

"Why is that?"

"Microgravity. There are all kinds of problems that can arise due to prolonged exposure to low gravity, and trust me Calvin, you don't want to experience them if you don't have to."

"Wait, don't the passengers have this problem too?"

She tapped at the gray hair around her temple, and then pointed at Calvin's forehead. "Remember how your cut didn't heal even though five years had passed?"

"Yeah."

"Well, as it turns out, biostasis seems to have the same effect on these microgravity issues. Our guests may well be asleep for forty or so years, but they will only have experienced the equivalent of a month's exposure," she explained. "Sure, they won't be as strong as the day they went to sleep, but they should still be able to function and contribute."

The thought of hundreds of people coming out of stasis all at once did not sit well with Cal. The idea that they might also be weaker coming out was even worse.

What if they can't function and contribute? Who is going to take care of all of them?

He followed Dr. Taylor as she departed the sleeper pod. They made their way down into the lower level of the ship and forward to a door at the end of the lower gallery. Dr. Taylor keyed her access code into a small pad next to the door and the magnetic lock released. She opened the door and turned on the light inside, revealing a small compartment that contained several sets of exercise equipment.

Cal noticed that all of the equipment seemed to be based on resistance bands rather than the usual weight plates. He moved his way in and touched the cold steel of one of the machines. Upon inspection, he determined it to be something designed to work various leg muscle groups.

"Pick your torture device," Dr. Taylor said.

"I guess this is as good as any to start with." He pulled himself into position and secured his body to the apparatus. "How do I adjust this thing?"

"The knob by your right hip. Forward for more resistance, back for less," she said as she maneuvered into another machine.

He twisted the knob forward and pumped his legs. The motion was too easy, so he went through a series of dialing up the equipment and testing it before he found a reasonable setting. Cal proceeded to slowly work his leg muscles while Dr. Taylor positioned her machine for lateral pulls. After a short time, he found himself straining against the equipment and short of breath. The doctor didn't seem to be affected, and she reconfigured her device for curls.

Either she's buff, or I'm getting soft. I don't get it, I used the weight room back in school a bit and it was never this hard. He recalled the earlier conversation in the pod. *I hope I'm just out of shape. If this is how quickly we get weak, I don't know if these passengers will even be able to stand when we get there.*

Cal and Dr. Taylor worked their muscles in silence, rotating every few minutes between the machines. After completing a full rotation, Dr. Taylor retrieved a pair of neatly folded towels from a locker and handed one to Cal.

"Ready for another set, Cal?"

Cal rubbed his face and neck with the towel to mop up the sweat clinging to his skin. His muscled burned and he breathed heavily. "No thank you."

"Alright. Will I see you at dinner? Hunter wants to join us; he's pretty fascinated with hearing the experience of others while in hibernation."

Cal considered her offer. *It would probably do me good to spend time with the crew.*

"Yeah, that sounds fine." He smiled at Dr. Taylor and took his leave.

A rush of cold air hit him as he left the gym for the lower gallery. He shivered and goose bumps quickly rose on his skin. Cal grimaced as the body heat from his workout quickly dissipated. He worked his way aft to where Lieutenant Ceretti had told him the library storage pod was. He typed his code in the pad next to the door and could hear the click of the lock release.

The door of the pod slid open and Cal took a whiff of the cold, stale air within. Cal brought up the light level so he could see the neatly stacked containers in perfect rows. These looked odd to Cal, as they were built more like cupboards than boxes. He drifted inside and was hit with an even colder wall of air. His shivering became nearly uncontrollable and spasms wracked his arms.

Jesus, the colonel wasn't kidding about bundling up.

Cal opened the nearest storage unit and tried to read the titles. Between the cold and the low light, he couldn't concentrate on making a selection and ended up grabbing three random books before exiting the pod like a rabbit flushed from its burrow. He slammed the metal door behind him and made his way for pod twelve above.

Once Cal reached his quarters he looked at the books he had grabbed. He found one to be a guide on furniture making and another to be about carpentry. He frowned as he looked at the covers, and then placed them inside his berth. The third was very plainly bound, and bore the simple title of *Practical Chemistry*. Cal opened this one and paged to the table of contents. He scanned the chapters and decided to read on.

After a moment he realized that he was upside down and slowly somersaulting as he was reading. Cal flailed and managed to right himself. He growled and looked around for a way to stay still but found none. Cal began to search through the pod. He came back to the door at the front of the pod marked "AUTHORIZED PERSONNEL ONLY".

Hmm. I wonder...

Cal punched his security code into the pad and the door unlocked. Inside he saw two seats and computer terminals, as well as countless switches and buttons that were black and devoid of life. There were several windows, and he could faintly make out the form of another ship section in front of him.

I'm not sure Ceretti meant to give me this access. Oh well.

He pulled himself into a seat, let the book float freely, and buckled in. As he grabbed for the book again, he looked up and saw thousands of twinkling stars through the canopy windows. His jaw dropped and he sat motionless for several minutes.

This may actually be better than the bridge. Same view, but more private.

As Cal continued his wondrous stargazing, the book slowly made its way to the cockpit wall and out of his attention altogether. His mind was filled with a peace he had not felt in years.

Thank you, Dad. I wish you could see this with me. His thoughts wandered back to the pod. *I wish... I don't need to wish, I CAN.*

. . .

"Having you help sure makes quick work of this." Dr. Taylor turned off her screen and stretched.

Cal nodded and cycled to his final pair of vital signs. He gave a satisfied grin and turned off his own terminal. His neck was stiff from staring at the screen, and his muscles were tired from working out the previous day. "Anything I can do to help, Doc."

"It's time for the gym. Are you coming with me?"

"Nah, not this time. I've got to study up on something that Hunter showed me," he replied. *Well, half true, anyway.*

"Alright. But don't forget lunch, Cal. Hunter and I want to hear more about your experiences when you were in stasis."

"Sure thing."

Dr. Taylor gently spun around and pulled her way through the hatch. Cal waited for a minute to make sure she was gone and then turned on his terminal once more. His heart began to race as he searched for a specific berth. As he narrowed in, butterflies rose in his stomach. He looked nervously over his shoulder. A voice inside him told him to stop, but he suppressed it and called up the passenger's vitals. His finger hovered over the emergency button.

Her discomfort will be momentary. She'll forgive you for that.

Cal pressed the emergency button and then executed the revival sequence. A loud alarm chirp rang out, but he quickly shut it off and powered down the computer before racing out of the pod. His heart pounded furiously in his chest, and he felt as if it might explode. His legs complained as he kicked off of a cart and shot into the darkness toward pod twelve.

He misjudged his course and careened shoulder first into the airlock wall. Cal tried to muffle his yelp of pain as best he could as he used his other arm to pull himself into the corridor. The pain was forgotten in moments as he closed in on section delta and laid eyes on the silver hatch and deeply tinted window of her sleeper berth. There was a slight hiss coming from within. Cal knew this was part of the revival process.

Minutes passed and the hissing slowly subsided. Cal retrieved a small plastic bag he had hidden inside his flight suit. His anxiety grew as he waited. He had a sudden thought.

What if she doesn't want to see me? Uhh… crap, I can't go back on this now. Oh well.

He heard a faint scratching noise and a rattle, followed by a click as the lock disengaged. The berth door nearly hit Cal as it burst open. Cal could hear Alexis gagging as he moved in front of the berth and ducked just under the open hatch. He unfurled the plastic bag and gently placed one hand on her back as he moved the sack towards her lips.

"Easy, here… here you go."

Her neck hurtled forward and her hands shot up to grasp the bag as a violent spasm shook her body. With a great heave, she vomited into the bag. The force sent chunks flying back into her face, making a vile ring around her mouth. She gagged and hurled again. Alexis gasped for air as her body was wracked by another fit of coughing. Cal rubbed her back and tried to soothe her with his voice.

Alexis coughed and spat up several more times before she was able to catch her breath. Cal withdrew the bag, twisted it several times at the top, and sealed it with a knot, then pushed the bag away from the berth. Alexis looked up at him, her hair a tangled mess, half sobbing through her watery eyes.

"C-Calvin?" Her voice was weak and hoarse.

He smiled at her and rubbed his hand on her shoulder. Even though she was a mess, Cal thought that she was as beautiful as she had been in his dreams. He reached into his flight suit and pulled out a napkin and a mint package that he had saved from his last dinner. He reached towards her with the napkin and she recoiled slightly.

"Shh, it's ok. Let me help you." Alexis froze as Cal wiped around her mouth. He discarded the towel and offered her the mint, which she eyed with suspicion. "Here, take it. Grandma always used to say peppermint helps with nausea."

"T-Thanks," she said as she took the mint in her hand as a timid dog would take a treat. Alexis flipped it over in her hand, inspected it, and then put it in her mouth. She closed her eyes and rolled her body back into the berth. Cal's palm brushed across her stomach as she withdrew. A euphoric calm began to spread through Cal's body.

She's here. I can touch her.

Cal drew his hands to her side. He clasped her hand between his and slowly stroked her skin. He watched as her breasts rose and fell with each breath. His eyes traced her lines until they fell upon her sweet face. Cal was aware that he was gawking, but because she couldn't see him he didn't care.

"There's no gravity. How long until we land?" Her lips were mesmerizing. Cal made no effort to answer, he just watched her. Alexis turned her head towards him and opened her green eyes. "Calvin?"

His smile waned and he opened his mouth to speak, but no words came out. He squeezed her hand and withdrew his own. *Great job, Cal. Way to think things through.*

"There's something wrong, isn't there?" Her eyebrows raised and her eyes widened, and a slight frown came to her lips. She tried to move upright but winced as she jammed her body against her restraints.

"No, no. Everything is fine. I… I just…" As Alexis unbuckled her restraints she gave Cal the look of a deer in the headlights. He sighed and hung his head. "I wanted to show you something."

"Wait," she said as she drew herself from the berth and steadied herself with her hands. "You woke me up? I thought you were a refugee? Where are we? How long until we land?"

The speed of the questions almost made Cal's head spin.

"Ah… eh…" he stumbled, "Look, let me just show you first and then I'll answer all of your questions. One at a time."

Cal extended his hand to her, palm up. She floated next to her berth and gawked at him.

Please, he silently begged of her, *just come with me.*

Time ticked away as the weight of her stare and the near silence of *Michael* wore on his nerves. Slowly, and with the same manner of caution as she took the mint, she reached for Cal's hand. Her warm, soft skin almost tickled as she gingerly gripped his hand. With a smile, he turned for the front of the pod, tugging at her to follow.

Cal led her to the pod's cockpit and opened the door. He smiled again and said, "Go ahead, strap in."

Alexis paused at the door and looked at the control panels and the seats in front of her. She drifted her way to the left seat and maneuvered into the restraints. Cal entered and buckled in to the other station.

"What is this? Do you fly this or something?"

"Nah, I just come here when I want to read. Or to see this."

He jabbed his finger straight up at the canopy. Alexis turned her attention to the windows and her jaw dropped wide open. Her body froze completely and for a moment Cal could have sworn she wasn't breathing. Cal leaned his head back and gazed at the endless backdrop of stars. As he drew in a deep breath, he fixated on one particularly bright white star just above Alexis's head.

He cleared his throat. "They tell me that you can't see the North Star. It's behind the ship or something. But I like to imagine that one over there is." He pointed past her head and out of the canopy. "It helps me make sense of things, since north has always been up to me."

Alexis did not break her stare. Her voice was almost a whisper. "I've never seen anything so beautiful."

"I saw a lot of stars back in Texas when I went camping with my friends. But I think I see more stars out these two windows than in the whole sky back home."

A slight smile formed on her lips. "I think I could say the same. I remember going home over Mount Hood really late at night this one time a few years back. Dad had this car where the whole roof was made of glass. He and Mom were in the front seat, and my brother Derek was asleep in the seat next to me. I was asleep most of the time too, but I woke up as we came over the mountain. The stars were amazing then, but nothing compared to now."

Cal raised his brows. "Oh, you have a brother?"

Alexis bit her lower lip. "Had. He was deployed to Iraq just after the trip. We got the call a month later…"

Cal's heart dropped as he knew he had accidentally hit a nerve. "I'm so sorry, I had no idea."

She shook her head and waved her hand in a dismissive gesture. "No, you had no way of knowing. Besides, we were proud of him serving his country. We knew that if he was to die, he wanted it to be for us, for the US." Alexis paused and looked at Cal. Her eyes seemed full of sadness. "That doesn't mean I miss him any less."

He placed his hand on hers and squeezed lightly. It seemed to Cal that her sadness entered his own body through her touch. He began to think of his father. It dawned on Cal that he may have made his own sacrifices in the end for Cal, and he felt his eyes begin to water.

"Are you thinking of your dad?"

He nodded and turned his head back towards the canopy windows. He squeezed Alexis's fingers again. "I'm still trying to make sense of it all. Dad and I had our troubles, but now they all seem so stupid. At first I was angry when he sent me to be here, then I was scared." Cal let out a nervous laugh and looked down at the lifeless control panel. "To be honest, I'm still scared."

He felt her fingers curl against his own. "Look at me, Calvin." He turned his head and looked straight into her bright green eyes. "I'm scared too. And at least until I met you, very much alone. You have no idea how glad I am that you are here."

I could say the same. Cal was lost in her eyes. He felt sudden butterflies in his stomach and his throat tightened a little. He could see her eyes watering even more, and a great pout formed on her face.

"No, no, don't cry, Alexis."

It was too late, she burst out sobbing and tears pooled up and floated away from her face. Cal took his free hand and wiped a tear from her right eye. Her face was contorted, and snot bubbles formed in her nostrils as her wailing became louder.

"Shhh, it's ok. Shhh."

Cal searched the compartments of the cockpit for a tissue or towel of some sort. He found an unused paper napkin from one of his previous meals and offered it to her. Alexis snatched it from his hand. She withdrew her other hand from his grasp, raised the napkin to her nose, and blew for a long time.

"You don't get it. I'm *all alone.* My whole family is dead, not just my brother."

Cal's heart sank. "I'm so sorry, Alexis."

"Oh God, Mom… Dad," she broke down and sobbed again, then unleashed a scream of anguish. Cal could do nothing but look at her and rub her arm. Tears welled in her eyes again. "I was in Yellowstone on a trip when the Chinese invaded. I didn't know it at the time. I tried calling my parents, but I couldn't get through. Not by phone, not by email. Then the rangers rounded up all of the tourists and took us to Colorado."

Her voice went cold and she wavered, "It was only after I landed myself in that refugee camp in Denver that I found out what happened. About how those bastards murdered innocent civilians in the street to provoke a counterattack by the National Guard. My parents were used as bait."

Alexis cried for ten minutes as Cal sat next to her, attempting to comfort her. He felt a twinge of guilt. *I shouldn't have awakened her. This was a mistake, I didn't want to hurt her.* He rubbed his hand down the back of her head as she cried into his shoulder. Her chestnut hair was soft and tickled at his hand as it slithered like a snake in the weightlessness.

She looked at him and drew in a deep breath as if to push her cries deep within. "I-I'm sorry, Calvin. I didn't mean to do that. You showed me this nice thing and I ruined it by being a mess and telling you my sad story. I shouldn't have put that on you. It's not fair, I'm so sorry, I ruined everything."

Cal smiled at her and brushed her cheek. "Please, call me Cal. And don't worry about it. Remember, when we first got here, I wasn't exactly a shining example of my finest."

They both laughed nervously. Alexis opened her lips as if to speak, but she paused. Something burned within Cal, and he felt as if he had to do something. He quickly unbuckled from his seat.

Alexis's eyes widened. "Wait, Cal, what…"

She did not get the rest of her question out as Cal swiftly moved between the seats, grabbed her around the shoulders, and pressed his lips to her mouth. Her lips were tight and her body was rigid. Cal could feel her breath on his cheek, but she did not press back against him. He withdrew and sighed.

"Cal, that… that was…" She paused as if she could not find the words to express herself.

"I know. Inappropriate. Stupid." He was exasperated with himself.

"Reckless," she added.

"I'm sorry, it's just that…"

"I'm not done," she interrupted. Alexis reached towards Cal and wrapped her hand around the back of his neck and stared him directly in the eye. "I have one more word to describe everything you have done today. Romantic."

Cal froze in a moment of shock as Alexis pulled him forward and kissed him. Her lips this time were soft, and her breath was like a warm tickling breeze on his skin. Cal closed his eyes and let the warmth of her kiss wash away the cold of the cockpit. Nothing else mattered in the moment. Cal forgot about the war and his father. Having been shot at did not seem to matter, nor did his hibernation dreams. Alexis slowly pulled away. Cal opened his eyes to see her smiling at him.

And then it hit him like a ton of bricks.

I have to put her back in stasis.

. . .

"Weyler, where are you?"

Haruka heard the echo of her voice bounce back to her, each report ever quieter until they faded to nothing. No response followed, only silence. She looked through the wispy cloud made by her frozen breath into the dark, cramped service hallway.

What's taking her so long? I already finished all of the thrusters aft of the midline.

She shivered hard enough for her to alsmost lose the grasp on her toolbox. Her attempts to rub her arms to keep warm had become futile; the tips of her fingers felt as if they were being pricked by a dozen tiny needles, and her lips were dry and cracked.

"Airman, can you hear me?"

Haruka waited for her echo to subside. She turned her head and strained to hear, but once more she was greeted by silence. She sneezed suddenly and the force sent her tumbling backward and her feet slammed into the roof of the corridor.

This is ridiculous, if I stay here any longer I'm going to get sick.

Carefully, she turned around and crawled with her hands back to the access hatch on the side wall she had entered through. Haruka grasped the lock lever with both hands and tugged. Metal screeched and then clunked as the hatch gave way. She hoisted herself into the lower gallery and secured the hatch. Haruka made her way down the nearly dark corridor to a terminal, then turned it on and activated the com.

"Lieutenant Kimura to Airman Weyler."

As she waited, she wrung her hands and breathed into them, trying to chase away the prickling cold.

"Weyler here, what can I do for you Lieutenant?"

What the hell? There aren't any stations in the access corridors.

"Where are you?"

"I'm in the computer core running simulations."

Haruka raised her voice slightly. "How long have you been there?"

There was a pause for a few seconds. "Maybe fifteen minutes?"

"Nova, you were supposed to check in with me." Haruka tapped her index finger impatiently on the wall.

"I'm sorry, it won't happen again."

"Alright, I'm coming up."

Haruka sighed and turned off the terminal. *She's almost as bad as Marco in her own way. I wonder if I should just call myself Lieutenant Babysitter.* She maneuvered towards the aft and started up the ladder to the upper gallery.

As she pulled her way up she heard voices up above. They were elevated, almost panicked. Haruka drew in a deep breath and pulled as hard as she could. She lifted herself into the gallery and quickly snapped her hand closed over the railing at the top to stop. She could make out three shapes darting toward the bridge. She tried to listen to what they were saying but could not make out all of the words, just a single phrase: "Hurry, Doctor."

Shit. Haruka's heart dropped. She immediately started down the long hallway after the trio. She wondered just what had happened to require the attention of Dr. Nelson. *It has to be an injury, probably a serious one. God, I hope Marco isn't involved.* Haruka shook her head at that. *No, he was in the propulsion section, last I checked.*

She grabbed at a brace and threw herself off of it to gain more speed. *Is it one of the bridge crew?* She snapped her arms to her side as she sailed forth. Ahead she could see two figures inside the forward airlock, going downward. *They're headed for the crew quarters.*

Haruka reached the airlock and darted to the stairs down. In her haste she almost knocked over Captain Bartrand. Her eyes adjusted to the light, but she could not see through the other crew that had gathered in front of her. She could hear conversation from deeper within the sleeper pod.

"How the hell did this happen, Doctor?" Colonel Fox demanded.

"I can't tell for sure. Judging by the smell, I'd say sulfide poisoning. Maybe you should have his sleeper checked out."

Haruka got a sudden chill. *A sleeper unit...*

"Maynard, look into it. I want a report as soon as you find something. Ellsworth, I want you to help the doctor with the body. Once he's done with his autopsy, I want it ejected into space."

"Yes, Colonel," Ellsworth's voice rang from beyond her sight.

"The rest of you, get back to work. We have a ship to run."

Haruka knew better than to wait for the colonel to see her. She immediately turned around and bolted for the airlock, and hoped that Bartrand hadn't seen her either. Haruka navigated her way out into the gallery and pulled herself around the corner. She clung to the wall as best as she could, and hoped that the crew would dissipate quickly.

They did just that, scattering like frightened rabbits. Haruka saw Mancini bolt for the propulsion section. She kicked off from the wall as hard as she could in pursuit.

"Marco, wait," she whispered loudly. He kept going. She repeated herself and the command came out hoarse as she tried to whisper louder. Mancini rolled over and turned to face Haruka. His momentum carried him backwards, but Haruka was still able to catch up to him.

"Damn it, Kimura. Where were you?"

"I heard Doctor Nelson and the others going toward the crew pod and I followed."

"No, before that."

"Down below looking for Nova. Why?"

Mancini looked over his shoulder and then tilted his head to the side to look behind Haruka. He pulled Haruka inside the connecting hall to one of the sleeper pods. His voice hushed. "Something stinks. The doctor says it's a sleeper unit failure, but something's not right."

"What's going on, Marco? Who was it?" A knot tightened in her stomach. She wasn't sure that she wanted to know the answer.

"It was Shipp."

"Shit." Haruka looked around to see if they were being watched. *Fox isn't going to be happy about this. I'd swear that she was looking forward to his trial.*

Mancini looked at her, concern evident on his face. "This is bad, Haruka. You know that if they find out that this is anything other than a complete freak accident, Fox is going to think you had something to do with it."

She let out an exasperated sigh. *He's right; she will try to pin this on me somehow. I wouldn't even put it past her to blame me even if it is an accident.*

"We need help, Marco. I overheard Fox assigning Captain Maynard to the investigation. I'm not sure if I trust him or if Fox has sway over him."

Mancini thought for a moment. "Maybe we could get Nova to offer him help? She could keep an eye on him and make sure he's on the level."

Haruka shook her head. "Fox would never buy into it. She knows that Nova is friendly to us. That would just give her the ammo she needs to stuff us in our berths for the rest of the voyage."

"Does she?"

"Does she what?"

A devilish grin crossed Mancini's lips. "When's the last time the mighty Colonel Fox has taken a trip to the propulsion section? Or the thruster access corridors? Has she ever seen the three of us interact?"

Dear Lord, his brain just fired on all synapses. He's right, she doesn't know about Nova.

"Marco, you're nuts. That might just work."

His grin broadened and his teeth showed through his lips. "See? I'm not *just* here because I'm pretty."

Haruka rolled her eyes. "Ugh, get out of here. Nova should be in the computer core. I need to think of a backup plan, though."

Mancini's grin turned to a frown and his brow furrowed. "Why? My plan will work."

"Not sure you've noticed yet, but things haven't exactly gone our way since we lifted off the pad at Laramie," she retorted. "This time I want to be better prepared."

"Good point. I'll catch up with you later."

She watched Mancini depart for the rear of the ship, and then made her way down to the lower gallery. She moved forward and made her way to the crew gym; this seemed to be one of the best places to hide from Fox. Once inside, she belted into an upper body machine and began working out. She paid little mind to the physical labor, which had become utterly routine. Haruka worked through scenarios in her head in an attempt to come up with another defense to a baseless accusation of murder.

The whole ship has gone crazy, hasn't it? Nothing has gone the way it should, except for the fact that somehow we've managed to point the ship in the right direction.

The thrum of the resistance bands broke her train of thought for a moment. She realized how hypnotic the repetitive noise and motion could be. She adjusted the machine to work a different set of muscles and then continued her workout.

I've had my share of nasty CO's, but Colonel Fox is just nuts. She stopped dead in her tracks and released the hand grips. The bands gave a loud twang as they snapped back to rest.

Fox is nuts. She's not just a little weird or cranky, she's full on insane. Why wasn't this caught before she was placed in command? Haruka shuddered. *This isn't about me anymore. This woman is unpredictable and irrational. She should not be in command of this mission.*

Haruka was no longer thinking about a defensive strategy. She knew she needed to go on the offensive against Colonel Fox. She knew she would need the support of more than just Lieutenant Marco Mancini and Airman Nova Weyler, too. She would need to figure out how to get the support of Dr. Nelson, as well as a higher ranking officer.

I need the major's help.

. . .

Calvin looked at Alexis as she sobbed uncontrollably.

Way to be a jerk, Cal. Try thinking something through some day, ok?

"Why the hell are you doing this to me?" she wailed. "Why did you wake me up if you had to put me right back to sleep again?"

Cal sighed, "I don't know. I guess I didn't think that far ahead."

"Jesus, Cal. You thought I'd just want to be popped out, played with for a bit, and then put back on the shelf?" Her voice escalated to a near scream. Cal hoped that nobody was on the other side of the pod door. "What am I? Some sort of teddy bear? Or video game?"

Cal's voice cracked as it raised an octave. "No, that's not it at all."

"Then what reason could you possibly have had?"

"I have two. Promise to let me explain?"

She glared at him and her breathing was erratic as she choked back her tears, but she nodded.

"The first may sound pretty stupid. I wanted to show you something that few people have seen. Or will ever see, for that matter."

Alexis drummed her fingers on her crossed arms, "and the second reason?"

Cal looked away from her. He could feel heat rise in his face, and he knew he was blushing. "I'm not sure if I should say."

"No, you promised."

He sighed and closed his eyes. "It's really hard for me to explain. Frankly I'm not sure you'd believe me." Cal paused and then looked at Alexis. "Did you dream much when you were asleep?"

"A little, I think. I can't really remember."

"Well, I had more than a few dreams. They were very vivid, and some of them I remember very well." Cal scratched nervously at his arm. "There is one in particular that I had over and over, as if I was being forced to face my demons in my sleep. Yet every single nightmare ended with you stopping it. It's weird. It was like you would pull me out of the dream and protect me."

Her eyes widened and her lips parted slightly. There was an awkward silence for several seconds. "What are you trying to say?"

You're going to scare her off, Cal. Don't say it.

"Remember when we first got to space, you told me that you thought that I might just be the person to keep you sane?"

Alexis gave a slow nod.

"I guess I'm trying to say the same thing." Cal paused. His eyes wandered to the forward windows and he caught a glimpse of the back of pod ten. "No. It's not the same thing." His eyes returned to look at hers. "I need you, Alexis. This isn't a sanity thing. This sure as hell isn't an entertainment thing. I may not think things out, as you have figured out already. But I do know that I need you. I couldn't wait until we reach the planet to see you again. I know it sounds crazy…"

"You're damn right," she cut in. "Look, as far as I see it, we've really only known each other for a few days."

Cal grinned and placed his hand on hers. "I seem to remember you kissing me first."

Alexis shifted slightly in her seat and her eyes dipped for a moment. "That's just because I had kicked you in the head. I felt bad."

Cal felt a clammy sensation in his hand. He withdrew his hand and balled it, stroking his palm with his fingers. He found his hand was warm and dry. *That was her, not me,* he thought.

"So you're the type of girl that goes to comfort a strange guy if he freaks out in front of you? It must have been interesting to watch you ride a city bus, then."

Alexis wrinkled her nose and furrowed her brow. "God no. And that's not what I meant, either."

"Which part? Comforting freaked out strangers, or riding the bus?"

Damn it, Cal. Stop poking at her. You're not helping yourself.

"You know what I meant."

"Actually, I don't. And quit avoiding the issue."

"What issue?" she asked innocently.

"Why you came after me, tried to comfort me, and kissed me."

Alexis avoided his stare. "Just trying to be nice, that's all."

Cal reached for her chin and gently turned her face towards him. His stomach suddenly churned. He closed his eyes for a moment and concentrated on the question he knew he had to ask. His eyes opened slowly and he locked his gaze with hers.

"So you're saying that I mean nothing to you?"

She bit her lower lip. "That's right. I think you're a nice kid and probably well intentioned, but you're also a bit screwed up." Cal felt a cold sweat throughout his body and a lump formed in his throat. Alexis continued, "I think you may have read a bit too much into things, and this is getting out of control." She gently grabbed his wrist with her hand, drew his hand to her mouth, and kissed it. "Thank you for showing me the galaxy, but I think I'm ready to go back to sleep now."

Tears began to cloud Cal's vision. Through them he could see a gentle smile on her face, and her own watery green eyes. His heart sunk into his feet as she released his wrist and he pulled back from her. He wanted to say something but could not for fear of upsetting her more. He just nodded and escorted her out of the cockpit and back to her sleeper.

Without a word, she climbed inside and buckled her restraint harness. Cal reached for her hand once more. As they exchanged one last touch, Cal again felt the rise of butterflies in his stomach.

Cal closed the hatch and heard the lock click. He bowed his head forward until his brow rested on the cold aluminum door. Cal could feel nothing on the inside. Only the sound of his breathing and the metal touching his forehead reminded him that he still existed. He did not move for quite some time. His mind was haunted by Alexis's crying, as if they were tormenting echoes of his failure.

No, he reassured himself. *She said it herself. You mean nothing to her.* He turned to the opposite wall where a terminal was located. He pushed himself slowly toward it and activated the sleeper berth program. *It's just like Brittany all over again. You want her, but she doesn't want you.*

Cal called up Alexis's berth on the screen. *No, that's not right. She's scared. She needs you just as much as you need her.* He stared at her vitals. Her heartbeat was fast for a conscious passenger, and her respiration line showed erratic breathing. *See? She's crying, you idiot.* He craned his neck and looked at her sleeper unit. *But she wants to go back into sleep.* He shook his head and turned back to the terminal. He pressed the button to engage the biostasis cycle.

She would never have forgiven you if you hadn't, Cal. His fists balled up and rage swelled within him. His anger spewed forth as he screamed at the top of his lungs and punched a sleeper unit. The metal clanged like a rock had hit it. Cal felt a pop and saw the dent his fist made in the door. It took his body several seconds to realize what happened; he howled in pain when it caught up.

Cal floated in the hallway, clutching his hand. He tried to squeeze the pain away by digging his fingers in to his wrists, but it would not abate. He breathed in deeply which helped somewhat, but it felt as if he had stabbed his finger.

He bumped and crashed his way out of the sleeper pod and headed for the belly of the ship. Maneuvering down the ladder proved to be very difficult with one good hand, and Cal hurtled end over end into the railing at the top. He muttered and swore, then sucked in another great breath and continued on.

Cal struggled through the dark corridor, almost blinded by pain. He fumbled as he input his security code into the key pad for the gym door and then slid it open. He was relieved to find Dr. Taylor still inside, working on an abdominal machine. She startled when he opened the door.

"Ugh, Cal. How many times do I have to tell you not to sneak up on an old woman," she said after she recovered.

"A few more times," he replied sarcastically. Pain shot through his hand again and he winced.

Dr. Taylor wiped the sweat from her arms with a towel and then rubbed it across her brow. "You hurt yourself again?" Cal nodded. "Come here, let me take a look."

"I think I busted something," he said as he advanced toward her.

Dr. Taylor took his bandaged hand. "Tell me where it hurts."

Cal pointed at his middle finger. Dr. Taylor squeezed it and he tried to stifle a yelp. She grunted and then scrutinized his other fingers, and then worker her way down the hand. "Does any of *that* hurt?"

"No, just the finger." Cal felt as if he had been stabbed again. He gritted his teeth and drew in a deep breath.

"I see. How did this happen?"

"I ah… had a little run in with my sleeper berth."

The doctor finished her examination and looked at Cal with her wizened brown eyes. "A word of advice, Calvin. Punching hard objects is a great way to break a finger, which it looks like you've done. If the hard object happens to be a piece of equipment on this ship, it's also a great way to upset a commanding officer."

Cal's eyes dropped as if he were a scolded puppy. "I know, but I couldn't help it."

"Well, you could have spared yourself a lot of pain by coming down here and working out your frustrations. Come with me and let's take care of that finger."

Dr. Taylor led Cal back down the lower gallery to a pod three rows away. She indicated for Cal to wait outside while she went in. After about a minute she came out with some tape and a few tiny packets. She taped his middle and ring fingers together in two spots as Cal bit his lip.

"Nothing more strenuous than eating or using your computer with this hand, and these fingers stay together until I tell you otherwise, understood?" Cal nodded. She handed him the packets. "Ibuprofen for the pain and swelling. If you think it is swelling too much, it probably is. Get an ice pack and come find me."

Cal gave her a pained smile. "Thanks, Doc. One of these days I'll go without you patching me up, I swear."

She did not return the smile. Instead, the wrinkles on her forehead became more pronounced and her eyebrows arched. "Calvin, I don't want you to be alarmed, but this is serious. I need you to tell me if you have any sort of sudden mood swings. You will not upset me by coming to me with problems. But you have to trust me on this, it's extremely important that you tell me about these kinds of things if they happen."

An eerie chill washed over Cal. "Why?"

Dr. Taylor pursed her lips and shook her head. "I can't tell you that. You just have to trust me, Calvin."

"I do, Doc. But you're kind of freaking me out a little bit."

"You wouldn't be the first person to be a little unsettled about *something* on this mission," she replied in a flat tone.

Cal flashed back to his earlier encounter with Alexis. *I wonder if she knows just how true that is.*

"In any case, Mr. McLaughlin, I do believe it is lunch time. I'm sure Hunter is off duty and looking for us."

Cal did not want company, not even from Dr. Taylor. He thought for a second, searching for a polite way to decline, but decided on an honest approach. "Sorry. And tell Hunter I'm sorry too. I just want to be alone right now. Maybe catch up on some reading."

She nodded. "Just remember what I said. I will see you later for passenger scans."

Cal quickly retreated to pod twelve and settled himself into the cockpit with a meal pouch and *Practical Chemistry*. He paged through the book to the last section he had been reading. *If I'm going to screw up everything here, I might as well learn something useful for when we land.*

The stresses of the day had taken a toll on him. No sooner than he had eaten lunch and read three pages, he fell asleep, harnessed in the seat of the lonely control room.

. . .

"Just a minute, Lieutenant, my head is still spinning."

Haruka idled by as Major Nathan Emberley rubbed his temples. His brow glistened with sweat and his salt and pepper hair was a tussled mess. Mercifully for both of them, the major did not throw up when Haruka revived him from hibernation.

He pulled himself out of the berth and stretched his long, lean frame. He squinted one eye and rubbed a hand across his stomach.

"Get me something to eat please, Lieutenant. Then tell me again what it is you need. I'm not quite sure I heard you right the first time." His voice was a soothing baritone.

Haruka saluted and raced to a locker in the adjacent corridor. She retrieved a meal packet from within and returned to the major, who was still stretching various muscles. Haruka tore open the package and handed it to Emberley.

He opened a smaller package and produced a biscuit, which he attacked like a starved wolf. Haruka watched as he consumed the piece in two bites. His eyes met hers as he looked up.

"I'm sorry. Please, explain the situation again. I'm listening," he said as he smacked his lips.

"Thank you, sir. I believe that Colonel Fox may be jeopardizing *Raphael*, her crew, and passengers. She has been acting in a very bizarre manner and has given orders that do not make sense. She has also at times acted in an abusive or paranoid manner," Haruka said, enunciating every word.

Major Emberley took a bite of scrambled egg from another pouch. He chewed with great deliberation as he gave a Haruka a pensive look. "Can you provide me examples of actions she has taken?"

"Yes, sir. She has baselessly suspected other officers of attempting to undermine her authority. She has stripped officers of their duties based on her idea that they are part of a conspiracy, when an admitted conspirator has denied their involvement in anything. She has placed unnecessary time constraints or demands on the propulsion crew during the maintenance cycle.

"These are just the items that I know about, Major. I am fairly certain that other crew members will have seen other incidents. The worst part, sir, is that she refuses to listen to the possibility that one of her nav crewmen may have miscalculated our course after she initiated a low-orbit slingshot, counter to mission plan."

Emberley took a deep drink from a packet of coffee. He wiped his mouth with the back of his hand and placed his collective wrappers in the outer packaging.

"So you say that the colonel doesn't want to review the course calculations, correct?"

"Yes, sir."

"And do you know if this officer took up the issue with the crewman who allegedly made the mistake?"

Haruka cleared her throat, "I know for a fact they have not, sir."

Emberley's brows raised and the corner of his mouth tightened. "Do you know why, Lieutenant?"

"This crewman is aware that he may have made a previous mistake that almost ended in disaster, but is unwilling to acknowledge it, sir."

"I take it by your knowledge that you are the one confronting Fox and this crewman, correct?"

"Yes, sir."

"So you want to spite Fox by bringing me in to watch her?"

"No, sir."

The major scratched at his short stubble of a beard. "Do you believe that Colonel Fox is an imminent threat to the safety of the crew and the security of the mission?"

"Yes, sir," she said with absolute confidence.

"I see. And what is your direct reasoning for this?"

"The low orbit slingshot forced a course change for *Raphael*. It also meant that she gained speed faster, requiring a recalculation of burn time for the plasma drive as well. If either factor is off even just a little, then the ship could be in grave danger. We could possibly miss our target altogether, sir."

Emberley stretched again and yawned. "And you want this reviewed, correct?"

"Yes, sir. But I believe she is also unstable, sir. If I were to make the request again, I am certain I would be relieved of duty for it."

Or worse.

"Very well, Lieutenant. I will see that Colonel Fox allows for a review of the course corrections."

Haruka sighed. "There's more, sir."

Emberley quirked his eyebrows. "Oh? What's that, Lieutenant?"

She wrung her hands together. "Earlier today, a crewman was found dead. Not just any crewman, he was the conspirator I had referred to earlier. She has ordered an investigation into his death. My gut tells me that she's going to make assumptions and accusations, no matter what the result of the investigation is."

"And this is why you believe she is a threat to the crew?"

"Yes, sir."

"Understood," he replied in a solemn tone. "I will watch for this behavior as well."

"Major, be careful. If she sees you snooping around, she might just snap."

"Thank you, Lieutenant. You've made your point clear. Now I suggest you return to your duties before *you* draw unwanted attention from her."

Haruka saluted him and then snaked her way out of the crew pod. She hurried down the gallery and into the propulsion section. At the last moment, she turned away from the propulsion control room as she remembered that Nova had been in the computer core earlier. Haruka slipped through the hatch leading to the core chamber.

She made her way past the racks to the mainframe interface terminal. Instantly she recognized Mancini's squat frame belted into the chair as she approached. She moved up next to him, and he looked up from the terminal.

Mancini smiled brightly. "Hey, Kimura. How's it going?"

She gave a slight smile in return. "Feeling a little better now, thanks."

"I take it your little meeting went well?"

"As well as it could." Haruka looked around the room. "Where's Nova?"

Mancini's grin took on a devilish look. "Assisting Captain Maynard, of course. Which is why I'm pushing buttons on this terminal. She can't be in two places at once, so I get to run her thruster sims. Exciting, huh?"

Haruka rolled her eyes at him. "Yeah, I'm sure you're thrilled. Want me to take over?"

"Not a chance. I'd rather be doing this than the last item on our checklist for the day." He pulled a clipboard from the side of the workstation; the Velcro that attached it made a sick ripping sound as it peeled apart. Mancini flung it toward Haruka like a Frisbee. She snatched it from the air and read the list.

"Reactor physical inspection." She flung the clipboard back at him. "Yeah, thanks you jerk," she said with biting sarcasm.

"Hey," he chuckled, "the early bird gets the worm. The late one gets to play with the nuclear device."

Haruka gave him one last sneer as she turned around to leave the core. She made her way through the propulsion control room and down the ladder to the reactor. The eerie glow from the reactor sent shivers down Haruka's spine.

God, I hate being near this thing. I know it's safe, but still...

Haruka grabbed a Geiger counter from a locker at the base of the ladder and began her physical inspection of the reactor casing. She listened carefully for unusual clicks from the counter as she moved slowly down the length of the reactor shielding.

Her thoughts wandered from the inspection. Her attention drifted to her parents, and to her sister. She wondered if they were safe. The failure of Shipp's sleeper unit chilled her, and dark thoughts of widespread problems came to her. She closed her eyes and pushed back the images of her family, gasping for air and dying.

You can do nothing to help them. All you can do is to help make sure this ship makes it intact.

Haruka suppressed her feelings and resumed her work as the twin generators cried a mechanical song of solitude.

· · ·

Calvin awoke with a start. The sound of metal scraping behind him made him jerk hard against his harness. He grunted and looked behind him. Lieutenant Hunter Ceretti poked his head through the cockpit door. Just beyond him was the blond lieutenant that Cal had accosted when he had arrived from the transport.

Hunter spoke, "What are you doing here, Calvin?"

Cal rubbed his eyes and stretched. His face twisted as his calf cramped. "Ugh. I fell asleep, sorry."

"Well, Dr. Taylor has been looking for you. She got worried when you didn't show up to help her with monitoring."

Cal tapped a button on the terminal in front of him and the time flashed on the screen. "Crap. I'm sorry, Hunter. I didn't mean to sleep so long."

The blonde lieutenant interjected in a shrill voice, "That's *Lieutenant Ceretti* to you, Mr. McLaughlin."

Hunter glanced over his shoulder. "No it's not, Josephson. He's not military so he's not required to address me by rank. And I'd thank you not to yell at my friend." He turned his attention back to Cal. "Anyway, that didn't quite answer my question. What are you doing in *here*?"

Cal suddenly remembered the markings on the door. He sat bolt upright, which made him jam into his harness again. "I'm sorry, I'm not supposed to be here, am I? I haven't touched anything but the clock button, I swear."

Hunter reached out and placed his hand on Cal's shoulder. "Take it easy. It's not like you can cause much damage in here."

Josephson protested, "But the ESAARC pods are for emergency…"

"Calm down, Lieutenant. We both know that Calvin can't accidentally eject the pod. The system has to be activated elsewhere first."

Emergency pod? What the hell? Cal grabbed at his buckles but forgot about his finger. He yelped as he pushed against the release too hard. He grabbed at his hand with his uninjured one in an attempt to quell the pain.

"E-eject the pod? Wait, what is this thing I'm sitting in?" His voice cracked from the pain burning in his finger.

"It's an ESAARC pod. There's one attached to each sleeper pod, as well as one on the crew pod under the bridge. Jesus, Calvin." Hunter looked at Cal with great concern. "What did you do to your finger?"

Cal sucked in a breath and held it for a moment before he let it go in a rush. "Ah, broke it being my usual stupid self. What's an ESAARC pod?"

Hunter winced in sympathy. "Josephson. Care to tell him what it does?"

She let out an exasperated sigh. "Really, Ceretti? He's a civilian."

"Who happens to be a crew member. Would you treat Doctor Taylor this way?" There was a momentary silence. "I didn't think so. So just tell him."

"Fine," she said, almost pouting. "ESAARC stands for Emergency Semi Autonomous Atmospheric Reentry Control. In a nutshell, if *Michael* has an emergency in planetary orbit, she can detach all of the pods. Two crew members then control the chemical thrusters attached to the sleeper pods to hopefully navigate a safe landing."

Cal's face contorted as he processed the information. "Wait, you said these are attached to the sleeper pods, and so are the thrusters. What about the cargo pods?"

Hunter smiled broadly. "You caught that, didn't you. They detach too, but they come down differently. Josephson?"

She cleared her throat and looked around. "Aerodynamic freefall and parachutes. And if all else fails, litho braking."

"I'm sorry, lithawhat?" asked Cal

"It means they smash into the ground and we pray they don't crater," replied Hunter.

"That's… special," said Cal. "Why don't they have thrusters too?"

Josephson scoffed, "Because it would cost too much, weigh too much, and require about four times the crew that we have."

"The passengers are more important than the cargo," added Hunter. He motioned out of the pod with his hand. "Come on, it's almost chow time. Josephson, can you go get Doctor Taylor, please?"

"Yes, *sir*," she sneered and then left the hallway.

Hunter craned his neck to watch her as she departed. He then pulled himself into the seat next to Cal and reached for his buckles. "Here, let me get those for you."

"Thanks. The last thing I need right now is to go to Doc and tell her I've broken myself again." Hunter grinned at Cal. Cal looked around to make sure they were alone, and then spoke in a hushed voice. "You don't get along well with Josephson, do you?"

"Actually, we're fine. She just doesn't seem to like *you* for some reason."

"I can't imagine why. I only pushed her into a wall, escaped hibernation, and became an unwanted burden on the crew."

Hunter released Cal's restraint and then looked him dead in the eye. "Your awakening was a shock to us all, no doubt. But don't think for a second that you are a burden." Cal scoffed, but Hunter ignored him. "Both Doctor Taylor and I are very glad to spend time with you. I like hanging out during meal time and talking with you."

"Yeah, that's great Hunter, but…"

"I wasn't finished. You've also made an impression on Colonel Dayton. He's been asking about you, how you've been fitting in, and how you've been performing."

Cal blinked. "Why?"

Hunter shrugged. "I don't know. It's not my place to question him. But I can't imagine it would be anything bad." He floated out of his seat and headed for the pod door. "I'm hungry. You coming?"

Cal was not particularly hungry, but he couldn't deny himself company this time. "Yeah, right behind you." He pulled his arms out of the straps and fell in behind Hunter and he exited the sleeper pod.

It took a moment for Cal's vision to adjust to the darker expanse of the gallery. Hunter was already moving ahead of him as he made way for a meal and conversation.

"Can I have a moment of your time, Mr. McLaughlin?" The voice from the shadows behind him startled Cal, and he flailed like a cat in free fall.

Cal turned and faced Colonel Dayton. He cocked his head sideways and put his hand over his heart. "Sorry, sir. You surprised me. What can I do for you?"

Dayton's beard hooked upward as he smiled. "Funny you should put it that way, Mr. McLaughlin. How has your training with Doctor Taylor been going?"

Cal was puzzled. "I'm done training, sir. I've been helping her monitor the passengers for several days now."

"And you're enjoying it?"

"I'm quite happy to be helping, sir."

"Good. Would you like to continue helping for the next maintenance cycle?"

Cal's heart beat hard within his chest. His mouth twitched as he tried to stifle a smile. "You mean you want me to wake up with the crew next time?" Colonel Dayton nodded. "Yes, sir!"

"Good." He slapped Cal on the shoulder. "I look forward to it. I think you work well with Doctor Taylor. I was skeptical at first, but you've proven that you do truly want to work, and this is your reward for that. Now, go join your friends for supper."

"Yes, sir. Thank you, sir," Cal said excitedly.

He pushed hard off of a cart, eager to tell Hunter and Dr. Taylor the news.

· · ·

The com system crackled to life. "Fox to Lieutenant Kimura."

Haruka chewed hastily and swallowed the bite of sandwich. She drifted to the workstation at the end of the sleeper row and pressed the com button. "Kimura here, yes Colonel?"

"Took you long enough. Where the hell are you?"

Really, Colonel? That was maybe ten seconds. "Sorry, I was eating. I am in the crew pod, ma'am," she said, concealing her irritation.

"Report to the bridge immediately." The colonel's voice was curt.

Haruka opened her mouth to reply, but the com system had already shut off. *Oh, she's definitely not a happy camper today.* She rolled up the rest of her half eaten sandwich inside her mostly untouched meal pouch, stowed it her sleeper unit, and bolted for the stairway up to the bridge.

As she crested the stairway and found herself on the command platform, she realized that Colonel Fox was waiting for her. The command chair was facing Haruka already and Fox sat upon it, her back hunched as she leaned on an elbow, her expression twisted in an almost evil smile. She was flanked by Captain Bartrand and Lieutenant Singh.

Haruka felt a lump rise in her throat and her palms began to sweat. Her nerves had not been on edge this much since Whiskey Zero Four's flight. She did not hesitate as she approached the command chair, although a voice in her head screamed at her to run away, growing louder every inch closer to the colonel she came.

"Lieutenant Kimura, reporting as requested, Colonel," she said, trying to sound confident.

"I will make this brief, Lieutenant. The bridge recorders are on. I will give you one last chance to confess to everything you have been involved in." Fox's smirk grew wider. Even her crow's feet stretched in an almost arrogant manner. "I promise you that leniency will be shown at your court martial if you do this."

"I'm sorry, Colonel. I cannot confess to anything. I have done nothing but serve my country, and to serve you as my commanding officer," she replied in a calm tone.

In an instant, Fox's expression turned sour. "Very well, Lieutenant.

You had your chance, but now you leave me no choice." She reached for the command panel on her chair and pressed two buttons. Her voice echoed through the ship's speakers, taking on a tinny quality. "Attention, all crew report immediately to the bridge. Doctor Nelson, please come to the bridge."

You're about to do what I think you are, aren't you? The corner of Haruka's mouth tightened, but she did not speak. She knew she would have to choose her words carefully with the recorders operating. Haruka stared at Colonel Fox, unflinching. She was a ball of emotions on the inside, but she would be damned if she would let Fox see that. She was barely aware of time passing as she thought of every accusation she might have thrown at her, every defense to whatever phantom schemes that Fox had concocted in her twisted mind.

Haruka was shaken from her concentration when Mancini came up from behind her and placed his hand on her shoulder. She looked at him and then surveyed the bridge; nearly all of the crew had assembled. Nova was making her way onto the bridge right on the heels of Captain Maynard. Haruka did not see Major Emberley, nor did she spot Doctor Nelson or Airman Ellsworth.

Where is he? Despair began to brew in her mind, and her heart pounded so hard that she feared that Fox could hear it from the command chair. Haruka gulped as Fox opened her mouth. The colonel stopped and looked past the throng of crew that had gathered at the back of the bridge. She tapped impatiently at her terminal.

"Doctor Nelson, we're waiting on you. Please report to the bridge. *Now,*" her voice rang over the address system once more.

"Sorry, I'm here now Colonel," panted Dr. Nelson as he pulled his way past Haruka and to the railing beside the command chair.

"Very well, it's time to begin." Fox shifted forward and upright in her seat, making her look rigid as a board. Her smirk returned and she took a deep breath. "I have assembled the crew so that we may all hear the results of the investigation." Her gaze burned deep into Haruka. "If any party should be responsible, I intend to try them immediately."

Haruka could hear whispers amongst the crew behind her. She tried to pay no mind to them. All she could do was to continue her staring match with *Raphael's* commander.

"Doctor Nelson, have you completed your autopsy on Lieutenant William Shipp?"

"Yes, Colonel," he puffed, still out of breath. "Lieutenant Shipp died of pulmonary edema. I believe the cause of this was sulfide poisoning.

Given that he was in biostasis at the time, the most likely source would be from the sleeper unit."

"Thank you, Doctor. That will be all." Colonel Fox tented her fingers and drew her hands toward her face. "Captain Maynard, have you completed the diagnostics on Lieutenant Shipp's sleeper berth?"

Maynard ran his right hand through his close-trimmed brown hair. "Yes, ma'am."

"And what did you find?"

"I couldn't find anything wrong with the unit at first, Colonel. It was actually Airman Weyler who found the problem."

I'm going to get blamed for this somehow, Haruka thought.

The grin on Fox's face dissipated. "Very well then. Airman, can you please tell us what you found?"

Nova snapped to attention. "Yes, Colonel. I found that the GDS sensor inside the berth had failed. This caused dangerous levels of hydrogen sulfide to build up inside the unit."

"I don't speak engineer, Airman," the Colonel snapped back. "Explain it to me in English, please."

Nova stumbled for words for a moment before regaining composure. "The GDS, or Gas Distribution System sensor, monitors the composition of the air inside each berth. It's there because hydrogen sulfide is used in low concentrations to help with maintaining biostasis, but it's also a toxic gas. The system needs to regulate..."

Fox's hand shot up in the air. "Fine, fine." Again the twisted, evil smirk returned to the Colonel's face. "And you found evidence of sabotage?"

Nova and Maynard looked at each other. Haruka could see a look of shock on Nova's face. More whispers came from the crew.

Maynard stuttered, "N-no ma'am. The sensor appeared undamaged, it just failed."

Fox rose from her seat and pointed a weathered finger at Haruka. "And there's your saboteur, Captain. Bartrand, Singh, seize her."

Silence engulfed the bridge. Haruka could not even hear any breathing, as if all air had suddenly been sucked from the room. Not a soul moved.

"But Colonel," Maynard's voice shattered the silence. "There was no sabotage. There would be no *way* to sabotage the unit while closed and locked."

"Don't try to defend her, Captain, or you'll suffer the same fate."

Haruka's heart sank. *What fate? Where are you, Major?*

Mancini chimed in, his voice clearly concerned, "But Colonel, if Captain Maynard said there was no sabotage, then why are you..."

"That's it," she interrupted. "Seize Mancini as well, Captain Bartrand." Bartrand and Singh exchanged confused glances. "*Now*, Captain!"

"Belay that order, Captain," rang a deep, smooth voice from behind Haruka. She turned around. Major Emberley drifted his way through an opening in the crowd, flanked on either side by a pair of lieutenants that she did not recognize. All three had holsters on their hips, and a small black grip protruded from each.

"What's the meaning of this?" shrieked Fox.

"I should ask the same of *you*, Colonel," he said.

Anger burned within her eyes as she locked on to Emberley's face. "I am conducting a trial here. Who authorized you to be out of stasis, Major?"

He dismissed her question. "I am conducting an investigation, and I have come across some rather disturbing information."

Fox scoffed, "So let me finish my trial here and you can investigate whatever little thing is it that's caused you to wake up."

"I'm afraid that I have to stop your so-called trial here, ma'am, because my investigation is very pertinent to what is happening on this bridge." He cleared his throat. "Doctor Nelson?"

"Ah, yes sir," he replied in a soft tone.

"Has Colonel Fox exhibited any irrational or unbecoming behavior lately?"

"How dare you," she screamed, spittle flying from her lips. "Major, I will not have you question my authority here. Bartrand!"

"Stay where you are, Captain," Emberley ordered as his fingers shot up in Bartrand's direction. "Doctor, please answer the question."

"Y-yes, sir," he stammered, his voice shaky. "There have been several incidents recently where she has treated crew members in an unusually... ah... harsh manner. Also, it's almost like she is ignoring evidence that she has asked for while she is conducting this... trial, I guess it is?"

"How would *you* know how to run a ship, Doctor?" she roared.

Major Emberley calmly continued. "No, I already know that last part, Doctor. I could hear quite well for myself. Tell me, do you know of a condition that Doctor Tadashi Kimura warned all command staff and ships' doctors about during the briefings on the stasis units?"

Fox fumed, "That information is classified, Major."

Doctor Nelson seemed to be gaining in confidence the longer Major Emberley questioned him. "Yes, sir. Hibernation Psychosis. It's an uncommon side effect of biostasis, but it was demonstrated in at least two test subjects back on Earth."

"What are the symptoms, Doctor?"

Fox narrowed her eyes at Emberley. "You piece of shit, you're going back to sleep now. Bartrand, seize him!"

"Ignore her, Captain," he repeated. Bartrand flinched but settled back to where he was. "Doctor, what are the symptoms?"

"They vary. However, the two most common physical effects were fever and loss of appetite, and the two most common psychological effects were delusions and paranoia. The effects last only a few days with proper treatment, and are believed to be temporary even without treatment," The doctor squinted as he recalled.

Haruka felt a lump rise in her throat. *Wait, so this could happen again with any crewmember who has been in stasis? Or any passenger?* She watched Colonel Fox sputter, unable to respond to what was happening around her. The whispers of the crew were now no longer whispers, but mutters.

Major Emberley tugged at his flight suit. "In your opinion, Doctor, has Colonel Fox exhibited symptoms of hibernation psychosis?"

"Yes, Major."

"Lies," she hissed.

"Very well. Colonel Marissa Fox, you are hereby relieved of duty on the grounds that you are not mentally fit for duty. You will be placed in stasis until we reach Demeter, at which time you will be treated for your illness," he said, his gaze firmly locked on her.

Fox's eyes widened like a cornered beast. "Mutiny! I'll have your heads for this. Bartrand, Singh, arrest them all!"

Bartrand hesitated as he looked at the colonel. He moved forward slightly. Major Emberley reached to his hip and drew his weapon. The fat, contrasting black and yellow tip told Haruka that he was brandishing a Taser.

"Belay that order, Captain, unless you also want to be relieved," Emberley warned.

Haruka heard a voice inside that was egging on Bartrand. A part of her wanted to see him back in stasis for not owning up to his failures. She bit her lip and forced her feelings aside, remaining a stone wall on her exterior. Bartrand did not take the bait. He gripped the railing and steadied himself.

"Cormack, Morado," Emberley signaled to his lieutenants. "Take Colonel Fox into custody and put her in stasis. Bartrand and Singh, too, if they intervene."

The two looked like misfits as they moved towards Fox. One was very tall and muscular, Haruka estimated him to be well over six feet tall. The other was a slender Hispanic man, probably close to Haruka's height. They grabbed the arms of Colonel Fox and pulled her toward the rear of the bridge, spitting and screaming the entire way.

"All of you are going to pay. Mutineers! Worthless swine," she cursed as she looked into the eyes of every man and woman on the bridge. As she neared, she spat directly in Haruka's face. Haruka flinched and closed her eyes, but did nothing in response.

She waited a few seconds until she could hear the colonel behind her before she wiped the spit from her face with her sleeve. She opened her eyes and felt Mancini's hand on her shoulder again. "You did it," he whispered in her ear.

She dropped her head toward the floor and shook it. "No, my father's biostasis research did this. All of it. If she is suffering psychosis, it's because of that."

A commotion broke out at the top of the staircase, and the two spun to face it. They turned just in time to see Fox throw her elbow into Cormack's throat and reach for his holster with her hand. As she pulled the Taser free, Morado trained his own on her and pulled the trigger.

Chaos ensued. Fox screamed in pain as her muscles seized up. Cormack tumbled slowly head over heels as he gasped for air. Haruka felt herself being shoved to the ground by Mancini's hand.

Mancini yelled, "Look out, Major!"

Haruka's fingers scrabbled at the cold deck plate and she rolled onto her back. She saw Bartrand and Emberley fighting over the major's weapon for a split second before Mancini smashed headlong into Bartrand, sending both of them hurtling over the railing and into the canopy beyond. She saw Emberley struggle to regain control of his motion.

There was a dark blue blur. Haruka turned her head and realized that something was coming at her. She tried to throw her hands up to protect her face, but it smashed into her and her world went black.

• • •

Cal's gaze drifted down the bank of sleepers across from him. He could not pick out any specific detail on them; his mind was occupied with an endless replay of his encounter with Alexis. He felt his pulse quicken when he remembered her face as she gazed at the star field for the first time. Lingering warmth tickled his lips when he recalled her kiss. And it all turned to despair when she pulled away from him and enclosed herself within her aluminum prison.

I had to fuck it up. It's what I always do. I lost her just like I lost Brittany.

He conjured an image of the tough blonde girl he had known back on Earth. Cal realized he would never see her again. He had only aged a few days, according to Dr. Taylor, while five years had actually passed.

Five years of war, no doubt. He sighed. *She may not even be alive. No, I didn't lose her. She was taken from me. Twice.*

"You know, you just got some damn good news. Why do you look like someone punched your grandma?"

Cal blinked and turned to face Hunter. "I'm sorry, what?"

"Seriously, Calvin. What gives? I thought you'd be happy to hear that Dayton wants you to help out next cycle."

"My mind's just not in it right now, Hunter." Cal shifted his weight and winced as he pushed his injured hand against the deck plate.

"Easy there," soothed Dr. Taylor. "Don't hurt yourself again. Remember what you promised me?"

"Yeah, Doc. Sorry."

Hunter pawed at his sandy hair. "So where *is* your mind?"

If only I could tell you.

"Just… having memories of someone."

There was a brief pause, and then Hunter asked, "Someone who got left behind?"

Cal nodded half-heartedly. He hoped that Hunter wouldn't probe any further. Dr. Taylor put her hand on his arm, and Cal began to feel more at ease.

"We've all had to leave friends and loved ones behind, Calvin. I know it's not easy at all," she said. "But at the same time, I can't fathom how hard this must be on you." Cal nodded again and sniffed. "Remember, though. You aren't alone, despite what you may feel. Lieutenant Ceretti and I are here for you, no matter what."

"Thanks guys. I don't mean to be a party pooper. You've all had a lot longer to adjust to what's going on here than I have."

"Okay then," Hunter said. "It's time to leave the stress behind for now. We're done with the maintenance cycle. We just chill and relax for a couple hours, go to sleep, and wake up again in five years. No biggie, right?"

Cal grimaced. *That depends. Do I go back to five years of torment and nightmares?*

"I don't know, man. I guess I'll have to wait and see."

Hunter pushed off from the sleeper and activated the computer terminal. "Seriously, you're still too stressed. Let's see if I can help with that." His fingers flew across the screen almost faster than Cal had ever seen anyone type. "How about a little trance?"

The hallway filled with pulsing beats and almost hypnotic patterns. The sounds were clear, and the bass hits were not distorted.

"Trance?" he asked. "And how is it playing so clearly? I didn't know that terminals could do that."

Hunter gave Cal a broad smile. "You like it? I made a slight… ah… modification to this terminal." He pointed to the corner of the ceiling where a speaker box had been hidden. "The good stuff deserves to be played on something better than the crappy com speakers."

Cal rose up as he felt the music beat as if it was within him. "Wait, so why did you modify this one and not one in the crew pod?"

Hunter laughed. "I did. Dayton caught me doing it and told me I couldn't modify the crew pod. He never said anything about passenger pods, though. So here we are."

Cal chuckled. "Yeah, this is pretty good. I could listen to this for a bit."

"It's a deal, then we'll listen to something else. Your choice."

Dr. Taylor pulled herself to the exit. "Sorry, boys. This isn't my cup of tea. I'm off to go find something a little quieter to do."

"Give my regards to Elvis," Hunter joked as she left.

Cal listened to the music for several minutes as he watched Hunter attempt to dance. The lack of gravity made him seem more like a cat having convulsions in midair. When the lieutenant tried to make a spin move and lost control, Cal had to dart out of the way. Watching

Hunter bounce off of the wall did make him laugh however.

They were joined a few minutes later by two crew members. The first was Cameron Drisko, the ops officer whom Cal had recently learned was quite talented with the guitar. The second was the acting chief engineer, Vince Hartley.

Hunter greeted them as soon as they entered. "Hey Cap. Hey Drisko. Have you heard the news?"

Drisko replied, "No. What's up?"

Hunter placed his arm across Cal's shoulders and squeezed his hand into Cal's clavicle. "Colonel Dayton asked Calvin here to help out Doctor Taylor during the next cycle."

"Really? That's great!" Drisko extended his right hand towards Cal. There was an awkward moment as Cal returned his left hand instead of his injured right. The two figured it out and shook hands.

"Congratulations, kid," said Hartley as they shook hands as well.

"Thank you, Captain," Cal replied. "I'm still surprised by it all."

"You're not military. Please, call me Vince. And I'm not all that surprised, to be honest."

"Oh? Why is that, Cap... I mean, Vince?"

"Colonel Dayton is really interested in you. He's had me monitor your work now and then, and I know he has asked the doctor about you many times."

Cal was shocked. All he could manage to say is "why?"

Hartley shrugged. "I don't know, you'd have to ask him that yourself. But what I do know is that he hasn't been asking if you've been getting in trouble, but rather how efficiently you have been doing your tasks. Obviously, he liked the answers he received."

Cal gave a short, nervous laugh. *There's a first time for everything, I guess.*

He watched as the three others chatted and laughed, smiling at this little bit of normalcy. It was the first thing that made him feel even a slight bit at home since he had left Earth. The music pulsed and swayed as he answered questions about himself, his home, and his injuries. He asked Drisko and Hartley about their families, and was intrigued to find out that Drisko's mother was Korean. As time passed, a song came on that grabbed Cal's attention. Its beat was fast, and he recognized that it was meant to be a love song. The lyrics struck a chord with him, and at once he felt a sadness he could not bear.

He took Hunter aside and lowered his voice, "I'm sorry, Hunter.

I've got to go."

"Why? What's wrong?"

Cal looked around. "Look, I appreciate everything you've done for me. You've helped me take my mind off of things, but I'm still not really in the party mood if you know what I mean." Hunter nodded in slow acknowledgement. "See you next cycle?"

"Yeah, Calvin. Take care." They shook hands and Cal departed.

As he slowly snaked his way out of the sleeper pod, the music faded and the walls made it echo horribly. Cal could barely hear it once he reached the solitude of the gallery. He worked his way aft and into Dr. Taylor's pod.

He searched each of the four sleeper hallways, but he could find no sign of her. A cold emptiness consumed him. His shoulders slumped and he made his way for the ESAARC pod. He opened the pod door and was startled to find Dr. Taylor inside.

"Calvin?" she asked as she looked over her shoulder.

"Jeez, Doc. I didn't expect to find you in here." He maneuvered to the seat next to her and worked his way into the restraints.

"I find it's a quiet place to go when I want to read, or when I want to be alone with the stars."

Cal nodded. "Same for me. I don't see a book in your hands, am I disturbing your alone time?"

She straightened up in the seat. "No, not at all. Just getting another good look at them before we all go to sleep."

Cal smiled and leaned his head back to look out the canopy windows. He searched for his "Polaris", such as it was. It took him a good two minutes to pick it out of the field. He breathed in deeply.

"You said I should come to you if I have any extreme mood shifts, right?"

"That's right. Have you experienced one?"

"I'm pretty sure I just have, a few minutes ago. Hunter was trying to cheer me up, but a song I heard made me feel really sad."

"Well, music can be a powerful emotional tool. What can you tell me about the song?"

Cal sighed. "Here's the thing. It was a really upbeat love song. But something about the lyrics just really got to me."

"I see. Did you have any suicidal or violent thoughts because of it?"

Cal glanced over at Dr. Taylor. "You're kidding, right?" She shook her head. "Dear God no. That just wouldn't make any sense."

She reached to her side and produced what looked like a long leather pouch, but at the end it had a valve similar to the drink pouches. "You'd be surprised what makes sense to an irrational person. That's why they're called irrational. Here have some of this." She gently floated the pouch over to Cal.

He opened the valve and sniffed, and was greeted by the smell of alcohol. His brows raised and he asked, "Really, Doctor?" She nodded. "I'm underage, you know."

"This is for medicinal purposes. I'm administering a treatment to you, Calvin. Now please, drink. Not just a sip either. Take a good long drink."

This has got to be the strangest treatment anyone has ever administered to me. He put the valve to his mouth and squeezed hard. Cold liquid streamed into his mouth, but as soon as he swallowed he nearly gagged, and his throat felt like it was on fire. He flinched and he jammed his shoulder into the belt.

"What the hell is this?"

"Tequila. Another drink please, Calvin."

"Does Colonel Dayton know you have this stuff?"

"Dayton is well aware that I have alcohol in my possession. Just not this particular alcohol. Drink."

Cal took a deep breath and held it as he forced more of the tequila down his throat. The second swig burned worse than the first, and his stomach churned. He coughed twice hard, but stayed himself from vomiting as he passed the alcohol back to Dr. Taylor.

She took a swig and returned the pouch to its hiding place. "I know, it's not the greatest stuff on the planet. There wasn't a whole lot to choose from before we left Earth."

"I take it that's not standard military issue," he said, almost choking on the words.

"Not in the slightest," she replied. "And as far as I know, I'm the only one on any of the ships who has one of these things."

Cal's eyes darted to where she had hidden the pouch. "What is it, exactly? It looks kind of like our drink pouches."

Dr. Taylor nodded. "It's similar in several ways. Except unlike the ration drink pouches, this is reusable. I got the idea from the ancient wineskin. I figured that they worked in the same basic way as the zero-G rated drink pouches, so I could fill it up on Earth with whatever and drink it up here."

"Clever." Cal could feel his fingers tingle slightly.

"Thank you. In any case, I had Dr. Kimura's wife, Sarah, make a few for me. The only problem is that you can't refill them while in space; they still need gravity for that."

"So I hope that this doesn't mean that our ship's doctor is a space lush."

She smiled at Cal. "Not at all. This is only the second time I've had a drink. The first was five years ago, before I went into biostasis."

He could feel the effects of the alcohol take hold. The chill of the ESAARC pod was less pronounced, his fingers were almost numb, and the stars seemed to be dancing above his head.

"So, feeling better now, Calvin?"

He considered his reply for a few seconds. "I'm not sure if better is the term, but definitely buzzed."

"But a love song made you sad. Are you still sad?"

Cal remembered the lyrics one more time. He bit his lip and nodded.

"So who is she?"

His jaw slacked open. *How does she know?* He recovered and tried to play it off. "What? What do you mean?"

"*Who* do I mean? The girl that you're in love with," she replied, staring Cal dead in the eye.

Cal sat dumbfounded in silence. He looked down at his right hand and flexed the fingers slightly. They responded with a dull throb.

"That's why you broke your finger, isn't it? Oh, Calvin."

She released her restraints and wrapped him in a hug. He wanted to cry, he wanted to express his rage, but he was too numb. There was another emotion that he couldn't put his finger on. Dr. Taylor's embrace was comforting, almost like his mother's had been, and yet he still felt unsettled. He wrapped his arms around her but that did little to help.

"Do you want to tell me about it?" she whispered in his ear.

"There's not much to tell. I screwed it up. I acted before I thought, and I drove her away." His voice cracked as he spoke in a hushed tone.

"I am so sorry." She broke her embrace but held him by the shoulders as she looked at his face. "If I can ever do anything for you, let me know."

Cal nodded.

I wish there was something you could do. But you can't change the past or make me forget about her. Sorry, Doctor.

He took his leave and made way for his sleeper berth. When he arrived, he opened the door and stared at the darkness within for a minute. He was unsure of what awaited him once he entered hibernation, but he steeled his resolve and secured himself within the berth.

If there are demons, they are mine to face. No more running for Calvin McLaughlin. Ever.

. . .

Haruka groaned and her head throbbed. Her eyes adjusted to the soft light as she opened them. She could see an airy, vaulted ceiling. She shifted, but was stopped by a harness across her chest.

What the hell? She jerked and fumbled in an attempt to release the buckle.

"Easy, Lieutenant," soothed Dr. Nelson. "Here, let me get that for you." He drifted to the table that Haruka was strapped to and released the restraint.

"Where am I?" she asked as she pulled herself upright and looked around the unfamiliar room. There were a few other tables scattered about, and several storage carts were secured along each wall.

"You're in medical pod one. I'm glad to see you're awake, but please don't exert yourself." He looked at her with sad eyes, and his voice lowered. "I'm sorry, I didn't mean to hurt you."

Haruka reached up to her aching head and felt a bandage near her temple. "What happened? You did this?"

"It was purely on accident, Lieutenant. When the struggle broke out on the bridge and I saw Cormack get hit in the trachea, I rushed to help him." He looked down at the deck. "I admit, I should have watched where I was going. In my haste, I hit you in the head with my knee pretty hard. You hit the deck plate, and I guess I knocked you out."

Crap, the bridge. Marco and Emberley were in trouble.

She swung her legs around to push off from the table. Dr. Nelson put his hand out in front of her.

"Whoa, where are you going?"

"To find Lieutenant Mancini," she said quickly as she pushed the doctor's arm away.

"He's in stasis."

Haruka froze for a moment. Her heart began to beat hard within her chest. "Then the major needs me."

"Relax, Lieutenant. He's on his way here. He wanted to speak with you as soon as you woke up."

Dr. Nelson's words seemed to melt away Haruka's anxiety. She breathed a sigh of relief and slowly swung her legs back up onto the table. *That means that Fox is not in command. Which means Marco must be okay.*

"Is everyone ok? How's Cormack doing?"

Nelson moved to a storage cart and rummaged through it. "Cormack is fine; the colonel didn't do him any permanent harm. Lieutenant Mancini will probably have a nasty shiner from his fight with Captain Bartrand. As for Bartrand and Colonel Fox, they shouldn't have any lasting effects from the shocks they received.

"Now, for a little bad news," continued Dr. Nelson. "You may have a concussion. I've volunteered to stay awake with Major Emberley to make sure that you recover properly if you do indeed have one."

"Stay awake? How long have I been out?" Haruka massaged her head in a vain effort to dull the throbbing.

Dr. Nelson looked at his wrist watch. "About six hours. Since the maintenance cycle is over, most of the crew has reported to their berths for hibernation. Although I had to practically order Mancini to his sleeper berth. He was very insistent on making sure that you were alright."

"You said most of the crew? How many are left?"

"Besides the doctor and myself, two. But we will get to that in a moment," came a deep voice from behind her.

Haruka turned around and faced Major Emberley. His tall, slender frame almost filled the entire doorway vertically. His arms were stretched to either side, bracing against the sides of the doorframe. Haruka snapped her body straight and saluted.

"At ease, Lieutenant," he said. Haruka dropped her hand to her side and eased her shoulders. "How are you feeling?"

"Fine, sir."

"I imagine your head hurts, but can you still perform duties?"

"Yes, sir." She paused as the Major nodded. "Sir, may I go back to my original assignment?"

Emberley pursed his lips and shuffled a wrist up and down the door frame. "I've reviewed the logs and there is something that I saw in there. As much as I loathe admitting it, it would seem that Colonel Fox accidentally stumbled on a way to increase our maintenance efficiency. We don't need a full time pilot during maintenance, and we don't need two ops crewmen either."

Her heart sank. She knew now that Emberley was not going to return her to her duties as a pilot, and it didn't seem as if he was keen on returning Mancini to his duties as well.

"The propulsion work gets done much quicker with three crewmen," he continued. "As such, both you and Mancini will continue your propulsion duties going forth."

Haruka let out a loud sigh. "Yes, sir."

"Don't despair, Lieutenant. When you are done with your propulsion duties, I'd like you to report to the bridge to see if you can sort out whether or not Captain Bartrand put us off course."

Or, I could be wrong about him. She could not contain her smile. "Yes, sir!"

"Now, I need your help with some special duties right now."

"Only light ones, Major. I don't want her lifting anything, or doing systems maintenance, or anything like that," protested Dr. Nelson.

Emberley flicked his fingers dismissively. "Nothing like that. I just need her to help coordinate a grid search of the ship."

Haruka tilted her head, "Sir?"

"We seem to be missing a crew member, Lieutenant Kimura. That is unless you happen to know where Airman Ellsworth is."

"No, sir."

The major grunted. "Nobody seems to know. Doctor Nelson was the last one to see him, if I have my timeline straight."

"I had left him at the airlock after the autopsy of Lieutenant Shipp," the doctor added. "He said he wanted to give Shipp a more proper burial than just being dumped naked into space. I went back to the medical pod to finish cleaning up."

Haruka was filled with a sense of dread. She didn't know Ellsworth well, but one thing she knew is that he always performed his duties. The idea that he would simply vanish was unsettling.

"Sir, you don't suppose…" she trailed off.

"I suppose nothing at this point, Lieutenant. Do you have any information that may be useful to finding him?"

"Was Shipp's body gone, sir?"

"Yes it was. I had Captain Maynard look through the systems logs as well. It showed the airlock cycled once, about thirty minutes after the doctor left Ellsworth alone."

Cycled once. You were just imagining things, Haruka. She pushed off of the table and moved toward Major Emberley. A nagging voice in her head told her that something still wasn't right.

"Major, can we check the airlock one more time?"

His mouth twisted as he considered the request. "I suppose. Doctor Nelson tells me you need to stay awake for a while just in case, so we've got time to kill." His head swiveled to look at Dr. Nelson. "Would you like to accompany us and make sure our patient doesn't exert herself too much?"

"Of course, Major," replied Dr. Nelson. He retrieved a stethoscope from the drawer of the cart and stuffed it in the pocket of his flight suit.

The trio silently made their way out of the medical pod, through the upper gallery, and into the belly of *Raphael*. Haruka tried to think of where Ellsworth might have gone after Nelson departed. *If I can recreate his steps, maybe we can find out something about his disappearance.*

They arrived at the forward airlock. The massive door was slightly recessed into the floor of the gallery. Haruka pulled herself to the edge and crept her way around it.

Emberley cleared his throat. "What are you looking for, Kimura?"

I'm not sure. She paused for a moment to think. "Has anyone opened the airlock, sir?"

Dr. Nelson and Major Emberley exchanged quick glances. "Only to make sure there wasn't a body inside."

He would have had to go inside to put Shipp's body inside. Haruka rubbed her chin as she thought. *He shouldn't have been able to cycle the airlock from inside, right? There shouldn't even be a terminal in there.* She floated to the terminal on the wall and commanded it to open the airlock door. It heaved open with a deep groan, exposing the dark maw. She punched in another set of codes and bright lights flickered to life within the hole.

Haruka sidled to the edge of the airlock and pulled herself inside. She glanced at the walls just inside the door and saw a terminal. *Of course, how could I be so dumb? They would have built one there to prevent crew from being trapped inside the airlock.* She pulled her body over to it, hoping to see if there were any finger smudges on the touch panel. What she saw made her gasp loudly.

"Doctor, come here," she exclaimed as she touched a brownish red stain on the wall next to the terminal, just above block lettering that read "RAPHAEL". It flaked off easily on her finger. Dr. Nelson drifted his way next to her. "Is that… blood?"

He reached out, scratched his finger along the stain, and then examined the substance. "It is indeed, Lieutenant." He looked at the wall and then the opening. "Shipp was long dead, and his autopsy already completed before he ever got here. This is someone else's blood."

Emberley balled his hand into a fist and brought it to his mouth. After a moment, he moved to the terminal that Haruka had used to open the airlock, and turned on the ship broadcast com.

"Morado and Maynard," his voice echoed. "Please come to the forward dock, immediately." ·

"I'll need to test this against what we have in the personnel files. Maybe I can confirm whose blood this is," said Dr. Nelson.

I already know whose it is. Ellsworth's. Something happened to him. Haruka just nodded at the doctor.

"We must assume this is a murder investigation, Lieutenant," she heard Major Emberley from behind her. "I would like for you to help Doctor Nelson with anything he needs."

"Yes, sir."

"Come, Lieutenant. We need to get some supplies from the medical pod," Nelson said as he hurried off. Haruka followed close behind. "Too many problems, Lieutenant. I'd like a couple quiet days on this ship for once."

"No arguments here, Doctor."

You probably don't know the half of it.

· · ·

A set of vital signs glowed on the terminal screen in front of Cal.

"Beautiful, isn't it?" Dr. Taylor admired the screen, her gray hair in an immaculate braid resting on her shoulder.

Cal rubbed his eyes and scrutinized the data. "It looks normal to me."

"Exactly what we want. Serene. Tranquil."

"I don't get it, Doc. What am I missing?"

He heard a tapping noise to his side. Cal glanced to his left and watched Captain Hartley inspect something just inside his open stasis chamber.

"Almost done here, Mr. McLaughlin," he said.

Cal turned his attention back to the terminal. He traced lines in the air in front of him to mimic the pulse and respiratory lines. This exercise proved futile, as he still could not figure out what she was talking about.

"It's a pulse. So?"

"It's life. Not just any life either," she said. "It's *Michael*."

That doesn't make any sense.

"All ready," said Hartley. "Time for you to get in."

Cal took three steps toward the berth. *That's not right.* He glanced back at Dr. Taylor and realized her hair was not floating. *Gravity. I'm dreaming again.* He walked to the sleeper and climbed in. *If I'm already asleep, what's this going to do to me, anyway?* He laid back and closed the hatch.

Time passed, what felt like a few minutes to Cal. He felt his equilibrium change, and he realized that he was now standing vertical instead of laying down. There was a dim glow, and he could taste humidity in the air around him.

Cal turned around. Light reflected off of the swirling mist that danced in front of him. The shimmer reminded him somewhat of the surface of a lake on a lazy autumn day. Complete silence met his ears, and despite the motion of the mist, the world felt still.

He stepped forward with trepidation. His footfall made no sound, and the ground felt smooth and flat. Cal noticed darkness surround him as he went deeper inside; the growing fog seemed to filter out the light.

Alone again, he thought.

He couldn't help but wonder what the significance of this was. The words of Dr. Taylor came back to him and gave him pause. He had been hanging out with Hunter quite a bit lately. Hunter treated Cal very differently from his old friends on Earth; Hunter never once disrespected Cal for anything he had said or done.

Cal continued despite his obscured vision. He stopped in his tracks as he heard a noise drift into his ears. He strained to hear, but just as quickly as it had come, the sound was gone. Cal turned to where he thought it had come from and plodded forth. Again he heard the sound and turned, but it eluded him.

Am I facing ghosts now?

He trudged on. The ground beneath his feet began to crunch, and the texture changed; there were bumps now. Cal knelt down and felt the ground. It was moist, and he could feel leaves and sticks, obscured by the mist. He grabbed a fist full and brought it to his nose. A hint of wet earth wafted from the soft debris in his hand. He rose to his feet and dropped the muck, which was devoured by the swirling mist. Cal could hear a whispering ahead of him. It did not abate this time, and he sprung ahead to find the source. The fog thinned somewhat, and he could see gaps moving around. He saw a dark shape ahead and pressed onward.

Before him he saw Alexis, sitting on the ground with her knees to her chest and her arms wrapped around them. She seemed to be crying. Cal moved in front of her and dropped down. He placed his hands on hers and found her touch as cold as the walls of *Michael*.

"What's wrong?" he asked. She gave no response; she did not even look at him. He repeated his question, but she did not react. "I know you're upset with me, but I want to help you."

She continued to sob and gave Cal no regard. He took his hand and brushed her cheek. It too was as cold as the metal which caged them.

"Alexis, why are you shutting me out?" He squeezed her frozen hands.

"I can't do it, Cal," she croaked feebly.

"Can't do what?"

"Why do you keep hurting me?"

"It was only that once," he protested.

"You don't get it, do you?"

"I guess I don't. But please, I want to hear it."

Her hands rose to her head and tangled in her long hair. She wailed and tears streaked down her face. Cal moved behind her and held her. The iciness of her body next to his made him gasp for air and his hands felt like they were burning, but he did not dare let go of her. He tried to soothe her as he embraced her, but she just screamed louder when he did so. Anxiety welled within him. His throat tightened as he fought back tears.

"Let me in, Alexis. Please."

"No, I can't."

"Why not? What are you so afraid of?"

"Go away, you monster," she screamed and pushed her arms outward on his.

It was becoming much harder for Cal to hold back his feelings. "Don't say that, please," he choked as he tried to swallow the lump in his throat. "*Please.*"

Alexis tore out of his grasp and scrambled to her feet. She bolted into the mist as soon as her feet gained purchase. Cal stumbled to his feet to give chase, but something held him back. He looked down at his feet and found them sunk in mud.

"Alexis, wait!" He tried yanking his feet free but they would not budge. "Come back!" He started to cry. He whimpered for her to return, but only his own voice echoed back through the swirling mist. He knelt back down and sobbed. His hand ached. Cal looked at it and saw his hand bandaged and taped together, where as only moments before it had been whole. His hand dropped limp at his side and he bowed his head.

What does it matter? She hates me. She's right, I am a monster. Who else in their right mind would revive someone only to put them back in hibernation right after?

"Doctor David Benedict would," said a vaguely familiar voice from his right. Startled, Cal looked and saw a tall, hard-faced man with a tight gray crew cut walking toward him in dress blues. "The only difference was that David only asked people to do so voluntarily."

"G-grandpa?" he stuttered.

"You weren't ready for this," continued the apparition. "Neither was she. Do you remember how you reacted when you woke up?"

Cal paused and thought for a second. "I hurled."

"Besides the physiological aspect, how did you react?"

"I… I was scared. I didn't see anyone. I didn't hear anything. For a moment, I thought I was dead."

His grandfather stopped at arm's reach from him. "And how did she react when she woke up? Besides vomiting."

Again Cal took a moment to recall. "She asked me questions. And she was fascinated by the stars."

"You had to come to grips with your mortality; all she had to do was some stargazing. Do you think that might have had any impact on her preparedness?"

Cal knew the answer. He hung his head again. He closed his eyes and played the scenario from the ESAARC pod out again. He could almost taste her lips when he remembered her kiss.

"It was reckless, she said. And romantic," Cal said.

The voice that responded was more familiar and harsher. "You've been too reckless lately. How many times do I have to save you before you understand? Actions have consequences." Cal looked up and saw his father's stern face. His eyes flashed angrily at Cal.

"Look, I'm trying, Dad. It's just that…"

"Forget about her, son," General McLaughlin interrupted. "You've caused enough damage already. You need something new to do, maybe learn a new skill."

"Damn it, Dad." Cal could feel his temper flaring. "Can't you see I've been doing that too? I've been working with Doctor Taylor, I've been studying books, what more do you want of me?"

The visage of his tormentor changed once more. Rob's face was dominated by his arrogant grin. "I think he wants you to be a man. Like that will ever happen, loser."

"What the fuck, Rob?" Cal seethed with anger, and his hand curled into a fist.

"That's right, you want to make something of it?" Rob thumped his chest and flung his arms outward and sneered. "We know you won't."

"And how do you know that?"

Rob just laughed, "Because Brittany said you were too much of a pussy to go after her. She got tired of waiting for you. And hey, that worked out for me, didn't it?"

Cal let out a primal scream and lunged at Rob as he tore his feet free of the mud. He landed on top of Rob and pummeled his face with a haymaker. His fist protested with sharp stabbing pains, but Cal pushed through. He wanted to punch every tooth out of his so-called friend's head, the costs be damned. Blow after blow rained down on his opponent. Blood ran from his knuckles as well as the mouth of his target, but Cal did not relent. Tears blurred his vision and rage fueled him.

"Stop it, Cal, you're hurting me," shrieked a voice. He ignored the plea and threw another punch. "Oh God, please no. Stop it." He land- ed another blow. "What did I do? I promise I'll stop! Just stop hurting me!"

Oh God... Cal stumbled backward as he realized that he was punching Alexis instead. He rolled off of her and landed on the soft mud with his hip. *No.. I didn't mean to!*

She curled her knees to her chest and hugged them, and blood dripped from her nose. Her cries of pain and fear stabbed Cal in his heart. Cal scrambled to his knees and reached for her, but she recoiled as he approached.

"S-stay away from me, you monster!" Alexis bolted once more into the mist.

"No," he yelled after her. "Come back. This isn't me! God, Alexis please..."

Monster. Her voice echoed within his mind as he sat alone and cold in the vapors.

. . .

Darius felt his way along the sleeper hall to a storage locker, unwilling to open his eyes more than the barest squint. He knew the light was not particularly bright, but the dark coffin of the sleeper berth made it almost painful by comparison. He groped along the smooth metal surface until he came to an indent in the metal. He knew this was the handle, so he twisted and the locker popped open. The door gave some protection from the lighting, and Darius slowly opened his eyes and adjusted to the light.

He reached inside and retrieved two meal pouches from the top shelf and then closed the locker. The bang of the metal door sent a stabbing pain through his already sensitive head. Darius grunted and grabbed his temples with his free hand.

Darius had heard of other crew members getting sick and throwing up when they came out of stasis. He had never experienced that for himself, but the migraine headache he had at the beginning of the last cycle almost made him prefer the alternative. This one was not much better. He took a minute to compose himself before he exited the crew pod and made his way down the deserted gallery to sleeper pod four. As he approached he could hear the gentle chirps of a terminal being used within.

Figures he'd be awake already.

Darius found his way to where Dr. Kimura was working. It seemed to Darius that the doctor had again aged while in stasis, although he knew that was false.

"Excuse me, Doctor," he said in a voice barely louder than a whisper. "I don't mean to interrupt, but I brought you breakfast."

Dr. Kimura glanced over at Darius, blinked his eyes, and yawned. "Thank you, Darius," he smiled. "Sometimes I think I might starve if not for you."

Darius passed a meal to him and tore into his own. The sound of the bag ripping open caused another throb of pain in his head, and he winced.

"Is there something wrong, Darius?"

"Ah, my head just feels like someone stuck it in a vise grip, that's all."

"I am sorry to hear that. Would you like me to get you something for it?"

Darius grimaced as another wave of pain came over him. "That's okay. I know which pods contain medical supplies, I can get something myself."

"Very well."

Darius took a bite of his scrambled eggs. "Colonel Eriksen is going to want an update on you. Is there anything to report?"

Dr. Kimura shook his head. "Everything seems normal so far. I have completed an initial check on fifty eight percent of the passengers so far."

You've been awake a while, haven't you Doctor?

Darius and Dr. Kimura consumed their meals in silence. Darius could barely concentrate on getting his food down, but he was aware of the doctor's heavy gaze upon him. He wondered at what Kimura could be thinking. The scientist's problems must be far more significant that those of Darius, so it seemed odd that the elder man looked at him with such concern.

When they finished eating, Darius disposed of the waste and pocketed a half consumed pouch of coffee. Dr. Kimura went back to work, but Darius noticed him glancing over periodically as if to check on him.

"Is there something wrong, Doctor?" he asked.

"You do not seem yourself today, Darius."

He looked down and waved his hand. "It's just the headache, I swear." Darius locked his eyes on Dr. Kimura once more. "You know, I don't get something about you."

Dr. Kimura stopped his work and turned toward Darius. His eyebrows seemed to shoot straight at the ceiling. "What is that?"

"Well, a bunch of things, I guess. First, how you get up before everyone else and do your work. Second, despite how I haven't exactly been friendly to you as of late you still seem to care about me. Finally, how the hell can you even work at all given what has happened to you."

The elder man simply smiled at Darius. "The second point is the easiest to answer. You are my friend, Darius. Your orders, my treason, do not change this. I will always have a place in my heart for you, no matter what."

Darius felt an odd peace. This had not crossed his mind, but it made sense. Darius himself felt affection towards Dr. Kimura that had not been seriously dampened by the accusations leveled against him.

"The first," he continued, "is also easy. I gained my work ethic early in my life, from my father and uncle. They taught me the value of discipline and hard work, traits that certainly helped me in my early studies." The scientist gave a quick laugh. "I should thank them and their lessons for helping me earn my Doctorate so early, and attract the attention of the minds behind Project Columbus."

Dr. Kimura's smile did not last long, as the corners of his mouth turned down and he returned his gaze to his work. "The third, I try not to think of. They are the undoing of the other two."

You must be a very strong man to be able to suppress your feelings like that, Doctor. Darius nodded, even though Dr. Kimura could not see him. Minutes of awkward silence passed as Darius alternated between thinking of Dr. Kimura's situation and attempting to assuage his own physical pain. The silence was only interrupted by the occasional chirp of the terminal processing requests that had been made of it. Darius concluded that he should concentrate on his own work and well being.

The fact that Colonel Eriksen has us constantly monitoring him is a little absurd, he thought to himself. *The man is not going to do anything stupid. He's not going to hurt anyone. And from what I've learned of him today, he is never going to abandon his duty.*

Darius pulled himself from the hallway and navigated his way through the upper gallery to the cold bowels of the ship. He sought out one of the forward cargo pods and exposed the absolute darkness within. With a flick of his fingers on the computer, dim lights flared within, allowing him to rummage through the contents of the crates within. He procured some migraine medication and washed it down with the coffee he had saved from earlier.

He then made his way slowly toward the rear of the ship. The cold of the lower gallery made him shiver, and he rubbed his muscled arms together for warmth. The medication would take some time to take effect, and he knew that the mainframe terminal screen would only make his headache worse. His thoughts drifted from his work and he found himself thinking of the future.

There are two decent, hard working men whose lives will be at stake when we reach Demeter, he thought. *Lord knows I owe one of them a debt I'm not sure I can ever repay.*

He reached out and touched one of the walls, near frozen from its position far from any active heating system. Darius closed his eyes and let himself be consumed by his vision.

He found himself in his mother's hospital room. An IV was stuck in her frail, flabby arm and she wore a breathing mask over her nose and mouth. A monitor beeped nearby as her vital signs marched across its screen like a solemn banner. She coughed, but her body seemed too weak to affect any change in her condition.

Mama. Her bony, veined hand drew her mask down from her face as she beckoned Darius to come closer. *Mama, don't,* he pleaded in silent desperation.

"D-Darius," she whispered. He leaned in towards her. "You a good boy, Darius."

He could feel tears well within him as he recalled the moment with utter clarity.

"Mama, it's okay. I'm here for you. Just please, rest. Doctor said you need rest," he pleaded.

Her hand rose up and stroked his face. He could feel her warmth, even in his dream state. "Look at you, all handsome in your uniform. Your daddy would be proud."

Darius choked up, "Mama, please, just sleep. I'll be here for you, but you need to sleep for us, okay?"

He reached for her mask but she pushed his hand away. "Ain't no sense fussin about it. I know the cancer is shuttin everything down. I know I'm out of time on Earth and the Lord will be comin for me soon." Darius tried to hold back tears as his lip pouted. Her hand wrapped around the back of his shaved head. "No, don't cry. You got your whole life ahead of you, sweet child. And the Lord gonna see what a fine man you are and take care of you, you hear?"

Darius leaned his head against his arm, his brow resting on the cold steel of *Gabriel*. In his mind he bit his lip and nodded an acknowledgement to his dying mother.

"You promise me one thing, Darius?"

He nodded without hesitation.

"Never forget what your daddy and granddaddy did for our country. Never forget the men that they were. Always strive to be the man that your daddy was, you hear?"

"I promise, Mama," he said, tears streaking down his face.

She smiled at him one last time, and her eyes closed as she slipped into her final coma.

I promise, Mama. Now and forever, with God as my witness.

Darius wiped his tears on the sleeve of his flight suit. He took his bearings and continued his journey aft and up into the gallery. He made his way down the lonely corridor into the propulsion section and finally to the computer core. He strapped into the chair and looked at the blank screen for a minute.

There are two decent, hard working men whose lives are at stake, he thought. *There will be trials. One civilian, one a court martial. I will do what I must.*

Darius turned on the mainframe terminal.

XCS-02 MAINFRAME LOGIN:

He entered his username and password.

XCS-02 LOGIN ACCEPTED. OWENS, LT. DARIUS. MAIN-FRAME ACCESS ENABLED. ENABLE VOICE INTERFACE?

Darius entered a negative response.

COMMAND?

He entered a command to open the communication system, and then proceeded to the null mailbox he had created. His eyes widened at the number of files contained within. Thousands of communications had been received by the main communication array over the past five years. They varied greatly in size from just a few bytes to almost a giga-byte in size.

Darius stretched and then cracked his knuckles.

Time to get to work.

. . .

Haruka grimaced as Dr. Nelson lifted her left eyelid and shined the light from his ophthalmoscope in her eye. He repeated the procedure on her other eye. After he let go, green dots scattered across her line of vision. She tried to blink them off, but they followed her movement as if to taunt her.

"Any headaches?" he asked. Haruka shook her head. "Any confusion? Sensation of missed time?" Again she indicated in the negative. "In that case, I don't believe this to be related to your recent concussion. You probably just have a mild case of hibernation sickness. I do, of course, want you to come see me if any of those things happen, or if you experience severe mood swings."

"Thank you, Doctor," she said with a sigh of relief. The spots had mostly vanished and she could see his face again. Dark circles under his eyes made her wonder if his sleep was not restful, or if he was getting any at all.

The investigation is taking its toll on him, she thought.

Haruka could still remember the look on his face when he confirmed that the blood found inside the airlock matched Airman Ellsworth. She was glad that Major Emberley ordered the doctor to go into hibernation before the remaining crew recreated the events as they believed they had occurred. As it was, he had turned white as a ghost and looked as if he wanted to pass out when the major explained their belief that Colonel Fox had fought with Ellsworth, locked him in the airlock, and then murdered him by cycling it.

But why would she have done such a thing? She shook her head and tried not to speculate. *Major Emberley will find out. He should be interrogating her again right now.*

"Are you okay, Lieutenant?"

Her attention returned to Dr. Nelson. "Yes, sorry. Just lost in thought." She quickly looked around the medical pod. "I must get back to my duties now."

"Alright, but remember what I said. If you have any more symptoms, come see me right away."

She nodded and made her way out of the pod. She paused for a moment and looked longingly toward the bridge, hoping to see it beyond the wall of darkness. *I will be up there soon enough. I just have to help Nova and Marco finish the propulsion checks.* She turned and wandered to the rear of *Raphael*. Haruka knew that the sooner she finished her primary task, the sooner she would be able to join the bridge crew. Still, she could not make herself go any faster. Her dislike of crawling through the bowels of the ship and the sinister glow of the reactor made her almost dread the task at hand.

As she drifted down the propulsion section hallway, she listened to the din coming from ahead of her. It was not as loud as usual, and the echo was not a chaotic jumble. *Marco must have one of the generators offline already.* She would have to perform a physical inspection of the reactor. The thought made her shudder.

Haruka passed through the empty propulsion control room and down into the generator room. Generator one lay silent; its access door was open and a faint light glowed within. She looked around at the otherwise empty room and sighed. As she approached the generator's casing, she could hear Mancini at work.

"Marco," she yelled. There was a clang, and the generator casing thrummed for a moment.

"Ow! God damn it, Kimura," Mancini cursed as his head popped out of the casing with his hand clutched to his scalp. "Don't sneak up on people like that. Not cool."

A wry grin crossed her lips. "I'm sorry, should I kiss it and make it feel better?"

"Ha, ha. Very funny." He closed one eye and rubbed his head where he had bumped it. His sleeves were streaked with grease, and Haruka saw flashes of light in his hair that made it look like he had managed to transfer some from his hand to his hair. "What do you want?"

"Have you seen Nova?"

"Maybe thirty minutes ago. She said she wanted to get a head start on inspecting the thrusters. Why?"

"Oh, just hoping, I guess."

"Yeah, well if you want to get out of inspecting the reactor, you need to wake up earlier. Now you gonna help us or not?"

Haruka scoffed. "Fine, I'll look at the stupid reactor."

She turned away and glared at the reactor. *Nova's the damned nuke tech, she should be inspecting this thing.* Haruka retrieved a Geiger counter and a flashlight and began her inspection with the fuel loading system. Inch by inch she moved down the length of the reactor. She looked for cracks in the shielding and listened to the counter for anomalies in the radiation level.

Haruka had just completed the inspection when she heard something from a nearby terminal. She moved toward it. "Emberley to Kimura," she heard as she sidled up to the workstation.

"Kimura here. Yes, sir?"

"Where are you, Lieutenant?"

"Generator room, sir. I've completed the reactor casing inspection."

"Good," he said. His even tone was a refreshing change from the Fox's squawking. "Please report to medical pod one. I need to speak with you."

"Right away, sir," she said and disconnected the com system. She turned for the ladder and nearly knocked over Mancini. "Sorry, Marco."

"Whoa, whoa, what's the rush, Kimura?"

"Emberley wants to see me. Can you hold down the fort until I arrive?"

He smiled. "Yeah, sure thing."

"Great." She floated over to the ladder and grabbed it. Haruka paused and turned back. "If you see Nova, make sure she did both sides of the ship, ok?"

Mancini nodded his head and waved two fingers at her. She climbed up the ladder, glanced at the reactor readouts on a workstation, and then bolted for the medical pod. *This is as urgent as I have ever heard the major sound. I wonder what he wants.* She passed the dark voids of tunnels leading to pods on both sides as she made her way amidships to her meeting with the major.

"Ah, good," said Emberley as Haruka entered the room.

Dr. Nelson was at his side. He was frowning as he rubbed the bridge of his nose. "If you don't mind, I will take my leave, Major." He did not wait for a response as he hurriedly shot past Haruka and out of the pod.

"Don't mind him, Lieutenant. He's got a lot on his mind, and a new task to complete." Major Emberley paused and scratched at his chin. "He's not the only one. How are your team members coming along with the propulsion maintenance?"

"It looks like we're a little ahead of schedule, sir. Airman Weyler is already inspecting the thrusters, and Lieutenant Mancini should be done with the first generator by now."

"Good. I don't want to be a burden to them, but it looks like the rest of your team might have to carry a heavier work load. I have need of you."

Haruka felt her heart flutter a bit. "What do you need me to do, sir?"

"Captain Maynard is hunting down an anomaly in the com system. I'm doing a little rotation of crew right now to make sure stations are covered on the bridge, but unless we pull from elsewhere or wake a reserve crew member, we'll still be one short." He gave Haruka a warm grin. "So I need you at nav. I'm probably going to have you monitor ops as well while you're up there."

She tried to contain herself, but could not help letting a broad grin escape. "Yes, sir. Thank you, sir."

"I want you to start your calculations to see if Captain Bartrand brought us off course with his maneuvering." His face one again bore a flat expression. "But there's more. I got some disturbing information from Colonel Fox when I interrogated her. It is clear that she cannot be restored to command. I have assumed full command of the mission."

Haruka nodded. "I understand, sir."

"Hopefully you understand as much as I think. I have not had an opportunity to observe you in action for very long, but back in Laramie I saw your files and was impressed with your service record. I also know that your actions helped stop Colonel Fox, who was clearly a danger to the ship."

"Thank you, sir."

He held up one hand. "I'll admit, you were not my first choice for this. However, my first choice turned down the position. I hope you will accept, given your service thus far."

"Accept what, sir?"

"The position of First Officer."

Haruka was struck speechless. *Me? First Officer?* Her heart began to beat furiously and her fingers tingled. She struggled to find words but still could not.

"Do you need some time?" he asked.

"No, sir. I accept," she blurted.

"Very well. I am glad to hear it. I'm giving you a field promotion so your rank can accommodate the position." Emberley extended his long, slender arm. "Congratulations, Captain Kimura." She reached out and grasped his hand. Emberley's grip was deceivingly strong, and she felt as if he might crush hers was they shook hands. "Now, please report to your new station, Captain."

"Yes, sir," she grinned and exited the pod.

Marco's going to hate me for this, she thought to herself in a moment of selfish delight. *But I won't have to touch that reactor again.*

. . .

Calvin McLaughlin
22 September 2024, 06:58
Michael
>|

Cal slowly floated down the silent gallery toward the bridge. A knot grew in his stomach and the hairs on his neck seemed to stand on end. Something was not right, but he could not say what for sure. A metallic groan sounded through the darkness ahead of him as if *Michael* complained about an ache. He stopped and cocked his head to listen as the sound faded and the echoes died off.

Get out of here, you idiot. You're in danger, a voice screamed from the back of his mind. Cal screwed up his courage and continued forth. He heard the ship creak and moan once again, deeper and louder than before. *This is wrong, turn back now!*

Too late Cal reacted. Before he could turn he saw a deep gash form in the canopy of the gallery, and the steel hull of *Michael* tore open. Cal was violently sucked, screaming in futility, through the massive hole made by the explosive decompression.

He awoke to the sounds of his own screaming, his body twisted and jammed in his sleeper's harness. Sweat drenched his flight suit. His screams gave way to weak sobs and fits of coughing.

It was only a dream. Cal exhaled a breath of relief. *No, it was a nightmare. But still not real.*

He spent several minutes taking deep breaths and convincing his fragile nerves that he was safe. He reached for the com panel and activated the clock.

9-22-2024 07:04

And I'm probably late for duty to top it off.

Cal opened the hatch and squinted as the light filtered in. His stomach churned, but he took a deep breath and fought back the urge to vomit. With a single heave, he pulled his gangly body from the berth. A sharp pain in his hand reminded him that he needed to be more cautious. Cal winced and again struggled to keep his stomach from turning. He glanced for a moment at the berth containing Alexis.

It's not me.

Cal sought out a meal pouch and consumed it in the hallway. He could not bring himself to take it inside the ESAARC pod today, lest he revisit his failure with Alexis. He reserved a small amount of coffee from his meal and fished his hand into his pocket, where he found

J.C. Rainier

a small pack containing two ibuprofen pills that he had stashed. He tore the pack open with his teeth and washed the pills down with the remaining drink, and then set off to find Dr. Taylor to begin his work. He found her at work in her sleeper pod, staring at her usual terminal. She looked at Cal as he moved past her to the other terminal.

"Good morning, Calvin," she said in a soft voice. Cal grunted and turned on his workstation, and then pulled up a pair of passenger vitals. "Is something wrong?"

"Oh no, everything's just peachy," he said, his voice laden with sarcasm.

Cal saw Dr. Taylor out of the corner of his eye as she turned off her console and turned to face him. "Do you need to talk to someone about it? I'm here for you."

"Nope."

"Are you experiencing any depression? Anger that's difficult to control?"

Cal clenched his teeth. "Yes to the first, no to the second."

"Please, Calvin, I want to make sure of something. So you need to talk to me about this."

He pressed the power button on his terminal in a very deliberate manner with his left hand and then slowly turned to face the doctor. "You want to talk about it, huh?"

"Yes," she reached out to brace her arm against a sleeper as she spoke.

"Alright. Let's talk about it." Cal's voice dropped an octave and he spoke in a hushed tone. "Let's talk about how I've spent what seems like months trapped in the worst hell that you can possibly imagine. Let's talk about how just a few minutes ago I was sucked out of a hole when the hull of *Michael* blew wide open. Or how about how I've had a thousand fights with my father. Or maybe how half the time I end up trying to make amends with him but he ends up running away from me and right into machine gun fire."

A look that could have been either pity or horror washed across Dr. Taylor's face. Cal didn't care which it was. He did not think that she could possibly fathom the situation he was in.

"Or maybe you'd like to hear my favorite one," he continued, "about how over and over again I beat the living shit out of the woman I love."

"Oh, my," she gasped.

"So yeah, you'll just have to pardon me if I don't really want to talk about it, Doctor." He turned to face the terminal again and brought it back to life.

He caught motion out of the corner of his eye. Cal felt the urge to flinch, but refrained from doing so. He felt Dr. Taylor wrap her thin, spotted arms around him. Her embrace did little to temper his emotions although he did appreciate the gesture. He made no eye contact with her as he continued his work.

"Please don't keep things bottled up. Especially not out here," she said. He could feel her breath in his ear.

Cal changed pages and something scrolled across the screen that made him sick. He froze for a moment.

"Do you hear me, Calvin?" she asked.

"Doctor, look!" He tapped his fingers emphatically on the screen.

"Oh no!" Her hand flew to the com button on the terminal. "Dr. Taylor to bridge. Medical emergency in pod twelve. Send assistance immediately." She clicked off the system and turned to Cal. "Begin emergency revival. Catch up with me as soon as you can." She shot off out of the hallway as fast as an arrow.

Cal quickly keyed the sequence to revive the passenger and initiated the amyl nitrite injector program. He stared at the screen and hoped with every second that the weak vitals would grow stronger. He had no clue what would happen in a real passenger, and the simulator never went this far. Cal felt as if his heart stopped for a moment when the pulse on the screen twitched briefly higher. He sucked in a breath and held it. Again the pulse flicked higher, and did not drop back down.

He took that as his cue to exit the pod. He kicked off of carts and staved off structural braces as he hurried his way aft toward pod twelve. Cal's heart raced as he approached the dimly lit maw of the sleeper pod. A sudden realization struck him; he had not checked which passenger berth was affected.

Oh God, if it's Alexis…

He shuddered at the thought as he pulled his way into the first corridor. His haste was taking its toll. He huffed and sweat beaded on his brow as he rounded the corner into the crowded hallway that contained his sleeper. He could see Dr. Taylor braced against the wall and tending to what Cal assumed was the distressed passenger. He could not see who it was, as his vision was blocked by the backs of two crew members floating in front of him, whom he recognized as Hunter and Colonel Dayton.

Oh God. Please...

Cal heard a fit of coughing from the passenger. Relief washed over him and he took a deep breath. His head darted from side to side to get a view around Hunter. He felt something brush against his left arm, and was startled as Lieutenant Josephson moved past him. A flash of color caught the corner of his eye. He looked down and saw the black and yellow outline of a Taser strapped to her hip.

"Deep breaths, Major," he heard Dr. Taylor say.

Major?

Hunter moved to the top of the hallway to allow Josephson to pass. As he did so, Cal could see a middle aged man in a flight suit nearly doubled over. His brown hair was a tussled mess, and he clutched a pair of horn rimmed glasses in his hand. He coughed and spat for a few minutes at Dr. Taylor soothed him.

Cal noticed that Hunter had sidled up beside him. He turned to the lieutenant. "Who is that?"

"Major Forrest," Hunter replied quietly. "One of your father's alleged co-conspirators."

Cal looked back at Forrest. He seemed to tremble as he uncurled and looked around. He mumbled something, but Cal could not make out what was said. He was only barely able to make out Dr. Taylor's voice as she said, "You nearly died. My assistant saw your distressed heart rate, alerted me, and revived you."

Colonel Dayton looked over his shoulder and saw Cal. He gave a quick nod before his eyes darted between Lieutenant Josephson and Hunter. "Ceretti, Josephson, please escort the major to the crew pod so that Doctor Taylor can treat him there."

"Yes, sir," they replied in chorus. Hunter gently grabbed Forrest's arm and righted him, and then escorted him out of the pod. Josephson followed suit with her hand resting on the grip of her weapon the whole time.

Dr. Taylor looked at Cal and beamed. "Great catch. And you did a marvelous job of waking him up."

"Will he recover?" asked Dayton.

"I will have to monitor him for a while, but I do not believe that he will suffer any permanent damage from his ordeal."

Michael's commander nodded. "Thank you, Doctor Taylor. Go see to it. I want to speak with Mr. McLaughlin alone." She bowed slightly and then took her leave using the far hallway exit. Dayton straightened his flight suit and scratched at his beard. "That was a close call. You did very well."

Cal shrugged. "I just did what Doctor Taylor taught me to do."

"Without hesitation, from what I hear. That in itself may have saved the major's life."

Cal was puzzled by the merits of saving an accused man from death. "I don't get it, sir. You're accusing him of treason, but thanking me for saving him. Isn't that kind of a mixed message?"

Dayton placed a strong hand on Cal's shoulder. "Not at all. It's the right thing to do. Major Forrest may be accused of a capital crime, but he will have a chance to defend himself at his court martial. Had he died, it could have been seen as a premature execution. That's not even mentioning the fact that we hope to hear his reasoning from his testimony. A lot of truth might have died with him, and you saved that as well." His beard stretched upward with the corners of his mouth as he smiled. "Please, if there is anything I can do for you, let me know."

Cal nodded and then shrugged off the colonel's hand. "I'll think about it. In the meantime, I have work to do."

"Very well, Mr. McLaughlin."

Cal snaked his way out of pod twelve and forward through the backbone of the ship. *So I've just delayed what's coming for the major. I still don't exactly see that as fair to him.* He entered the pod where he and Doctor Taylor worked side by side. The hallway felt still and empty, as she was not there. Cal turned on his workstation and resumed his task. He stopped on the readout of Alexis Decker. *She's still asleep. No clue that someone just a few feet from her almost died.*

He continued his duty alone. Cal did not expect Dr. Taylor to return for this round of monitoring, based on the conversation between her and Dayton. As the minutes ticked away, he felt alone again. He had never completed a full round without the doctor working at his side. As much as Cal didn't want to talk to anyone right now, he did wish that she was helping him. Her presence made Cal feel more at ease.

Cal's mind snapped back to attention. Something inside him told him that he had missed something a few screens back, so he rolled back one passenger at a time. After the fourth screen, an anomaly showed on his screen. His heart dropped.

This one is dead.

He activated the com. "Calvin to bridge."

"Bridge here, Sergeant Drisko speaking."

"Cameron, I... there's..."

"Calvin? Is something wrong?"

"Is Colonel Dayton up there?"

"Yes, why?"

"Please send him to pod seven, section bravo. There's... there's been a... one of the passengers... is dead."

The speaker crackled with static for a moment. Then Drisko's voice came back, clearly dejected. "Understood. Bridge out."

The com system shut off as Drisko cut the connection. Cal floated in the empty hallway and stared at the passenger's completely flat lined vitals. *We're not safe. This must be what my last dream was about.* He swallowed hard. *Oh God. I don't know what would be worse, dying as the sleeper chokes you, or getting sucked out into space.*

Cal exited the pod and made his way to a sleeper pod on the opposite side of the gallery. He pulled his way into one of the sections and searched for the unit that contained the victim, which he found it just as Colonel Dayton and Captain Hartley made their way into the section.

"Which one is it?" Dayton demanded. Cal pointed to a unit on the top row of the inboard side. "Open it, Captain."

Hartley put an override command into one of the terminals and the magnetic lock on the berth popped. As Colonel Dayton opened the hatch there was a stench of rotten eggs. Dayton crawled part of the way into the unit. Cal could hear the restraints of the passenger being released as Dayton grunted and cursed under his breath. Dr. Taylor arrived and placed her hand on Cal's shoulder. A sudden feeling of worry gripped him.

Dayton and Hartley freed the body from its tether and removed it from the unit. Cal could see he was an older, heavy set man, whose little remaining hair was completely gray. Cal could feel his heart sink. He felt tears well up, but it did not make sense to him. This man was a complete stranger, yet he felt a great sorrow for the loss.

"He looks familiar. Check the passenger matrix, Hartley," said Dayton.

"No need to do that, Colonel," Dr. Taylor stopped him. "I know who this is." She bit her lower lip.

Dayton looked at her with surprise. "Who is it, Doctor?"

"Doctor Jonathan Fairweather. One of the head researchers of

Project Columbus, and a dear friend," she said as her voice cracked slightly.

The color seemed to drain from Dayton's cheeks. Silence blanketed the crowded hallway. Dr. Taylor drew her hands to her face and wiped her eyes. Hartley stared at the body.

"Captain Hartley," Dayton broke the silence.

"Yes sir?"

"Activate all engineering crew members." His voice had a serious tone to it that filled Cal with dread. "Activate anyone else that has computer maintenance or programming experience. I want you to head up an investigation and find out what happened here, see if these units have failed. If they have, I want the ship torn apart stem to stern until you find and fix the problem."

"Yes sir." Hartley beat a hasty retreat from the pod.

"Doctor, I want you to start working from the crew pod for now. Josephson will be assigned to guard you in case the major tries to escape custody." She nodded and turned to exit. Dayton focused his attention to Cal. "Mr. McLaughlin, I would be further in your debt if you would help Lieutenant Ceretti with any tasks he needs you to do during this investigation. I am granting you temporary access to the computer core."

"But sir," he blurted. "One passenger has died, another almost did just a little bit ago. Shouldn't we wake the passengers to keep them safe?"

And by the passengers, I mean Alexis.

Colonel Dayton's stare hardened and his brow furrowed. "Absolutely not. We don't want to panic them, and we certainly don't want to put that much stress on our food supply."

"Then maybe…"

Dayton put his hand up to interrupt. "The passengers aren't in any danger. I don't think this is a coincidence, Mr. McLaughlin."

"What do you mean, sir?"

"The two men had something in common. Both were accused of conspiracy for their alleged parts in the theft of Project Columbus."

Cal's jaw dropped. "Wait, so that means…"

Dayton shrugged. "Probably. That's why we have to investigate. There's another reason I'm granting you more access, however. It could be that someone is targeting conspirators. That means that you're either lucky, or whoever is doing this thinks that you're innocent."

Wait, you think that I was a target too? Cal's hands went numb and his vision started to narrow. *No, pull yourself together.*

"You need to give Ceretti an order from me," he continued. "He is to move you from your current sleeper berth to one of the spares in the crew pod. We have a few Marines on board. Have Ceretti put you in a berth next to one of them. Also have him make sure that you are still listed in your original berth, and that the new one is marked as empty and shows as offline, even when it is in use. Make sure he keeps absolutely quiet about this. If there is a suspect on board, I don't want them to know about this."

Cal took a few deep breaths to calm down. "Okay. But what if Hunter is the one doing this?"

Dayton shook his head. "I can't guarantee anything. I chose Ceretti because he seems to like you more than anyone else on this ship. I just hope that translates into him being protective of you. Now please, go find him and get that done before half of the crew wakes up and you lose the chance."

"Yes sir," Cal replied nervously as he departed for the bridge.

For the first time in his life, Cal felt as if his life was in the hands of someone else.

I hope you're a true friend, Hunter. I need to rely on you now.

• • •

```
1st Lt Darius Owens
22 September 2024, 09:05
Gabriel
>|
```

Darius felt his stomach churn and knot as he read computer code from the screen in front of him. *This is terrible,* he thought. *If this hadn't been routed to the null mailbox...* The result was horrible enough that Darius dared not finish that thought, not even in his head.

"Owens to bridge," he said as he activated the com.

"Bridge here, Airman Garza speaking."

"Garza, can you please have Colonel Eriksen meet me in the computer core?"

"Yes sir."

"Owens out." He switched off the com system and let out a great sigh.

He leaned forward and rested his head in his hands. The restraints across his chest reminded him of their presence with a slight bite, but he ignored it. The torrent of white noise made by the racks of computers seemed to grow louder as Darius took a moment to close his eyes and rest.

Darius had listened for hours to the files received by the null box. At first he was not sure what to expect, perhaps a message from one of the other sleeper ships. Most of the files contained blips and blurps of background noise from the cosmos. But then he had stumbled on to two files that were very different. Both files sounded like an old modem carrier, a sound that Darius had not heard in years. He knew at once that these were intelligent transmissions, yet they were not voice messages from the other ships.

What he found when he compiled and opened them was chilling. Whoever sent them knew the exact weakness in the communications system to exploit. As Darius read the code, the purpose of the transmission became clear: to assassinate a passenger.

"You requested to see me, Lieutenant?" The voice of Colonel Eriksen startled him.

He regained his composure and turned to face the massive, square commander of *Gabriel.* "Yes sir. I've been working on a problem with the com system since last maintenance cycle. I created a null mail file to capture any incoming transmissions to the ship to make sure no accidental issues were created."

Eriksen's brows perked up. "Accidental issues? What are you talking about?"

"When I did some redundant system checks ten years ago," he explained, "I found that our com system software had been rolled back to an earlier version. The mainframe's firmware was damaged too and I had to rebuild that."

"Uh huh?" The colonel's expression went flat and he looked at his watch.

"Well, it's a good thing I did, sir. Someone sent us a transmission." He punched a button on the mainframe terminal and a horrible cacophonous screech filled the computer core. Eriksen winced and brought his hands to his ears. Darius stopped the playback.

"What the hell was that?"

"A carrier wave, Colonel. Someone sent us a program through the com system."

"Are we talking aliens here or one of the other ships?" Eriksen closed the gap between the two men and looked over Darius's shoulder.

"It's definitely from one of the other ships, sir. The code is written in binary. It's extremely eloquent, too. When I compiled the files and looked at them in a sandbox, I found that not only are they written for Unix, there were none of the notation tags that you'd expect to see from a dev team to mark what sections of code do what."

"Sounds thrilling. Why would they do that? And why would they send it to us?"

"Sir, I think whoever sent this meant to assassinate someone."

Eriksen froze. His hand gripped Darius's shoulder. The colonel seemed to splutter for a moment before he asked, "Do you know who they intended to kill, Lieutenant?"

Darius nodded. "Yes sir. Each file was coded with a target sleeper. I matched them against the matrix. The targets were Lieutenant Reid and Doctor Kimura."

"Damn." Colonel Eriksen wrung his hands together. "I've seen the doctor, so I know he's alright. Is Reid in danger?"

"No sir. Between the null mailbox and the sandbox, these files never hit our actual mainframe."

"Good. Can you tell who sent them?"

"Well," Darius said as he sifted through another section of code. "I can't tell who wrote this, and the authorization signature has been wiped from the file. There's a pretty sophisticated bit in here that deleted the signature once the file was opened, even in the sandbox. It looks like whoever did this may have messed up, though."

"How so? Do you have something?"

"I'm not sure yet, Colonel." Darius tapped on the screen. "This section here looks damaged. I'll work on finding out what it was supposed to be, but if the position within the file is correct, it's probably the mainframe identifier. It should at least tell us which ship this came from."

"How long will it take you?"

"Maybe a minute or two. We're talking about just a few bytes of data here."

"Do it." Eriksen activated the com. "Eriksen to bridge."

"Bridge here, Airman Garza speaking. Yes, Colonel?"

"Send Captain Quinn to get Doctor Kimura, and have him escort the doctor to the computer core."

"Yes sir."

Darius started work on the damaged code. He opened a parallel window that contained a communication file from *Gabriel's* mainframe and compared the structure against the mystery code. With a few adjustments he was able to reconstruct the signature code.

"Sir, look at this."

XCS-03-R

"*Raphael.*" The lines on Eriksen's face hardened into a scowl. "Who on that ship would want to kill the doctor and Reid?"

"I don't know sir. I don't know much about the active crew on that ship, other than her commander is Colonel Fox and that Lieutenant Kimura is over there instead of *Michael.*"

"Wait, why is Kimura over there?"

"From what the doctor told me, she was on that damaged transport that had to make an emergency docking with *Raphael.*"

The hatch to the computer core slid open with a scraping noise. Darius and Colonel Eriksen turned as Dr. Kimura entered with Captain Quinn on his heels. The two men were a comedic mismatch of size; the slender gray scientist was dwarfed by the great redhead. Eriksen motioned for them to come closer.

"Doctor," he said in a hushed voice. "Do you know of anyone on *Raphael* that would want to harm you?"

Dr. Kimura's face registered his shock and confusion. "No, Colonel. Why?"

The colonel ignored the question. "Think hard. Any enemies? Anyone who might hold a grudge?" Kimura paused and shook his head. "Very well. Return to your work."

"Colonel Eriksen, may I ask what…"

"No you may not," he said abruptly. "Now return to your work."

Dr. Kimura hesitated for a moment, but bowed and took his leave from the core. Captain Quinn watched him go with a puzzled look and then looked at the colonel. "Sir?"

Eriksen lowered his voice even more, to the point where Darius had to strain to hear him. "Captain, what I tell you in this room goes no further, understood?" There was a nod of acknowledgement. "It would appear that there is an assassin onboard *Raphael*. I want you to go through all crew and passenger profiles to see if you can find any discrepancies that might lead us to a possible identity."

"Like what, sir?"

"I'm not sure. At this point we're grasping at straws. But if you find anything funny at all, I want you to make a note of it and bring it to my attention. I also don't want you drawing attention to yourself, so I need you to do it from one of the workstations in the propulsion section."

"What about Smith, sir?" asked Quinn.

"Find a way to reassign him. I don't care where to."

Quinn thought for a moment. "I could have him inspect the thrusters early."

Eriksen nodded in approval. "Lieutenant Owens, I want you to send a message to *Michael* and inform them of the danger you found in the com system. Let them know the problem is a threat to their passengers and how to fix it, but don't give too many details. Then send a coded message to *Raphael*, for Colonel Fox alone. Notify her that she may have a saboteur with extensive knowledge of the com system. Maybe she can help us out."

"Yes sir."

Quinn and Eriksen turned and departed from the room. Darius was left once again with only the whir of the cooling fans to keep him company. As he stared at the graphic of the com system on his screen, a sickening thought hit him.

Michael was probably already hit.

• • •

The parabola looks right, if not a bit tall. Haruka squinted as she scrutinized the trajectory of *Raphael* on her nav screen. She zoomed in to the end point of Alpha Centauri B and opened a map that depicted the known stellar system. She sighed. *I may have been wrong. It looks like Captain Bartrand put us on the exact correct course.*

Haruka stretched her arms above her and yawned as the simulation continued. Her eyelids drooped and her back ached from sitting hunched in the chair without moving for hours. A sphere that represented the planet Demeter lazily arced its way around the orange star in the center. Two smaller, dotted spheres rotated in orbit around the planet. These were suspected to be moons but had never been fully confirmed. The outer moon was much larger, and its trajectory followed its smaller sibling at a more leisurely pace.

I wonder what it's like there, she pondered. *Dad said that Dr. Benedict said it was probably habitable.* The word "probably" stuck in her mind. *There's no guarantee of that, even if we make it there in one piece. It could just as easily be a dead world. I suppose the approach probe will answer that question.*

She zoomed out slightly so that she could see the remaining planets in the same window. Demeter was the second planet from the sun. The inner orbit was occupied by a rocky planet that was somewhat larger than Mercury, but also more distant. Haruka had heard that this one was tidally locked to Alpha Centauri B. *Burning death on one side, frozen doom on the other.* Two known planets lay beyond Demeter's orbit. The first was a gas giant that was believed to be just over 1 Astronomical Unit farther out, but also hypothesized to be not much larger than Neptune. The second known outer planet was also a gas giant, but it had a different orbit type altogether. Haruka tried to remember the term that her father had used.

Circumbinary? Yeah, that's what it was. She zoomed out a little more and watched the projected path of the massive, gaseous planet as it slowly traversed from Alpha Centauri B to its binary companion. Then she saw the blip that represented *Raphael* close in on the system. Again she zoomed in toward Demeter. She waited for the ship to enter the screen again. It did, and she gasped.

We're coming in way too hot. Haruka watched as *Raphael* passed well in front of Demeter and off into oblivion. She closed her eyes and breathed deeply. *Don't panic, you can fix this. Just tell the major what's going on.*

Haruka loosened her harness and made her way past the empty command chair and rows of empty stations to both sides; with Emberley's reassignments, she was the only one on the bridge. She traveled down the staircase into the crew pod and knocked on Major Emberley's closed sleeper berth door.

C'mon, Major. Open up. She waited and listened for any response, or for the lock to open. Silence greeted her. She knocked again on the cold aluminum, but the result was no different.

Haruka sighed and made her way to her own berth with a quick detour to grab a meal on her way. As she consumed the preserved spaghetti and garlic flavored bread, Mancini returned from his duty. He was covered from head to toe in grease, and Haruka did not know whether to laugh or take pity on him. Despite the fact that she no longer had her companion to talk to while working, she did not miss propulsion maintenance at all.

When he saw her, Mancini grinned and gave her a dramatic, sweeping salute. "Reporting for dinner, Captain."

She giggled. "At ease, soldier. Besides," she said as she patted him on the stomach, "you've never missed a dinner in your life."

"Why let perfectly good food go to waste, right Kimura?"

"Funny you should put it that way." Haruka peered inside the pouch of spaghetti. "Perfectly good food is great, but I'm not sure how much longer I can live off of these things. Everything's starting to taste the same."

Marco tore into his meal pouch like a starved wolf. "That so, huh? Alright, princess. After we land this thing and get set up, I'll make you breakfast. How about that?"

"Hah," she snorted. "You only wish you could make me breakfast. That's for your booty call girls, not me."

"Tsk. You wound me. I'd never do that to you."

"Right. Because you remember I always try to keep you from getting punched in the face when you're in trouble?"

"Yeah."

She grinned. "There will be no one to protect that pretty face of yours if you get in trouble with me."

Mancini's grin widened and his eyes seemed to dance with light. "So it's a date then?"

"Ugh, fine," she conceded and rolled her eyes. "Breakfast only, nothing else. Try anything funny and I swear I'll break your nose myself, Marco." He raised his hands and cocked his head slightly, then went back to his dinner. "Say, have you seen the major lately?"

"Yeah, he's in the gym. I just came from there."

Good, he's still awake. Haruka smiled and left the hallway. "Hey, where are you going?" she heard Marco ask, but she hurried her way out into the ship and down into the lower level, then sailed forward to the gym and opened the door.

Major Emberley was still inside, working on what looked like a leg press exercise. He glanced at Haruka and nodded at her before he continued his routine. "Come on in, Captain. There's plenty of room."

"Sir, I'm not here to work out. I have something to report." She tried to mask her nervousness. The information she was about to divulge could be catastrophic if not resolved. *I just hope he has faith in me to fix it.*

Emberley stopped his workout, released himself from the apparatus, and then turned to face her. He reached for a towel and wiped away the sweat that had beaded on his forehead. "Go ahead," he said, out of breath.

"Sir, it appears that Captain Bartrand did indeed make an error in his calculations after the low orbit slingshot." She drew in a deep breath through her nose so as not to make a sound. "His course is on target for the planetary orbit of Demeter, but the computer sims show that we're moving too fast. As it sits right now, we will cross the orbit about two months before the planet itself reaches the target point."

Emberley's eyes widened. "My God. We can't just stop the ship in the middle of space and wait for the planet to catch up. Can you slow us down a little bit so that our target is there at the same time as us?"

She opened her mouth to speak, but something inside her told her that slowing down now would be wrong. "I need to do some more research on our options, sir. If we hadn't discovered this mistake, it would have been fatal. I want to make sure that I don't make any mistakes myself."

He nodded. "Very prudent, Captain. By all means, take all the time you need. I don't care if it takes you a day or six maintenance cycles to figure it out. The safety of the ship and its passengers can't be left to a chance decision."

"Thank you, sir." She saluted and took her leave. After she closed the door she let out a great sigh. She hadn't noticed before that her

J.C. Rainier

hands were shaking. She rubbed them together as she kicked off of the wall in search of the ladder up.

I have to say, she thought. *It sure is nice having a commanding officer who actually cares about the mission. Now, what to do about bringing the ship back on course...*

A huge yawn parted her lips, and she stretched her lean body.

I've got thirty years to figure this out. No sense in starting calculations now when I'm so tired.

Haruka changed her course once more, and this time she headed for her berth.

. . .

"That should just about do it."

Cal sighed in relief as Hunter put the final touches on the routine that would mask his new berth's location. "Thanks, man. I owe you one."

Hunter shook his head. "No, not at all. If there's even a chance that what the colonel says is true, you need to be protected. Whatever your father did, you had no idea."

I have no idea. There's an understatement for you.

Cal looked around the computer core room at the racks of computers in precise rows. The song of their cooling fans was akin to the heartbeat of the ship. One thing that he knew about *Michael* was that every system in the so-called "support section" was absolutely vital to operation. The computers regulated the sleeper pods and kept track of various navigation sensors while the crew was asleep. The reactor and generator, farther aft, powered the whole ship. Cal marveled at how these few systems would keep everyone alive all the way to this new planet that Hunter had talked about. There was also the constant nagging idea that something might go wrong.

Like in my last dream. He shook the thought from his head and looked at his friend. Hunter had put on a headset that was plugged into the mainframe terminal. He stared intently at the screen.

Cal cleared his throat and asked, "So what now?" Hunter did not look up at Cal, but instead held up his hand with one finger up to his lips, as if to silence him. Cal looked at the screen and saw the active com indicator. "What is it?"

Hunter sighed and placed the headset on a Velcroed hook that was attached to the side of the terminal. "Well, it looks like Captain Hartley and his crew can stop their investigation."

Cal gulped. *That doesn't sound good.* "What were you listening to?"

Lieutenant Hunter Ceretti turned to meet Cal's uneasy gaze. For a moment, Cal thought he saw fear in his friend's eyes.

"We just got an incoming transmission from *Gabriel*. They said they found an... exploit. It was in their com system." Hunter's voice was hushed and solemn. "They think the same problem may exist in our computers as well."

"What do you mean by exploit?"

Hunter seemed to ignore his question. He turned back to the terminal and brought up a schematic of the ship. Cal watched as screen after screen flashed by, until at last Hunter stopped at one particular drawing. He traced the screen with one finger as a sneer marred his face. Hunter slammed his fist into the terminal, making Cal flinch.

"Damn it," he seethed. "They're right. This is the wrong com software version. How damn long have they known about this?" Cal gulped but did not say a word. He watched as Hunter's fist slowly balled up and relaxed, over and over. "They want us to create a null mailbox for the com system so transmissions don't go right through. Would be kind of nice if they just gave us the program, wouldn't it?"

"Maybe they don't know how to," Cal suggested.

"Oh, they know how and have done so already. How do you think they knew it would work?"

Ugh, he's right. Cal put his hand on his friend's shoulder. Uneasiness gave way to a feeling of bitterness. He forced this aside for a moment and asked, "Is there anything I can do to help you?"

Hunter scoffed and pulled from his grasp, and Cal took a deep breath and settled down. Hunter cleared his throat and confidence returned to his voice. "I've got my work cut out for me. For the good of the ship I need to get to it right away. Go tell Hartley and Dayton about the message. Tell them to stop looking for the problem with the sleepers, and that *Gabriel* may be hiding something from us."

"Sure thing, but do you have any idea what that might be in case the colonel asks me?"

"With any certainty? No. But from the way this guy Lieutenant Owens from *Gabriel* was talking, it sounds like they may have experienced the same thing. Only they were prepared and we weren't. He specifically said that this exploit was a threat to the passengers."

Cal nodded. "Sounds like you're right, they do know something." He pursed his lips as he took a moment to think. "Hey, this means that the computer thing would have to be started from somewhere off the ship, right?"

"The thought had crossed my mind. It makes total sense. Make sure you tell the colonel that as well. Personally I don't think that we have a saboteur on board. I know all the guys we work with and I don't think any of them could or would do something like this." Hunter started typing on a blank terminal screen. "Anyway, I've got to get started on this right away. Go, tell them."

"You got it."

Cal pulled himself along the walls and out of the core. He paused for a moment in the smaller, dim hallway of the support section. He looked aft and could make out the form of a hatch in the distance. *I guess the reactor is back there, from the plans of the ship,* he thought. *Captain Hartley will be back there.* Cal floated toward the hatch but stopped again before he got there and heard a loud whine from the rear of the ship. *I don't have access, and he'll never hear me over that noise anyway.*

Instead, Cal turned about and shot forward into the gallery. He made his way toward the bridge of *Michael.* His gaze was locked forward and he ignored the dark maws of pods on either side as he sought out Colonel Dayton. He came at last to the open airlock that went to the crew section, then passed through it and went up the staircase to the bridge. Cal grabbed the railing and came to a stop as he passed under the massive glass canopy. He looked up and took in the panoramic view of the stars, smattered all over the sky like glitter cast off by a child.

Colonel Dayton's voice reminded him of his purpose. "Can I do something for you, Mr. McLaughlin?"

Cal straightened his posture as he locked eyes with the ship's commander. "Yes, Colonel. Lieutenant Ceretti reports that he has received a message from *Gabriel.*"

"I know. We received the same message up here. Do you know if he's applying the fix they talked about?"

"Yes sir."

"Good," Dayton said as he nodded. "Should just be a matter of time before we catch Doctor Fairweather's assassin, then we can put this whole matter to bed."

Cal glanced around at the workstations surrounding the command chair. He could see Sergeant Drisko seated at one of the workstations to the right of Dayton, but the rest sat vacant. Cal made a gesture toward the commanding officer. "Sir, may I?" Dayton nodded and Cal pushed gently from the railing and stopped at the command chair. He bent his head next to the colonel's and lowered his voice. "Are you sure the killer is on board?"

Dayton turned and looked directly into Cal's eyes. "Do you know something that I don't, Mr. McLaughlin?"

"Well, Ceretti says that the exploit can only be triggered from outside the ship. He also said that the officer that placed the call to us seemed to be holding back about something."

There was a pause.

"Does he know what?"

Cal shook his head. "He's a smart guy, sir, but I don't think he's a mind reader."

Dayton's brown eyes seemed to burn a hole in Cal as his stare continued for almost a minute. Then his eyes broke away from Cal, he raised his voice and barked, "Drisko, clear the bridge. Take Mr. McLaughlin with you. Make sure no one enters the bridge until I order otherwise."

"Yes sir," he heard Drisko reply.

Dayton again locked his eyes on Cal. "I have some business to attend to up here. Something isn't right, I'll give you that."

Cal could feel his temper rising quickly. He flexed his right hand, which gave him a painful reminder of the last time this happened. "Colonel, sir," he said through gritted teeth. "I need to report to Doctor Taylor immediately. I can have Josephson take my place if you need."

"Are you ill?" Dayton asked as he sized up Cal.

"Maybe. I'm experiencing a symptom that she wanted me to look out for."

Colonel Dayton nodded. "Very well. But Josephson is only to take your place guarding the bridge if Major Forrest is resting. If he's awake, I want her there guarding the doctor."

With a nod, Cal leaped toward the end of the bridge and pulled his way down the stairs past a surprised Drisko. He did not as much as pause to acknowledge the sergeant's query as to where he was going. He made his way into the sleeper section that contained the new berths of both himself and Forrest. He found Dr. Taylor and Lieutenant Josephson within.

Dr. Taylor was using one of the terminals; Cal presumed that she was doing her work. Lieutenant Josephson was rigid against a bank of sleepers. If Cal had not known better, he would have sworn that she had been glued to the wall. Her eyes fell on Cal with a watchful gaze as he passed.

"Is the major asleep?" he asked as he came to as stop next to Dr. Taylor.

She nodded. "Resting, but not in hibernation. I still need to monitor him for another day or so."

He turned to see the blonde lieutenant eyeing him. "Colonel Dayton said that if the major was resting, he wanted you to guard the entry to the bridge."

Her lip curled and she drummed her fingers on the grip of her Taser. "Isn't that nice. I don't take orders from you, kid."

Cal sighed and shook his head. "Look, I already said I'm sorry for shoving you. I really don't know what your beef with me is, but it's starting to get old. If we're going to keep working together, can you at least be civil with me?"

Josephson's lips parted in what could be either a sneer or a grin; Cal couldn't make up his mind as to which it was. "I don't work with you. You're just the doctor's pet."

"Hey," Dr. Taylor protested.

"Look," Cal continued. "The order came from Colonel Dayton. Does it matter who the messenger is? Because I can just go outside and get Drisko to tell you the same thing."

"Hmph. And so quickly you run to go tell on me. Tsk tsk." Josephson crossed her arms. "Well go on, I'm calling your bluff, little man."

"Enough!" Dr. Taylor's voice boomed and echoed through the hallway. "Go guard the bridge, Lieutenant."

Josephson did not budge. "Sorry, Doctor. Civilian authority ends at the airlock. Up here I don't take orders from you either."

"Wrong, Lieutenant. Colonel Dayton ordered me to treat Major Forrest up here, as well as move my work here," the elder woman said, standing her ground. "Which means that according to the operational guidelines of Project Columbus, this hallway is de facto designated a hospital. And that means that *my* authority is supreme here." The smirk disappeared from Josephson's face and all color seemed to drain from her. "Now get your ass out of my hospital and follow your damned CO's orders."

"Y-yes Doctor," she stuttered as she beat a hasty retreat from the crew pod.

As soon as the lieutenant was out of sight, Dr. Taylor turned back to Cal with a grin. "I see you've made a friend."

Cal shook his head. "Seriously, who keeps pissing in her oatmeal? I don't know what else to do about her. I've tried to make nice, but she just refuses."

"Turn the other cheek, Calvin. That's about all you can do right now."

"Doc, I've got symptoms. These mood swings that you warned me about."

Dr. Taylor turned off her workstation and gave him her full attention. "Can you describe these mood swings? What kind of moods, what's happening when they strike you?"

He looked up at the ceiling. "Oh, God. How do I even begin to describe them?" He dropped his eyes back down and stared Dr. Taylor in the eyes. "Well, up on the bridge, I felt a burst of anger for no reason whatsoever. Then there was when we found Doctor Fairweather's body, I almost burst into tears."

"Hmm. I don't know about the anger, but generally speaking, crying is an appropriate response to grief."

"That's part of the thing, Doc. I didn't know that guy from Adam, yet I felt almost as bad as the moment I found out Dad was killed. I would have expected to feel shocked or numb, yes. But that kind of reaction for a guy I've never seen in my life?"

Dr. Taylor pursed her lips and nodded.

"There have been a bunch of other times where I've felt something that just didn't fit the situation. Numbness, fear, happiness, anger, you name it. It's almost like the part of my brain that sends out emotions is spinning a wheel every few minutes to see what is next." He averted his eyes and laughed nervously. "I can't tell if being awake or asleep is worse at this point. When I'm asleep, I'm battling my demons, but at least I feel how I expect to feel. But when I'm awake, it's almost like a different kind of nightmare. I feel like I'm losing my mind, Doc."

Dr. Taylor sighed and placed her hands on Cal's shoulders. He felt more at ease, as if a load had been lifted from his shoulders.

"I love working with you, Calvin. Your work ethic is great for someone of your generation. I consider you a good friend, and that's why I worry about how you're going to take this," she said. There was a dramatic pause and Cal could feel a knot tighten in his stomach as she withdrew her hands. "I need you to come with me to talk to the colonel as soon as he is available."

"Why? Is it bad?" He dreaded the answer.

"I believe you may have a rare condition known as Hibernation Psychosis."

His heart sunk.

Then it's true. I am living a nightmare.

• • •

"Are you joking, Lieutenant?"

Colonel Eriksen glared at Darius. It seemed that his superior was judging Darius for what he had reported. *I'm just the messenger,* he thought. *You're not supposed to shoot the messenger, right?* Darius shook his head and replied, "No sir. He was very clear, it was an order."

"Who the hell does he think he is? This is *my* ship!" Eriksen's voice bellowed and he drew the attention of Tyler Quinn; the engineer gave a curious glance toward the command chair. "Not to mention that it's also my investigation."

"He seemed convinced, sir."

"And did he say why?"

"He just said it was classified," Darius replied.

Eriksen scoffed. "Two can play at that game. Reply with my compliments," his voice was thick with sarcasm. "Inform him that we regret that we cannot divulge any classified information without proper clearance."

Darius sighed heavily. *I don't want to argue with one colonel, let alone two.* He tugged at the cuff of his flight suit. "With all due respect, sir, I do not believe that Colonel Dayton will accept that coming from me. Shouldn't you speak with him yourself?"

Colonel Eriksen clenched his jaw and his eyes narrowed. Darius glanced over his shoulder and was reminded that Captain Quinn was still watching the spectacle unfold. He drew in a breath and held it. *Lord, I just disrespected his command in front of others. That won't help at all.*

Instead, Eriksen relaxed and breathed in deeply. "I suppose you're right, Owens. Let's just nip this in the bud." Darius exhaled in relief. "Is there still a headset in the computer core?"

"Yes sir," he replied.

"Good. I will use the terminal back there to contact *Michael.* See to it that I'm not disturbed."

"Yes sir."

Darius watched as his commanding officer rose from the chair and propelled himself off of the bridge. He then looked back at the engineering console and saw Captain Quinn, a wry grin etched on his pale face.

"Good job, Owens."

Darius drew his eyebrows together as he tried to figure out what Quinn was talking about. "What for, sir?"

"Wrangling the colonel. I've never actually seen anyone back him down like that before."

"I-I didn't really do anything, I just thought that if they talked to each other it would save a huge headache."

Quinn's lips parted in a toothy smile. "No doubt for you."

None at all. It would have been like getting wedged between two rocks. He nodded. There was a brief silence while Darius thought. "Sir, are you done with the colonel's request?"

"No, working on it right now."

"I thought you were going to do that back in propulsion?"

Quinn sighed and his shoulders slumped. "I couldn't get rid of Smith, so I came up here. Turns out that nav's already done for the day, so it's just been me and the colonel up here." He ran a hand through his fiery hair. "So what was that all about, anyway?"

Darius drifted to the railing next to Quinn. "Colonel Dayton of *Michael* ordered us to divulge all information on our investigation and to send a copy of my null mailbox file. He wouldn't say why."

Quinn whistled. "Did you send the file to him? I know you built it to protect the ship."

"Couldn't if I wanted to. I programmed it as an add-on to the existing system. If I sent it to them, it would just sound like a fax machine arguing with a parrot. It would never install."

A puzzled look came over the captain's face. "So how would a transmission from *Raphael* trigger anything on a ship if you can't get this mailbox to install?"

"Good question, sir. Whoever designed the transmission took advantage of specific exploits. In many ways..." he trailed off and then corrected himself, "no, I take that back. In *every* way, it acts like a virus."

"A virus, huh? That might just help me in my search."

Darius craned his neck to look at the file displayed on Quinn's terminal. "Had any luck with that, sir?"

Quinn turned back to the terminal and flipped to another profile.

"I've got a few discrepancies, but I'm not sure that any of them are useful. Take this one here," he said as he tapped the screen with a freckled finger. "Lieutenant Julio Morado. Turns out he's actually a Mexican citizen. We've got quite a few Hispanic passengers and a couple crew scattered about, but this guy is the only one of them that wasn't actually born in the US."

"That doesn't seem useful," Darius said in a flat tone.

"Tell me about it." Quinn advanced to another file. "Here we've got one from the other border. Major Nathan Emberley, Royal Canadian Air Force. Again, the only Canadian citizen I've come across."

"Hmm, what else have you come across?" Darius leaned over the railing a bit to get a closer look.

Another profile popped up. "Let's see here. Airman Nova Weyler. This looks more like a clerical error than anything. Her enlistment date and entry into basic are way too far apart."

"How far?"

"Three years."

Darius shook his head. "That sounds like someone slipped on a ten key, sir. Do you have any favorites so far?"

"I've got two. They're real thin stretches, but at this point it's all I've got. There's this guy, Lieutenant Mancini. He was supposed to be on board *Michael* but ended up on *Raphael* after his transport took fire on the way up. He might possibly have the skill set to pull this off, and his record has a couple incidents. At first glance they look like minor things, but they are also linked to the last name Kimura."

Darius nodded. *That's pretty thin, Captain.*

"The other pick is Harjit Singh."

Darius looked at the picture of Singh. He was a reasonably young man; by the date of birth on his file, he was twenty seven when the ships launched. In his file photo, Singh's dark beard was neatly trimmed, and his hair was slicked back in an equally tidy manner. His lips were expressionless but his dark brown eyes seemed to burn with an inner fire. His dress blues almost seemed to flow into his dark skin.

"What's the anomaly with him?" Darius asked.

"Nothing in his file," replied Quinn. "But there's just something about him. Look at those eyes, they're pretty sinister looking, right?"

Darius shot a glance over at Captain Quinn as if the man had grown a second head on his shoulder. *Sinister looking eyes?* He shook his head and looked at the screen once more. "I don't see it, sir."

"C'mon now, Owens. Don't tell me it hasn't crossed your mind that some terrorist group has placed someone on board."

Darius could not believe what he had just heard. *He thinks that Singh is a terrorist. Because what, he's brown?* His fingers began to tingle. There was something definitely wrong with the captain's search if all he was going on was a gut instinct about a colored man's eyes.

"Sir, permission to speak freely?"

Captain Quinn stopped for a moment, seemingly stunned by the request. "Of course."

"I don't see anything odd about him or the file, sir. Are you sure you haven't selected him because of the color of his skin?"

Quinn looked at Darius, clearly contemplating his words. "Are you accusing me of something, Mr. Owens?"

"Just trying to understand something. Do you think that Lieutenant Singh might possibly *be* a terrorist?"

The captain sat in stupor. He blinked at Darius and lowered his voice. "Is this a trick question?"

He shook his head. "Only if you want it to be, sir."

"Frankly, yes."

"Then with all due respect," Darius said without skipping a beat, "remove him from your suspects list and move on. We're looking for an assassin."

"Not that there's a difference."

"Respectfully, sir, there is quite a difference. A terrorist would have just found a way to breach *Raphael's* hull and killed everyone on board. What we have is an assassin who is precise, calculating, and extremely cautious." He reached over and tapped the screen emphatically. "There's a good chance that they aren't even on the list you've compiled. They probably already know what we'd be looking for."

Quinn looked up at Darius. He seemed deflated, and exhaustion was evident in his expression. "So I've done all this work for nothing?"

Darius scratched at his cheek as he stared at the picture of Harjit Singh. "Maybe, maybe not. But if there's someone on this list that did it, it's that little blonde girl. What's her name again? Weyler?"

The captain looked at Darius with a bewildered look. "What? Why?"

He smiled. "Because you know the innocent looking blonde girl is the one who's the biggest problem, right? The prom queen? The girl in the grocery store parking lot that backs into your car and drives off without leaving a note? Yeah, she's the one who's most likely to kill someone from thousands of miles away by making a phone call."

Quinn burst out laughing. Darius joined him. When they caught their breaths after a minute, Quinn added, "No you've got it wrong. It's that damn Canadian. You know it's all a vast conspiracy to overthrow baseball and replace it with hockey. I mean, you can't trust a man whose bacon is round."

The two men started laughing again. For a shining moment, Darius forgot the gravity of the situation and remembered that he needed moments of levity to balance against the cruel reality in which he lived.

. . .

Calvin McLaughlin
22 September 2024, 20:05
Michael
>|

Cal held on to the railing with one hand as his other came to his mouth in a vain attempt to conceal a yawn. Quiet settled in on the hallway just inside the crew section airlock.

I wonder if Colonel Dayton is done arguing with whoever he was talking to.

As Cal waited at the bottom of the staircase with Sergeant Drisko and Dr. Taylor, the trio had been subjected to occasional bits of Dayton's tirade. There was no one on the bridge that anyone knew of, so they presumed he was having a radio conversation. Based on the large gaps of time in between outbursts, it must have been a fairly long range conversation as well.

Drisko had suggested that Colonel Dayton was having a "discussion" with another one of the sleepers. It made sense, but only an occasional word was clear enough to understand. Several of them were curse words, twisted by Dayton's New England accent. Cal had to keep from laughing several times from how silly it sounded, but took a ribbing from Drisko about his own drawl.

"I don't know. If it's another colonel, they could be arguing all night," Drisko quipped. "I saw the three of them together once back on Earth. Talk about making mountains out of molehills, I swear they were trying to pull rank on each other over a sandwich in the cafeteria."

Cal blinked. "Are you serious? A sandwich?"

His friend smiled. "You obviously never had the sandwiches there." Drisko's facial expression flattened out again. "In all seriousness, I did happen to be walking by a room where they were having a staff meeting and heard them all yelling at each other. I don't think they liked each other very much before all this crap started happening."

"Hmm," Cal said out loud as he thought. *Dad always said that there was unity and structure in the armed forces. From what Cameron is saying, there's a big rift here. Let's hope they can keep it together at least until we land.*

"We don't have our peacemakers with us," added Dr. Taylor in a sad tone. "Dr. Benedict was always quite good at soothing the command staff when their feathers got ruffled. And I don't know a man alive that could stand against the kindness and reasoning of Dr. Kimura."

An awkward silence descended again as the three avoided eye contact with each other. After a minute, Colonel Dayton yelled down from the bridge.

"Drisko! Are you still down there?"

"Yes sir," he replied.

"Get your butt up here."

"Yes sir." Drisko heaved once and shot up the staircase to the bridge.

Cal remained at the landing with Dr. Taylor. He decided to press her for more information.

"Forgive me, Doc. I don't know a whole lot about some people. My dad was kind of vague when he described what Grandpa did for Project Columbus, but in my dreams Grandpa keeps referring to this Dr. Benedict. Who was he, exactly?"

Her brown eyes met with his and she grabbed her braided hair as a young girl might. "He's the man who dared to dream about the potential of Project Columbus, and then dared to make it happen. Possibly one of the most dedicated men that I have ever worked with." Her eyes wandered off into the distance and she seemed to be lost in a memory. "A man who sacrificed so much, both inadvertently and intentionally."

"What do you mean by that?"

She laughed nervously and looked at the ceiling. "My husband, God rest his soul, was not the first man I chose. My heart belonged to the dashing and handsome young David Benedict. I tried to get him to notice me, to take me on a date, to woo me. But after a couple years I came to the realization that he was too absorbed in his work. I wanted a family, so I got married and settled down." Dr. Taylor paused and twirled her braid. "Dr. Benedict was married to Project Columbus. He never married or raised a family. We *are* his family, in a way."

Cal took a moment to consider her words. *I don't know, it still sounds like a lonely life to me.*

"Actually," she laughed as she continued, "in a way he *did* raise a family. He introduced Doctor Kimura to his wife Sarah, and was the godfather of both of the Kimura girls. He had so much influence in our lives outside of the project, just through who he was."

"I see." Cal waited for Dr. Taylor to meet his gaze. "So why did he stay behind?"

She sighed. "I can only imagine. He may have got it in his head somehow that his sacrifice would somehow keep us safer."

"And you don't believe that," Cal finished.

Dr. Taylor shook her head, her hair slowly whipping behind her. "I think we could have used a brilliant astrophysicist and an amazing leader." She craned her neck as if to listen. Cal stopped and listened as well, but heard nothing. "I think it's just about time. You have a choice to make. Do you know what you're going to do?"

Cal sighed and dropped his head. "Not a clue."

Dr. Taylor gently pushed from her railing and floated over to Cal. She placed her hand on his. Her touch was comforting, but raised doubt within him at the same time. "You've always been honest with me. Just be honest with yourself."

He nodded. *What do I want, honestly? She told me what the choices were: stay on the maintenance revival list and take anti-psychotic drugs, or be placed in hibernation and receive treatment after arrival.* Cal reached to his temple and ran his fingers across the scab of the wound he received years ago on the transport. *The drugs should help fix my issues, but Doc said the more times I go in and out of hibernation, the greater the chances I'll lose my mind completely.* He looked at his taped hand and slowly flexed his fingers. He closed his eyes as the dull pain throbbed in his digits. *But if I go to sleep, I will have no break from my nightmares for over thirty years.*

"Calvin," he heard Cameron Drisko say, "Colonel Dayton will see you and Doctor Taylor now."

Cal opened his eyes and looked to the top of the staircase. Drisko floated there in a pose close to attention. Cal thought that his friend looked every bit the soldier, and could not help but feel a measure of envy. Every one of his friends on the ship has a clear place and purpose. Cal had a job, but he was replaceable.

Josephson was right. I am nothing but Dr. Taylor's pet. I don't belong with the crew.

Cal kicked gently off of the deck plate and rose to the command platform. Drisko motioned to the command chair, where Dayton was already waiting, before himself departing back down the stairs.

He looks almost like a king there, he thought. *He might as well be, on this ship. And I'm just the peasant who is about to beg for his fate.*

Cal halted his motion a few feet from the colonel. Dr. Taylor took a similar position on the opposite railing, and spoke. "Colonel Dayton, I have some troubling news."

Dayton folded his hands. Cal could see the man's knuckles turn white as he clasped his fingers tightly together. "This seems to be the day for it. What's going on?"

Dr. Taylor frowned slightly. "Calvin came to me with some medical concerns. After speaking with him and performing a diagnosis, I believe it likely that he has Hibernation Psychosis."

The commanding officer of *Michael* stared at Cal intently for a moment, and then bowed his head and brought his locked hands to his face. Silence blanketed the bridge for minutes; the weight felt as if it would suffocate Cal.

I'm a burden, as always.

Dayton glanced up again. "Very well, Doctor. Have you explained to him what this means and what his options are?"

"Yes, Colonel."

"Have you made your choice, Mr. McLaughlin?"

Cal hesitated for a moment. "I have, sir."

Dayton looked crestfallen as he sighed. "I see. May I speak my mind before you tell me your decision, Mr. McLaughlin?"

"It's your ship, sir. I believe you can do whatever you like."

The colonel dropped his hands to his lap. "Let me rephrase that. Are you going to listen to me if I speak my mind?"

"Of course, sir." *But probably not for long.*

"This cycle has started off absolutely terribly," he started, as if giving a lecture. "One passenger is dead, and one of my crew almost suffered the same fate. I've got the commanding officer of another ship stonewalling me for no good reason. The other commanding officer is ignoring me altogether." Dayton paused and beat his hands against his lap, clearly frustrated. "We're all in a sticky situation here. I could use you. You're clearly bright, you learn quickly, and have earned the respect of the crew. Please consider taking the meds and staying on with us."

Cal let the colonel's plea sink in. It seemed contrary to the view that Cal held of himself. *I'm not a hero. I'm a pet. How useful could I possibly be?* Cal searched inside for an answer to the question. The response came in the form of Dr. Taylor's voice, recalled from his mind.

You've always been honest with me. Just be honest with yourself.

"Sir, I don't think you should rely on me," he said as he tried to mask his anger with himself.

Dayton closed his eyes and asked, "Why not?"

"Because I haven't been completely honest with you, sir. You place more faith in me than what I have returned to you." Cal paused. "Colonel Dayton, sir. Please look at me." Dayton opened his eyes and locked gaze with Cal. A lump rose within Cal's throat, but he continued. "I used the knowledge that I learned from Doctor Taylor and the security code that you had Hunter issue to me for a very selfish purpose."

"Something tells me I don't want to know what that is, Mr. McLaughlin," Dayton interrupted.

"With all due respect, sir, too bad," he continued, unfazed. He was aware of the weight of Dr. Taylor's stare just as keenly as that of the colonel's. "During the last maintenance cycle I revived one of the passengers and showed her the stars from the ESAARC cockpit on my sleeper pod. I spent a couple hours talking with her before placing her back in stasis, at which point I broke my hand by punching my sleeper berth."

Dayton looked at Cal in utter shock. "Why on Earth would you do that?"

Cal sighed. "Because I'm a bigger idiot than you think, sir."

"He's in love with her, Colonel," added Dr. Taylor.

Dayton glanced back and forth between Cal and the doctor. "You knew about this?"

"Only that he was in love, not what he had done."

Don't defend me, Doctor. Maybe he'll change his mind about me. Cal sighed. *Then I wouldn't have to make the decision myself.*

Colonel Dayton shook his head and laughed softly. "Mother Mary and all the saints, Mr. McLaughlin. Thank you for reminding me of what it means to be eighteen and in love."

"Sir?"

"I have to say, that's probably both the grandest and dumbest thing I've ever heard a kid do for love. You've got moxie, I'll give you that much." The smile disappeared from his face and his glare became harsher. "But I know you won't be doing that again. Not till we make it to Demeter, at least. Now hurry up and tell me what your decision is."

Cal nodded. His jaw slacked as he tried to speak, but he stopped himself.

What will it be? Potentially losing your mind, or endless nightmares? He considered both options, and what it would mean to himself and to his new friends on the ship. *Hmm... Colonel Dayton said he owes me a favor, didn't he?*

"Sir, may I suggest a compromise alternative?"

Dayton scratched his beard. "What do you have in mind?"

"I don't like the idea of going completely crazy," he admitted. "As terrifying as my issues are when I am in hibernation, I think I've learned to handle them. I don't want you to think of me as a complete shirk, though. Wake me up for the final approach cycle. Have Doctor Taylor put me on meds then."

Colonel Dayton nodded in agreement. "I suppose that's better than losing you completely. I accept."

"Great." Cal smiled and tried his best to put on a puppy face. "Oh, and you told me that if you could do anything for me to let you know, right?"

"That I did, Mr. McLaughlin."

"Wonderful. I'd like to cash in that favor, then."

Next time don't use the word "anything", Colonel. Cal steeled his resolve and prepared to argue with the exhausted officer for what he wanted.

. . .

1st Lt Darius Owens
23 September 2024, 06:15
Michael
>|

Darius sat at his ops console on the bridge. His headset gently caressed his head, but he left the boom raised and away from his mouth. He squirted a swig of coffee from his ration pouch as he listened to another file from the com system null box. The sound of static pierced with an occasional tick told Darius that this was just the background noise of the cosmos.

The bridge was nearly abandoned. Captain Quinn sat on the other side of the command platform at the engineering stations. Quinn worked in dead silence; if Darius had not seen him on the way in, he would not have known of the engineer's presence.

Colonel Eriksen had not arrived for duty. Darius knew that the colonel had stayed up late the night before in an attempt to come to an understanding with *Gabriel's* commanding officer. From the rumors that were flying, Darius did not believe that endeavor ended well.

Darius stretched and yawned, and then opened another file. More white noise filled his ear. He put the valve of his coffee pouch to his lips and took another drink.

"You know that I don't want liquids around any of the bridge stations, Mr. Owens." The stern voice of Colonel Eriksen made him jump. He coughed as the warm liquid made its way down his windpipe. "And now you know why."

Darius hacked and spluttered for a moment as he recovered. He twisted the valve shut and stashed the coffee. "Sorry, sir," he said as he glanced over his shoulder.

"Finish it outside when you're done with your monitoring." Eriksen paused. "Speaking of, are there any messages for us this morning?"

"Let me check these last two files, sir." He called up the first one and began listening. There seemed to be no difference from any of the previous files. Darius examined his commanding officer's movements. *He's a lot more tense than normal,* Darius thought. "Sir, did your conversation with Colonel Dayton go well?"

Eriksen glared at Darius. "Just listen to the files, Lieutenant."

I guess that's a no.

He turned back to his station and opened the second file; this contained yet more cosmic noise. "No messages, sir."

Eriksen's beard twisted as he tried to contain whatever was eating him inside. Darius could see a bulge in the colonel's cheek from where his tongue was pressed against it. He knew this would not mean good things for whoever had upset Eriksen. Darius shuddered in a moment of panic.

Don't worry, he told himself, *you're just reporting what he asked about. He's not upset with you, this is about Colonel Dayton.*

"Not even a response from *Raphael,*" Eriksen asked. His calm voice reaffirmed Darius's apprehension.

"No sir." *He's not mad at you,* he repeated to himself.

A metallic ping echoed through the quiet bridge as the colonel drummed his fingers on the railing. "Captain Quinn, do you still need use of the com system for your investigation?"

"No sir."

"Shut it down, Mr. Owens."

Darius stopped for a moment and played back what he had just heard in his mind. "Colonel?"

"You heard me, Lieutenant," Eriksen said sternly. "Shut down the external com system. I want radio silence all the way to Demeter."

"Y-yes sir." Darius unbuckled and pulled himself to the command platform.

"I mean now, Lieutenant," barked Eriksen as he blocked Darius's path.

"Yes sir. I don't have the proper access up here. I have to do it from the computer core," he responded nervously.
The colonel shook his head and spun his body out of the way. "I'm sorry. I don't mean to take this out on you, Mr. Owens." The bars of the railing squeaked as he wrung his hands on them. "I gave both of them every chance to cooperate. They can listen to static the rest of the way as far as I care."

So it's not just Dayton, it's Fox too. Darius nodded at Colonel Eriksen and then scrambled from the bridge.

The gallery seemed even colder than usual as Darius made his way to the support section. He scanned the walls and floors as he drifted, wondering about the environmental system operation or the condition of the network cables as they ran through the ship. He tried every trick he knew to keep from thinking about the implications of the order he was about to carry out. It did little good.

There will be no way to call for help from the other ships in an emergency, he thought. *Especially if the other colonels order their com systems offline in retaliation.* Shivers wracked his body, but they were not from the cold. *We also need our com system to receive data from the approach probe when the time comes. No, you can't let him forget that. That would be a fatal mistake.*

Darius entered the core and secured his frame to the terminal chair.

XCS-02 MAINFRAME LOGIN:

Darius logged in.

OWENS, LT. DARIUS. ENABLE VOICE INTERFACE?

Not today, computer. Darius answered with keystrokes.

COMMAND?

His hands rested along the edges of the screen as he stared at the cursor flashing back at him. He hesitated several times as he brought his hands to the screen and started work on disabling the communications system. He fought himself every time he drilled down to a new layer of the software.

This isn't right. Darius removed his hands from the terminal screen and folded them in his lap. *I could simply not do it.* He nodded to himself, but cut himself short. *And if Colonel Eriksen finds out, I get put in stasis for the rest of the trip. If we survive and land, I get a hearing for my insubordination.*

He placed his hands on the smooth screen and within minutes had executed the colonel's order. *I guess this is called the lesser of two evils.* Darius turned off the mainframe terminal screen, closed his eyes, and hung his head. A seed of doubt grew within his mind.

This mission is dangerous enough as it is. Even with everything going smoothly our chances of landing and surviving aren't great. Despite all that, our COs can't seem to see eye to eye with each other. He shook his head and sighed. *We might as well just open the airlocks and get it over with if we can't get someone to lead around here.*

Darius unbuckled the restraints and shrugged them off, then made his way out of the core and back into the gallery. Emptiness washed over him. He had no duty to perform, and no desire to seek entertainment. He drifted forward aimlessly, propelling himself from brace to brace, over the rows of silent carts, and past the great dark maw leading to the lower level.

Darius grabbed a brace just outside of one of the sleeper pods and halted his momentum. As he clung to it, the bitter cold of the steel felt as if it would burn his hands, but he did not care. He put his cheek to the bare metal and closed his eyes.

Atlanta was never this cold, not even in the winter.

He looked back on how his life had put him aboard this ship, a light year from Earth. Darius had always been smart and athletic, but never stood out at any one thing. He was one of the most talented offensive tackles on his team in high school, but he was nowhere near good enough to get a scholarship for his play. Likewise he had shown a knack for puzzles and computers growing up, yet his other studies held him back in the increasingly competitive arena of college entrance.

Darius laughed under his breath when he remembered meeting the Air Force recruiter. His uniform was neat and crisp, his smile was as warm as the sun, but what Darius remembered most were the words he used. The recruiter filled Darius with confidence that the Air Force could fulfill his dreams of college and travel as easily as a clown might blow up a balloon. Darius had run home to his mother to tell her about the opportunity. Darius remembered how she looked at him with such a cautious expression, but how she relayed to him the stories of what the Army had done for his father, both during and after his service.

That was all the encouragement that Darius needed. He signed up the first chance he could get and was shipped to Basic weeks later.

They gave me training, and the travel that I have done so far has exceeded the dreams of any high school kid. Although at this point I don't think I'll get to go to college when I'm out.

"I see I'm not the only one who daydreams around here." A soft, accented voice brought him back to the ship.

"No man is an angel, Doc. Every man is a dreamer."

Dr. Kimura smiled warmly at Darius. "This is true. A man cannot hope to find his path without a dream. Tell me, what is it that you dream of so fondly that you can't let go of that beam?"

"Home. Years past." He let go of the brace and gave it a short glance.

"Undoubtedly happy memories of family and friends."

"I'll take anything I can get at this point," Darius replied.

Dr. Kimura paused briefly and the smile evaporated from his face. "Something troubles you, then?"

"Yeah."

"Please, tell me. Maybe I can help."

"I would if I could, believe me. But you can't help in the matter."

"I can try if you let me, Darius."

He shook his head. "I can't even get that far. I have orders."

"I see." Kimura paused again. "If there ever *is* anything I can do for you, do not hesitate to ask. I know that you saved my life."

Darius gave Kimura a shocked look. He hushed his voice to a whisper and asked, "How do you know that?"

"Please," the doctor responded with a slight laugh. "I was not told by anyone. Do not forget who helped design this ship. I pieced together what happened based on Colonel Eriksen's investigation and the project I know you've been working on since we left Earth. The colonel's precious classified information is still a secret."

Darius gave a weak smile. "Good point. I'll remember to ask you if I need something." He bowed courteously toward Dr. Kimura, which caused him to flip over forward. Kimura laughed and retreated to his sleeper pod. Darius sighed and frowned.

You may not have your freedom when we get there, Doc. I hope I can actually take you up on that promise.

• • •

Haruka struggled to right herself as she caught the handle of a cart. It groaned as it pulled at its shackles. One of the three meal pouches tucked under her arm tried to squirt free. She carefully pulled her crooked arm forward and let go of the cart to quickly adjust her load. Her lungs drew in a deep breath, which she pushed out as she prepared herself for the next push toward the propulsion section.

Damn, this is harder than it looks. I'll be lucky if I can surprise them. Her stomach grumbled at her. *Then again they may not care about the surprise, just the food.*

She was thankful that she had chosen to raid food from pod fourteen, one of the rearmost sleeper pods. Anything farther forward would have made her journey with lunch that much harder. Haruka pulled herself down to the deck, braced her legs on the plating, and shot toward the rear airlock. She could feel the cold air rush past her cheeks as she flew, hugging the meals to her chest.

She realized too late that her trajectory through the mouth of the airlock was slightly off. She tried to twist around to avoid impacting the wall head-first and managed to get her shoulder in front of her just before she bumped onto it. This broke her grasp, and the meal pouches scattered down the hallway. Haruka cursed under her breath and carefully navigated the hallway, collecting the pouches as she went.

She reached the hatch to the propulsion control room and found that she could not open the latch while holding lunch, so she carefully set it adrift and yanked on the handle. It gave way and the hatch opened with a metallic groan. Once more she rounded up the food and brought it in.

Lieutenant Mancini watched her entrance from his control station. Airman Nova Weyler had her back turned, her attention squarely on whatever she was monitoring on her terminal.

"Look who's here, Nova," Mancini smiled.

"And with lunch," Haruka added as she lightly flung a pouch at Mancini.

"So the Princess not only graces us with her presence, but also serves us. What did us humble little folk do so right?" Mancini teased.

"Oh, stow it Marco." She looked at Nova, who was still staring at the screen. "Nova, are you even alive over there?"

Her head snapped up and whipped around, and her blonde hair wrapped across her face a split second later. Nova reached up and parted her locks from her face. "Huh? What?"

"Food." Haruka tossed a pouch at the younger woman. "Try not to forget to eat since starvation makes work a lot harder."

"Sorry, Captain. I'll try not to."

"I keep telling you it's ok to call me Haruka."

"Haruka," Nova corrected. "Sorry. Just not used to being on a first name basis with officers."

"Don't worry about it." Haruka took the last open seat and strapped in, then tore her provisions open and produced a bag of stroganoff. "Yuck."

Mancini chuckled. "Did the Princess forget to check what meal she had before opening it?"

"Shut it, Marco."

There was truth to what he said, however. Haruka had forgotten to check the meals before handing them out. Mancini dug his fork into his bag, drew out a bite of chicken, and ate it with as much dramatic flair as he could muster.

"Mmm. Tastes like chicken. How 'bout yours, Kimura?"

She shook her head as she gave an exasperated sigh. *I'm so glad we are only awake for a week at a time. I'd throttle him if it were much longer.*

"So how is life on the bridge, Capt... I mean, Haruka," Nova asked.

She glanced over her shoulder at Nova before returning her attention to lunch. "Well, other than wracking my brains on these course corrections, not too shabby."

"Course corrections," Mancini repeated. "What course corrections would those be?"

Haruka froze mid-bite. *Crap. I wasn't supposed to tell them.* She quickly thought of what she should say to her friends.

"Nothing important," she bluffed. "Just trying to figure out when I'm going to fire the attitude thrusters, just in case."

"Why, what's wrong?"

She searched for her next lie. "It looks like we've been doing a very slow corkscrew motion," she said as she motioned with her finger. "We might end up upside down when we reach the planet, so we're going to have to roll and correct that at some point. I've just been trying to figure out the best time to do it, that's all." She turned again to Nova. "I trust the thrusters are still in good shape?"

"What?" Nova seemed lost in thought for a moment. "Oh, yeah. They're fine."

"Good. Then we have nothing to worry about."

Mancini grinned again. "Good. I'd hate to have to enjoy those warm, sunny beaches I've been dreaming of dangling from a harness."

"Yeah, that would spoil your quest for a margarita, wouldn't it Prince Marco?"

"Yep. And we can't have that."

Haruka chuckled. "So how's life back here in the ass end of space?"

"Oh, just peachy," replied Mancini. "Since you've been gone I haven't been more than thirty feet from that damned reactor, since little miss cherry picker over here gets on duty first and bolts."

"Hey," Nova protested.

Haruka laughed. "It sounds like karma's been biting you, Marco. You stuck me with the reactor enough yourself."

He sighed. "Yeah, there is that. But in truth, we'll probably be done early. Nova is really fast with her work. In fact, I'd say that unless Major Emberley has any other operational items or you still need to crunch your numbers, we can probably all head off to sleep tonight for a nice five year nap."

"I can't complain about that idea. The fewer days we stay awake, the better in my opinion."

"That's right. Fewer days in this tin can, more days working on my tan."

Haruka gagged mockingly. "How poetic."

They continued eating in silence. Haruka occasionally shot a glance at Nova, who sat in silence with only the back of her head visible over the seat. *She's been awfully quiet. I wonder if she's ok.*

Mancini belched loudly. A moment later, Haruka could smell the tang of marinated chicken.

"Ugh, really Marco," she complained.

"What? Couldn't hold it in forever."

"Whatever. I think the computer core is calling your name, maybe you want to make friends with it."

He frowned. "That's harsh, Kimura."

"Seriously," she said sternly. "Beat it before I make you listen to girl talk."

She heard him quickly unbuckle. "Alright, I know what's best for my own health." Mancini made his way through the hatch and closed it behind him.

Haruka released her straps and collected the trash floating around the compartment. She watched Nova as she worked, but the young airman seemed to avoid eye contact with her. After she rounded up the errant bits of packaging, she stowed them.

"What's wrong, Nova?"

"Huh? Oh, nothing," she replied with a slight hesitation.

Haruka moved to the side of Nova's workstation. She steadied herself with one arm on the terminal and the other on the bulkhead. "That's not what it looks like to me. Are you upset? Have I done something? Has Marco?" Nova bit her lip and turned her head away from Haruka. Haruka leaned to her left, trying to regain eye contact. "It's Marco, isn't it?"

"I don't want to cause any trouble, Captain."

"Please, it's Haruka," she said. She was beginning to wonder if she sounded like a broken record. "And if he's doing something wrong, just let me know. I can make him stop, whatever it is."

The blonde girl looked up at Haruka and sighed. "I'm sure he's a nice guy, but he keeps hitting on me. It creeps me out."

That hairy, pint-sized jerk. I told him to leave her alone...

Haruka smiled at Nova. "Say no more, I'll make sure he keeps it professional from now on."

"Please, forget I said anything. I don't want him to take this out on me."

"Don't worry. Marco's really harmless. He just gets... ah... excited sometimes."

"Are you sure?" asked Nova, her voice almost a squeak.

"Positive. Now if you're as far ahead as Marco said you are, go ahead and get back to work." Haruka looked at the hatch that led to the core and gallery. "The sooner we can get this over with, the better."

"Yes, Captain."

"Haruka," she said with an exasperated sigh.

"Sorry. Haruka."

"You're never going to get used to that, are you?"

"Probably not."

"Alright. Well, see you for chow, Nova." Haruka received a nod from Nova, and then she exited through the hatch. She made a bee line for the computer core and flung its door open.

Mancini was at the mainframe terminal. His head was down and he listened to a headset that he cradled to his ear in one hand; he had a tendency not to wear such equipment if he was not going to use it for long.

Haruka pushed herself straight down an aisle between server racks, straight to the chair where Mancini sat. She halted herself with the chair, which jostled Mancini.

"Hey, what the…" was all he got out of his mouth before Haruka delivered a sickening slap to the back of his head. The headset flew from his hand and yanked back as it reached the end of its cord. "Ow. What the hell, Kimura?"

"Just jogging your memory, Marco," she said, trying to hold back her fury. "Is it working?"

"Well, you've got my attention at least." He rubbed the back of his head. "Would you mind just telling me what this is about? I don't want to play 20 Questions for Marco because I know what you give for wrong answers."

"Nova."

"What about her?"

"Stop trying to get in her flight suit."

Mancini's eyes narrowed and his jaw slacked; Haruka knew he was thinking. "What the hell are you talking about?"

Haruka growled and raised her hand. She brought it down to smack him again, but he caught her by the wrist.

"Whoa, whoa, seriously Kimura," he said as his voice rose. "I don't know what you're talking about."

"Right, so that's why she told me that you've been hitting on her and creeping me out I suppose."

"What? When?"

"When you've been working together," she snapped back. She pushed her legs back from the chair and yanked free of his grip. The momentum sent her crashing into a server rack behind her.

J.C. Rainier

"When I've been working with…" he trailed off as he processed. "I've seen her a grand total of maybe a half hour this cycle. Most of that was just before you came in with lunch. The rest of the time I've been inspecting that god damned reactor or my butt's been stuck in a generator tube."

"Don't lie to me, Marco, I swear to God."

"I'm not lying, Kimura. Look at me." He looked directly at her, as if he was begging her to look in his eyes. "I'm telling you the truth. You told me last cycle not to mess with her and I'm not."

Haruka moved back to Marco and looked him square in the eye. *He's telling the truth.* She sighed. "I'm sorry, Marco. I believe you."

Mancini rubbed his head again. "I know you're protective of your girl there, but that was kind of overboard, don't you think?"

Haruka felt her cheeks flush. She averted her eyes. "I'm sorry. Can you forgive me?"

Mancini gave a laugh that was half snort. "Don't worry about it. I'm still your man, no matter what." She felt his hand clasp her forearm.

"Thanks. I'll make it up to you, I swear."

"I'll tell you how," he said with a devilish grin. "We're upgrading from a breakfast date to a dinner date when we get to the planet."

"Okay, fine. But the same rules apply. Try anything funny and I'll break your nose myself."

"Alright, it's a date then," he said cheerfully.

Haruka turned and left the computer core. She slid the hatch shut behind her. With one hand still on the lever, she dropped her head, and imagined the awkward date she had just signed herself up for.

I really don't want to get deeper in debt with him. If I keep up at this rate, he'll say I owe him a kiss. She shuddered and made way for the bridge.

. . .

Calvin McLaughlin
Date and time unknown
Michael
>|

The deck plate clanked with every footfall. Faint echoes bounced off of the dark walls and tickled his ears. Calvin did not stop running; his heart pounded and his lungs swallowed great breaths of air, yet his legs did not tire. They could not, for he could not afford to stop.

The echoes of his steps were drowned out by another chorus of voices from the darkness behind. At best they spoke gibberish, but most either laughed at him or hurled unintelligible insults at him. He clutched his ears as he ran in a vain attempt to block the assault on his mind.

Make them stop! When will they stop?

Cal could not be sure how long he had been running. His mind was aware that he was dreaming, but time had no reference in stasis. All he knew is that he had been running since he fell asleep, and it felt like a week. Two days ago he had stopped trying to figure out if his legs were still attached or if they had actually fallen off. Two days prior to that, he had stopped contemplating just how long *Michael* had to be for him to run in a straight line for so long.

He could no longer hear the voices. Cal dropped his arms from his head and resumed pumping them in a renewed sprint. He laughed maniacally.

"I'm beating them! I can run faster than sound," he shouted.

A few moments later, the cacophony came back. He screeched and threw his hands back to his ears in an ineffective bid to stop it.

"Oh God, make it stop," he pled to the darkness.

This pattern played itself out for the next fifteen minutes. Every time Cal thought he had shaken the voices, they seemed to come back a little stronger. Each time he ran with a more fevered stride, until he could no longer outrun them.

Coward, a single word tore through his mind like scissors through paper.

Cal faltered, and he tumbled to a stop on the deck plating; his right hand complained with a sharp stabbing pain. He looked at his hand and saw his fingers taped together, where moments earlier it had been free and whole.

Cal rose to his knees and looked around the dim corridor. A pair of dark braces jutted up from behind him like teeth in the shadows. He was alone, and defenseless.

"Come on, bring it on," he challenged the darkness.

Coward, the voice said again. The tone was clearer and it had a peculiar familiarity to it.

His hands began to tremble. "Show yourself," he said as his voice cracked. "If you're going to call me a coward, show your damned face."

Cal heard an echoing in the distance. It was not a voice, but rather a metallic noise that was moving slowly closer. He strained for a moment and realized that it was the echo of footsteps on the deck plating.

"About time," he taunted as he looked down the gallery.

He could make out a shadowy figure walking toward him about fifty feet away. Whoever it was had a long stride, and was very tall; possibly as tall as Calvin himself. As the apparition approached, he saw that it was also slender and walked in an ungainly fashion. Then a detail caught his eye, and Cal's jaw slacked.

The fingers on the right hand are taped together.

The figure emerged from the shadows behind the structural braces, shrouded in a disheveled blue flight suit bearing the name "Forrest" on the chest. Cal looked down at his own attire and saw the name on his own flight suit. He snapped his head up and found himself staring into his own blue eyes.

"You heard me, coward," sneered his doppelganger.

Cal could not form any words, nor could he even scoff in response. A lump rose in his throat and tightened it so hard he felt as if he was being strangled.

His clone began to circle to his left. "No wonder Dad said you're a loser. Look at you."

No...

"A little trouble comes up and you run away," it continued. "You know you're taking the easy way out. Just admit it."

"NO!"

"No? Funny, because it seems to me that you could have worked it all out if you had just tried."

"I'm losing my mind, you should know that," Cal retorted.

"*Could* be losing your mind," it corrected as it walked behind him. Cal could feel the weight of its stare as the hairs on his neck rose. "Or you could just be stressed out, ever thought of that?"

"No, not at all. Life on this bucket is a peach." He managed to force a spate of sarcasm from his tightened throat.

The doppelganger ignored him. "You were learning a skill. No, make that two skills. But hey, you've thrown that away too just to go hide in a hole."

"That wasn't a skill. Doctor Taylor was just using me to make her job easier. Any monkey could learn to do that. As for the book, I just got bored."

"Bull," it spat as it crossed back into Cal's line of vision. "Nobody has ever read a chemistry book because they were bored. The only thing worse than a coward is a lying coward."

Cal closed his eyes and tried to shake off the sting of that slight.

"What the hell were you hoping to learn, anyway?"

"Something I could do to help on the planet," he replied as he opened his eyes. The apparition had stopped in front of him and was glaring daggers.

"There you go. You had to go and read a book because you knew somewhere inside that thick skull of yours that you were a waste of space on this mission." It tapped on its temple in a dramatic manner. "And guess what? You were right."

Cal clenched his jaw, barely missing his tongue as he bit down. He balled his left hand into a fist.

It looked down at his hand for a moment, and then back to his eyes and laughed. "You're going to hit me? I think that's the dumbest in a long line of dumb decisions you've made."

Cal narrowed his eyes and stared into its piercing blue eyes. It seemed as if it could peer through him and read him like a book.

Of course it can, it's me.

He straightened up and relaxed his hand as he tried to regain composure. "I'm not perfect, but I'm trying."

"You *were* trying." It seemed to fashion each correction into its own insult. "You just ended up doing what you always do; giving up and running away."
Cal could feel his temper rise. "Just how am I running away this time?"

"Duh, by going into stasis for the rest of the trip. You've stopped your studies, you've shown Colonel Dayton and the crew that you can't handle life…" It trailed off and then grinned evilly. "Did I forget to mention how you gave up on Alexis?"

"I did *not* give up on her. She wanted to go into…"

"She was testing you, jackass," his double interrupted. It cupped its hands to its mouth. "News flash: you failed."

Cal spun quickly around so he could not see his own face judging him. His arms went rigid and he curled both hands into fists, despite the protests from his broken finger. His gaze peered deep into the darkness.

"No," Cal said sternly.

"Yes, you failed."

"No I didn't." He wheeled around to face his assailant once more. "She wanted to be put in stasis. Knowing what I know now, I still would have put her in stasis. Do you think that either one of us would have enjoyed watching me spin out of control and go insane?" Cal waited for a response that never came. "How much more damage would that have caused? No thank you, I'd rather fail the test."

"She's still going to think you're weak when she wakes up."

"She'll get over it."

"Will she?"

Cal wished that he could wipe the smirk off of the apparition's face. *It does have a point. Will she get over it?*

"That's not the worst that she'll think, and you know it," it continued.

Cal tried to force the lump from his throat. "I know it. That's something I just have to face."

"How?"

"I don't have to explain it to you. You already know how."

Cal could see his double's jaw clench. He recognized the look of frustration on his own face. "I hope you know what you're doing, then. Remember, your plan hinges on technical prowess that you don't actually have thanks to slacking off in school."

"Again, leave that to me," he said as he stood his ground.

The doppelganger sized him up and nodded. "Good luck with that. Oh and tell Dad hi next time you see him." It turned and walked quickly back into the darkness.

A chill went down Cal's spine. The words of his double struck a chord with him.

I'm not going to wake up any time soon. There are more nightmares to come.

Cal took a deep breath and screwed up his courage. He walked into the darkness beyond the shadowy fangs.

• • •

The course projections on Haruka's screen blurred into a thick, white mass. She blinked and rubbed her eyes, but it did nothing to clarify her vision. Her back ached and her stomach growled like an upset lap dog.

It's no good. I can't get it any closer, she thought. *If I stare at this screen any longer today, my head will pop.*

Yesterday she stayed at her terminal for twelve straight hours running nav simulations. She was aware that she was well over ten hours today. Once again, Nova was ahead of schedule with her propulsion maintenance. Ops was running on a light schedule this cycle. Everything seemed to be pushing Haruka into a position where she had less and less time to solve the course correction problem.

Haruka did not seem to be nearing a solution, either. She had been taking an approach of testing one variable set at a time to isolate its effect on the ship's trajectory. In her latest calculations, she was able to get *Raphael* as far as the planet, but the massive sleeper ship was still carrying too much speed, and skipped right through the atmosphere.

She had even tried a slow burn of the braking drive during the final maintenance cycle, but the results of those simulations were even more horrifying; *Raphael* became unpredictable and would veer wildly off course. Some predictions even showed the ship crashing into one of Demeter's projected moons, or the massive gas giant that circled both stars.

If I don't find the solution, we're as good as dead. I have to keep going. She was caught by surprise by a massive yawn. *Ugh. Okay, maybe just one more simulation tonight.*

Haruka rubbed her eyes again and reset the parameters for the simulation. The computer populated all known variables based on the ship's present course. She read each individual field carefully, desperate to find a clue hidden within that she had overlooked before. Nothing stood out, every reading from ship speed to roll rate and thrust power remained exactly the same as every other time she had tried to analyze the data.

She sighed and smashed the palms of her hands into the terminal in frustration. *There's not enough time. Not enough time to figure out this problem, not enough time to turn the ship, not enough time to slow the ship down.*

She looked at the time clock on her screen as it flipped over a minute mark. *One would think that with twenty five years left, I'd be able to figure this...*

Her head snapped up and she looked directly in front of her at an orange dot far in the distance, larger than any of the other stars in the field.

"That's it," she yelled excitedly. "Time!"

Haruka scrolled her finger over the parameters until she found the start time for the braking maneuver. *I don't need to brake three years early, that's why the ship kept going too far off course.* She laughed at herself and shook her head as she plugged a new number in for the braking start. *If I can get an extra week on approach, that should give us enough time. Maybe even some room for error.*

She started the simulation one more time. As she watched the final approach of *Raphael*, she drew in a deep breath and held it. Seconds ticked by and the tiny white dot neared the planet. Haruka had not realized that she still held her breath until she nearly passed out. The air rushed from her lungs and she panted as her lungs forced her to breathe.

Damn it, Haruka, breathe. You can run the sim again if it doesn't work.

Raphael approached the orbital path of Demeter. A smile crept across Haruka's face as the ship appeared to be dead on course for the entry plane. A movement from the corner of her eye caught her attention, and she glanced at the side of the screen. Demeter's closer moon bore down on *Raphael*. The tiny ship disappeared from view as it appeared to get sucked into the gravity well of the satellite.

The words she had come to dread flashed across the screen in bold, red letters: SIMULATION TERMINATED. SURVIVAL CHANCE: 0%

Haruka slammed her fist on the terminal again. *Damn it. Damn you, Fox. Damn you, Bartrand. You've killed us all.* She grabbed her long, black hair in her hands and screamed. *Damn your arrogance!* She found herself growling as a way to keep from screaming her lungs inside out. Her hands shook furiously, and she thought at any minute that she might tear clumps of her hair from her skull.

"Bad day, Captain?" Major Emberley snuck up from behind her; not a difficult task given how much of a ruckus she had made.

"Sir," she straightened herself up and saluted, "apologies for my

J.C. Rainier

poor behavior. It won't happen again."

Emberley hoisted himself gently over the railing and into the seat next to Haruka. He looked at the slash of red across her terminal. "Still no luck with the course corrections?" His voice was calm, almost to the point of being unsettling.

"Very close, sir. This is the closest sim I've run yet, but we cross the inner moon's orbit at the wrong time."

"I see. So why the outburst? I'm sure that a minor tweak of what you're working on here will get us there." He smiled softly at Haruka. "You've almost got us there already."

Haruka closed her eyes and rubbed the bridge of her nose. *He's right. God, how could I have been so childish? I can fix this. I just need… uhh…*

"Captain?"

"Sorry, sir. Just thinking." She opened her eyes to see her commanding officer looking at her with apparent concern.

"Well, you look like hell. Go to sleep, Kimura."

"I can do this, sir," she protested.

"That's right, you can. Just not tonight. Go to sleep, that's an order," Emberley said, his voice firm.

She sighed and stretched her legs one at a time. "Yes sir." Haruka loosened her harness and pulled herself over the bar, down the length of the bridge. She spiraled down the staircase and into the crew pod, where she bumped into Mancini.

"Hey, watch it," he grumbled.

Haruka flailed her arm out and steadied against the wall. "Sorry, Marco."

He squinted at her. "Jesus, you look like someone gave you a bunch of sugared up kids to watch."

Haruka realized how sapped she was. "Kinda feel like it too. It's been a really long day. How're things going for you?"

A slight frown drooped across Mancini's face. "Lonely. It's really great that you found your way back to the bridge, but I really miss talking with you. Nova hasn't been around again."

Haruka paused for a moment in thought. "Has she been reporting for duty?"

"Yeah, the girl's a real hard worker. She's got all the thrusters inspected, and is almost done with the plasma drive. But it's almost like she's avoiding me."

No wonders there, not after she made up that shit about Marco.

"Sorry to hear that." She put her hand on his shoulder and grinned. "But I might just have some good news for you."

His eyes perked up. "Yeah?"

"Yeah. I'm going to ask the major if I can borrow you from propulsion for a bit. I might need you to tweak something in the computer core for me as part of my course corrections."

Just as quickly, his expression became deflated. "Yeah, I guess that's better than sitting alone in propulsion."

He really does just want some company, doesn't he? Haruka felt sorry for Mancini; she was so absorbed in her work that she didn't consider what her absence meant to him.

She smiled and feigned a cheerful voice. "Hey, I need to tell you what to fix, right? I'm coming into the core with you to hammer this out."

Again Mancini's face lit up. "Oh yeah, I suppose that makes more sense, huh?"

"I just have to get one more thing done on the bridge, so we'll probably do this tomorrow after lunch. Thirteen hundred hours?"

"You got it, Captain."

"Good night, Lieutenant," she said as she opened her sleeper berth and pulled her body inside. Haruka buckled her restraint and closed the hatch.

Having Marco give me the extra time I need will be a snap. Figuring out how to get around that damned moon, on the other hand... just how the hell am I going to do that?

. . .

Darius and Captain Quinn waited on the bridge, facing each other across the empty command chair. Each man grasped the railing behind him and avoided eye contact with the other. The silence was awkward, but they had nothing to talk about; conversation on *Gabriel* had long turned stale. Though each crew member spent only a few days awake each cycle, the long hibernations were taking their toll on morale.

The fact that Colonel Eriksen seemed to be increasingly late for his duty or to meetings was also starting to wear on Darius. While he was by no means punctual as a youth, Darius had come to appreciate both structure and punctuality after he joined the service.

He drummed his fingers impatiently on the metal railing. Quinn glanced up at him, a bored look on his face. "Give him a minute, Lieutenant."

Darius just shrugged and rolled his head toward the rear of the bridge. *I've already given him fifteen. Besides, it's not like I have any choice but to wait.* The mouth of the bridge remained a dark hole; Darius watched for Eriksen to emerge as a child might watch a pot on the stove in anticipation of when it would boil.

Several minutes later, Colonel Eriksen emerged from the darkness and made his way to the command chair. Darius watched as he secured his broad frame to the chair and cleared his throat.

"Sorry for the delay, gentlemen," he said, his voice devoid of all emotion. "Let's get started. I would like an update from each of you regarding the investigation. Lieutenant Owens, any progress in identifying who wrote the assassination program?"

Darius did his best to straighten his posture. "I've analyzed the code from end to end, Colonel. Whoever wrote it was extremely thorough. Beyond the knowledge of which ship it came from, all I have been able to find out is that it had to be sent from *Raphael's* computer core. None of the terminal workstations could have sent this due to a specific exploit that the program uses."

Eriksen scratched his beard and frowned. "So nothing that would shed any light on who might have done it, then?"

Darius thought for a moment. "I'm not sure if it helps, but they may have intimate knowledge of the Oort and approach probes. The exploit is the same one those probes use to feed data to the nav system."

"Hmm. Alright." Colonel Eriksen turned to face Captain Quinn. "Captain, have you made any progress in identifying a suspect?"

"I have reviewed the files of every crew member and passenger on *Raphael*," Quinn replied quickly. "I think we can conclusively rule out any civilian in this matter based on what Owens just said, Colonel. There doesn't appear to be a civilian in the file who has any connection to Project Columbus, except for the ship's doctor."

"What about the crew?"

"Only the thinnest of anomalies, sir. I've got a lieutenant who has significant computer experience who was originally assigned to *Michael*, and an airman whose enlistment date and basic training camp were in different years. Even thinner threads still are those of the only Canadian and Mexican citizens on board the ship. One is a major we received in an officer exchange from the RCAF, and the other enlisted in our service, possibly to gain citizenship."

He didn't bring up Singh, Darius thought. *Maybe he thinks I'm right about the terrorism idea.*

Eriksen appeared to yawn as he scratched his beard again. "We can probably ignore those last two." He paused for a second. "Scratch that, the last three. The only thing that sounds plausible so far is that crewman assigned originally to *Michael*. What do we know about him, Quinn?"

"Just a moment, sir." Quinn did a neat back flip over the bar and landed in his workstation chair. His fingers flew across the screen in precise motion as he recalled a file from the computer. "First Lieutenant Marco Mancini. Born March 9th, 1989 in Brooklyn, New York. He got his computer science degree from NYU and joined the service through AFROTC. There are a couple marks on his disciplinary record. They look like minor incidents, but two of them refer to a…" his voice trailed off as he peered at the screen. "Lieutenant Haruka Kimura."

"Kimura," Eriksen repeated. "Any relationship to Doctor Kimura?"

"Yes sir. She's his daughter."

"These incidents you speak of, what are they?"

Quinn tapped his screen a few times. "Looks like they were bar fights, sir." He cocked his head to the side and whistled. "This guy is a bit out of control, if you ask me. I wonder why he's even assigned to this mission."

Eriksen waved dismissively at Quinn, a gesture that Darius found odd since the engineer could not see it from where he sat. "We can't question that part right now. What did Lieutenant Kimura have to do with them?"

"Just a second, sir". Quinn took a moment before he came back with an answer. "It seems that in both of the incidents, Lieutenant Mancini provoked fights with the boyfriend and the brother of two different women. Each time, Lieutenant Kimura intervened, apparently by beating the tar out of the other men."

Darius chuckled. He stopped quickly when Eriksen shot him a dirty look. "Sorry, sir." He smiled at the colonel. "It was just kind of funny."

"Try to be serious, Mr. Owens," he said in a scolding tone, then turned back to the engineering terminals. "There might be something there, but I'm having a hard time seeing how it helps. Lieutenant Kimura came to the aid of Mancini in these occasions. Why would he try to kill Doctor Kimura?"

Quinn turned around in his seat. "Beats me, sir. This whole thing doesn't make sense to me."

Eriksen sighed. "If only that damned arrogant fool Fox would talk to me, we might be getting somewhere."

Darius intervened quickly, "May I make a suggestion, Colonel?"

"Of course, Mr. Owens."

"It occurred to me that the assassin might be afraid of the exploit being used against them if they were discovered. If they were able to send a program that sophisticated, certainly they know enough about *Raphael* to disable the external com system."

Eriksen bolted upright and the clasps on his harness rattled. "So Fox can't even hear me when I call her." His fist slammed into the arm rest of his chair. "Damn, you're right." He unlocked his chair and swiveled to face the bow of the ship. Darius could only see his receding red hair over the top of the chair. "And she's out there, probably unaware of what has happened."

"And we have no way of informing her, sir," added Darius.

"Very well," Eriksen said in his command voice. "We've done all we can do from here. Once we arrive we can join forces with Colonel Fox to catch this assassin. Resume your normal duties, gentlemen."

"Yes sir," Darius and Quinn responded simultaneously.

Darius exited the bridge and floated down the gallery toward the computer core.

Add that to the list of tasks when we get to the planet. We better not get too many more, or we won't have any time to set up a colony.

. . .

Haruka's eyes were glued to the terminal screen. She had to remind herself to keep breathing. A thin white line drew from the bottom directly to the entry plane of Demeter's atmosphere.

C'mon, be right this time. I was so close on the last try.

The blip that represented *Raphael* emerged from the lower edge and glided along the projection line. Haruka glanced at the left side of her screen; the dotted outline of Demeter's near moon swooped onto the screen.

Show time, she thought. With a flick of her wrist, the view changed from a top-down to an angled 3D model. The moon now appeared spherical, and the course of *Raphael* was a thin arc that seemed to skip by the planet near its northern pole. Haruka watched as the moon bore down on the ship. A grin crept across her face. *It's going to clear this time.*

Raphael passed over the moon, and the approach arc dipped down close to the equator. The ship pitched down with the new course and finished its approach to the planet.

SIMULATION TERMINATED. SURVIVAL CHANCE: 97.82%

"Yes!" she screamed and threw her hands into the air in triumph. She unbuckled, spun in her seat, and pulled herself up on the railing. "Calculations for course correction are complete, Major."

The gray haired commander gave her a toothy smile. "Excellent work, Captain. What do you need to make it work?"

"I need Mancini to modify the proximity program for crew revival, sir."

Emberley nodded. "How much extra time will you need at the start of the approach cycle?"

Haruka glanced back at her terminal to read the start time for the maneuver. "Four days."

"Permission granted, Captain Kimura. Have him revive both you and I early. Do you need anyone else to join us?"

She nodded. "We'll need an engineer to help fire up the braking drive and the plasma thrusters."

"Indeed. Have Lieutenant Mancini revive Captain Maynard as well."

Maynard? Why not Nova?

"Sir, with all due respect," she said, "why not Airman Weyler? She has been on propulsion maintenance the whole time."

"I appreciate the suggestion," replied Emberley, "but I want the best crew available to work on this solution. We have no more room for error."

"Yes sir," she said. *Nova has a lot of hands on experience, but I guess Captain Maynard will do. I've won enough of a victory today.*

"Kimura…"

"Yes sir?"

"When we land, I do believe we will all owe you something. Will you… will you have a drink with me?" His voice sounded almost like an awkward teenager asking for a date.

Haruka was taken aback. Her mouth dropped open and she wondered if she had heard that correctly. "Sir?"

"A drink. Will you share one with me? I've got a private stash on board."

"I… I don't know what to say." Haruka paused again. "Only if the whole crew gets to toast, sir. We were all in this together. They should share the rewards."

Emberley smiled. "Of course. I wouldn't have it any other way." He glanced out the forward windows. "You're a hero, Kimura."

"Heroes get themselves killed, sir."

The colonel looked at Haruka, confusion written on his face. "Excuse me, Captain?"

"Just a saying, sir. If you don't mind, I'd like to go get started with Mancini."

"Of course. Carry on."

Haruka gave a quick salute and left the bridge. She reached the open airlock to the gallery when her stomach reminded her that she needed to eat. She grabbed the frame of the airlock and turned about, then made her way to the crew pod. She made her way into the storage locker and took a moment to select a suitable meal. Haruka then made her way out of the pod once more, tucked the pouch under her arm, and made off down the gallery toward the propulsion section.

She looked around at her surroundings as she drew in the stale, sterile air. She could faintly see her breath cloud up as she exhaled. *It's getting colder in here. I should probably bring that up with Marco.*

Minutes passed before Haruka reached the airlock to the propulsion section. She made her way to the propulsion control room and opened the hatch. Mancini was inside, with his neck craned toward the door to see who had come to visit.

"C'mon, Marco. Time to go to the core," she said.

Mancini tore his harness off faster than Haruka had ever seen before. "Finally," he exclaimed and shot past her.

Haruka laughed and chased after him down the hall and into the computer core. He beat her through the door and raced between the server racks to the mainframe. Haruka caught up a moment later and stopped herself at the back of the chair. She grabbed her meal pouch from under her arm and tore it open.

"Alright," he said as he fired up the mainframe. She watched over his shoulder. "Let's do this."

XCS-03-R MAINFRAME LOGIN:

Mancini put his credentials into the terminal as Haruka began to eat a neatly formed sandwich.

XCS-03-R LOGIN ACCEPTED. MANCINI, LT. MARCO. MAINFRAME ACCESS ENABLED. VOICE INTERFACE ERROR, MANUAL COMMANDS ONLY.

Mancini paused when he read the error from the screen. "Huh, that's odd."

Haruka almost choked on her bite of food. *Odd? No, no odd. I don't need any more odd, Marco.* She shuddered at the thought of another issue with the ship. "Odd like trivia knowledge, or odd like 'my God, we're all going to die'?"

"Oh, probably nothing," he assured her. "It just looks like there's something wrong with the voice routine. So, what do you need me to do for you here?"

"I need a few more days at the beginning of the approach cycle."

"Days, huh? The proximity cycle is programmed based on calculated distance, not time," he said as he pecked at buttons on the screen. "Have you figured out how much distance that is?"

"Damn," she cursed. "No. Let me see if I can do the math."

"Do you at least know how fast we're moving?"

"Yeah, that's easy. I had to figure that out so I could calculate braking. We're doing point one zero zero four *c*."

Haruka watched as Mancini placed a set of calculations into the mainframe for processing. The computer whirred for a second and then chirped. "Got it. This will be a breeze."

One less thing to worry about.
"I'm really glad that you can help with this, Marco. It's going to make my life so much easier later on."

"Yeah, sure thing, Kimura. It's good to be away from…" Mancini's voice trailed off.

"Away from the reactor, right?" Haruka waited for a response from Mancini, but he said nothing. "Marco? Is something wrong?"

"Something's screwy. Look at this," He tapped on the last response from the mainframe.

WARNING. PROXIMITY ROUTINE OFFLINE. SYSTEM FAILURE.

"Crap, that can't be good. Can you fix it?"

"Gotta find out what's wrong first." He tapped away at the virtual keyboard.

PROXIMITY ROUTINE LINK TO COMMUNICATION SYSTEM BROKEN. SYSTEM FAILURE.

"Somewhere in the com system, it looks like. Just another moment." Again he tackled the stubborn system.

EXTERNAL COMMUNICATION SYSTEM OFFLINE.

"Well, let me just go ahead and enable you then," he said.

SYSTEM OVERRIDE REQUIRES AUTHORIZATION. ACCESS DENIED.

Mancini paused as he stared at the screen. "You're going to ask me for authorization, you piece of junk?" It appeared that he had forgotten about Haruka floating behind him. "Yeah, let me give you an authorization right here." His fingers pounded furiously into the keyboard.

ACCESS DENIED. AUTHORIZATION REQUIRED.

Mancini growled at the screen. He glanced over his shoulder and said through gritted teeth, "Kimura, you mind going outside for a bit? I need to… persuade this pile of garbage."

She thought about making a joke to lighten the mood, but she had never seen Mancini this irritated before, and thought twice. She simply nodded, rolled up her half eaten meal pouch, and retreated from the room.

And now one more thing to worry about.

. . .

Damn it, Marco, where are you? Haruka wiggled her foot impatiently as she sat at a workstation in the propulsion control room. Captain Maynard was strapped to the chair at the end workstation, snoring lightly. *How can he sleep at a time like this? We're running out of time, and he's taking a nap.* She sneered, even though she knew he was out of it, and couldn't see her.

Haruka tried to occupy her mind, but the gravity of the situation was too great for her to ignore; every attempt that Lieutenant Mancini and Captain Maynard had made to try to crack the com system access codes had failed. Even Major Emberley's command codes didn't work. Every maintenance cycle, Maynard and Mancini had stayed awake for an extra week in an attempt to resolve the issue, with no luck. The com system was linked to the revival cycle through the approach probe, and without access to the system, Haruka could not have her precious four days added to the beginning of the cycle.

Equally disturbing was that Captain Maynard could not tell if the approach probe would even launch with the external com system disabled. He was certain that the ship could not receive data from the probe, and without that data *Raphael's* crew might as well be blindfolded. The ship's nav system could not avoid any comets or asteroids on approach. The crew would have no idea if the speculated moons of Demeter existed. For that matter, they could not tell if the atmosphere of the planet was hospitable or if the temperature range was suitable for human life.

She looked again at Maynard and sighed. *I should cut him some slack. He has put in a lot of extra work on this problem.* She felt a twinge of guilt at her earlier frustration with the engineer.

Haruka sighed and called up a display of the reactor status. All readings showed nominal. She flipped through other readings available to her, looking for something to do with her time. For the first time since launch, Haruka was disappointed by the fact that the ship was working properly. She had no duties left to perform until the approach cycle, but she could not bear to go back to stasis until she knew that she would be revived early enough to correct the ship's course. The wait was nearly unbearable, as was the knowledge that she could do nothing to help.

She picked at the arm rest of the chair. The foam on the leading edge had started to pull apart from repeated scratching over the course of weeks. Haruka saw this, and bored her index finger into the foam to see if she could separate it from the metal inside.

She startled when the hatch door groaned and swung open, and Maynard awoke with a sharp snort. Mancini pulled his way into the compartment and stopped himself on the open chair. He looked as if he hadn't slept in days.

"Please tell me you have good news, Marco," she begged.

Mancini sighed loudly and shook his head. "The weirdest thing just happened."

"I don't want weird, I want fixed." Her stomach began to knot. *Why can't it ever be good news?*

"Hmm? Oh, yeah. You've got your four days. I finally got that programmed in the system," he said, as if they were having a casual conversation.

Haruka let out a huge sigh of relief, but held back a squeal of delight. "Thanks, Marco. I owe you one."

"That's the thing, Kimura, I don't think that you do," Mancini said, clearly exhausted.

"Was it the brute force tool that finally got through?" asked Maynard.

Mancini looked over at the engineering captain. "No, sir. That's the weird part. I didn't do anything at all."

Maynard looked back at him in shock. "Nothing?"

"I swear to God," Mancini replied. "I left the core to go to the can and find some grub, and when I came back, all of the systems were online. Well, except voice command. But everything else: approach probe, external com, approach revival control."

Maynard dug his hands into the armrests of his chair hard enough for his knuckles to turn white. "Are you kidding me, Lieutenant?"

"No sir," he shot back quickly. "I swear. Go look at it yourself if you don't believe me."

"With how much work we put in, I don't believe it. I need to see for myself." Maynard unbuckled his straps and kicked off from his chair. Mancini and Maynard made their way through the door as Haruka released her harness and followed suit.

The trio made the short trip down the hall to the computer core. Maynard led the way and took the mainframe terminal chair for himself. Mancini hovered over his left shoulder, and Haruka floated over his right. Maynard swiped a finger over the screen and brought the terminal out of sleep.

XCS-03-R SUBSYS CHECK: COMMUNICATIONS

INTERCOM: ONLINE

EXTRACOM: ONLINE

PROBE LINK: ONLINE

BIOSTASIS LINK: ONLINE

NAVIGATION LINK: ONLINE

TELEMATICS: ONLINE

VOICE INTERFACE: SYSTEM ERROR

Haruka rubbed her eyes and looked at the screen, as if doing so would rub away a cruel illusion that all was well. Her eyes confirmed that this was no trick; all communications subsystems were online, except for the mainframe voice control.

"Incredible," remarked Captain Maynard. "And you didn't do anything at all, Mancini?"

"Honest to God. I just left the room for fifteen minutes and came back to this."

Maynard tapped a red button in the corner of the screen. "Maynard to bridge."

There was a long pause before a crackle heralded the response. "Bridge here, Major Emberley speaking. Go ahead, Captain."

"Sir, the com system has been restored. Captain Kimura's modifications have been entered into the mainframe."

"Excellent news," the major's voice rang through cheerfully. "When the maintenance is completed, I want all crew to report to stasis for the final time. Good job, Captain. Lieutenant Mancini, too. Tell him when you see him."

Emberley didn't even ask what was wrong, Haruka thought to herself.

"He's right next to me, sir. He can hear you."

"Well, it bears repeating. Good job, both of you. Emberley out." The light on the com link went dark as the connection ended. Mancini clapped Maynard on the shoulder and turned to leave. Maynard fiddled with his harness.

"That's it?" Haruka's words came out before she could stop them.

Both men looked at her, a mixture of confusion and exhaustion on both of their faces.

"Did we miss something, Captain?"

Her eyes darted between the screen and the engineer. "The system just turns itself back on and we're not going to find out why?"

The two men exchanged a quick glance. "Uh, no," Mancini said with a slight hesitation.

"C'mon, don't you think it's a little weird?"

"Yup," he replied quickly. "But we've been working on this almost every waking moment since I first came across the problem. And there's an old saying I love to live by: If it ain't broke, don't fix it."

But it is broken. Computers don't just fix themselves. Haruka wanted to scream the words at Mancini, but all she managed was a stuttered "but".

"We're going to get some rest, Kimura. I know you've still got work to do back there in propulsion, but try to take it easy tonight when you get off. It's fixed, got it?"

She sighed. "Yeah, you're right Marco." Haruka managed a smile. "Sleep well. You've earned it."

Haruka watched Mancini and Maynard leave the core. The hatch slid shut behind them, sealing her alone in the core with only the monotonous whir of the server cooling fans to keep her company. She maneuvered into the seat and pulled the straps loosely over her shoulders. With a few key strokes, she logged into the nav system and brought up her course corrections. *One more time, just to make sure.*

She watched as the simulation ran its course. Once more, *Raphael* maneuvered successfully over the near moon and into the approach plane.

Everything is fixed. We're going to make it, and I will get to see Mom, Dad, and Saika as they walk off of the ship. Haruka chewed on a thumbnail and thought about her father's situation. *Maybe I won't get to see Dad. They've accused him of a serious crime. Will they even let him walk off the ship?* Her thoughts began to race. *Saika will be devastated. Not only is Dad being accused, Brandon is as well.*

Haruka leaned back and closed her eyes. She could see her sister's face in her mind. Saika was in the first wave of launches, but Haruka had to remain behind one more day to pilot her own transport. Haruka remembered a conversation with Saika on the day her sister boarded a rocket bound for *Gabriel*. Saika was extremely excited about something, but no matter how hard Haruka tried, she could not get her sister to tell her. "Just wait," she kept saying. "I'll tell you, Mom, and Dad at the same time."

That was the last time Haruka had spoken with her sister. By the calendar, that was over forty years ago. It had only been a few weeks for Haruka, thanks to hibernation. Haruka now worried about what her sister meant. *If I had to guess, she probably wanted to say she's pregnant. Oh, Saika… this is a terrible situation you're in.* Haruka could feel anxiety well from deep within her. *I know you love Brandon with all your heart, so how will you react to his arrest?*

Haruka tried to project her feelings out, as if the walls of the computer core could not stop them. She imagined reaching with her mind through hull of *Raphael* as if the distance of space were nothing. Haruka willed herself to talk to her sister, asleep and far away. *If you're pregnant, Saika, you have to stay strong. Whatever happens, don't lose that baby.*

. . .

The heat of the Texas sun washed over Cal. He could see the bright orange glow through his closed eyelids and the grass beneath his body tickled the back of his neck and ears as he stretched, soaking in the warmth. The smell of food grilling on a barbecue taunted him from afar.

"Finally found yourself a little slice of heaven, huh?"

Cal's eyes slowly opened to see his doppelganger standing over his head, his face hard to recognize upside down.

"Just working on my tan," Cal responded as he closed his eyes again.

"Shouldn't you be working?" He could hear the disdain in his clone's voice.

"I'm on vacation."

"From what? You haven't done anything yet, you slacker. Hell, you don't even have a job. Not a real one, anyway."

Cal gave a half hearted laugh. "That depends on how you define work." He folded his hands across his chest. "I survived you, that's a good start."

His mirror self laughed in an unnerving way. "Did you? Then why am I still here?"

"You're here because I'm going nuts. Crazy people talk to themselves and hear voices, they say." Cal took in a deep breath through his nose and relished the smell of burgers being grilled. *Can't wait to have one of those again.*

"Or I'm here because you've still got issues that you're trying to figure out," his voice shot back. Cal ignored his double and started to hum a song. He was not sure where he had heard it, but it was certainly catchy. "Now you're just plain being rude."

"Shhh," he hissed. "This is the best part." He hummed his way to the bridge in the song. *I think this was something that Hunter was playing through his hidden stereo.*

"Show some respect, Calvin," his father's voice cut through the song.

Cal opened his eyes and looked up at his father's inverted face; His cheeks were red and his nostrils flared. Cal slowly sat up and turned to face him. His father's face was no longer distorted in his mind as he looked at him from an upright position. Cal crossed one leg over the other and twisted to the side. His body reacted with a series of pops as he cracked his back.

"Are you trying to get deep with me there, Dad? A little bit of a crack at how I have no self respect?"

General Andrew McLaughlin took the hat off of his short, blonde hair and tucked it in the armpit of his pressed dress blues. "Can you blame me? With what all happened in the last couple of months, it seemed that you didn't respect *anyone*. Including you."

Cal sighed and looked down at the grass. He passed the palm of his hand over it and felt the teasing blades run across his skin. *This is starting to feel too real,* he thought.

"What happened to you, Calvin?" his father asked.

He picked a handful of grass and tossed it aside. "It won't do any good. You're already dead."

"Maybe you should blame me. We had a rough go at the end there, didn't we?"

Cal motioned to a spot on the ground in front of him. "Sit down, Dad."

The elder McLaughlin walked forward and sat cross-legged in front of Cal. His dress pants wrinkled slightly, and blades of cut grass dotted the fabric.

Cal looked into his father's sad, blue eyes. "I don't hate you, Dad. I'm certainly not going to blame you for anything."

"I got you into this mess," his father retorted quickly.

"Yes you did." Cal smiled gently. "I should be thanking you for that, not blaming you. If I had stayed on Earth, I probably would have gone to war and been killed."

"I never told you what I was planning."

"Do you think I would have allowed you to send me here if you had told me?" Cal hesitated as he reached for his father, but pulled his hand back and turned his gaze to the ground once more. "As angry as I felt in the moment, I now know that everything that you have done has given me another chance. A chance I never deserved."

Cal looked up and saw past the dress blues of the soldier at the man behind them. Andrew McLaughlin was fighting back his emotion, and Cal saw tears roll from each of his eyes. "You are my son," he said, choking up. "You deserve every chance that I can give you."

"I was terrible to you, Dad," he said as he jumped to his feet. "All of the drinking and trying weed was because I was getting back at you for Mom leaving us."

Andrew rose quickly to his feet, a look of devastation on his face. He turned to walk away but Cal grabbed his arm and spun him around. His father pushed Cal and he stumbled backward and fell on his butt. "That wasn't my fault!" He spun and tried to run off.

Cal launched himself from the ground and sprinted after his father. *No, I am not going to let you run away this time, Dad.* He pumped his arms and legs furiously as he slowly caught up with his father. Cal lurched one more time and grabbed Andrew firmly by the wrist. He dug his heels into the ground. Andrew wheeled around as his shoulder jerked backward and his hat was sent flying.

Cal grabbed hold of his father as hard as he could with both arms. "I know it wasn't your fault. Mom didn't love either one of us, that's why she left," his voice cracked as he almost shouted at his father.

"Don't say that, Calvin." Andrew could no longer hold back his emotion. He was crying, tears streaming down his face. "Your mother may not have loved me, but she loved you. How could you say that about her?"

"Because it's true, Dad," Cal spat back, half sobbing himself. "You weren't around often enough to know it, but she changed. Five years ago, something about her was different. She'd barely talk to me, she wouldn't tell me she loved me, she wouldn't hug me. She never asked me about school or my friends. She'd leave sometimes and come home late at night, smelling like booze and cigarettes."

"No, it's not true," Andrew whimpered.

"It's all true." Cal looked up at the blue sky above. "Dad, you were more of a parent than she was. You were almost never around because of your duties, I got that. But when you *were* around, you made me feel like I was your whole world."

"Cal..."

"I miss you, Dad." Cal couldn't hold back any longer. He buried his face in his father's shoulder and wept. "And the worst part is that I never got to tell you that I love you. I never got to say goodbye to you. You died protecting me, and all I could think of at the time is how pissed I was at you for taking me away from my friends. Friends that really couldn't give a shit about me."

Cal felt his father return his embrace. It had a warm familiarity about it, and reminded Cal of when he was a young child; how his father could make any care in the world disappear with a simple hug.

"I love you, Calvin," Andrew whispered in his ear, choked up by the words.

"I love you too, Dad," Cal sobbed. The words made Calvin feel as if he were weightless and on *Michael* again. He pushed his father out to the edge of his grasp, arms on his shoulders, and looked him in the eye. "Just know that you didn't die for nothing. You protected me. You protected everyone on these ships. I owe you a debt that I can never repay, but I will work every day of my life to make sure that I do the best I can to make up for it. I'll make sure that everyone whose life I touch lives their lives to the fullest. For you, Dad."

Andrew McLaughlin bit his lip and nodded. He turned around and walked with his head down to where his hat had landed. He reached down, picked it up, and seated it precisely on his head. With one sad glance back, General Andrew McLaughlin walked over the crest of the hill and out of sight.

"Goodbye, Dad," Cal said to himself.

• • •

Haruka stowed her soiled flight suit in a locker stuffed full of other laundry items. She opened the adjacent locker and rifled through a disheveled pile of clean suits to find one in her size. Goose bumps rose on her naked skin as the cold air teased her body. She unfurled the fresh suit with a snap, pulled it over her body, and zipped it up.

So this is what final approach feels like, she thought. Somehow Haruka had imagined that when she awoke from hibernation for the final time that everything would feel different, brighter and more vibrant. Instead she was greeted by the soft sounds of the life support system as it cycled air through the crew pod.

She heard a click from behind her and turned around. The hatch of one of the sleeper berths opened, and a groggy, shaggy Captain Maynard emerged. He groaned and threw an arm up to his eyes, shielding them from the light in the pod. She heard a loud sigh from him. "Are we really awake for the last time, Kimura?"

"It doesn't feel like it," she replied, "but we are."

Maynard rubbed his eyes. "I didn't look at the clock before I came out. How long?"

"A little over three years since the end of the last cycle. Forty three years since we left Earth."

"That's a long time." Maynard paused and looked off into the distance, then shook his head. "Best not to think of that." He unzipped his flight suit and quickly disrobed.

Haruka was caught off guard by the captain choosing to strip in front of her. Her eyes fell momentarily to his waist, and realized that he had removed his underwear as well. Her cheeks flushed, and she turned around to face the sleeper unit. Maynard chuckled from behind her.

"Don't tell me you've never seen one of those before, Kimura," he quipped.

"Sorry, sir. I didn't mean to look."

"I'm not your superior any more, Kimura. I won't salute if you won't." Haruka heard the scrape of metal on metal as he opened a locker.

"Sorry, force of habit." A smile crossed her face. *Now I sound like Nova.*

"Well, get used to it," he replied. Haruka jumped slightly as the locker banged shut.

Déjà vu. Creepy. I wonder if I sounded like that to Nova.

There was a moment of awkward silence, and the sound of rustling fabric. "It's safe now, I'm decent," Maynard said as the zipper of his flight suit confirmed the completion of his wardrobe change.

Haruka turned around. Maynard's flight suit was fresh, but it did little to improve his disheveled look. He looked around the hallway.

"No one else is up," he noted.

"Major Emberley is," she replied. "The rest are going to be asleep for another four days. The three of us are needed a little early. This is why Marco needed access to the com system."

"I see. So what are we doing?"

"Course corrections," she said, hoping that her voice would not tip Maynard off to the severity of the situation. "Major Emberley wanted you to bring the propulsion systems online for me."

Maynard rubbed his face and tried to stifle a yawn. "What's wrong with our course?"

Damn. I was hoping he wouldn't ask. Haruka shrugged. "We're a little off the approach plane. I just need to make a few corrections so we hit the atmospheric entry window correctly." Haruka saw Major Emberley enter the hallway from behind Maynard. The engineer did not turn around, oblivious to the commanding officer of *Raphael*.

Maynard's brow furrowed. "Something doesn't sound right about that. Why do you need so much time?"

Haruka looked at Emberley. The major nodded and spoke, startling Maynard. "It's okay to tell him, Captain. By the time the rest of the crew wakes up it won't matter."

"Tell me what? What's going on, Kimura?" Haruka could hear the worry in Maynard's voice.

Haruka sighed. "After Captain Bartrand executed the low orbit slingshot maneuver around Earth that Colonel Fox ordered, he tried to recalculate our course for Demeter. His calculations for speed were off." She looked into Maynard's eyes and lowered her voice. "We're two months ahead of schedule. If I don't slow down *Raphael* and make course adjustments, we will fly right past the planet to our deaths."

All color drained from the engineer's face and his jaw slacked.

"You can see just how dire this problem is, Mr. Maynard," Emberley added. "We didn't want to panic the crew, so only Captain Kimura and I knew the extent of the problem. Once the corrections are made, it won't matter."

"Y-yes s-sir," he stuttered.

"Enough talk for now." Emberley swept one arm grandly toward the exit. "Captains, if you will please take your stations. Maynard, is the telemetry link between the bridge and propulsion room up?"

"No sir."

"Very well. Please go to propulsion control and bring all of the plasma systems online. You can then work on the telemetry link and join us on the bridge once that is established."

"Yes sir."

"Kimura, you're with me." Emberley grabbed the frame of the exit hatch and pulled himself out of the hallway. Haruka followed; Maynard brought up the rear. When they reached the top of the stairs, Major Emberley and Haruka spiraled up to the bridge while Maynard departed for the rear of the ship.

Haruka glided to her workstation at the front of the bridge. As she passed the command chair, Haruka saw Alpha Centauri B for the first time. *Raphael* was still far away; the orange star was a dot just below the horizon of the canopy, no larger than the tip of an eraser. She maneuvered to her seat and secured her restraints, then stared out at the star. She smiled as the idea that their journey was nearly at an end began to sink in.

I don't care if we don't land next to Marco's white sand beach, she thought. *I'll just be happy to stretch my legs and feel the sun again.*

Haruka heard a *thunk* as Major Emberley locked the command chair in place. "Are we receiving data from the approach probe?"

She looked down at her screen and brought the workstation to life. "Just a moment, Major." With a few swift taps and swipes, she brought up the probe data file. She opened the file and saw data within, and a pair of green arrows showed an active link with the device. "Yes, we have a data stream from the probe."

"What do we know about Demeter?" There was an air of anxiety in his words.

Haruka scrolled through the dizzying array of information that the probe had already sent back to *Raphael's* computer. "What would you like, sir? I have information on satellites, mass, diameter and gravity. It looks like the probe has made several passes and compiled maps of the planet. We're receiving more data, too." She paused a moment as she read several lines of incoming data. "It looks like atmospheric data."

"Atmospheric. I'd like to know if the air on that rock is breathable."

"Just a moment, sir." Haruka called up the atmospheric data stream. She beamed and her voice boomed as she read the data off. "Nitrogen-oxygen atmosphere. Seventy seven point nine percent nitrogen, twenty point nine percent oxygen. Trace amounts of water vapor, carbon dioxide, methane, and noble gases. Average atmospheric pressure of nine seven zero millibars." She turned and looked at Major Emberley. His eyes were closed, and his mouth moved in what appeared to be a silent prayer. "It's breathable, Major. It's almost identical to Earth's."

His eyes dropped to meet Haruka's and he exhaled loudly enough for her to hear. "Breathable," he repeated. "That's a very sweet word to hear right now."

"Agreed, sir." *Sweeter than any word I have ever heard.*

"I want to hear more. Does it have any moons? What's the gravity like? How big is the planet?"

Haruka turned back to her terminal for the answers. "Two moons, just like Doctor Benedict predicted. The inner moon is much smaller than the outer moon. Gravity is point nine two *g*. The probe estimates the circumference of the planet Demeter to be about 37,000 kilometers. Axial tilt is estimated at nineteen percent." She paused and tapped through several photographic images of the planet. "Sir, this is… beautiful."

"What is?"

"Demeter. The probe has sent back pictures of the planet. I'm sending them to your screen now." She transferred a group of photographs to the command chair's terminal.

"Thank you, Captain."

She stared at a photograph of a large archipelago near the equator. Haruka's thoughts drifted to the planet out in the distance, somewhere in the void between *Raphael* and the tiny orange star. She wondered if the planet was warm and what kinds of life they might find there. She considered what the beaches of those islands might look like. Images of sunsets and warm breezes teased her senses, as if she could see and feel them from millions of miles away. She yearned to feel sand squeeze between her toes as she walked lazily along the shore.

Now I understand why that's what you've been looking for, Marco.

Now we just have to find you a foofy tropical drink, and your dream is complete.

Haruka rejoined her senses in her seat on the cold bridge when she heard voices muttering behind her. She glanced over her shoulder and saw Emberley and Maynard engaged in a conversation, taking turns pointing at the command screen and making a discussion point. They were far enough away that their hushed words came to her as nothing more than incoherent babbling.

"Captain Maynard," she interrupted. His head snapped up and met her gaze. "Are the propulsion systems online?"

"Yes, Captain Kimura. They're all at your command."

"Thank you." She turned and gave one more glance at the star ahead. "You might want to strap in, Captain. Some of these maneuvers may be a bit disorienting."

Haruka placed her hands at the edges of the screen and patted them as one might praise a dog. *Let's bring you home, Raphael.*

· · ·

Calvin McLaughlin
Date and time unknown
Michael
>|

He opened his eyes slowly. The stench of body odor permeated the air. When Cal felt along his body, his hands became slick with sweat. His back rested firmly on the sleeper's bed, and his restraints lay gently on his chest.

Gravity.

He reached over and clicked his clock on. 4-3-2058 14:37.

Colonel Dayton honored my wish, he thought. Cal gently unbuckled his harness and opened his berth door. Bright light flooded his sleeper berth, and he was blinded for a moment. He recovered and slid out of the berth, dropping to the deck plate with a slight wobble.

No, this isn't right. He was supposed to wake me up for the approach cycle.

The com system crackled to life, and Dr. Taylor's somber voice came through. "Taylor to Cal. Please step outside of the ship. It's time."

Cal's feet steadied beneath him and he trudged out of the sleeper pod and into the fully lit backbone gallery. He looked in both directions, but saw no one. Even the gallery itself seemed devoid; no carts lined the sides of the massive hall. He marched forward awkwardly, his legs still not used to bearing weight.

Where is she?

A bright light from the lower gallery beckoned as he passed the great hole in the floor leading down. Cal swung himself onto the ladder and descended. To the rear of the ship, he could see a slash of green. He moved toward it, and realized that the rear air lock was open, and the outer ramp had been lowered.

Cal jogged to the ramp, stumbling every few strides. When he stopped at the edge of the ramp, his eyes were greeted by the verdant glow of wild grasses, and the smells of flowers beckoned his nose. With renewed vigor, he charged down the ramp and somersaulted on the grass the moment he felt the blades touch his feet. He laughed and rolled onto his back when the maneuver failed.

"Shhh," hissed a chorus of voices from nearby.

"What? We're here. We're finally here," he cried out.

"Shhh."

Cal rolled to his knees and looked around. Dozens of faceless men and women dressed in blue flight suits marched in two perfect columns from *Michael* to the top of a knoll directly behind. From there they fanned out precisely, in perfect silence, along the ridge.

"What's going on?" He sprang to his feet and sprinted to the hill, ignoring the angry hisses directed at him.

He reached the top of the hill and jerked to a stop. Almost immediately he collapsed to his knees and screamed. The first scream was primal; meaningless other than to express his horror. The second scream was a simple "NO!"

Spread across the far hillside opposite a shallow valley was a sleeper ship. Its pods lay scattered and burning, and the backbone had been broken like a tinder twig.

"Oh, God no! We have to help them," Cal screamed as he struggled to his feet. He started to move forward, but two arms locked with his and held him back. "Let go," he yelled as he tried in vain to break free.

Cal looked to either side at the faces of those who would hold him back. Lieutenant Ceretti and Doctor Taylor ignored his pleas and stared stone faced across the valley at the wreck.

"Hunter? Doc? Let me go," he pleaded. "Please, we've got to help them. Someone might have survived, and they need our help!"

"Shhh," they hissed in unison.

"What's wrong with you two? Let me go!"

"Shhh."

A motion from the corner of his eye caught Cal's attention. He craned his neck further to see. Cal watched as Colonel Dayton marched past the shoulder of Lieutenant Ceretti, made a crisp right turn, and marched directly in front of Cal. The commander of *Michael* halted and sharply turned left to face the valley.

"Parade... *Rest*," he barked.

Ceretti and Taylor released Cal's arms. With a great stomp and clap, every man and woman in both lines spread their legs to shoulder width and clasped their hands behind their backs. Cal hesitated for a moment, turned to face the wreck, and duplicated the pose.

What the hell? Are we just going to watch as they burn?

"Men and women of Concordia," Dayton called in a commanding tone. "Citizens and servicemen."

Cal looked around in confusion. *What citizens? These people are all wearing uniforms.*

"Today we grieve the loss of our own," Dayton continued. "Over two thousand innocent and brave souls have been lost." Cal gulped and felt his heart plummet. "Some were friends and some were strangers. All of them were family, not of blood but of spirit. Every one embarked on a journey with us to a new world. In this world we hoped to build a new life and new peace together, far from the ravages of war. Though their lives may have been cut short, their spirit and courage will endure in each of you for generations to come. Live your lives in honor of those that were lost before you, both on Earth and Demeter. Keep your loved ones close, and live in honor and unity with all around you."

"Honor and Unity," the crowd chanted in response.

"May God watch over them in Heaven. Amen." Dayton raised his hand with two fingers extended and drew a cross in the air. He turned to Ceretti and nodded.

Ceretti stepped forward to the colonel's flank. Dr. Taylor joined the lines of blue that stretched over the side of the knoll

"Honor Guard, forward *march*," Ceretti barked. Seven men marched in slow unison from the line, bearing rifles.

Where the hell did those come from?

"Flight *halt*." The Honor Guard came to a crisp halt. Cal stared at their rifles. He could recognize that model anywhere. The M4 carbine was the standard rifle for most service members, no matter what branch they served in. He fixated on the motions of the barrels as the Honor Guard performed maneuvers that Ceretti barked out.

All seven aimed at an exact angle over the valley. The terrible crack of seven rifles firing simultaneously made Cal reel and his ears ring. He knelt down on the ground and pressed his hands over his ears.

The second round of fire was only barely less brutal. Cal tried to curl head first into a ball. He knew what this all meant, and the emptiness he felt inside was a chasm too wide for his mind to bridge after years of fighting his own demons.

A final peal signaled the third round of the salute. Cal dropped his hands from his ears and into his lap. Through the ringing he could faintly hear the distant echo of the gunfire as it bounced off of hillsides all around. The blue-clad throng marched their way in neat lines back to *Michael*. Cal sat back on his heels and turned his head across the valley to the sickening red glow pulsing deep within the thick black clouds of smoke.

This is no end for a family trying to flee war. He clenched his fists and looked skyward. He yelled with a defiant snarl, "Is this how you treat the innocent, God?"

Cal tore at his chest and beat his fist into his skill as hard as he can. "Wake up, damn you. You need to wake up and warn them." He jumped to his feet and bolted down the back side of the hill as fast as he could toward the burning wreckage. He could feel no heat from the flames at all.

He ran into a burning pod and scoured within. He did not burn, nor did he choke on the smoke. Though Cal could barely see within, he saw neither people nor bodies. His strength seemed to sap from him as he staggered from the pod and back to the valley.

Cal let out an anguished howl and collapsed into the cold, damp grass, sobbing. *I'm trapped. Their death is on my hands.*

· · ·

Demeter dominated the left side of the bridge canopy. Brilliant blue oceans and vibrant green land masses darted in and out of cover from fluffy white clouds. Haruka felt butterflies in her stomach. For the first time since Earth, they were from excitement rather than worry or fear. She smiled and looked to her left at Lieutenant Julio Morado. Her new nav partner seemed just as pleased, his broad grin unable to hide his slightly crooked teeth.

Haruka's body ached, but her hours in the chair no longer fatigued her. After *Raphael* cleared the dark, near moon that Emberley had dubbed "Arion", and used its gravity to dip into the approach plane hours earlier, Haruka had been riding a near constant euphoric energy. The bright sphere of the other moon, which had been named "Persephone", was trying to slink behind Demeter, but the speed of the sleeper ship had kept the moon in sight for the approach.

Here we are, within an hour of atmospheric entry. She looked forward at the massive, encroaching planet. *All those setbacks and problems are history. There's the planet. There's home.* She bit her lip. *Here's Dad's dream, and Marco's.*

There was a slight bitterness to that last thought. Travel to Demeter was never Haruka's dream. She had always wanted to be a combat pilot. She was stunned when she was groomed for space flight just weeks after she had started combat flight training. *If the rumors are true, Dad had everything to do with that.*

"Captain Kimura," Emberley called from the command chair. "How is our course looking?"

She glanced down at her screen just as *Raphael* rumbled with a slight jerk. "Course is true, Major. Captain Maynard can shut down the main and braking plasma drives at any time. I still need plasma thrusters, and it's only a few minutes before I'll need to switch to chemical thrusters."

"Understood. Maynard, prepare the drive systems for entry."

Raphael shook again. Haruka heard a confirmation from Maynard.

"Emberley to Lieutenant Mancini." There was a momentary pause. "Are the final inventory checks completed and entered into the mainframe?"

Haruka could not hear the com system over the increasing noise in the cockpit. She reached for her headset, but a jerk from the ship made it slip from her fingers and clatter at her feet in slow motion.

"What about pre landing resource distribution?" she heard the major ask.

"Major, we've got gravity again," she yelled as she retrieved the headset and positioned the boom.

"...fully stocked with the standard supplies on the checklist, from stem to stern. I'm also shutting down the second redundant server as a precaution, Major." She heard Mancini's voice through her headset. "It's starting to get a bit bumpy and I don't want every computer on the ship to fry if something goes wrong. Mancini out."

"Emberley to Doctor Nelson," the major's voice rang clear through the com.

"Nelson here."

"Status of the final passenger checks please, Doctor."

Raphael rumbled and jittered. "...confirmed that biostasis system is offline. No alarms from station monitors. It's getting a little rough back here so I'm going to sign off and take refuge in medical pod one."

"Emberley to Lieutenant Singh."

"Singh here."

"Did the radio marker buoy land at the target site?"

"Yes sir. Confirmed that the buoy is transmitting on all frequencies. *Michael* and *Gabriel* should be able to pick up the signal in a few days, if my calculations are correct."

"Kimura to Emberley," she said as she grabbed the boom with her right hand. "Major, I'm picking up a slight port roll. Firing thrusters to compensate."

"Understood."

"Maynard to Kimura. Main and braking plasma..."

Raphael shuddered violently and began to roll to the starboard.

"What the hell was that?" screamed Major Emberley.

Haruka fired her starboard elevation thrusters on full burn. The roll slowed, and she backed off until it was neutralized.

BRRZT. BRRZT. BRRZT. BRRZT.

Oh shit, she thought. *Not again.*

"Major," Maynard yelled through the com. "Reactor core temperature is rising. Generator two is overheating, and I'm reading a pressure loss in service corridor eleven. I think we've lost a heat exchanger in the drive section."

"Can you reduce reactor power to bring the temperature down?"

Haruka's heart pounded and her palms began to sweat. She glanced at Morado. His eyes were locked on her in terror. She smiled and mouthed the words, "Don't worry. I land these all the time."

"Negative, Major," Maynard responded. "The temperature is rising too quickly. A core breach is imminent. If we try to land, the friction will aggravate the cooling issue and we'll just explode somewhere between here and the ground."

"Damn it all." The com went eerily silent as *Raphael* careened toward the planet. "Kimura, Maynard, get back to the propulsion room and transfer all control to the workstations when you get there. We'll keep us afloat until you get back there."

"Sir, what do you intend for us to do when we're back there?" Maynard's voice was nearing panic. Haruka's stomach was in knots.

No, I don't want to go back to the reactor. It's going to blow.

"Try to bring us to emergency drop range. We'll scramble the crew to the ESAARC pods and prepare for drop."

Haruka nearly fainted at the words. An emergency drop was the worst possible scenario for any of the ships, and her commander wanted her in the propulsion section instead of an ESAARC pod. There were escape pods in the rear section, and the control room was directly above an emergency launch vehicle as well, but the critical state of the reactor terrified Haruka.

"Once the pods are away," Emberley continued, "pull *Raphael* back from the planet for as long as you can before ejecting yourselves. Lock onto one of the pod beacons and follow us down. We'll try to make for the landing beacon if practical, but our first priority is a safe landing."

"Yes sir," Maynard shot back.

"Sir, why me?" Haruka cringed as the words came out of her mouth without thinking.

"I need my best pilot to steer this wreck away from the pods. Now go, Kimura."

"Yes sir." She unbuckled and stumbled down the bridge. Gravity was present, but it was lighter than normal. She tumbled down the stairs and slammed her shoulder into the deck plate, grunting in pain. For a moment, Haruka froze on the ground. The impending destruction of the glowing monstrosity at the back of the ship was almost more than she could bear.

"C'mon, Kimura, get up," Maynard yelled as he clumsily sprinted past her.

Haruka forced herself to her feet and ran after the engineer.

C'mon, Kimura. Don't you know that heroes get themselves killed?

• • •

Gabrielle Serrano
Civilian
30 March 2058, 09:32
Raphael
>|

It was very dark, and strange noises startled her every few seconds when her bed shook. A faint red light looked at her from the darkness, like an evil, winking cat. She could move her arms, but she could not get up. Something held her in place.

"Mama?" Her voice was weak.

Again her bed lurched and threw her against whatever it was that held her fast. A deep rumble echoed in the tiny space, and Gabi's lip trembled.

"Mama," she repeated as her voice quaked.

Gabi groped around in the darkness, trying to feel anything around her. Across her chest were some straps, like those on her car seat. She tried to find the latch to take them off, but it was too dark. She looked to her side at the menacing light. With no warning, it flared brighter, and she let out a shrill shriek.

A man's voice came from somewhere in the dark. "Attention passengers, this is Major Nathan Emberley of the sleeper ship *Raphael*. We are about thirty minutes from landing. For your own safety, please remain in your assigned berths with your safety restraints on. Do not remove your restraints or open your berth until you are instructed to do so, or you are assisted by a member of the crew."

Gabi traced the straps on her chest with her tiny fingers. *That man says I need to keep these on because it's not safe. I'm going to keep them on until Mama takes them off.*

Gabi heard the man's voice again. "All crew report to ESAARC position two. Com flash when ready."

After the voice went away, the scary eye dimmed. It still looked at Gabi through the darkness. Fear grew within her. Her bed lurched and rumbled again.

"Mama," she screamed. "Mama, Mamaaaaaaa!"

"I'm here, Gabi." Her mother's voice was muffled and faint, like she was yelling through the walls of their house. "It's okay, Mama will get you out when we land."

"Mama, I'm scared," Gabi wailed.

J.C. Rainier

"Don't be scared. I'm right here. I'm not going anywhere."

Gabi flailed her arms around to find her mother. "Mama, where are you?" She waited for her mom to answer. Panic set in as she searched the darkness. Above her was nothing but a cold wall. The tips of her fingers brushed against something cold and metal to her sides. Her mom was nowhere to be found.

The walls of her bed rattled, and the noise did not go away. Gabi covered her ears, which helped for a moment. But the noise kept growing and growing, and even her hands could not keep the noise out.

"Mamaaaaaaaaaa," she screamed and burst into tears.

Her mother did not answer her terrified cry.

. . .

Haruka's legs burned as she tore down the length of the gallery. Her sprint from the bridge had left her breathless. She bled from scrapes on her left knee and elbow from where she had fallen again in the gallery; the light gravity played nothing but havoc with her balance. Captain Maynard was already halfway down the propulsion corridor by the time Haruka reached it.

She skidded to a halt just inside the airlock. Alarms blared from both sides of the junction in a chilling discord. Haruka grabbed the heavy door and pulled against it, grunting hard. It slowly swung with a mournful creak. She ducked her way around it as it swung, and then closed and sealed it. Terror gripped her for a moment; she had just closed herself into the aft section with the crippled nuclear reactor.

Pull yourself together, damn it, her mind screamed at her. *Protect the passengers. Do your duty, Captain.*

Haruka wheeled down the hall and bounded toward the control room. At the side of the hallway, the hatch to the computer core opened and Lieutenant Mancini stumbled out. He gave her a frightened glance as he struggled to a knee.

"What the hell is going on, Kimura?" he yelled as she ran past.

"No time," she huffed. "Hurry up." She reached for his outstretched hand and pulled him to his feet. Mancini stumbled as they raced down the hall, but Haruka steadied him and pushed him through the open hatch ahead and into the control room. She leaped inside, spun around, and slammed the hatch shut.

Nova sat in her usual seat near the ladder to the reactor, her pale hands gripping the armrests of her chair. Maynard sat at the left station and keyed away at his terminal with alacrity. A great heave from the ship threw Haruka to the floor next to Mancini. *Raphael* rattled like a can of ball bearings in a paint shaker. Haruka knew the only way she would be able to hear anyone would be to get to her station and headset.

Haruka lunged for the back of the chair and wrapped her arms around it. She struggled to regain her feet, and then maneuvered into the seat. Her hand shot to the headset that was secured by Velcro and jammed it on her head.

"…running out of time, Captain," she heard Emberley through the com.

"Transferring nav control to Captain Kimura now, Major," Maynard boomed. "Captain Kimura, vid link to the bridge should be up on your station. We will evacuate the bridge on your order."

"Standby," she barked into her microphone. The familiar bridge camera that she used to monitor during maintenance cycles popped on her screen, as well as an array of touch sliders and controls for the propulsion system.

Damn, she thought. *No physical controls. No canopy view.* She shook her hands out. *No time to worry about precision, just get the job done.*

Haruka looked at the nearly empty bridge. Only three stations sat occupied, and Major Emberley sat fast in the command chair. She recognized the slicked, dark hair of Lieutenant Morado at nav. *Hang on, kid. I'll get you out of there in a second.*

Haruka tested her thruster control. *Raphael* groaned in response, but her telemetry indicated that the ship was very slow to respond.

"Maynard, did you bring the chemical thrusters online?" She tapped her thrusters again with little response.

"No, standby." More rattling and rocking came from the sleeper ship. "Chemical thrusters online. Go light on them, the ESAARC pods need them for landing."

She tapped the thrusters again and *Raphael's* descent halted for a moment. "We're good to go. Evacuate the bridge, Major."

"Understood. Morado, Perez, go for pod one. Overton, you're with me. Pod two. *Move!*"

Haruka watched the video feed as the four men released their restraints. Something at the bottom of the image caught her eye. Haruka looked on in horror as she realized someone was walking up the bridge steps toward the command chair. Emberley turned to the rear of the bridge as he rose, and for a split second Haruka saw the major frozen in place.

A glint came from the side of the scruffy long-haired visitor. Haruka's heart sank as she instantly recognized the M4 carbine that Colonel Fox leveled at her former first officer.

"Major, look out," she screamed into her boom.

Her warning came too late. Time seemed to slow to a crawl. Haruka heard the first shot through her headset. Major Emberley's shoulder jerked back. Two more *cracks* came in rapid succession, and he started to fall backward to the deck.

"NO!" Haruka screamed.

Fox swung the weapon around and squeezed off three more rounds at the nav station. Morado caught one round to the face and fell limp instantly. Haruka watched in horror as the other two rounds slammed into the front canopy, damaging the glass. The colonel turned to her right. Haruka saw a twisted, sadistic grin on her face. Crack, crack, crack, CRACK. Fox placed two rounds in Overton's chest, and he spun and fell over his station.

In just over a second, a massive crack spread through the canopy glass from the nav station to just off the right side of the screen. The last thing that Haruka saw before the video feed failed was the shattered canopy blowing out into space, dragging Fox, Perez, and the bodies with it.

Her screams were drowned out by alarms that rang out in the control room. Haruka stared at the video feed, but all that remained was static. *No. Oh God, no. That didn't just happen, did it?*

Maynard's urgent voice in her headset brought her back to task. "Kimura, get us out of here!"

"You have to drop the pods first, Captain," she shot back.

"They auto-dropped when the gallery lost pressure. They're gone. Full thrust, *now.*"

"Yes sir." Haruka slid her thruster controls to maximum. She watched her altimeter carefully. Their rate of descent slowed, but did not stop. Warning lights flashed on her console that indicated atmospheric entry was beginning.

We're not going to make it. The plasma thrusters are too weak to use this close to the planet, and I only have one bank of chemical thrusters left. She gulped and flipped desperately between gauges. Something caught her eye. *Our tail is dropping. Maybe if…*

"Captain Maynard, bring the main plasma drive online."

"What? Are you nuts?"

"Just do it," she barked.

"It's already done, Captain Kimura." Nova's voice was barely audible in her headset. Haruka glanced over and the young blonde gave her a weak thumbs up.

Haruka cut power to all thrusters in the aft half of the ship. She winced as the tail of the ship dropped and slammed her forward into her harness. Alarms rang through the cabin, but she ignored them and steadied herself.

Wait for it...

"What are you doing, Captain?" Maynard screamed.

The tail of *Raphael* dropped perilously close to 90 degrees. Mancini could no longer hold on to his perch and slammed into the back of Nova's chair. Haruka strained against her harness as she pushed the throttle of the main plasma drive to full and cut the remaining thrusters. The stricken ship responded by hanging in place for what seemed like an eternity, and then slowly *Raphael* built up speed directly away from the planet.

"We need altitude, Kimura."

"Check your gauges, Captain. That's what I'm giving you."

Maynard responded, "We need it faster. Generator two is criti..."

The control room shook from a blast beyond its walls. Haruka was dazed and her ears rung. The screen blurred as she fought for consciousness. She clutched her head and shook it for a moment. The ringing was replaced by the whine of a generator at full speed that filled the compartment. A new alarm blared, and a yellow and black radiation symbol flashed on Haruka's screen.

"Radiation leak," Nova screamed. "We have to get out of here."

"Just a few..."

"Generator two is gone," Nova cut her off. "Number one is overheating and the reactor is about to go critical. We have to leave now!"

"Damn it." Haruka set her controls to lock the drive at full. "Abandon ship." She dangled her feet onto the wall behind the terminal and unstrapped. She shuffled to the corner and dropped to her knees, then opened a hatch in the floor plating.

Haruka looked up into the control room. Gaping holes had been torn in the steel walls of the control room by shrapnel from the failed generator. Nova had made her way down to her corner and crawled through the escape hatch. Mancini had climbed his way up to Maynard. She saw the engineer's arms limp and bloodied, and his head bent backwards over the chair, blood dripping from a deep gash across his forehead. Mancini yelled at her, but she could not hear. She did not need to; Haruka knew that Captain Maynard was dead.

"Come on," she yelled at Mancini and waved her arms furiously at the hatch. He jumped down to the bulkhead that Haruka stood on and crawled through the up-ended floor hatch. As soon as his feet cleared the hatch, Haruka knelt down and crawled behind him along the ladder.

Haruka's bloodied knee had opened again by the time they made their way along the long, metal ladder and into the escape skiff. Nova was already inside, and had started the craft's systems. Mancini dropped into the seat next to Nova and grabbed for his restraints. Haruka winced as she lifted herself into the pilot's seat. She secured herself and donned a headset while Nova closed the hatch leading to *Raphael*.

"Marco, tell me when Nova is strapped in so we can launch," she said.

"You got it."

Haruka checked to make sure all of her controls were ready and active. Her finger hovered over a large red button bordered with yellow and black stripes.

"Alright, let's go," Mancini barked.

Haruka pressed the button. With a lurch, the escape skiff detached from *Raphael* and cleared its underside. Through the cockpit windows, Haruka could see the moon Arion and the remnants of *Raphael*. The ship looked like a sad shell of itself; it had no sleeper or cargo pods attached to it. As it slowly turned like a corkscrew, Haruka saw the black maw at the front where the bridge had been torn apart. A scar across the top of the propulsion section marked the damage that sealed the sleeper's demise.

"My God," Mancini said and pointed at the torn hull. "What the hell caused it?"

"It's blown out from the inside," Nova stated. "Something failed, big time."

Haruka replied. "Hang on, this will probably get bumpy." She fired her nose thruster and the craft did a slow back flip. Arion and *Raphael* dropped out of view, and the vast blue expanse of Demeter's oceans dropped down from the top of the canopy.

"I've locked on to one of the pods' emergency beacons, Captain," Nova said. "Feeding the info to the nav system now."

Haruka performed a half roll and pitched the nose up slightly. Demeter now covered the lower portion of their forward view. "Beginning atmospheric entry," she exclaimed.

The skiff began to rattle and blue wisps of light flowed over the nose of the craft. After a twenty or so seconds, the blue light was overpowered by orange flames dancing off the nose. The bumps and jitters intensified, and Haruka felt herself clutching the controls even tighter.

"Nose up, Kimura," Mancini called through the com. "You're coming in too hot."

"We're fine. Demeter's approach path is more forgiving than Earth's. I need the speed to catch the pods." She tweaked the roll of the vessel slightly to compensate her course.

"We've lost computer link to *Raphael*, Captain," Nova said.

Then it's done. The reactor breached. Haruka gulped and adjusted her grip on the attitude controls.

The darkness of space drifted out of view, and only Demeter itself was visible. A vast blue ocean extended in front of her. Only a faint trace of land could be seen, at the very edge of the horizon. Haruka activated the HUD. A broad, broken green oval encircled a wide path of her forward view, while crosshairs slashed the center. A red blip showed in the lower left quadrant, moving erratically.

There's the pod, she thought. The escape skiff was losing speed quickly, but it still gained ground on the ESAARC pod. Haruka banked toward the pod and dipped the nose to gain more speed.

"This is Captain Haruka Kimura to unidentified emergency pod. Requesting status check." The com crackled with static, then silence. "I repeat, this is Captain Kimura requesting status from unidentified emergency pod."

Again, static and silence filled her ear. Then a muffled voice squeaked through the com. "This is Lieutenant Harjit Singh in sleeper pod nine. We hit a patch of turbulence and lost automated control. My pilot is unconscious and we're losing altitude fast. Help us, Kimura!"

Damn it! "Are your thrusters firing, Lieutenant?"

"I.. I don't know. How do I tell?" Singh's voice was laced with panic.

Haruka closed her eyes and imagined the touch controls in *Raphael's* engine room. "Do you see the altimeter in the center of your console?"

"Yes. Please hurry!"

"Okay, the two bars to either side of that. Take your fingers and slide them all the way up," she said, trying to keep her voice calm.

"Okay." There was a pause. "It's not working, Captain!" A warning beep sounded through the headset. "I've got a warning. Altitude critical." Singh screamed in terror, then Haruka heard a loud bang, and silence. The red blip on her HUD vanished.

Her stomach revolted against her. She closed her eyes for a moment and used every bit of her concentration to keep from throwing up.

"Nova," she choked, "get me another pod to follow."

"Y-yes ma'am," she responded.

Haruka opened her eyes. A landmass was now clearly visible ahead of them, though still very distant.

"Pod beacon linked to nav system, Captain." A blip appeared on Haruka's HUD, this time to the right and above her horizon.

Damn it, were we following Singh into the sea? Haruka fired her pitch thruster hard, and the skiff's nose soared into the air. "This is Captain Kimura to unknown emergency pod. Status check, please."

The response was almost immediate this time. "Lieutenant Cormack here, pod seven. We're on final approach right now. There's a lot of trees down here. Wait… there's a clean place to land, right there. See it, Daniels? Right there, set it down right there."

"Is everything alright, Lieutenant?"

"Yes, ma'am. Our pilot is headed for a clearing in the woods. Can't talk anymore, but I'll see you on the ground," he said, and cut the com link.

Haruka sighed in relief. *That's where we go, then.*

"Alright, Marco, Nova. We're going to make for that pod. Start tracking the other pods so we can round up the other passengers." Haruka dipped her wing and banked for the red dot on her screen.

• • •

Gabi's bed rocked. She sobbed quietly, but dared not remove the straps that held her down.

The nice man told me I can't take them off. Mama said she will when she can.

She glanced to her side, but the evil cat's eye was no longer there. It had disappeared a while ago and had not returned. Gabi was now all alone in this dark, scary place.

The rattling and creaking had died down and only an occasional sway was left to startle her. Gabi grabbed the straps that lay across her chest and pulled at them. They reassured her in a way; her mother always said the straps on her car seat were to keep her safe in case they crashed in the car.

Suddenly, there was a loud roaring noise, and Gabi felt as if she was being pressed into her bed. She cried out for her mother, but could barely even hear her own voice. The walls shook with a terrible clatter. Gabi dug her fingers into the fabric of the bed and closed her eyes as tears streamed down her face.

Gabi wondered how long it would be before her mom would come and take her out of this dark place. It had been a long time since she had heard anyone's voice. Even the nice man who talked to her through the walls wasn't talking to her any more.

The bed shifted and pitched hard to the left. Gabi slammed into her straps, which bit into her skin. She screamed, though she didn't know if it was more from terror or from pain. She tried to hold back against the straps, but she could not pull herself up to do anything.

There was another lurch, and her bed rolled more and more, until Gabi landed on her back. Her head slammed into the pillow as everything lurched to a stop. She could not hear anything at all, but her chest throbbed and there was a sharp pain in her hand.

Gabi cried with a blood curdling scream, "Mama!"

She wailed as she waited for her mother to respond. As she waited, she saw a crack of light cut through the darkness near the edge of the bed. Gabi reached for the crack and her fingers brushed against the metal wall, which gave way and swung upward with a slight creak. She squinted as her eyes adjusted to the brightness pouring in from outside her berth.

She sobbed and cried out again. "Mama? Papa? Where are you?" For a few seconds, there was no noise. Then Gabi heard a creak, like the sound made by the door of her father's truck. "Papa?" She heard the creak again.

Panic gripped her. She knew something was wrong, but not what. She grabbed at her harness and ran her fingers along their length until she found the buckles. Gabi's fingers fumbled as she tried to release the latch. Her tiny fingers were not strong enough to work the mechanism. She tried to get the latch open over and over, sobbing and trembling as she did so. In a fit of frustration, she screamed and yanked at the harness.

To her surprise, Gabi was able to loosen the straps themselves. She yanked again and they loosened even more. She shrugged the shoulder straps off of her small body, and then wiggled her legs free.

I'm supposed to keep that on. It's supposed to keep me safe. Gabi felt guilty about disobeying the nice man and her mother, but nobody was around to see her do it. Gabi shoved against the door to her bed and it swung open with a groan. She saw a metal floor and what looked like a long, low door across from her.

Gabi crawled from her bed into the hallway and stood up. She looked around and saw more doors like hers on both sides, in long rows, stacked two tall. Besides the door to her bed, there were two other open doors at the far end of the hall. Two people lay on the floor next to those open doors. They looked like they were sleeping.

Maybe they know where Mama is. She felt another twinge of guilt. She didn't want to wake them up, but she really wanted her mom.

Gabi sneaked down the hall to the two people. As she neared them, her foot slipped and she put her hands out in front of her to catch her fall. They landed in something slick and red. Gabi stood back up and looked at the thick liquid, and then back to the two people.

The man was facing down and she could not see his face, but the woman stared straight at the ceiling with dull brown eyes. Her skin was paler than any Gabi had ever seen, and her mouth was stained with blood. Gabi's eyes fell to the woman's stomach, and she realized that there was a piece of metal barely poking through her belly. A trail of red ran down the woman's side and to Gabi's feet.

Gabi remembered something that her mom had told her one day when Gabi had unbuckled her car seat while they were driving; People can be very badly hurt in crashes without their seatbelts, and sometimes they even die.

These people are dead.

She gasped, as if her lungs could not find any air. When she finally drew in a huge gasp, she screamed at the top of her lungs. Her scream echoed through the metal hallway. Gabi turned away from the bodies and ran to the other end of the hall. She saw a small open doorway at the other end that looked like a crawlspace. Gabi bolted into it and crawled along the ladder that was inside.

She came out to a short, dark hallway. She ran a few feet and came to a skidding halt when she saw another body crumpled against the wall at the end of the hall. Groans and angry shouts echoed from beyond. Gabi sobbed and looked around. To her right was a heavy looking door with some words on it that she could barely understand: "something PERSONsomething ONLY". She looked to her left down another dark hallway lined with cabinets.

At first, Gabi thought she would hide in one of the cabinets, but as she ran down the hall she saw a ladder going up, with light filtering down from somewhere above. She bounded the few extra paces and grabbed the ladder. When she looked up, she saw blue sky mixed with wisps of black smoke.

Gabi struggled to climb the ladder. The rungs were made for an adult, and her short legs and arms strained to make it to each of the next rungs. Her hands left smears of blood every time she grabbed one, and she nearly slipped from the ladder when her blood soaked foot pushed off of one of the steel rungs.

She reached the top of the ladder and scrambled her way onto the top of the giant metal cylinder. There were scrapes and mud all over the outside, as well as tears of many sizes. Smoke seemed to filter into the air from all around. Gabi surveyed the surrounding area and saw a wide path of trees that had looked like they had been snapped. On the far side of the cylinder, a few trees close by leaned as if they might fall down, but the rest of the forest beyond looked untouched.

Gabi was thrown down to the skin of the craft as a loud *boom* rocked everything. She hit her head on the steel. The force made her bite her lip hard enough to bleed, and she started crying. She looked back over her feet and saw a column of smoke and wisps of flame rise up from just beyond the edge of the craft. The fire filled her with dread, and her panic was renewed.

She sat up and curled her knees to her chest, then looked down the side of the craft at the ground below. She knew it would be too high up for her to jump, and that she would hurt herself if she tried. She rested her head on her knees and wailed, rocking back and forth.

She cried for minutes, alone on the top of the wreck. A warm breeze that tickled her neck made her open her bleary eyes. Through the tears, she saw rungs built into the side of the cylinder that led down. She scrambled to her knees and crawled over to them, her mind locked in single focus.

Gabi grabbed a rung with her hand, then slid her foot precariously down to another. She cautiously worked her way down the side of the craft, past scars and gashes. Part of the way down the ladder, it straightened out, and the side of the craft dropped straight down. Gabi kept going, making sure she could put both feet on a rung before moving her hands down.

She was still high above the ground when her foot moved for a rung and slipped. Her other foot could not find the rung either. Gabi screamed and looked down as she dangled helplessly by her hands. She saw that the next few steps of the ladder were missing; only a large hole in the metal remained where they should have been.

Gabi's feet flailed as she tried to find some place to brace them. Her right foot kicked the top of the gash and her hands slipped loose from the rungs. With a terrified scream, Gabrielle Serrano fell from the side of the pod.

. . .

There was no doubt that the skiff had descended into Demeter's troposphere. The horizon was dominated by lush, green land, edged by a long, pencil thin white beach that separated from the contrasting blue seas.

We'll be lucky if we see any of it, at this rate, Haruka thought.

"Hey Kimura," Mancini said, "we look like we're coming in a little low to you?"

Haruka feigned a glance out the window. "No, we're fine," she lied.

Too damn much time chasing Singh. Haruka clenched her teeth. *We can't possibly make Cormack's landing site.*

"Hey Marco. There are your white sand beaches," she pointed as she swung the skiff in a lazy left turn. She searched the ground beyond, trying to find any signs of a break in the endless foliage on land. *I could try crashing on a beach. That might be a softer landing.*

"Great. Remind me to go play on them when we land." Haruka tried to ignore the cutting sarcasm in his tone.

"Captain," Nova queried, "can you turn the other way? I think I saw something on the ground."

Haruka swept her eyes across the ground one more time and sighed. She saw no clearings ahead, so she reversed the turn of the skiff. A plume of smoke rose from the beach far in the distance.

"What do you think it is, Nova?"

"I can't tell from here, ma'am."

"It's probably a pod." Mancini's voice was becoming more sullen every time he spoke. Haruka felt pained in her soul. She had always known Marco Mancini to be one of the most upbeat and comedic people she had ever met, but he seemed to be in an uncontrolled spiral.

She shrugged off the thought. *None of us are having a good day today. I just need to keep us safe and we can start over tomorrow.*

"Looks like a cargo pod," Nova remarked. "The sleeper pods should have used up most of their fuel on the way down. They shouldn't burn like that."

"And just which cargo pod would burn like that?" sneered Mancini

"We should have been carrying four pods of fuel for the power equipment."

"Diesel fuel, *Airman.*"

"Well then just what do you think it is, *Lieutenant?*"

"Enough! Stop fighting, you two," Haruka snapped into her boom.

Airman Weyler and Lieutenant Mancini both fell silent. Haruka could feel the hairs on the back of her neck stand up. Everyone was on edge, but she had never had to pull rank before to get her way. The power tasted like a bitter pill to her.

Haruka scanned the ground all the way to the far edge of the ocean, but the only thing she could see besides the blue sea was an endless green one marking the land beyond. She leveled her flight and fired all of the thrusters for five seconds.

She curled her lip and bit it. *That's the last of it.* The thruster reserves were dangerously low, and Haruka knew that if she fired them again, she would be unable to slow their descent, and a crash landing would be unavoidable.

The ocean dropped out of the lower view of the skiff's windows. They were close to land, and Haruka's passing thought of a beach landing became infeasible. She desperately scanned the horizon for a patch of grass or a bald hilltop. She turned the craft left once more.

A quick flash of brown in the sea of green caught her eye. *A clearing!* It was not far off, maybe five or ten miles. In an instant, Haruka aimed the nose of the skiff at it and put the nose in a slight dive.

"What are you doing, Kimura? Pod seven is off to the right," Mancini protested.

"Yes it is," she responded coolly.

"So turn back."

"Can't do that, Marco. We don't have enough fuel or altitude left."

Nova shrieked, "What?"

"You said we were fine, Kimura!" She could hear the escalation in his voice.

"I lied. So court martial me," she responded without skipping a beat. "Just remember that when you *do* court martial me, it's because I saved your life by not trying to make the pod seven site."

Mancini spluttered for a moment before he formed a reply. "Just who the hell do you think you are?"

"The pilot, and your commanding officer. Get those pod beacons loaded into the radio tracker so that we can follow them once we're on the ground."

"Yes ma'am," he shot back. Haruka could hear the slight against her in his tone, but ignored it.

The skiff glided closer to the tree line. The density of the tree canopy gave Haruka the impression that this might be a jungle or tropical area. She used her flaps to tip the nose up slightly, and she felt the tightness of her harnesses as the craft slowed down.

Almost there, she thought.

She dipped the right wing down hard and banked into a turn. The edge of the brown clearing passed into her line of vision. Haruka's heart plummeted and her hands froze on the controls.

We can't land here, she screamed in her own mind. *This is a crash site!*

"Captain," Nova yelled through her headset, "there's a crashed pod over there."

Haruka quickly leveled the skiff and fired the thrusters to gain altitude. The trees dropped below them and Haruka saw white, fluffy clouds ahead of her. *Don't stall... DON'T STALL!*

She leveled the nose out just before the thrusters sputtered and coughed out. A warning light blinked on her terminal. Haruka dared not look at it for fear that it would be the stall indicator.

She nosed down slightly to build up speed and the tree canopy again dominated her view. Once more she pulled up and the skiff gained altitude at the costly price of speed.

I can't keep doing this. She nosed down again and caught a glimpse of blue mixed in with the green tree line. She closed her eyes and blindly aimed for the image in her mind.

"Kimura?" Mancini no longer had anger in his voice, only terror.

"Brace for impact," she yelled.

There was a deafening noise of tearing metal, and the tail of the skiff suddenly jumped. Haruka squeezed her eyes tighter. The nose dipped to the left, then the craft felt as if it was doing a cartwheel. Shattered glass from the canopy showered her face, and her body bounced back and forth between the harness and the seat. There was a bright orange light and a brief searing sensation, and then water splashed her face.

Her eyes shot open just as the canopy rolled into water. Haruka tried to scream, but water forced its way into her lungs. She gagged and choked, then the skiff flipped once final time and came to a rest. Water quickly rushed into the cockpit, rising up to her chest.

Haruka coughed and vomited, then coughed more until she could feel her breath again. Her hands clawed at the restraints that held her, but her latch was jammed. She could taste blood; she brought her hand to her face and drew it back, stained in red. There was a sensation of backward motion and she could hear splashing noises. Haruka's hands shot to her headrest and her eyes closed.

"C'mon, Kimura, let's get out of here," Mancini said from behind her.

She opened her eyes and saw Nova Weyler staggering out of the water and to shore just ahead of the craft. Haruka looked down and tried to release her buckle again, to no avail.

"My latch is jammed."

"Hang on."

Haruka heard more splashing. She looked behind her, but Mancini was nowhere to be found. "Marco?" The skiff jerked again and slid backward a couple feet. The water level rose to her shoulders. "Marco, where are you? Help me!" The surface of the water thrashed and bubbled as she jerked desperately at her harness.

She heard a splash and a gasp from behind her, then the sound of metal plunging into cloth. Her left shoulder was freed. She looked to her right and grabbed for her harness.

"Wait, don't move," Mancini barked. Haruka saw the glint of a blade as he jabbed it through the right shoulder harness and into the cushion behind. He drew it out of the seat, flipped the handle around, and handed it to Haruka. "Cut the hip belt and let's go." He slung a pack over his shoulders and reached down to grab more equipment, then jumped from the skiff.

Haruka reached under the water and felt for the harness at her waist. She sawed furiously at the belt. The craft groaned and slid back another foot, and she took in a mouthful of water. Haruka coughed and drew in a gulp of air before her face went under. She doubled her efforts at cutting through the thick harness, and managed to free her torso. She kicked the last bit of webbing from her legs and clawed toward the surface, bursting through like a rocket. She gasped and choked. The water blurred her vision, and she could not tell if she was aimed at the right shore.

She felt a hand grab her flight suit and yank her back. "Hang on, Kimura," Mancini yelled. "I've gotcha. Just keep kicking."

Haruka obeyed and kicked her feet for dear life. Moments of her life flashed back to her, and she thought of her mother, sister, and father. She thought of how much she wanted to see their faces again, and to hold them. She muttered a prayer that she would not drown. Her feet brushed against something solid. She pushed with all her might and flopped onto the shore, casting the knife aside. Her lungs hacked as they tried to expel the remnants of the cruel, murderous waters. She curled a hand up and felt something soft between her fingers. Her eyes opened as she brought her hand to her nose and took a deep sniff.

Wet earth. Mud.

"Kimura, you alright?"

Haruka rolled onto her back and spread her arms out wide. Her face widened into a grin as she saw fluffy white clouds far above. She rolled her head to the side and saw Marco's worried face looking down at her, and Airman Weyler behind him, watching her as an angel might have watched.

Haruka started to laugh. Mancini's worried frown disappeared, and he chucked as well. Haruka grabbed him by the front of his flight suit and planted a kiss on his surprised lips, then shoved him away. Mancini landed on his butt with a look of complete shock.

"We're alive," she screamed in jubilation as she scrambled to her feet. Haruka looked up as the brilliant orange sun escaped from behind a cloud. She felt the warm radiance wash over her as she took in the smells of Demeter.

"Well, we won't be forever if we don't find shelter or more supplies," Mancini remarked. "I got everything off the skiff that I could before it sank, but we need to find a pod."

Haruka turned to the other two survivors, their faces again grim. She walked forward to look at the supplies that Mancini had managed to gather. *Three emergency survival packs. Three canteens. Two belts with an M9 bayonet and an M9A1 pistol each, one M4 carbine. The skiff's ammunitions box, and the radio tracker.* She sighed as she knelt beside the ammunition box and opened it. *Dry inside, good.*

She looked up at Mancini and Weyler. "Marco, Nova, each of you take a pack, canteen, and belt. Marco, I want you to take the tracker. The rifle is mine. We'll carry as much ammo in the packs as we reasonably can, but this box is not coming with us. Marco, toss me my pack."

Mancini lobbed a pack to her and then reached for a belt. Haruka unzipped the pack and took a quick tally of the contents, and retrieved a compass from inside. *Only four meals. At least they have matches and emergency blankets.* She grabbed three magazines for the rifle and shoved them in the pack between the emergency blanket and a coil of thin rope, then locked a fresh magazine into the rifle. She rooted through the remaining ammunition and found eight magazines for the pistols. *A shame that we have to leave the rest of it here.*

Haruka lifted her pack onto her shoulders, grabbed the rifle, and then distributed the ammunition to the others. "We have no idea what is out there in the wilderness, so be very careful. We want to move quickly, but don't be stupid or reckless. Marco, what's the closest pod reading on the tracker?"

Mancini held up the device and slowly turned in place. "I think the one we flew over was number eight. That's the closest by a long shot, but it also crashed."

Haruka considered for a moment. "How far away is the beacon for number seven?"

"About forty miles, and in the other direction too."

Haruka looked back at the water that they crashed in. It looked to be a sizeable lake, and that it might be several miles around either end to add to the journey. Beyond that loomed the dark silhouette of a mountain. "Nova, did you get a good look at eight when we flew over?"

"Sort of, why?"

"How broken up was the pod?"

"Actually it looked like it was mostly intact."

"How far away is eight, Marco?"

"Maybe six miles or so as the crow flies."

Haruka nodded. "We're going to pod eight. If there are any survivors, they may need help. There will also be supplies there."

Nova took a step back and her jaw dropped. "Ma'am? Shouldn't we go to a pod we know landed fine?"

Haruka shook her head emphatically. "It's not just forty miles. Look at that lake and tell me how long it will be to get around it. See the mountain behind it. Look in your pack and tell me how much food you have. If we're lucky we'll make it before we run out of food." She jerked her thumb over her shoulder. "Those people might well die without us, but I can guarantee we'll get there before we run out of supplies."

"I'm with Kimura on this one, Weyler," Mancini said as he fixed his canteen to his belt. "No use arguing about it with her either, she's the commanding officer now."

Mancini's words sunk in deep. In the skiff, Haruka had told him that she was the commanding officer partly as a tactic to get him to listen. She realized now that she had been made First Officer by Emberley, and that both he and Fox were dead.

I am now in command of the crew of Raphael.

Haruka straightened up, gripped her rifle, and walked toward the wilderness. Mancini fell in at her side, and she heard Nova scurry to catch up.

Let's see just what is left of my command.

. . .

>END PLAYBACK|

Credits and Acknowledgements
16 August 2012
The real Earth, somewhere in Washington State
>|

Lieutenant Darius Owens may have said that "no man is an angel", but it was John Donne that wrote that "no man is an island." In writing, these words have a particular ring of truth. Without those around us to support and guide us through the process, our literary scene would be very different. Many books might never exist but for the support of others, while some works would read very differently. In that light, I would like to thank the following people, for their contributions to this project:

Thank you to Jay, Rob and Melissa, Karie, and Sarah L. These were my test readers. Without them, I would not have known whether or not I was stringing together an intelligible plot thread, or if I was just wasting space on a page. In addition they assisted in catching a couple glaring inconsistencies that needed correction.

Thank you to Mathew Reuther, who helped steer me away from the rocks of "what not to do when writing." To Harrison Pierce and J.M. Foster, I am most grateful for the assistance in early proofreading and plot mechanics. Thanks go out to Bridgette Reuther for the fantastic cover art that wraps the book. A special nod goes to Beth Revis for snapping me out of my mid-editing doldrums and getting me back on track.

I'd like to thank my wife Megan and my three boys. They provided all the moral support I could have hoped for and more, and as well, Megan has been one of my most passionate test readers. To the point of harping on me to hurry up and send her more chapters when she knows I have a batch done. (I love you, babe!)

Finally, I'd like to thank you, the reader, without whom the writers of the world would not exist.

For more information on J.C. Rainier, his work, or upcoming projects, please visit http://jcrainier.com.

• • •

About the Author:

J.C. Rainier is product of the Pacific Northwest, born in the Seattle area in 1978, and living in the Puget Sound area his whole life. He is the younger of two children in his family, and his older brother proved to be a giant pest up through his teenage years (as siblings tend to be).

J.C.'s parents were both educators working at the middle school level, and he married into another family of educators. In his family, counting in-laws, there are now two retired principals, two retired teachers, a retired school counselor, and an active science teacher.

In his youth, J.C. read quite a lot. The Call of the Wild was one of his early favorites, and into middle school he began to devour other books such as Anne McCaffrey's Dragonriders of Pern series. Unfortunately, J.C. developed a form of dylexia that made reading from the page of a book difficult. It was later discovered that the curvature of the page itself caused the issue, and the advent of the eReader (with its perfectly flat screen) has allowed him to once again enjoy reading as he used to.

He enjoys both indoor and outdoor pursuits including computers, cars, and camping. J.C. and his wife enjoy hockey, and set aside time several times each season to watch the local WHL franchise.

J.C. and his wife are raising three boys, including a set of twins. If his blog ever fails to make sense, he's probably had a very long night just prior to writing it. If said writing is just a random set of characters similar to "adsk,wr3.1", then one of the children has managed a surprise attack on his laptop.

• • •